The Dreaming Swimmer

The Dreaming Swimmer

Elisabeth Ogilvie

I think the danger of the ocean lies
Not in the storm, but in the mermaid's eyes;
She closes them for kisses, unaware,
Enfolds the dreaming swimmer, and he dies.

A. R. Ogilvie

McGraw-Hill Book Company

New York   St. Louis   San Francisco
        Toronto   Düsseldorf   Mexico

23456789 F G F G 79876

Library of Congress Cataloging in Publication Data

Ogilvie, Elisabeth, date
The dreaming swimmer.

I. Title.
PZ3.0348Dr [PS3529.G39]   813'.5'2   76-5511
ISBN 0-07-047598-9

To Marian McNamara

I think the danger of the ocean lies
Not in the storm, but in the mermaid's eyes;
She closes them for kisses, unaware,
Enfolds the dreaming swimmer, and he dies

chapter 1

Seth came to us one February afternoon, tramping all the way from the mailboxes in the icy wind off Morgan Bay. With his round face burned scarlet with the cold, he took off his steamed glasses, embraced me, and shook hands with his brother as if he were Dr. Kissinger getting off a plane with a signed peace treaty.

"I just sold the Darby Homestead," he said. "A hundred thousand cash, and no dickering. The papers were passed today."

"It's outrageous." Barnaby looked outraged. "It's the worst kind of inflation. No wonder the state hauls back on the school subsidy, and our taxes go up and up! They think we're all millionaires down here. A few more sales like that will bankrupt the town."

"Don't you even rejoice," asked Seth with hurt dignity, "that I am doing pretty damn well out of this? That I made a special trip just to tell you the news before anyone else gets it? That I could have got frostbite on the way because you don't allow anything out here but the jeep?"

"Sure I rejoice for you, even if you won't get to keep much of that commission."

"My brother the crapehanger," said Seth.

There were just the three of us that afternoon. Sara Brownell, their young cousin who was staying with us, was out that afternoon, gone to the northern end of Cape Silver, where my aunt and uncle lived. She'd made a cake that morning, and I brought it with the coffee into the living room, where the sun and the open fire made for comfort. Seth told us about the new owner of the Darby Homestead.

"He came to Fremont first. He'd read that article about its being one of the most crime-free spots in the nation. Well, he was looking for something very quiet, but Fremont was too busy for him even in January, and when he heard what it was like in summer he was ready to quit. But not me." For Seth, being a salesman is a spiritual calling. "I've been driving him around the countryside, up hill and down dale; explored more mountainsides, looked at more spooky old places and run-down farms than I knew existed, and they were all a thousand miles from the nearest black road. At least it felt like a thousand miles. I did know enough to use the truck to get into those places. He just grunted at everything or made no sound at all. Then one day I remembered the Darby place and brought him down here. Love at first sight. But I didn't want to let you know until it was a sure thing." He knocked on wood, and gave us that wide unquenchable grin.

"Tell us about him," I urged, recklessly plying him with more cake. "Is he young, married, a painter, a writer, big business, retired Army, or what?"

"*What* is more like it," Seth said. "I asked in my usual art-less way, but got nowhere. In all those miles of deer tracks and cowpaths he never became what you'd call even moderately friendly. When I said it was love at first sight down here, my euphoria was carrying me away. What he did was look at everything without visible reaction, and not a glance at the view, which was spectacular that day. He walked out of the room when I mentioned some of the details that usually drive clients mad with lust, like hand-hewn beams and the original thumb latches. He does have a practical head on his shoulders when it comes to the heating system, plumbing, and so forth. And he wanted to know how much land there was, and I offered to walk the lines with him, but I gather he's no outdoorsman. Finally he grunted something which I construed as 'I'll take it.' I must have guessed right, because today he handed Rex Ashton a certified check from Chase Manhattan for a hundred thousand."

"Oh, *damn!*" I said. "We don't want any millionaire around here, cluttering up the bay with his friends' yachts and clogging the road with their Bentleys, and trying to bribe the selectmen to put a four-lane highway through Applecross."

"When's he moving in?" asked Barnaby.

"Just as soon as everything's turned on and working. They're selling the place furnished."

"If you don't know anything about him, at least you know what he looks like," I persisted.

"In his forties, I'd say. In good shape—slim, very erect—he could be a retired serviceman, from the way he carries himself, but in my experience they always let you know. Black hair cut short, clean shaven, wears dark glasses, and if you don't see someone's eyes you don't really know what that person looks like."

"That settles it," I said. "He's either a defector from the Mafia or he's a movie star. Gosh, Seth, except for your good luck in this I don't know how I feel about it. The harbor's such a little village in itself that a new person can make quite an impact. So far we've been lucky with our outsiders, but—"

"Where do you get that *we* stuff?" Barnaby kidded me. "Don't let any of the old-seed people hear that. Garfield snapped me up in the store the other day for saying *we*. Reminded me that my great-grandfather was a foreigner. According to Garf, you only get to be a citizen of Applecross if your ancestors stole their land from the Indians."

"Garf," I said, "is an old pain in the neck, and I'd have used another word if Seth hadn't been here."

"Don't mind me," Seth said with enthusiasm.

"Arse, then," I said. "Good old pure Elizabethan English. And if he says anything to me about the Weirs, I shall remind him that his great-great-grandfather only settled here because he was chased across the river from St. Andrews for dirty Tory tricks."

"I never heard that before," said Barnaby.

"Neither did I," I said. "I just made it up. But knowing Garf, I could believe it. . . . What name is this Croesus going under?"

"Cory Sanderson."

"An alias if I ever heard one," I said. "I'm dying to welcome him to town. That's one way to get a look at him."

Seth became as nearly uncomfortable as I'd ever seen him. He's been unflappable for as long as I've known him, since I was ten and he was a solid, competent thirteen-year-old with eyes both shrewd and calm behind his glasses. "The fact is, he's made it clear he doesn't want to be welcomed. If I'd mentioned having a brother nearby when I showed him the house, I don't think he'd have taken it. Rex mentioned Barnaby after the papers were passed, and from the look that went over Sanderson's face I half-expected him to repudiate the deal. Then he said stiffly that he'd come looking for complete privacy and isolation."

"He doesn't have to worry about us," Barnaby said at once, "and when the word gets around, he'll be so isolated he'll think he's in quarantine for bubonic plague."

"Well, it's what he wants, so you don't have to feel any neighborly responsibility," said Seth. He grinned. "Maybe I should have warned him about the clammers."

"By the time he's found out he can't win that little war, he'll be humbled down to human size," said Barnaby.

"What makes you think he needs humbling?" I asked. "Maybe he's already got an inferiority complex."

"If he can pay a hundred thousand cash for a place, what makes you think he's got an inferiority complex?"

"Tell me just how he looked when he heard about your brother," I said to Seth. "Startled? Sad? Aggressive? Hostile? *Scared?*"

"We will now psychoanalyze him, sight unseen." Barnaby headed for the kitchen and more cake.

"Well, his normal expression, or what I took for normal, is impassivity. It hardly changed when he got the deed. So the way he altered when Barnaby was mentioned as a neighbor was quite a change."

"Would you call it an ecstasy of disgust?"

"I'd call it a spasm of annoyance succeeded by alarm, as if a dog had just mistaken him for a tree . . . a large boxer."

"Thanks," said Barnaby, returning with the cake. "Just call me Rover. Have some more of this. I don't know which ashram or commune Sal learned in, but wherever it was it can't be all bad."

"They were never so sybaritic in the ashram," I said. "The keynote was asceticism. One thing she was kicked out for, in addition to giggling at the wrong moments and not being able to master the lotus position, was her addiction to surreptitious cheeseburgers."

Seth examined his cake with fascinated interest. "You sure those little things in it aren't chopped peyote?"

"Candied lemon rind, I *think*. If we all start taking off around here we'll know different."

"After a month of Sara," Barnaby said, "I'm pretty sure she'd never need any outside help to turn her on, unless it's the moon and the turn of the tide."

"How's the book going?" Seth asked. "Sara any help there?"

"Just by washing all the dishes she's a wonderful help," I said warmly. Barnaby and I were working up his grandfather's records and journals of life on Cape Silver into a book; the project had begun as the result of a letter from a publisher who specialized in such books, and whose son had once spent a week on Cape Silver photographing wildlife. Now, discussing the book with Seth, we forgot all about Cory Sanderson.

Sara came home in the early dark, exhilarated. "I steered by the stars," she told us, peeling off outer layers of clothing. "Boy, was it quiet in the woods! I never heard such silence. I kept standing still to listen. Where were all the deer?"

"Listening to you," Barnaby said.

"I kept hoping I'd meet a moose. I had my eye on all the good trees to climb, just in case." At last she was down to jeans and turtleneck jersey. She was a tall blonde girl with a long neck, she looked too thin and supple to be very durable; she reminded one somewhat of Botticelli's *Primavera*. She had green eyes, sometimes of a real tourmaline color. She was no beauty, not even pretty, but striking in her own way; she could look as dreamy, sexy, or mindless as any of Botticelli's girls, then give a sudden rake-hell grin, which slitted her eyes and showed an engaging space between her two front teeth. Then you knew why she'd been a disrupting influence at the ashram.

"Hey, know what I found out this afternoon? That place next to the Boones' has been sold."

"We never know anything till the last minute over here," I said mendaciously. "Who's buying it?"

"A rich oil man. Not Getty, but I forget who. *Or* a rich television personality. *Or*—well, it depends on whether you hear it from the oil man, the telephone man, the plumber, or the electric light man, who's somebody's brother-in-law."

There was no way to keep a secret in Applecross. People found out things by osmosis if they didn't have a brother-in-law in the power company. So we told her what Seth had told us, and we all became very wittily unkind at the mysterious stranger's expense.

Then all at once I remembered, with a pang of shame. "I wonder if Lorenzo knows yet," I said, and it put an end to our jokes.

"I hope the family had the decency to let him know in advance," Barnaby said.

"Why should they?" I asked. "They've taken him for granted all these years. I don't believe they've ever paid him a cent for his care and devotion to that house."

"He wouldn't have taken it," Barnaby said. "The house is a religion with him."

"It's been for sale, hasn't it?" Sara said. "He must know that."

"He's never really believed it," Barnaby said. "Because up till now nobody's wanted to pay a hundred thousand for it. I don't think he ever dreamed it would happen."

chapter 2

The Darby and Boone places are on the Morgan Bay side of the black road that comes down the hill, crosses the Neck, and ends at the Cape Silver mailboxes. The Boones' ten acres, nearer the Neck, were once part of the Darby land, and Joel Darby sold them to Kyle and Deirdre about fifteen years back, when they could afford to buy. I doubt if they could now, with the modern prices. They had a Williston man build their low unpretentious house on the granite terraces among the thick old spruces, but they were able to use it only on rare vacations until Kyle retired from building dams.

The Darby Homestead sat on the side of the hill, looking straight down Morgan Bay to open sea, so Horatio Darby could see his fishermen coming home. He ran a big weir for herring and mackerel, and his fishermen brought in doryloads of codfish, hake, and big pollock for salting down in wooden tubs, or to dry slack-salted on the flakes set out on the ledges. Vessels sailed up Morgan Bay to buy his fish and take them to our own southern ports, the West Indies, and to Africa.

College and travel for his descendants put an end to the life of the Homestead as Horatio Darby had known it. He would have seen his modern heirs as inhabitants of another planet, and perhaps they were. They became summer people with from-away accents; they came to Applecross less and less as the children grew up, and finally the visits were no more than rare weekends. No, Horatio wouldn't have recognized any of his heirs, but I think he and Lorenzo would have understood each other. Horatio had believed in the law of primogeniture, and Lorenzo descended from a third son who'd gone to sea when he saw no chance for him in Applecross. This branch had followed the sea, until one of them married a schoolteacher who grew deathly sick even when only in a dory and couldn't make voyages with him. Besides, the days of sail were almost gone, and so he retired and bought a farm in Applecross, and built boats in his barn. Lorenzo, the only child, could have gone to work for any Williston or Limerock yard by the time he was sixteen or so, but he wouldn't leave Applecross even to attend Williston High. My uncle, who'd started first grade with him, said Lorenzo was one of the brightest students the town had ever had.

"But Williston was foreign territory to him," Uncle Stewart said. "So the rest of us moved on—most of the rest of us—to high school, but not Lorenzo, and his folks wouldn't drive him. When 1941 came along and the Army was drafting anything that could move and breathe, even they realized there was something missing in Lorenzo. Or," he said with a smile, "something *additional*. Because who's to say Lorenzo isn't maybe more complete than the rest of us?"

His father had died when Lorenzo was nineteen, and he ran the farm devotedly until his mother died. He sold the farm then, keeping seventeen or so acres of woodlot fronting on Morgan Bay beyond the original Darby land. He built himself a log house down there, and became the Lorenzo we knew.

Like the gypsyish Jasons, he was at home outdoors at night as well as in daylight, with the difference that he was an observer instead of a poacher. He didn't even hunt legally. He made his living clamming, fishing, and lobstering from a dory, occasionally cutting wood for someone who wanted a woodlot cleaned up; but it was all done without a power saw, just as he wouldn't use an outboard motor in his dory. "I don't hold with gasoline engines. It's something personal between them and me."

His true north or his obsession, depending on how you regarded him, was the Darby Homestead. He knew the history of the house as if it had all happened in his lifetime. He could tell you where the fish-flakes stood, where the vessels had tied up to unload salt and take off fish. He knew where each of the children and the hired girls had slept, the names of the horses and dogs, where the pigpen had been, and what happened the year the Darbys boarded the schoolmaster.

Peripherally he had become an expert on the tools, the foods, the amusements, the politics, the manners of the time. In his log cabin he had a trunkful of Darby ledgers and letters, daguerreotypes and photographs, that constituted not only a family archive but that of a village. He was such a feast of information that just to look at him made the Historical Society's collective mouth water. He had refused to become a charter member, and he refused to contribute his treasures to the collection in their new building.

He revered the Homestead like a Chinese at the shrine of his ancestors, and with a careless and patronizing generosity, Joel Darby allowed him to keep watch over the place and hold the keys. One day Lorenzo had confided to Barnaby that he hoped to be able to buy the house; for that he would even sell his beloved woodlot. He saw no reason why the heir wouldn't be glad to let him have the place at a reasonable price, since the family came less and less, and it meant so much to him. Apparently the question of big money had never entered his unworldly mind. Barnaby tried to suggest it, but got nowhere. After all, Lorenzo was a Darby; he had the right.

They wrote him when they put the house on the market, telling him it was all right to let a local realtor borrow the keys. He didn't take it seriously, so it was a shock when the man himself hiked down from the black road looking for him; he had a client waiting in his car. In disbelief Lorenzo followed, and skulked around the outskirts during the viewing, making the prospect uncomfortable. The realtor complained to the Darbys' Limerock lawyer, Rex Ashton, who then wrote to the family, who sent him a separate set of keys. Thereafter Lorenzo missed a few viewings, but not all; he seemed to have a sixth sense about the Holy Place. Realtors muttered that it was like trying to sell a haunted house with the ghost visible. As months went on and winter set in, Lorenzo must have felt pretty secure. Then suddenly, this February, the man called Cory Sanderson bought the house while Lorenzo's back was turned.

We talked about Lorenzo at supper that night. Sara knew him, of course, but she didn't know his background, and when she heard it she told us the schoolteacher mother must have been a Yankee Elizabeth Barrett who got cheated out of Italy but was in love with the Medici, therefore the name *Lorenzo* . . .

"His father's name," Barnaby interrupted. "Also his great-uncle's."

"But I'll bet he had long curls till he was ten, which would be all right *now*, of course, but *then*—oh, poor little Lorenzo!"

"Lorenzo never needed pity when he was growing up," said Barnaby in annoyance.

She widened those green eyes at him. "You're so picky, you remind me of my father." She appealed to me. "Don't you ever wonder about Lorenzo? He's intelligent and vigorous, and really quite attractive behind those whiskers—he's got the *youngest* eyes—so why is he such a solitary? Did he ever have a sweetheart? Maybe his id has fastened on the Homestead because—"

"To be or not to be, that id the question," said Barnaby, and we groaned. We'd gotten a long way from Cory Sanderson, and I was relieved. Sight unseen the man had become like a splinter in one's thumb, too deep to be removed by a needle. Talk about Lorenzo being an oddity! This one sounded fantastic.

Sara left after supper with my skates, to be picked up by Ronnie Deming at the mailboxes for moonlight skating in North Applecross. Barnaby and I took advantage of the situation, and locked the doors. With a good fire in the fireplace and moonlight pouring in, the sea all a resplendent shimmer in the night, we were transported to our own secret continent.

The next morning the weather was softening, but it was too rough to haul, and Barnaby and I drove early to the store at Applecross Center. Seth had stopped in yesterday to say hello to Mr. Ives, and had told him about the sale. He asked us if Lorenzo knew.

"We don't know," Barnaby said. "We're stopping there on our way back."

Mr. Ives shook his head. It was enough of a comment; it expressed everything that concerned us about Lorenzo.

"*Lorenzo?*" someone said close by us. It was a man who'd been studying the bakery counter when we came in. I had just barely noticed a head of thick light brown hair, and amber glasses, as well as the usual outdoor winter outfit for around here. "Excuse me, I wasn't really eavesdropping," he said, sounding a little embarrassed, "but I heard that name. Mr. Ives, isn't that the man you told me about, who might help me with my sloop?"

"That's the one. You haven't met the Taggarts yet, have you?" He introduced him to us. "This is Max Kemper. He's just rented the Yule place in North Applecross and he's writing a book."

That wasn't extraordinary in Applecross these days. "And building a boat, too?" I asked.

"*Re*building. I bought the old girl for a hundred dollars and had her brought to the barn. I'm ignorant, but resolute." He lifted a clenched fist.

"I told him Lorenzo might give him some advice," said Mr. Ives.

"God knows I need all the help I can get. I'm not proud." He was our age or maybe older, with one of those angular, long-jawed faces that can be either very forbidding or very attractive. His mustache didn't hide a slightly lopsided and teasing smile, as if he were laughing at himself. "If I ever was, *Jemima C.* has really cut me down."

"Well, Lorenzo's our expert," said Barnaby. "But I don't know if you can get him up to North Applecross. The store's usually about as far as he'll go."

"Maybe I can appeal to his sense of pity," said Kemper. We wished him luck, and left. When the jeep had gotten clear of an incoming oil truck, the bread truck, and a passing school bus, and was on the way back to the harbor, I said, "I wonder what kind of a book he's writing."

"Oh, some sado-porn masterpiece."

"You cynic. It's probably something deep and scholarly."

"A deep and scholarly sado-porn masterpiece, then."

"He loves boats, so he can't be a pornographer. If that's what you call them," I added uncertainly.

"All you have to do to find out about him," said Barnaby, "is ask around and see if he owns a pornograph."

It got us to Lorenzo's road much too fast, but then we wouldn't have been ready anyway for what we dreaded. In glum silence we snowshoed through the woods to his cabin. His road was never plowed; he got in and out on snowshoes, or else rowed around to the Neck in his dory if the bay wasn't frozen or too rough.

Grosbeaks flew up in a rush from his feeders, and mourning doves took off from the ground, but only to the nearest trees. Smoke from the chimney was whipped about by the erratic gusts of damp wind, but Lorenzo wasn't home. The place was unlocked. He never locked anything but his trunkful of family records.

We took his path to the shore. The tide had gone far out from the rind of spill-powered snow and rotting ice, and gulls were picking around the purple mussel beds. The dory was gone, but we thought we could see it at the edge of the clam flats on the western rim of the bay, near the pale green aluminum skiff of another regular clammer in the area, an Amity man. Between us and them the shallow bay was a swirling expanse of gray and brown and green, whipping into crests that left clots of dirty foam at the edge of the tide.

"Well, he hasn't hanged himself in despair," said Barnaby.

"Do you suppose he hasn't found out yet?" I asked. Barnaby shrugged. We went back to the cabin and left a note on Lorenzo's kitchen table, inviting him to supper.

If I'd been alone I'd have detoured around the harbor to pick up the local talk from my friend Jean, and then I'd have stopped in at the Boones' for a nourishing discussion of the possibilities implicit in the arrival of a new neighbor. But you don't detour with Barnaby, and besides it was a good day for work on the book.

"What are you thinking?" I asked Barnaby when we passed the Darby drive.

"I was wondering if you'd found a quotation for the section on the many voices of the sea."

"You're lying, but I'll go along with it. Yes. Emerson's 'Seashore.' 'I too have arts and sorceries; illusion dwells forever with the wave . . . I know what spells are laid. Leave me to deal with credulous and imaginative men.' Only I didn't find it. Thomas Two did."

"I know," said Barnaby. " 'I make some coast alluring, some lone isle, to distant men, who must go there or die.' "

"How alluring is this coast to Cory Sanderson, I wonder?"

"I don't even want to guess," Barnaby said. "As far as I'm concerned, the man doesn't exist. And it's not just because he doesn't want *me* to exist, or you, or the rest of us. I have a feeling he's going to be a thorn in our flesh."

"That's funny, because I've been thinking of him as one of those deep, nasty splinters in a thumb, or even under a fingernail."

"Well, forget him," said Barnaby, as if a command from him was all it took to erase Cory Sanderson.

Sara was off on the shore somewhere; low tide was as enthralling to her as high. When she had asked to stay with us for a while, she had promised to make herself useful and not be in the way, and she had kept the promise. She liked people, she was both curious and compassionate, but she could be satisfied to spend long hours alone. Sometimes she sounded ten years old and sometimes sixty. She made bread like a farm woman, but would brood over her Tarot cards in such a fog of concentration it was like self-hypnosis.

"I've just been expelled from my ashram," she had told us within twenty minutes of her arrival on our doorstep that January night.

"Why?" I asked, imagining a sideline as amateur call girl or drug pusher.

"I flunked Yoga," she said. "That wasn't too bad. My goodness, in India it takes years to get where they expect to be in six months. But I used to get silently hysterical with laughing sometimes—did you ever have that happen in church? You nearly die, trying to hold it in. And I wasn't always successful. It was terribly irreverent and upsetting, and then I was hungry all the time too, so—" She shrugged, resembling Barnaby. "So I thought, well, I've never seen Cape Silver, and here's this perfectly genuine cousin who's up to his neck in the nature bit, so I'll make a pilgrimage, like going to Walden, and maybe you'll give me a corner of the barn to put my sleeping bag in, and I can stay till winter's over. Then there's a place in New Mexico I want to try."

"Listen," said Barnaby coldly. "Don't you have a home to go to? I think we'd better go around to Shallows and make some telephone calls."

"I'm *nineteen*." If he hadn't been a Taggart too, it would have withered him. "And I have a home. Home is where, when you go there, they have to take you in. Who wants to go home under those conditions?"

"Well, we had to take you in," said Barnaby. "You didn't think we'd turn you away tonight in the dark and at least ten snowflakes, did you?"

"But you can tomorrow. That's the difference. And I won't blame you. If you let me stay awhile, it won't be because you have to."

"That's right," Barnaby agreed. "I may drive you to Williston tomorrow and put you on the bus for Alexandria." His narrow face was severe. She looked from one to the other of us with those green eyes, and her jaunty pose became a terribly frail dignity.

"I called them from Williston," she offered. "They haven't

cast me out, or anything, if that's what you think. I really love them. I didn't mean to sound the way I did."

"Except that you're taller," said Barnaby thoughtfully, "you don't look a bit different from the last time I saw you. How old were you that time?"

"Thirteen. And I thought you were smashing. Can I sleep in your barn, if it's got hay in it?" She was pale and beginning to droop.

"Oh, shut up about the barn," I said, "and take off that pack." She burst into tears.

In February she was still with us, painlessly all around, and as if to underline a point she had washed the dishes while we were gone that morning, and set bread to rise.

chapter 3

L orenzo didn't come for supper that night, and the next
day we had our obligatory mid-February snowstorm. It
continued for two days, and the third morning we woke
up to a cloudless sunrise over the sea, the Deepwood spruces
decorated like the trees on Christmas cards even to the
sparkle, and the snowy fields flushed pink, with lilac shadows
to mark the contours. It looked like a calm day for hauling
lobster traps, and Barnaby went off early with his dinnerbox.
He plowed with the jeep over to Shallows, where he kept a
skiff at Uncle Stewart's wharf.

Sara and I could hardly wait to get out on snowshoes. We
followed a trail just inside the edge of Deepwood down to the
field above the Raven Hole. Around us the snow fell from
the spruce boughs in twinkling powdery showers. The chickadees and crows, tutelary spirits of the winter woods, were
active over our heads. We snowshoed across the Far Meadow,
then carried the snowshoes around the long beach of Mussel
Cove where the tide had left bare shingle and sand. Out there
the loons called as if it were spring, the buffleheads splashed
and chased. Deer had crossed the beach not long before us;
Sara studied the tracks hopefully, still watching for a moose.

We went all the way to Shallows and had a mug-up with
Aunt Jess and the two Aussies, and then we walked home by
the road. The Shallows drive goes along the high bank above
the inner loop of the harbor, where tall old birches and
younger moosewoods throw an involved pattern of shadows
over the water or clam flats below. This morning it was mud
and clammers down there. No Lorenzo, but the green aluminum skiff was there and the man's dog lay near it. The Ger-

man shepherd went everywhere with him, and was known to be a perfect gentleman as long as he and Gus Flint were ignored. Some other clammers worked off the sand curve of beach below the bank, and Sara shouted their names. Two heads came up. "Hi, Sara. Hi, Mirabell!" Across the flats the dog stood up and barked. "Hi, Hugo!" Sara called. That she knew the dog's name was to be expected of Sara. She had probably even patted it, but for me to approach any German shepherd past obvious puppyhood tightens my scalp and ices my stomach. This one was actually wagging his tail, though with restraint.

After supper the Boones walked out to Cape Silver in the clear starshine to tell us what had happened to them that day; Cory Sanderson had arrived, and the impact had made more than a slight dent.

Kyle Boone is very tall and spare, with fresh color. His neat, tawny Vandyke and his way of thoughtfully considering one from mild brown eyes gives him an aura of intellectuality, as if his proper background should be great universities instead of great rivers. Deirdre is a truly pretty woman, with short brown hair turning gray, and humorous blue eyes, a dimple in each cheek. She also has one of those sympathetic voices that can make a simple Good Morning sound like a special good will message to you alone.

On that day of Cory Sanderson's arrival, the man who had come around to plow out their lane, after the town had cleared the black road, told them that Rex Ashton had asked him to do the Darby drive because the new man was going to move in that afternoon. The Boones knew that the place had been sold. But they hadn't seen us, so they didn't know that the man wanted to be left alone.

In the late afternoon they walked up to the Darby house. They took a bubbling-hot clam pie, one of Deirdre's specialties, and a wedge of fresh apple cake. Their dog was with them. He was a very large and leggy mongrel who appeared to be made all of yarn fringe in assorted shades of brown, with a pair of lovely eyes under raveled bangs. They put him on a leash before they reached the house. Seeing some movement beyond the kitchen windows, they went to the back door.

Kyle knocked. There was silence inside, so he knocked again, and finally there were slow, very reluctant steps; they thought he must be lame, elderly, or otherwise feeble. Finally he opened the door and stood there without speaking, looking at them from behind square-shaped dark glasses. He was neither lame nor elderly. He was lean, straight, and conservatively but smartly dressed for country living.

His silence and the dark glasses were flattening. However, Kyle introduced Deirdre and himself, and said, "Welcome to Applecross." Deirdre held out the basket with her most beguiling smile. Most people find it impossible not to smile back at Deirdre.

"Something for supper," she said. "Getting a meal the first night is always such a nuisance."

Sanderson made no move to take the basket. He said in a toneless voice, "I don't wish to socialize."

"It was so unexpected," Kyle told us, "that I almost laughed out loud. Deirdre's mouth actually flew open, and that was funny too. Then I told him that he'd misunderstood us, we hadn't intended to move in on him, we were simply following the custom of welcoming new neighbors, and so forth. To which he replied, without a glimmer of expression, that if he'd wanted neighbors he'd have stayed where he came from."

"*Then* he added," said Deirdre, " 'And I don't want to see that dog on the premises again.' While Prince was standing there wagging his tail madly and smiling at him with his usual lack of discrimination. *Well!* After twenty-five years of trying to be a perfect representative of my country wherever I was, and never saying the wrong thing no matter what the provocation, I nearly blew my top."

"I make it a practice never to kick my wife in public,' said Kyle, "but I almost did that time. However, she got the message without violence on my part. Then I told Sanderson that from now on he might get a nod from us if we met—unavoidably—but probably not, if that would make him happier. And he said, unsmiling, that it would make him very happy. On that cooperative note we left."

"Did you *ever*?" demanded Deirdre. "It wasn't what he said about Prince. Some of my best friends can't stand dogs. It was the whole thing, beginning with that preposterous statement. 'I don't wish to socialize.' Where does he get his dialogue, for heaven's sake? It sounds like a cheap imitation of Henry James."

"Relax, Deirdre." Barnaby handed her a drink. "Wind down."

"That'll be enough of that from you, young man. I've been hearing it from Kyle all day." She took the drink.

"What's his voice like?" Sara asked. "James Cagney? Humphrey Bogart? Edward G. Robinson?" She'd been watching a lot of late movies with Uncle Stewart.

"I'm not sure how to describe it," said Kyle. "It's colorless, with no discernible accent. The whole effect is as negative as the dark glasses."

"Well, is he very dark? Could he be Sicilian?"

"He's dark, but—"

She took that and was gone like a flashing mackerel. "*Mafia!*"

"We're voting for Martin Bormann," said Kyle. "But he's too young, unless he's Martin Bormann with plastic surgery."

"No, he's got to be Cosa Nostra or whatever they call it among themselves," Sara told us. "I've been reading all about them. He's taken his money and gone legit, or maybe it's some of the Family's money, and he doesn't want them to find him, especially the Godfather. But I can't understand him being so stupid about hiding out in a place like Applecross. He ought to know enough not to go around in dark glasses being nasty. It just makes him stick out like a sore thumb. Somebody ought to tell him."

"Maybe somebody will," said Barnaby, "but it's not going to be you, in case you have any plans for making a call."

Sara looked blighted. Deirdre said, "He'll find it out for

himself, soon enough. I've met people like him before. He doesn't have to be a gangster to be hostile and suspicious; he's like a cat in a strange garret, that's all. . . . But it was such a total surprise that I was disoriented. Just for a moment, dear," she assured Kyle. "I wouldn't really have called him an arrogant and cantankerous son of a bitch."

We exploded.

After the Boones left we talked about the gratuitous rudeness tossed like mud into the faces of two very good, very kind people.

"What a difference between Sanderson and this other new man in town," I said wistfully. "Of course the nice creative people never have much money, so we get Cory Sanderson down here instead of What's-His-Name who's building a boat and writing books."

"But what about Lorenzo?" she asked.

"I saw him salvaging lumber out on Charlie's Island this morning," Barnaby said. "He's probably so mad he doesn't want to talk to anybody. There's a time when you can't stand sympathy."

"Just the same, I don't think he should be left to himself too much," said Sara.

"Lorenzo knows he has friends, Sara," Barnaby said. "If he wants to be left alone, we won't go busting in on him."

"I think he *needs* to be busted in on. He's probably not even eating."

"Listen, the way he was heaving those timbers around, he's not living on air."

Sara gave him an annoyed look. "I have a hunch about these gentle people like Lorenzo."

Barnaby was knitting trapheads. He tipped back in his chair, twine suspended, and grinned. "You think he's ticking away like a time bomb, and Sanderson's going up in a big bang one night?"

"It's not funny. I laid out my Tarot cards last night for Lorenzo, and they weren't good at all."

"Tell me something." He pointed the traphead needle at

her. "Do events influence the cards, or do the cards influence events? Or is it just the way you shuffle them?"

She arose, very straight of back, took her flashlight from the mantel, and went toward the back stairs. "Good night, *Mirabell*."

"I suppose you're going up to lay out the cards for me," Barnaby called after her. "Don't tell me the results. They'd probably scare me foolish."

"Some people aren't intelligent or sensitive enough to be scared," she said with immense dignity from the landing.

"You forgot your hot water bottle," I called, but was answered by the sound of a closing door.

"She won't be cold, she's too mad." Barnaby said.

"You shouldn't kid her about the cards, it's like knocking someone's religion."

"Then she'd better change her religion. That stuff's all right for a game, but she takes it too seriously."

We settled down to work. The publisher had asked Barnaby to compose a memoir of Thomas Two, and he began to write at the kitchen table, using a yellow legal pad. I brought books out to the kitchen, Palgrave's *Golden Treasury* and the *Oxford Dictionary of Quotations*, and put my feet up on the stove hearth. One of the nicest things about this job of ours was tracing the references to the great nature writers, both in poetry and prose. Thomas Two had been sparse in speech, but not in thought; a fragrance, a change of light, a shift in the wind, would often bring a particular phrase to his mind. Frequently he remembered enough to write it all out when he recorded the whole experience. Other times he put down a few words, occasionally only a name. In search, I would bumble around contentedly in his books like a bee in a rosebush, dipping into everything along the way.

Wood shifted softly in the stove, the teakettle steamily sang, Barnaby's pen moved over the paper in the lamplight, and I looked at him sometimes, with a secret joy in the long head with the rough bronze-colored hair, the perfect convolutions of an ear, the fold of an eyelid and angle of cheek-bone, the slightly frowning but serene involvement in what he was doing.

In the morning it was another good day to go to haul. Barnaby and I ate breakfast before daylight, watching Venus rise huge and dazzling over the southeastern sea. She was disappearing in the sunrise and Barnaby had gone when Sara came downstairs. She told me mischievously that she'd laid out the cards for Barnaby after all, and he was going to be rich, and fortunate. "That means he can enjoy his riches. But I won't tell him. When it happens, you'll remember this morning and tell him what I said."

"I'll write the promise in blood," I said. "After all, I should be rich and fortunate right along with him, shouldn't I? Or did it say anywhere he'd be a swinging single by then?"

"No domestic discord showed up, so I guess he'll let you share."

We set out later to walk to the harbor to collect the shrimp I'd ordered from Jean's husband. We stopped on the Neck to watch the buffleheads in the harbor and listen to the old-squaws on Morgan's Bay, making sounds like a clarinet quintet by Mozart. The sun was so warm that the snow was melting in the middle of the road. We walked up the hill making snowballs and throwing them at each other, laughing and dodging. We passed the Boones' mailbox, and after a little distance something like a cloudy cold came over us, though the sun didn't dim. At the next driveway there was no mailbox, nothing to announce that there was anything special about this particular private road. It curved off among white birches and big spruces and could have led anywhere, except that one knew Morgan's Bay lay at the end of it; it was so quiet we could still hear the old-squaws.

We stopped. Neither of us said anything, yet we didn't seem able to move along. Down below at the Boones', Prince's bark echoed awesomely through the woods. Someone whistled, and the barking stopped. A downy woodpecker tapped on one of the birches. There was a little rush of wings and a miniature snow flurry as chickadees swooped into a spruce top and dislodged a layer of snow.

"Let's go make a call," I said suddenly. "Let's pretend we don't know what he said to Seth and the Boones. We're just stopping by to say Feel free to cross onto Cape Silver when you want to look at the open ocean." I started off up the drive, but surprisingly, for one who had hitchhiked all over the country (attended by a very conscientious guardian angel, according to Barnaby), she hung back. More surprisingly she said, "Barnaby told me to stay away from there."

"He didn't tell *me* that. Come on." She approached slowly.

A crow called suddenly over our heads, and stopped us in our tracks. Then we heard footsteps crunching in the snow from beyond the next curve, and waited in suspense for the Mysterious Stranger. There was a tightening under my ribs, and Sara's eyes had such an awed, strained gaze that I wondered if she really believed her Mafia story.

Lorenzo tramped around the bend, hands in his pockets, head down. He wore his customary collection of odd jackets and sweaters, a visored tartan cap with earlaps, heavy lined jeans, and felts-and-rubbers on his feet.

"Wow," Sara breathed. "For a minute I thought it was Mr. Misanthrophe in person. Hi, Lorenzo!"

He appeared too dejected to be startled. "Oh. 'Morning. What'd you call him? Can't you think of anything worse?"

"We can, but it would probably shock you to hear it from these fair female lips," I said. "What's the matter, Lorenzo?"

"I blame it all on that Historical Society," he said savagely. "Well, maybe not on all of 'em, but Madam President was down here to see him this morning." He could never bear to refer to her by her name. "Rammed right in, you know her. Well, I showed up right in the middle of it, and she was yarning on about how important the house was, and maybe he didn't know all these things, so she came down to tell him. I spoke up and said if there was anything to tell about the house I'm the one to tell it, and she turned the color of a sculpin, then slaps me on the shoulder and says what a funny feller I am, and invited him for drinks tomorrow night to meet some of the neighbors."

He stopped. "And?" I prompted, unable to wait.

"He said he'd already met enough neighbors to do him for the rest of his life. She laughed like he'd said something comical enough to kill. 'I know what you mean,' she says, 'but you'll find out the rest of the town is a lot different from the harbor.' She gives me a *so there* look and prances out."

"Then what happened?" Sara asked, breathless.

"This is what I blame *her* for. Getting him so irritated he took it out on me. When I began telling him about the house being my special field, you might call it, and about all the stuff I've got to show him, well, he didn't let me more than get started before he was showing me the door." Lorenzo colored behind his reddish whiskers, and took off his glasses. As usual they were dirty, and as usual the clear hazel eyes were a surprise. Young, as Sara said, and defenseless. "You don't know what a funny feeling it gave me," he said in his soft country voice. "To be put out of my house. Because that's what it's been to me, all my life . . . I offered to keep on being handyman and caretaker, I said I'd do it for nothing. And he said if he needed a handyman he'd hire one in the usual way. And if I had any keys, he wanted them. On second thought, he'd have all the locks changed. Just as much as called me a thief. *Me!*"

"He's an ignorant oaf, Lorenzo," I said. "He's got money and nothing else."

"I was always welcome there," Lorenzo said. "I know the kids sometimes laughed at me when they got older, but I was good enough to take 'em clamming and fishing, and I taught 'em to sail, too. I've drunk many a beer in that house . . . To be told to get out and don't ever come back—"

He turned away from us, staring into the woods. Sara's eyes were watering and her face puckering up; she began searching her pockets. I handed her a tissue. My own throat felt tight. Lorenzo swung angrily back to us, his eyes bright with tears behind the smeared lenses. "I wish I hadn't told you about it!" he said in a fury. "Good Christ, where's my pride?"

"Well, I'm sorry you said it too," I said, "if you're going to hate us forever afterwards."

"Oh, I won't hate you, Mirabell," he muttered. He gave Sara a sidewise look. "You neither. If you're sniffling on my account, thanks, but there's no need of it."

He slogged off down the driveway. Sara blew her nose and swore in a whisper.

"My, but you have a picturesque vocabulary," I said. "I'm glad you save it for rare occasions. Keeps the luster on it."

"Well, I have to do something if I can't give Cory Sanderson the knee in his vital statistics."

"Let's go on to Jean's. Even if I weren't mad with him I wouldn't chance the reception we'd get after he's had both Madam President and Lorenzo telling him what to do with his house—"

"I have another suggestion," she said.

"That's what I'm afraid of. Nope. We'll still try it, but later." We walked back toward the road. "A few more mornings like this one and he'll be justified in fortifying the place."

"Don't you have any feeling at all for Lorenzo?"

"Of course I do! But to be absolutely fair, what would you think if you were in Cory Sanderson's position?"

"I would never be in Cory Sanderson's position!" she declaimed. "For one thing I'm a kind, sensitive, reasonable human being, and he's probably a criminal in hiding."

"All right," I said. "But a lot of people besides Cory Sanderson might not want to take on somebody like Lorenzo. We're all used to him, but what if you were a nervous stranger from the city—" She opened her mouth and I said hastily, "Forget that, you'd never be a nervous stranger from the city. But they do exist, and this is so foreign to them, they don't know whom to trust except familiar symbols like the oil man, the meter man, and so forth."

"Well," she said grudgingly.

"Look, when we get home from Jean's, lay out the cards for Cory, and maybe we'll get lucky and find out he's not going to stay around."

She grinned. "All right, I will!"

chapter 4

She did get out her cards after supper that night, with a good deal of unhelpful comment from Barnaby. But she shed him as easily as he could shed anyone who harassed him. She used what she called an ancient Celtic method, requiring only ten cards. There was something a little eerie about her low voice as she laid out the vividly patterned cards in the lamplight.

"This covers him . . . This crosses him . . . This crowns him . . ." She completed the design, saying, "This is what will come," and sat back to contemplate it. The display meant nothing to me, except that the sight of a man down and pierced by ten swords, a black knight labeled Death, and a gorgeously bestial Devil, didn't seem to offer much cheer.

"A nice lot of goodies you've got for him," I said.

"The death card doesn't have to mean literal death. It could mean the ruin of a plan or an idea. The ten of swords doesn't have to mean death either."

"But it would leave him as full of holes as a colander," said Barnaby.

"That's behind him, anyway. He's run away from it."

"Now I can understand his unfriendly attitude," said Barnaby dryly.

"I'm interested in what's ahead. What's to come." I touched the last card.

"The three of pentacles, reversed. I can't make anything out of that. It's not conclusive, it's no answer at all." She began to gather the cards up. "There's no sense in going through them all when there's nothing at the end."

"What's the Devil for?" I insisted.

She shrugged. "Violence, force, maybe even fatality, but still it's not necessarily evil, any more than the Death card. Anyway, like the swords, it already *is*. It's the basis of the matter. And don't ask me what *that* is."

"Somehow I get the feeling he doesn't come with very good references," I said. Still preoccupied, she shaped the pack and put it in its box. When she went up the back stairs with her hot water bottle and two apples she forgot to say goodnight.

"How about a fresh pot of coffee?" Barnaby asked. As I made it, the imagined face of Cory Sanderson, featureless unless you could call the dark glasses a feature, was very much in my mind, like the suspicion that a toothache is about to begin. I would be glad when I met him and could decide for myself that he was a retired professor or businessman turned sociopath after some scarifying tragedy. (The man pierced by ten swords?)

I carried the coffee and a plate of thin molasses cookies into the dining room. It is a large room that faces both east and south. Living alone, Thomas Two had turned it into a library and study. We kept it that way, and slept there too in the worst winter months. There is a fireplace on the inside wall, which shares the central chimney with the living room fireplace.

I chose a record of Guiomar Novaes playing Chopin nocturnes, put it on the little Philips player powered by six flashlight batteries, and settled down to work on my side of the big table.

With the familiar motions and the familiar music, and the small movements of the fire like a cat in the room, I was at once absorbed, forgetting Tarot cards and Cory Sanderson. So I was startled when Barnaby said quite a while later, "I suppose we're lucky she isn't into astrology."

That night Cory Sanderson turned up in an enthralling dream in which he told me all about himself. He was very nice, not a bit like everything I'd heard so far, and I told him so. "But that wasn't me at all," he explained. When I woke up I could remember how logical the whole thing seemed, at the same time knowing it was too idiotic a dream to tell at breakfast. Barnaby likes a meditative silence with his first cup of coffee, anyway. Even Sara had learned.

But I was even more determined to get a look at the man. Being naturally prudent, I kept my resolution to myself. After lunch Barnaby was leaving for Shallows to take his boat over to Elmo's wharf and gas up for tomorrow. He asked us if we wanted to ride along in the jeep and visit with Aunt Jess for a while or go across the harbor for anything. I told him truthfully that I was going for a walk, and Sara said she was going to walk too. It was the perfect time for it. The wind had gone around to the southwest again, blustery but mild and smelling of rain.

I gave him a decent interval to get out of the dooryard and then said to Sara, "Let's go call on Cory Sanderson."

She was pulling on her boots and looked up at me through her hair in astonishment. "You've got to be kidding."

"I said we'd do it, and we will. I'll take him a jar of something, just as if he were a real human being."

She clumped down the stairs after me into the roomy dirt-floored cellar and gave advice as I turned my flashlight on the shelves. "Don't take him any rose-hip jam, he'll think we're food freaks. Besides, it's too good for him. It's all too good for him. Currant?" she said in dismay when I chose a jar. "But that's a delicacy!"

"All my jellies are delicacies," I said haughtily. "I picked currant because most men like it."

"What makes you think he's like most men?"

"Well, I expect to come away from there with an opinion on the subject."

We followed a deer track down across the Indian Meadow, where the yellow–brown grasses and the odd fragile stalks of dill and asters poked up through melting snow. We watched a fox mousing, and then came out on the shore of Morgan Bay. We were having "low dreen" tides, and the clammers were far out on the soft flats not exposed at usual low tides.

They waded knee-deep or sometimes thigh-deep through the mud, pulling each leg out with an effort that made you ache to watch, pushing their hods ahead of them.

We wandered along the firm shingle and sand, investigating provocative objects entangled in rockweed; they usually turned out to be red, green, or blue detergent bottles. We made piles of them here and there along the shore for later burning. We found a couple of beautifully shaped and painted wooden buoys, which we purists prefer to the Styrofoam ones, but because of the law we couldn't take them without being larcenous; somebody without our principles (really Barnaby's) would probably pick them up later.

Among the rocks at the Neck we found a soggy tennis ball and saved it for Prince. When we came to the Boones' shore, he was frisking around a couple of clammers, sometimes doing a little digging on his own. When he saw us he splashed happily toward us with a dead crab in his mouth, dropped it in favor of the ball, and went loping off in a fine spray of mud to show his treasure to his new friends.

"Imagine anyone taking a dislike to Prince," Sara said. "That's another thing I despise about the man."

"Not liking dogs is no sign of a criminal nature. Maybe he was badly bitten once. Traumatized."

"Why do you have to be so fair to that fink?"

"It's because I have a really wonderful nature," I said. "Here's the famous inscription."

"Which now belongs to the fink," said Sara. We stood looking at it as people had been looking at it for at least two hundred years, and maybe longer. They had always found what they wanted in it. Roman numerals and letters and Runic writing were the most popular choices. They drew careful copies, made rubbings. In later days they photographed, trying all sorts of angles and filters to see if something else would be brought out that the human eye had missed.

Centuries of weather and the tides had eroded the sharpness, but the mystery was always there. "I like to think it was meant for some special person," I said. "Someone who was to come later. But how much later? Maybe he's been here and gone. Or maybe he hasn't come yet." There was gooseflesh on my arms; so do people invoke their own phantoms.

"Maybe it's Cory," said Sara. I laughed, but she was staring at the inscription the way she'd gazed at the cards last night. "He's so strange," she murmured. "Even allowing for eccentricity. Maybe there's a very good reason for it. Do you believe there's life on other planets?"

"I don't believe or disbelieve. I have an open mind."

"That carving could have been done by somebody from outer space. You're right about a message for someone in the future, and that's why Cory's here. He has some mission, but *what?*"

"He came to Fremont first, remember." I was taking it as her joke, but damn the gooseflesh. "What about all the places Seth showed him, back of beyond?"

"He was homing in. Fremont was as close as he could make it at first, but gradually his interior compass steadied. He knew none of those places was the right one."

"But he didn't know about Applecross. It was Seth who brought him—"

"Why did Seth think of it?" she demanded triumphantly.

"Because the Darby place was listed with him as well as with half a dozen others," I said in exasperation.

"If you could keep going back and back, for as long as that's been on that rock, I'll bet you could trace a clear pattern of predestination; everything falling into place to bring an entity here with the earth name of Cory Sanderson—"

"We interrupt 'The Twilight Zone' to bring you this special bulletin," I said. "The correct translation of the mysterious inscription on the eastern shore of Morgan Bay has been confirmed beyond all doubt. It's Martian for 'Kilroy was here'."

"Go ahead and laugh!" she defied me. "You'll see!"

"You mean when he comes out as his real self, all green

with pointy ears, and takes off those glasses and shoots a paralytic beam from his four eyes?"

She surrendered. "I hope he isn't watching," she gasped, turning her back toward the house. "He'll think we're laughing at him."

We straightened our faces with some effort, and began climbing up over the ledges. The natural terraces were carpeted in dead grass, reindeer moss, and shiny wine-colored wintergreen leaves. A few scarlet berries remained. I picked one and crushed it, releasing the fragrance that evoked bright pink fondant hearts on Valentine's Day, or those big chocolate-coated patties wrapped in foil.

The story-and-a-half house had a succession of three ells in graduated sizes, the smallest opening into the carriage house, which loomed over all the rest and had a codfish weather vane swinging madly in the gusts. Seen from the front, the classic pattern of the early 1800's was unflawed, if your eye could ignore the television antenna on the main house, and the power lines strung in from the road. The cedar shingles, though no more the originals than were the six-above six-below windows, had weathered to a silvery gray, and the trim was austerely white. In July the climbing ramblers on either side of the front door cascaded crimson from their trellises.

I admit I felt a painful twinge to know that the roses and codfish weather vane had passed into alien hands.

"You scared?" Sara whispered.

"Just wondering if anybody was home, that's all," I muttered. The bare canes of the ramblers rattled in a little burst of wind, and tapped against the strip windows on either side of the front door. Smoke blew down from the chimney and puffed into our faces.

"He has to be an earthling," I said, "because he likes a wood fire. Now that's something in his favor, isn't it?" I acted more confident than I felt when we stepped onto the granite doorstep. We were taking a chance on being insulted, or at least

[33]

snubbed, and I didn't know how I'd react. Whatever happened, it would be on our own heads.

"Here goes," I said jauntily, and lifted the knocker. It was wrought iron, the ring held in the mouth of a bear that a later Darby had brought from Switzerland.

The door was vehemently opened and the man stood there regarding us. At least the square dark glasses regarded us. His face wide at the cheekbones sloped in sharply to a narrow but not weak jaw. His mouth was set so hard his lips were almost invisible; the effect was of exasperation or pain. I went completely blank.

"*Well?*" he said. On the almost visible question mark his mouth snapped shut again. I came to my senses and subdued an impulse to say we were conducting a membership drive for the local Communist cell. Sara said coldly, "We aren't from the Historical Society, if that's what you're worried about. This is Mirabell Taggart and I'm Sara Brownell."

The dark squares turned on her. Then they were aimed past her at the shore and the broad reach of glimmering clam flats now darkening under a fog roller. The small figures of the men bent in work or laboring through mud enhanced the sense of great uncluttered distances. One of the clammers we'd seen earlier came into view just off the beach and began to dig. "Come in," said Sanderson. "Quickly. No sense letting in all outdoors."

The door shut behind us with a solid thud that echoed in my stomach. Given the right shape of beard he'd look like any one of several notorious murderers of women.

"We only wanted to say hello and leave this," I said, bringing the jar of jelly out of my pocket. But he was looking out the side windows.

"Who is that down there?" he asked abruptly. "Do you know?"

The fog roller went over, darkening the hall to twilight. Sara's eyes met mine behind his back. "I don't know his name," I said. "He comes from Amity, I think."

"But that's all you know about him?" Kyle had mentioned the colorless voice.

"There are plenty of clammers and wormers we get to know by sight, and never know their names. We don't think anything about it."

"But it's outrageous to have them come onto your property like this!" He turned to us. "Just going anywhere they please, with no permission. You don't know what some of them could have in mind! It's indefensible. You may put up with it, but I don't have to. I'm going to call the police."

You could hardly have called it an outburst, coming from that impassive face. It occurred to me that he might have had extensive plastic surgery after a terrible accident, but only on his face; he moved well, like a dancer or athlete. He was reaching for the wall telephone between two doors, and I said quickly, "He's on state property now, and he came by boat, so he hasn't trespassed."

"What do you mean, state property? I have a warranty deed that says that shore line is mine."

"Only the state can shut off the shore below mean high water mark. If you don't believe me, ask the police. Either they'll tell you what I did, or they'll refer you to the warden, and he'll tell you."

He took his hand away from the telephone. No visible change of expression below the dark glasses. There was an awkward silence. I set the jar of jelly on the hall table.

"We'll leave this and be going. You probably don't give a damn, but it's a local custom. Welcome to Applecross, Mr. Sanderson," I said insincerely. "You might find it more exciting if we sacrificed a cow in your honor, but that sort of thing went out a few years ago. At least around here."

I headed for the front door. Behind me Sara said in the clear and merciless voice of an innocent child, "I thought at first you might be blind, and that's why you wear those glasses even in the house. But you could see that man out there. So you aren't blind."

"Excuse me," he said. It was reluctant, but he did say it, and he took off his glasses. This change always takes me by surprise, because the eyes populate the face. Suddenly I remembered my dream, in which he had dark eyes, expressive with light and life. In reality they were a light clear bluish-gray, with a darker rim around the iris.

"That's better," Sara said, smiling. He didn't smile back.

"Are you Seth Taggart's sister?" he asked me.

"Sister-in-law. I'm married to his brother, Barnaby. Sara's their cousin."

He turned those pale bright eyes on her as if to carefully fit the name to the object. "Won't you come in and sit down?"

She glanced at me with an amused, questioning tilt of her head. I said graciously, "For a moment. I know you're busy, and we don't intend to pester."

"Well, as long as you're not from the Historical Society," he said to Sara, who laughed. I began to feel invisible, which was fine with me. I could do the observing while Sara did the distracting. We went into the long room, which had originally been the parlor and dining room in the very old days. It had a pine-beamed ceiling, off-white walls, and a fieldstone fireplace dominating the north wall, the mantel a polished pine plank. There were books and papers scattered around; at least he was literate. I tried to read names without being obvious. I recognized *The Wall Street Journal* and *The New York Times*. There were also a couple of new biographies of the man-against-the-sea-jungle-desert-Everest type.

"What a marvelous room!" Sara said. "Are these curtains and slipcovers your choice?"

"No, it's just as it was left. Are they right for it?"

"Oh, of course; but you'll want to make it your own, naturally." She wandered around like a cat making itself at home. "When you get your own pictures and your other treasures in place, and change the colors, then you'll feel settled in." She had taken on a reassuring, almost maternal tone.

I stood looking into the fire so I could concentrate on

voices. When you are just listening without seeing, you catch all sorts of nuances. Freed from association with his rigid face his voice had taken on a tint, faint but definite. "What do you think would be a good color for the curtains?" he was asking Sara. "This stuff's pretty neutral, it seems to me." There was also the ghost of an accent, but too elusive for me even to make a guess at its origin except that it was North American.

"Oh gosh," Sara was saying. "Don't ask *me*. Mirabell's the expert."

"Don't put the man on the spot, Sara."

He managed to look at me then, with the kind of politeness I can do without. It's worse than downright antagonism. But if he'd had plastic surgery he couldn't help the way his face was, so I said offhandedly, "This room gets sunshine from noon till sunset, and with the white walls it's so bright you could have any dark solid without sacrificing any of the light—wine, forest green, sea blue, even brown. Or combine one of them with some good print or a muted tartan." My professional instincts took over in spite of me. "A blend of earth colors would be both striking and restful."

"Thanks." He was back to Sara again. Not that he'd ever been away from her, in a manner of speaking. "Would you like a drink?"

There was a little smile brimming in her eyes; vanity or mischief, I couldn't tell. "Mirabell, what do you think?"

"Sit down, please," he urged with an approximation of hospitality. "What would you like? Scotch, vodka, sherry—*tea?*" he added as an afterthought and seemed almost pleased with himself, though one couldn't be sure.

We decided on sherry as restrained and ladylike, but less complicated than tea. He went out to the kitchen, and Sara followed him, chattily. "Do you mind? I've never been in this house, and it's so *old*. Look at those thumb latches ... Oh, a fireplace in the kitchen. That's tremendous! You can have indoor cookouts."

Ayuh, I thought cynically. I gave the reading material a closer look in search of a clue. Beside the solitary adventure-

and-conquest types, I found something else when I picked up a newspaper. Under it lay a new, thick book about Leonardo da Vinci.

It was a sight to cause ravening greed in even the gentlest soul, and I'm hardly that. Besides, he had it marked with slips of paper in different places, and I was avid to see what and why. As if Sara had telepathic reception, she went bubbling on like the Binnorie Brook in spring freshet, admiring the little brass buttons on the cupboard doors, exclaiming over the usefulness of a pantry, suggesting a driftwood arrangement for the kitchen mantel, and could she look into the next ell, which, she told him knowledgeably, was the summer kitchen. Her voice grew fainter but no less vibrant as she reached the third ell, which was the woodshed. In an ecstasy of adoration of wood, she asked which was maple and which was birch. All I could hear of Cory was an indistinct murmur now and then, and I wondered if desperation had him by the throat.

I sat down on the sofa before the fire, totally focused on the da Vinci book and the places he had marked.

But they were coming back. Sara had her jacket under her arm and looked quite at home, she winked at me past his shoulder. He brought in a round tray of heavy copper with glasses and a decanter, and poured the wine and handed me my glass without really looking at me. There was a faint color on his cheekbones. When he gave Sara her glass she lifted it to him and said gravely, "To a long and happy life in this house, Mr. Sanderson."

"Yes," I said, raising mine. He didn't say thanks, but drank his wine quickly while we still sipped. "This is very good sherry," I said, and was about to say something nice about the Leonardo book when he said to Sara, "I've never seen such green eyes. Are you a mermaid?"

"I don't think so," she said seriously. She looked down at her feet. "No tail, see?"

"Isn't there a fairy tale about a mermaid who wanted to

become human? I don't remember who granted her the feet, but they hurt with every step, as if she were walking on knives."

It was so much more fantastic than my dream had been that I didn't in the least mind being invisible. I kept thinking, Wait till I tell Barnaby.

"Well, it can't be about me," said Sara. "I've seen my own newborn footprint. You've got me mixed up with some other water baby."

He stood there silently regarding her. He couldn't ever have been a small boy, reading fairy tales; no, he'd arrived on earth exactly as he was now.

"I've always been fascinated by mermaids, though," Sara said, "and I know the story." She laughed. "And there's 'The Forsaken Merman.' I love that poem. I wonder if it hurt his Margaret to walk." It was no conversation, it was a monologue, because he seemed to have retreated completely after what he had said. Finishing my sherry as fast as I decently could, I got up and said, "We'd better be going. Thank you, Mr. Sanderson." I started toward the hall. "Any time you'd like a really long hike, come over onto Cape Silver."

My voice didn't even raise an echo in that wilderness.

"You can get a real ocean feeling on the outside beaches," Sara told him.

He was listening to *her* all right. "Thanks, but I'm not much for outdoors. Besides, I've got twenty-odd acres here to look over first."

"Like getting a little country all your own, isn't it?" I said cheerily. By now I knew better than to expect a positive response. We'd have been out on the doorstep in another moment, but Sara said suddenly, "Oh, have you seen the mysterious inscription carved on one of your rocks down front? Nobody knows when it was done. Even the very old people in town can't say." She sounded awed. "It could have been *before Christ.*"

"One theory is that the Romans got this far," I contributed.

"Or the Martians." Sara grinned at me. "So don't be surprised if you see people standing down there looking at something. It'll be your rock."

Without changing expression, his face flushed deeply all at once, and then paled. "I think I've heard it mentioned," he said evenly. By Madam President, I thought.

"Come on, Sara," I said. "I hate people who get ready to go and then stand and yak. Thanks again for the sherry, Mr. Sanderson."

Sara thanked him too, and got a nod, but he didn't thank us for the jelly, and he didn't say Come again.

chapter 5

We kept a mannerly restraint until we were out of sight of his windows. The incoming tide rippled across the flats, gleaming or dulling as thinning clouds passed over the sun. The diggers were gone; Prince too, though we could see the tracks of his big feet where he'd cavorted in the damp sand. Up the slope to our left the Boone house was snugged down among its spruces, its long windows reflecting sky and water back at us.

"Well, what do you think?"

"You're right. He's a Martian. But his cover's good. Imagine their knowing about the little mermaid, for instance. I think his green blood was stirred by the sight of you."

"I was thinking of some planet even farther out than Mars." She giggled. "That was a great line about the mermaid. I thought, Hmm, there's more in him than meets the eye. But he didn't follow it up."

"Are you disappointed?" I asked. "They probably never taught him to carry on that earthy badinage."

"Hey, that would be a good name for our bird list! The Earthy Badinage."

"A very gregarious and noisy bird," I said, "just the opposite of the Cory Crow, mutantis Sandersonious, who has square black eye rings—"

"And is an abnormally shy fellow who hides in dense coverts," recited Sara.

"And utters sharp aggressive cries when approached."

"Are we going to tell Barnaby where we've been?" Sara asked.

"Can you think of any other explanation for this sherry

breath besides an outright lie? Besides, I want to tell him about the books and the newspapers and so forth. But I won't mention the mermaid bit if you want to keep it sacred."

"*Sacred!*" she exploded. "My God, he must be forty, and older men aren't my bag. If you want to know what really turns me on, it's some gorgeous young guy in rubber boots."

"I've been through that. Are you thinking about Ronnie Deming, or Ruel Jason?"

"But seriously," she said, "I wouldn't want Barnaby to get mad. He's so darned much like my father." She blew hard and rolled her eyes to the sky. "So *male*."

"That's what I like about him," I said.

But Barnaby was not only amiable but interested. "What's your overall impression, based on intuition and so forth?" he asked me.

"Well, if I regard him as something dropped off from a flying saucer and not very comfortable in human disguise, I can forgive him for acting as if I didn't have one atom of charm. He certainly didn't turn *me* on, either. But still, I didn't think twenty-six was over the hill—"

"Is that what you went to find out? Isn't my word good enough for you? Mirabell, I didn't know you had this intense need for reassurance, for discovering your identity as a desirable woman, for—"

"Oh, shut up," I said.

"*I* think he's paranoid," said Sara. "He's not going to put up with clammers, and when we told him about the inscription he looked as if he were planning a machine gun nest in the juniper."

"He doesn't have to be paranoid," Barnaby said reasonably. "Maybe he's been mugged, robbed, or burgled often enough to condition him. Every time somebody wanders into view he probably thinks they're casing the joint."

"Anyway, Sara really scored," I said. "He asked her if she was a mermaid. And he said it straight-faced. Not a whiff of whimsy."

"Hey, that gives me another idea!" Sara said. "Maybe he has gills under that turtleneck sweater."

"Are you two so completely dazzled by the Creature from the Black Lagoon that you can't think about supper?"

Sara sank to her knees before him. "Less than the dust under thy chariot wheels, my lord."

"Wait till I get my boot off and you can kiss my big toe," said Barnaby.

We didn't mention Cory Sanderson again all through supper. I think we had tacitly agreed that the subject was closed for good. But in the evening Jean and Tony came around from the harbor, so Sanderson bounded to the surface again like a pot buoy in the wake of a lobster boat. His very elusiveness made him conspicuous, and speculation was always an indoor sport in a slack season. But after the guessing game wore itself out he would be half-forgotten as long as he was not visible.

He had been seen once at the store when he stopped for gas just before closing on a Saturday night, when the place was always crowded. He drove a Porsche, which attracted the innocent admiration of some teen-age boys. The experience must have been so unnerving that he wasn't likely to fill his tank there again if he could help it. His groceries were being delivered from Williston, and his mail didn't come to Applecross post office, so he must have got it in Williston.

"Maybe he doesn't get any mail," Sara suggested, "because nobody knows where he is, or else he's got nobody to write to him."

"He's sure as hell not getting his power and telephone for nothing, honey," Tony said. "He must get bills."

"His telephone's unlisted, by the way," Jean said. "*I* think he's in hiding from his wife, if you ask me. How do you manage an unlisted number, anyway? Don't you have to have a pretty good reason?"

"Obscene phone calls?" I asked. "Or maybe he said to

them, Excuse me but I'm really a spy so I don't want to be in the book where the FBI can find me."

"Or else it's protection from Madam President," Jean said. "But he'll find out it doesn't work. She'll keep driving down there. What do they call that, Barnaby, a war of attrition?"

"War of nerves is more like it."

"I think that's going on with the clammers," I said.

"If he starts giving Ruel Jason a hard time I'd like to be there," Sara said.

Of course we talked about Lorenzo. We were all sorry for him. But we thought he would get over it when spring came rushing in. Lorenzo was as much a creature of the seasons as any bird or four-legged thing.

If we were guilty that night of saying too glibly, *He'll be all right in time*, it was because we wished it to be so.

Saturday was carved out of a sapphire. I longed to go to haul with Barnaby, but my parents and Irenie and Todd were driving down from Limerock that afternoon, and we'd all gather at Shallows for supper, to which I was contributing a pot of beans. I wouldn't leave these to Sara; you have to have a psychic sense about when to add water, when to take off the lid to brown them, when to take the pot out of the oven. Tarot cards don't tell this.

Sara could have gone out with Ronnie Deming while he dragged for scallops, but she virtuously stayed home to wash some socks and underwear. I took my water colors out to the field that stretches from the house to the mica-sparkling tip of Cape Silver, and sat on the well curb. I wanted to get the little islands called the Andrews. They were really the St. Andrew's Islands and belonged to the township of St. Andrews, named by a Scottish grantee in 1648. They lay about two miles south of us, but in the curious larger-than-life bloom of the weather breeder they seemed much nearer. Tawny with dead grass and sunshine, they floated between sea and sky in the levitation of mirage. I could pick out the old stone walls crossing Charlie's (Prince Charlie's) steep meadow;

the three spruces on Little Cat; and at the northern end of long Herring there was the osprey's nest in the top of a dead spruce as tall as a mast. It seemed as if I could always remember it being there. The birds were gone now until spring, but the rest of the year we could watch them with the glasses, and they fished regularly over here and Morgan's Bay.

St. Andrew's Island, the biggest one, about fifty acres, was almost hidden by the other three, but its wooded height showed up with the velvety blue–black of damson plums. There were a few lobstermen's camps in a sheltered cove on Andrew's, but mostly the islands belonged to the nesting seabirds, seals, deer who sometimes swam out from the mainland to take refuge in Charlie's woods. (They weren't especially safe there, either.) There was good clamming out on the Andrews for anyone who wanted to go that far, and good picnicking, though not enough of that to overrun the islands and crowd the birds.

The long treeless ridge of Herring was so richly gemmed with wild strawberries that as I painted it I could smell and taste them. Whoever said you can't really recall scents was crazy; I was steeped and simmering in summertime. The gulls' calls echoing through sunny space enhanced the illusion. Crossbills chattered in the tips of Deepwood; Sara whistled while she hung out her washing. Even the stone flies drifting over the rotting snow were transmuted into summer insects.

I knew we could have a blizzard tomorrow, so I was dreamily in two seasons at once. Nicely schizophrenic. Barnaby wouldn't have been surprised.

I heard the boys coming long before I could see them, it was so quiet. Muttering damns, I left my work on the well curb and went back to the house. Most of our youngsters were no problem, but it was our policy to let them know someone was at home, especially if a gang came without an adult, and Sara had gone back into the house, as I'd supposed. As this group came up across the Indian Meadow they turned out to be the Applecross Boy Scouts with their leader and another man. Scott Thatcher was principal of our elementary school. The other man was a stranger. He stopped to examine and then photograph a section of stone wall.

The boys came streaming into the dooryard, shedding packs and jackets, blowing as if they'd just climbed Everest without oxygen. I received greetings ranging from vigorous to exhausted. They dropped like old clothes on doorstep, woodpile, and ledges.

"What a bunch of cream puffs," said Scott.

"For Pete's sake, we hiked all the way around the shore from way back of beyond," said a portly boy who looked exactly like his portly father. He panted ostentatiously.

"For Pete's sake," Scott mocked him. "I'm twenty years older than you are and I'm ready for ten miles more."

"That's because—" The boy stopped short with a funny abashed giggle.

"He almost called me a fitness freak, but he didn't quite dare," said Scott. "It's my iron discipline. . . . Do you know this guy?" The other man came toward us. At first glance everybody looks alike these days, with so much hair; they're early Christian hermits, Victorian poets, or dissolute Stewart princes. This one, because of his gray–green fatigues and serviceable boots, sheathed knife and hatchet at his belt, looked more like a guerrilla. He had his camera slung around his neck, so he was probably a peaceful nature lover who photographed birds.

"Hello," he said. "How are you?" He took off his cap in a courtly gesture not seen too often these days. "You don't remember me," he said. "I'm going to shave off my mustache and cut my hair. Otherwise I'm lost in the crowd. Everybody knows Scott because they can see his ears and his upper lip, but I'm beginning to be known as What's-His-Name."

"I know you now!" I almost said *the pornographer!* but decided he mightn't appreciate the joke. Yet. "The writer and boat builder."

"For those titles, I thank you!" He gave me a small bow, which caused unseemly laughter among the young. "I heard that," he said without looking around. His gaze shifted past my head, and Scott's round face began to flush a little brighter, so I knew Sara had come out. I introduced them to her.

"Hi, Scott," she said. "Hi, Max. Hi, men." It caused a surge of returning life. Some of the boys even got up.

"You know," Max said to Scott, "this place is the best antidote in the world for what just happened back around the shore."

"So you've met our man from outer space," said Sara.

"Oh, that explains it," said Max. "I thought he was a fugitive from a Gothic novel."

Sara laughed so hard at that the boys were fascinated.

Scott said, "We met Lorenzo when we came along his shore, I was going to tell him about Max's sloop, but he was all hawsed up about this character who bought the Darby place. He told us we were likely to be warned off by mortar fire, but we didn't believe that, and we stopped to look at the inscription, and Max began taking pictures."

No one climbed up onto the ledge or moved away from the group in any manner. When Cory appeared at his front door and shouted something, they thought he was calling a greeting, and they answered in kind. So he came down to the edge of the lawn where the ledges began.

"He was absolutely *white*," said Scott in awe. "Maybe it was the dark glasses that made him look more so, but he's either got galloping anemia or people *can* go white with rage. And he spoke so quietly that it made the whole scene all the weirder. Hadn't we heard him? he asked. Were we all deaf as well as insolent?"

"Jeest, what a nut!" said a skinny boy with the ethereal glow of a Christmas card chorister.

"He pointed at Max, and said, 'I forbid you to take any pictures on this property without permission, and I'm not giving permission. I consider this a serious invasion of privacy.' He actually said just that."

Max smiled. "I wasn't as astonished as Scott was by that. I'm used to people worrying about their privacy. There's so

little of it in some places. So I kept busy while he raved—
if you could call it raving, it was so soft and carefully
phrased—then I took off before he could demand the film."

Scott had tried to explain what they were doing, where
they'd come from and where they were going, and that the
rock was an important part of the region's history; the Darbys
had never objected to anyone coming to look at it or photograph it.

To which Sanderson had replied in that very level tight
voice, "The Darbys don't own it any longer. *Get out.*" They
left, with Scott sternly suppressing any comments from the
boys.

"Legally the inscription does belong to Sanderson," Scott
said. "So he was within his rights. I told the boys so then and
I'm repeating it now." He raised his voice and looked around
at every face. "Everybody's thought of it as something be-
longing to Applecross, because the Darbys felt the same way
and they belonged to Applecross too. They were here at the
start."

A very short scout piped, "Garfield Willy says *his* great-
great-grandfather *started* Applecross."

"I mean to go into that with Garfield one day," said Scott.

I said, "*Don't.* You may come out alive but witless."

Scott laughed. "Well, you know why men climb moun-
tains. Because they're there. Same like Mr. Willy. Come on,
men. We've got a lot to do today."

"Care to join us for a gourmet lunch?" Max asked Sara.

"Yes, how about it?" Scott said to me. Feeling like Sara's
mother being included for politeness' sake I said, "I've got
beans in the oven. But thanks, anyway."

"Well, as an old Girl Scout I'd like to go, if you guys don't
object to a woman tagging along," Sara said to the nearest
knot of boys who grinned, blushed, or stared elsewhere with
deep frowns.

"Come along, you superannuated Girl Scout," said Max.

"What's *that* mean?" inquired the chorister type, whom I

had by now placed as the son of a woman known in some quarters as the Scourge of Applecross.

"You can look it up," said Scott.

They went off down the field toward the Far Meadow, smaller boys eagerly ahead, taller boys with Scott, and Max and Sara were at the end, talking like old friends who were picking up where they left off. Son of the Scourge was at Sara's elbow, doubtless memorizing the conversation in his relentless little tape-recorder mind. If he was anything like his mother it would likely be reproduced in unrecognizable and spectacular version.

I went back to the well curb and got my work. It was pretty good, I thought, but there was a lot I didn't know. Then I added water to the beans, whose aroma was reaching the delectable stage. After that I concocted my own gourmet lunch of a fried-egg sandwich and a cup of instant coffee.

Sara was back in early afternoon. "Max is giving them a geology lesson."

"What's he like?" I asked.

"Very nice," she answered primly, then grinned. "He *is*. Brainy but nice. What a difference from Cory Sanderson! We can't figure out what *he* came here for, but Max came because he thought he'd like it, and he loves it and doesn't mind saying so. Hey, you know what?"

"What?"

"He showed me a rock that's millions of years old and told me how to recognize it."

"Tell me, then."

"I've forgotten its name," she confessed, and we both laughed.

"Because you were looking at his *beaux yeux*," I said.

"Well, they are *beaux* when he takes off his shades. A beautiful dark, smoky blue. Listen, next week he's going to take me to the museum to the opening of this exhibit of abstract sculpture."

Since I had worked at the museum in Limerock in my

school days, I received invitations to all the openings. I'd asked Sara if she'd like to go to this one and she'd been politely indifferent. I didn't remind her now as she rambled on and on about the Now-Person's obligation to be in vibration with all the chords of existence. "I mean, I was very limited until I came here," she told me. "And since then I've been in danger of becoming limited in another direction. Just being a child of nature is fine for a fox or a deer, but I have a human brain—" she tapped her forehead—"spirit, soul, and an infinite capacity for experience . . ."

"If this is Max's opening speech I'm afraid of what it's leading to."

"All he did was invite me to the museum and dinner somewhere afterward. And Mirabell, if he'd asked me just to go watch traffic lights I'd think that was exciting too."

"You like him that much."

"I like him that much. Don't tell me I've only known him about three hours and that's not really knowing someone. I'm not an infant. But I want to *get* to know him."

"But he isn't wearing rubber boots."

She looked mystified.

chapter 6

The weather breeder abundantly delivered; on Sunday we had a northeast snowstorm. Our house was somewhat sheltered by Deepwood, and we rode the storm out snugly. Shallows would be taking the full force of the gale, but that house had been doing so for over a hundred and fifty years.

Sometime during the day Sara found a photograph in an old magazine, of the Little Mermaid in Copenhagen. She cut it out and put it on the kitchen bulletin board. *Sara, waiting,* she wrote under it.

"For what?" Barnaby asked. "Or for whom?"

She smiled vaguely, Primavera in jeans and turtleneck jersey. "I'll know when I see him."

I went through the *Dictionary of Quotations*, and came up with Shakespeare.

> *Since once I sat upon a promontory,*
> *And heard a mermaid on a dolphin's back,*
> *Uttering such dulcet and harmonious breath,*
> *That the rude sea grew civil at her song,*
> *And certain stars shot madly from their spheres*
> *To hear the sea-maid's music.*

I typed it, signed it C.S. and put it up beside the picture. We laughed a good deal about it at supper and wondered callously how Cory would make out if he lost lights, heating, and plumbing; but all the time he seemed to be receding from us, so fast that by tomorrow he would be gone.

The intense storm was gone by the next morning, leaving

a heavy and sunless cold. Saturday's translucent water-color world had turned to a solid study in grays, white, and black. There was no wind, but a rough sea. Out on the Andrews, Charlie's northeasterly side was so constantly buried in white water that it looked as if the surf were breaking up in the meadow. Past Cat and the foaming easterly tip of Herring, we could see spray flying over the bar between Herring and Andrew's, and explosive spouts of white shooting high off the big island.

We went with Barnaby to plow the jeep track and dig out the mailboxes where the town plow had buried them. Then we went on to Shallows. Barnaby and Uncle Stewart rowed out to shovel snow and slush from their boats, and I called my mother to tell her we hadn't lost the roof or been air-lifted house and all out to the Andrews.

We stayed to lunch. Sara and I did the dishes, and then she left to walk home around the shore. When we drove back we saw her down on the inner harbor flats with Ruel Jason. She was sitting on her heels, talking while he dug.

"Living radio," said Barnaby. "The trouble with that is you can't change the station when you get tired of the program."

"But it's got no commercials," I pointed out.

Late in the afternoon Sara and Ruel appeared together. They made quite a pair, with her fairness and his Indian coloring. Both of them were red-cheeked and exhilarated; they had jogged all the way from where he'd left his filled clam hods in his truck at the Neck. While he was pulling off his boots in the entry, I felt like asking Sara if she was still turned on by rubber boots or if the Now-Person's essential vibrations had shaken the Then-Person out of focus.

Ruel told us that the Darby property had sprouted a crop of bright red NO TRESPASSING signs. "He must have planted them late Saturday, because he sure as hell didn't drive those posts during the storm yesterday, or through the drifts this morning. And he must have had a hell of a time getting them into the frozen ground, too. But there they are, blazing away like fire. Makes a nice cheery note of color, you might say."

"I'll bet you didn't say that," said Barnaby.

Ruel lifted his coffee mug like a beer stein. "*Skoal!* . . . Nope. We've already had one of those eyeball-to-eyeball confrontations. I went around there first today, and he came down on the shore and called to me. When I was ready to straighten up anyway I turned around and said, 'You speaking to me or would you like to?' " He grinned at the recollection. "I thought it sounded pretty good myself, but you can't tell a damn thing about him. Especially with those dark glasses. He says, 'Can't you read, or are you totally illiterate?' I said, 'What's them long words mean, Mister?' So he told me. . . . Good turnovers, whoever made them."

"Thanks," I said. "I made the mincemeat too. What'd you do?"

"Oh, just told him I knew my rights, and turned my back on him and went on digging. I could see between my legs when he walked away. Then I got to thinking he could be mental and maybe he'd gone for his gun. So I went back to the harbor. I had a good hodful by then anyway."

"How long do you think those signs'll last?" Barnaby asked him.

"Is that what they call a rhetorical question?" They both laughed. Then Ruel said piously, "After all, they don't mean *me*. I wasn't trespassing."

Jean and I drove to the store in her car a few days later, and the Scourge hailed us the instant we came in. "What kind of crazy coot have you got down to the harbor now?"

"I resent that," said Jean. "It sounds as if we had crazy coots down there all the time."

Her laugh could give pointers to an agitated crow. "Well, you do! You've got Lorenzo and the Jasons, haven't you? And some folks still think the Taggarts got a few buttons missing!" She gave me a strenuous tap on the shoulder to show it was all in fun.

I went to the dairy case and scowled at the cheese, but she called across the store to me. "All I can say is, a man who threatens a bunch of innocent young ones with a gun ought to be locked up."

"There wasn't any gun." I spoke very distinctly, for the benefit of everyone. "The man told them they were trespassing and to move on. They moved on. That's the story."

"My Keithie told me Cory had a gun, and my Keithie's no liar. He swore it to his father and me on Scout's honor."

"Let's say Keithie has a great imagination. There was no gun." I walked to the other end of the store. There was a suspenseful silence among the other customers, while she took in the fact that I may have slandered her child.

Then she came militantly around the oranges to confront me. "Now listen, Mirabell—"

"Oh, forget it, Doris," Jean said. "You know darn well Keithie gave you a good story to make your eyes pop, and get you raving, and now he can't go back on it because he's afraid you'll knock his ears off. Neither Scott nor the other boys mentioned a gun, and if there'd been one that's the only thing they'd have seen."

Doris, red-faced, took her groceries and left, stepping hard. "Poor Keithie," someone said. "Looks as if he'll get his ears knocked off after all."

When we went out, Garfield Willy was descending from his aged pickup by the gas pumps. "Beware the Ancient Mariner," I whispered, but he'd seen us and came to the car with his fast limp.

"Hey! What's going on down there?"

"What's going on where?" I asked. "Is something going on somewhere? You tell *us*."

Garfield looked like an evil brownie, for which there's probably a different name if you're up on the Little People. Whenever Garfield looked happy about anything, it was with the grin of a Being who's been souring milk, stealing babies, and putting nails in the beds of honest people.

"What about that new gink in the Darby place?" He was hardly out of breath; shrunken and sinewy, with a face like one of those dried-up apple dolls, eyes bright as diamond points amid the creases of years. "I hear he's queerer than a three-dollar bill." He used "queer" in its original meaning. "He's got his signs up; when's he gettin' the 'lectric fence and the guard dogs?"

"As soon as he hears about you, Garfield," Jean told him.

"I guess he's upset some folks considerable. Historical Society thought they was going to take him over. Scouts got drove off. He's threatening the clammers with the law." He snickered. "And Lorenzo, he's been sulkin'. I went all the way in there to see him, made a big effort, gettin' on as I am and havin' to go down that road on foot, and he'd hardly give me an aye, yes, or no."

"I wouldn't have spoken to you either, Garfield," I said. "You know you were just being nosy."

He accepted it as a compliment. "Ayuh. I asked him why he don't give up and hand his stuff over to the Historical Society, like I did, and *that* got a yelp out of him. 'They'll git it over my dead body,' he says, and I says, 'That's just how it's likely to be!' "

"And then you left," I said, "having spread sunshine all over the place."

He preened. "Well, as the oldest active citizen of Applecross and holder of the gold-headed cane—even if I don't have to use it—I think I do remarkable."

"You certainly do," said Jean, "and one of these days somebody's going to tell the State Police you're a menace behind the wheel, and then you'll have to go around on foot to sow your seeds of kindness."

"And while you've still got your wheels," I added, "why don't you go down and brighten Mr. Sanderson's life for him? He needs a friend."

"I'll do that. And I won't get arsed out in a hurry!" He went into the store, shaking and gasping with laughter.

"And he'll probably make it," said Jean wryly. "He's that brazen."

"Sanderson may be too tough even for Garfield's brass," I said. "Remember he's already been primed by Madam President and Lorenzo to beware of opening the door. And he suspects the clammers of planning armed robbery. So expect the electric fence and the guard dogs any time now.... Only he's afraid of dogs."

"Hey, he let you and Sara in, didn't he? And he gave Sara a second look."

"Most men do, when Sara's really projecting. But you can't compare Sara and Garfield, can you? One more local eccentric showing up on his doorstep, and he'll be selling out."

"How lucky can we get?" asked Jean. "But then we could get something worse, I suppose. He's unfriendly, but so what? He just wants to stay home and be left alone. What's the matter with that, when you come right down to it?"

"Nothing," I admitted. "But there's something about him that makes me almost believe in auras, because the one around him is—well, I don't know how to describe it, and I don't like to dwell on it."

"The trouble with us," said Jean briskly, "is that if anybody doesn't like us around here we get all upset and think there's some deep and awful reason. Nobody just says, 'All right, he hates people and that's the way he *is*, so forget him.' "

"Barnaby says it. Then he adds 'and to hell with him', and that's hardly objective, is it?" We laughed and got into the car.

chapter 7

Barnaby was working on gear in his fishhouse at Deep Cove and came up when he heard the jeep. Sara came home a few minutes later; she'd been all the way to Shallows and back on snowshoes through the woods. Now it was beginning to spit snow again, and the wind was rising. We had just settled down to coffee and the mail when Madam President's Volkswagen jounced into the dooryard.

Nobody moved. She slammed the car door and bounded onto the porch, and tapped shave-and-a-haircut-two-bits on the outside door. Barnaby stared into the depths of his coffee cup as if he expected Undine to surface. Then he got up, took his cup and his mail into the workroom, and shut the door behind him.

She tapped again, calling, "Anybody home?"

"Go in the other room and I'll lie for you," Sara whispered.

"I can't do that. We might as well find out first as last what she wants." So I went.

She was a big, rangy woman with a bony, equine cast of features, and broad hips crammed into stretch ski pants. She came in effusively apologizing. The cups were steaming on the table, I was parched for mine, so that and manners compelled me to offer her a cup. "Oh, I'd love it!" she cried, and settled into Barnaby's chair. Behind a closed door Chet Atkins gave Barnaby another protective screen.

After a few pleasantries she said, "I wanted to ask Barnaby something, but he seems to be busy."

"Yes, he is," I said.

"This is *really* a business errand, I wouldn't otherwise *barge* in. He could probably kill me because I *drove* in, but I'm getting over a sprained ankle. And this *is* urgent, believe me, Mirabell." She became terribly earnest. "Well, maybe *you* can tell me what I want to know. You must know as much about Cape Silver as Barnaby does."

"I should think so," Sara put in, "seeing as how the Weirs owned the whole place before Taggarts ever put a foot on it."

"*Right!*" said Madam President. She smiled at Sara. "I saw you at the Grange dance with Ruel Jason one night. You must be taming him."

"I didn't know he had to be tamed."

"Oh, my, yes! I've told my kitten never to be alone with a Jason." She laughed vigorously. "Of course *you're* pretty sophisticated, I imagine. But I tell my kitten the old rule still holds good. When a man marries he wants to be sure *he's* the first one."

Sara, with a smile of suspicious sweetness, said nothing. It was said around town that when the kitten got married Madam President would carry her across the threshold and supervise the first-night activities.

"What's your urgent errand, Polly?" I asked. "I can't stand the suspense."

"Garfield says there used to be a fort on Cape Silver, out on this point somewhere. Do you know anything about it?"

"No, and I've never heard my father or uncle mention it," I answered truthfully.

"Well, Garfield says his grandfather told him about it, and *he* had it from *his* grandfather. It was old then—tumbling in. It was built in the 1600's some time, to watch for Indians coming from the southwest. He and his friends played around it many a time."

"It's funny I've never heard of it before," I said doubtfully. "It wasn't written up in King's history, and he was pretty thorough about this region."

"Garfield says King only put in what suited him. He and Garfield's grandfather had a feud, so he ignored anything Old Squire could have told him."

I wondered if Uncle Stewart and my father knew that Eusebius Willy had been promoted to Squire. He'd been a drunken scoundrel whose wife and children had to be supported by the town.

"What I was thinking," Madame President rambled on, "is that the Historical Society could collect here some good morning after the snow's gone, and go through the woods looking for the foundations of the fort. It *could* have been overlooked, Mirabell, you *know* that. Maybe it's something your family and Barnaby's just never happened to know about."

I could see it would do no good to argue. "I'll talk to Barnaby," I said.

She whinnied with delight. "Oh, that will be just tremendous! Just think, if we *do* find something! We can organize a *dig* so we'll do it right, and we may have something even *better* than the Pemaquid project, who knows?"

I was glad Barnaby had music going. Sara and I avoided each other's eyes while Madam President finished her coffee. "That was wonderful. So was the doughnut. Well, I must be off now! Oh, would you try to let me know before next Monday? I'd like to announce the fort project at the meeting."

"I'll let you know," I promised. I walked out to the back doorstep with her, to be sure she went.

"I've really got some fantastic stuff lined up," she confided. "I'm going to get Max Kemper—he knows all about rocks, and it seems that our Applecross kind is pretty spectacular in places. . . . Right now I'm going to stop off at Boones' and talk to Kyle about speaking to us, and then I'm going to stop at Cory's."

It was always first names with her after the first meeting, and sometimes before.

"*Who?*" I asked.

"You mean you don't know your new *neighbor?* Well! He's very quiet—I should warn you of that—but what a sense of humor!" She laughed. "I stopped in one day to talk to him about his house, and he was really interested. I'm pretty sure we'll get him as a member. And wouldn't his place be marvelous for our midsummer picnic?"

We both laughed girlishly. She squeezed into the Volkswagen, and I waved her off into a blinding snow shower. When I got back in Sara had poured fresh coffee. "I thought you'd want a cup you could enjoy."

"Too right. I didn't notice any trace of a limp, by the way."

I gave her Madam President's account of her meeting with Cory. Barnaby came out to see what we were laughing about, and I passed on the request to search for the fort.

"No," he said very quietly. "Absolutely not. No wholesale search through these woods. I've nothing against the Society, I think they do a great job in collecting and keeping material that would otherwise be lost for good. But if there was ever a fort on Cape Silver, our grandfathers would have found the remains and they'd never have kept still about it." He smiled. "Why didn't you tell her you'd heard of a fort on Darby land?"

"I wish I had. Damn it, I can never think that fast. Or lie that fast."

The next day was clear, with a light northwest wind. Barnaby left the house before sunrise to go to haul. In the winter when the lobsters have moved out to deeper water, the men have a long run to the grounds, and Barnaby and Uncle Stewart went more or less in company, each in his own boat.

Late in the afternoon I walked alone to Shallows to meet Barnaby; Sara had been out all afternoon by herself. The slight wind had dropped and the air was still and cold, the almost bare ground hard underfoot. It was one of those sunsets that turn dead fields to a ruddy bronze, and wash white houses, birch trees, and gulls' wings with saffron. Our men were at Elmo's wharf selling their lobsters, so Aunt Jess and I and the dogs went down on the Shallows wharf to wait for them to row back from their moorings in the aureate light.

We had all just arrived in the yard when Ian Hamilton, the local coastal warden, drove in. We went into the house, where Uncle Stewart and Barnaby had the ritual drink they always had when they came in from winter hauling; Ian settled for coffee. During the mug-up he told us he'd just come from the Darby place. A trooper from the Williston barracks had called him and asked him to go around and straighten out Sanderson on what the clammers could and could not do.

Earlier, Cory had called the barracks and reported that he was being harassed by trespassers and a dangerous dog, so they had sent Bill Cartright down. The trespassers turned out to be Gus Flint and his son digging clams; they'd come by boat, so they hadn't crossed Sanderson's land to get to the flats. The dog was lying on a big clump of rockweed near Gus.

Bill went down and beckoned Gus. Gus told him that when they'd first come ashore that day, the boy had seen a pot buoy up on the beach and had gone to look at it, thinking it was his uncle's colors. The dog followed him, but came right back when Flint whistled.

"Cory probably called when he saw the dog coming up the beach," I said. "He's even afraid of Prince, so maybe he thought this one would come crashing through a window after him. Anybody who's afraid of Prince would expect the worst of a German shepherd."

"Bill went back and told Sanderson the dog was under firm control," Ian went on. "Then Sanderson pitched into him about the clammers and wouldn't take Bill's word for it about the tide limits. Bill told him he was entitled to post his property, but he couldn't keep anyone from walking past below mean high water line. When he came back he called me. So I went down."

We guessed from Ian's expression that Cory hadn't believed him either, or wouldn't admit that he did.

"He must have an inbuilt reaction to uniforms," Aunt Jess said.

"There could be a sinister secret there," I suggested. I began thinking up some, aloud. It was just idle foolery, perhaps not a very charitable kind of foolery, but it was without malice and it was among ourselves. Still, as I spoke nonsense I began picturing a man locked into his house, hiding even from himself with his dark glasses, going from window to window, nervous and sweating, his own prisoner.

"Poor cuss," I said, surprising even myself. Aunt Jess nodded.

"Maybe so," Ian said, skeptically. "I've talked to some prizes in my time, both natives and summer folks, but he's something new. Why don't you go and see him, Barnaby? Maybe some easy-going civilian could convince him."

"He sent word through Seth that he wanted to be ignored, so give me one good reason why I should go. Listen, he's had them coming out of the woodwork at him," said Barnaby. "Madam President, Lorenzo, my wife, and my chuckle-headed cousin. If he hasn't met anyone with a shotgun yet, I may be the one. Nope! I've got no interest in him whatsoever as long as he doesn't shoot or trap anything out of season or create any disturbance on Cape Silver."

"I'll go," said Uncle Stewart unexpectedly.

"Don't notify him beforehand," said Barnaby, "or he'll have the place fortified."

"Oh, that reminds me," I said. "Uncle Stewart, did you ever hear of a fort on Cape Silver?"

"No," he said. "As kids your father and I and Lorenzo, and the rest of the harbor gang, used to go hunting up the remains of all the forts we heard about, and we'd act out every story we heard about them." His thin face creased in delighted reminiscence. "We found part of the fort, or thought we did, over on Eastern Harbor point. There was a pile of wild apple trees around there then, and we had a great war with green apples. Your father commanded the fort and I was Captain Smart of the British Navy. It was the War of 1812. Well, my men and I came in dories and we stormed the fort, and the little green apples flew thick and fast, and we took the fort. Your father kept saying, 'You can't do that! It didn't happen that way! *We* won!' But we did it all right. We rewrote history, unpatriotic little scoundrels."

"Maybe the British should have used green apples," said Ian.

"But I never heard of a fort on Cape Silver. Logical place, though, isn't it?"

"So Garfield swears," I said.

"*That* one!" said Aunt Jess.

chapter 8

U ncle Stewart went to see Cory the next day, timing it for low tide so he could bring the conversation around to the clammers. Cory was civil, if just barely. He had already accepted, though unwillingly, the warden's explanation of the tide laws. Stewart made a few attempts to carry on. He mentioned the good fishing in Morgan Bay when the mackerel were running, and the possibility that the bluefish might return this year. Cory said tersely he didn't care about fishing in small boats, or even large ones. The subject of boats gave Stewart an opening to mention his own work, and the bookkeeping system inflicted upon fishermen by the Internal Revenue Service. Then he asked in a friendly man-to-man fashion what Cory's line had been before he retired.

"It's hard to explain," Cory replied. The following silence was not broken by the offer of a drink. Stewart decided to leave. At the back door he invited Cory to a Saturday night supper at Shallows and was not surprised when Cory said, "I don't go out."

So that was it. Once more we were prepared to forget him, and he seemed to be an extremely forgettable subject, especially when the end of winter was in sight, at least on the calendar. A good fight about zoning was shaping up for town meeting, and there'd been an epidemic of vandalism around the summer places at the center and northern end of town. We didn't have many around the harbor to worry about, but the spread of rural crime was anything but slow, and just because it wasn't happening here yet didn't mean that it couldn't. So that was a lot more immediate to us than Cory Sanderson.

You couldn't see his house from the road, you wouldn't

meet him at the store or post office, and he was rarely seen on the road. Except for the offensively blazing red letters on his signs, the house would look the same from Morgan Bay as it always had, and some night the signs would disappear; the ones farthest away from the house had probably gone already.

I did think of Cory once in a while, or rather of my own errant impulse of compassion toward him. It would be when I was alone on the shore or in the woods, or drinking a second cup of coffee in the early morning after Barnaby had gone. Or walking to meet Barnaby somewhere, happy, and then suddenly snapped out of myself and into that house where a man was wrapped tightly around with suspicion like barbed wire.

Why was I assuming that he was a pitiable prisoner of himself? That was sentimentality. He saw us with contempt if not outright loathing; he felt perfectly snug and secure inside the wall he had built around himself. I'd been sorry before for people who didn't need it, so why didn't I know better now? I did know better. Yet it was always there, a part of me I couldn't disown; the pity, as tender as a crushed finger, for the person whose unlikeability equals a disfiguring or painful affliction.

Sara wanted to be properly dressed for going to the opening at the museum with Max, and she'd brought nothing suitable in her pack, so we took the car on Saturday and went to Limerock to shop. (This fugitive from an ashram, this winter hitchhiker, carried a checkbook in her pack.)

Late Sunday afternoon she drove away in the jeep to meet Max and his car at the Neck. "You'd swear she was beautiful," I said, sighing. "I always wanted to be a tall and willowy blonde."

Barnaby ignored that. "Don't you think Kemper is too old for her?"

"Not to take her to the museum and to dinner. And Sara's heels are not round, if you want me to be vulgar about it."

"Yeah," he said breathily. "Come on. Be vulgar."

They came back in the middle of the evening. Barnaby is old-fashioned enough to believe that seductions can't take place before 11 P.M. at the earliest, so he was extremely cordial to Max.

Max had done what he'd threatened to do, shaved off his mustache and had his hair cut. He had a long mouth deeply indented at the corners, a good forehead, the thin high-bridged nose, prominent cheekbones and long jaw that go with his angular frame and aren't always so attractive. But with Max they were, and his eyes without the amber sunglasses were as Sara had described them, an unusual dark blue that looked almost black by lamplight.

There was so much to like about Max and so much to talk about that it seemed as if we'd never run dry. But after an hour or so he said reluctantly that he had to leave.

"I wake up around five, I always have," he said. "That's terrible in the city, in winter; it's sheer hell. But here I can hardly wait for the day to begin. I go for a walk, I watch the moon set and the sun rise, work on my boat awhile, and then get back to my book." His eyes shifted toward Sara and they smiled at each other. "It's perfection. I couldn't ask for anything more."

This obviously was not the time to ask him whether he was writing something scientific, historical, or biographical. (Or sado-porn.) Maybe Sara knew. But when she came back from driving him to the Neck, she was silent and expressionless. It discouraged questions.

Now we were having low tides in the morning and evening, and the next morning she and I decided to go to Mussel Cove and get mussels. She was pretty much herself today, hissing dramatic threats while she struggled with a troublesome zipper on her jacket. Waiting, I studied the Little Mermaid and my Shakespeare quote.

"Remember Cory asking if you were a mermaid?" I said. "It wasn't very long ago, but it seems like an age."

"Well, I've heard a lot about my green eyes, beginning

with my brother yelling at me, 'Green eyes, greedy-gut, Eat all the world up!' But I was never called a mermaid before, so I guess I'll remember Cory for that, if for nothing else . . . listen—" She got the zipper clear and pulled it up. "Did you ever hear of *Sabrina fair?* Somebody said it to me once." She was looking all around as if for her gloves, which were in plain sight. For *somebody*, I thought, read *Max*. "There's something in it about knitting under water."

I laughed, and she did too, boisterously as if with relief. "Well, did you?"

"I've seen it. Milton or somebody. Wait." I got out my Oxford Dictionary and found the verse. "Yes, it's Milton.

'Sabrina fair,
   Listen where thou art sitting
Under the glassy, cool, translucent wave,
   In twisted braids of lilies knitting
The loose train of thy amber-dropping hair.' "

"It's beautiful." She was transfixed.

"I think it's time to get rid of the Little Mermaid and Shakespeare," I said.

"Oh, no." Galatea came to life. "Leave it a little longer. For old times' sake."

The day had a damp calm, with a dim sun wading in a snowdrift. We took the short cut down through Deepwood, past the Devil's Den. The woods were dark and silent, the crows all somewhere else this morning. When we came out to Mussel Cove I was glad to see a few gulls walking around on the flats.

Beyond the sandbar the pewter-gray water seemed to stretch to Europe without motion or wrinkle. The loudest sound was made by our boots in the coarse sand of the beach, until a gull flew over and was either saluted or threatened by those on the flats.

The Long Ledges stood out like a miniature mountain

range. Their colors resounded in this dull light like bells ringing at midnight; reds and all variations of tawny, violet sinking into a deep purple crevasse.

Below high water line there was a white frost of barnacles, and the greenish-bronze seaweed lay in festoons over the slopes and in gleaming swags across the mud. The big blue mussels were bedded on the outside of the outermost ledge; the tide had just left them and wouldn't be long in returning. We squatted to pry them loose, and drop them into our plastic buckets. Our gloves were soon wet and our fingers chilly. Our noses began to run.

"I wish just for once Barnaby would let us try one of those recipes with all the wine and stuff," Sara said. "He's too young to be so conservative. Hey, look!"

Lorenzo's dory was coming up past Far Point. Sara wiped her nose on the back of her glove, then peeled off the glove, put two fingers in her mouth and whistled. Lorenzo looked over his shoulder and nodded. He turned the dory toward our end of the sandbar and beached her. We welcomed him with enthusiasm while he climbed out, but he said nothing, reached back in for clam hod and hoe, and set them down on the sandbar. Then he straightened up and gave us a long look over his glasses.

"He's had the inscription chipped off," he said. It sounded like gibberish, or the odd dissociated statements heard in dreams. But we knew what he meant, and Sara ignited instantly.

"That's criminal! Couldn't he be arrested for destroying valuable historic material or something?"

"Maybe it doesn't have any historic value," I said.

"What are you, the devil's advocate or something?" Sara asked.

"Look, somebody has to be a realist—"

"In the absence of Barnaby," she said sardonically.

"Maybe the inscription doesn't mean anything at all. Besides, there've been plenty of pictures and rubbings made of it for reference. Max Kemper must have gotten some darn good shots last week. Face facts," I urged them both. "It was on his property and he had a right to get rid of it."

"I'd like to go over there and paint some nasty message on that rock," Sara said.

"Ayuh!" Lorenzo cheered up. "Me too."

"You'd better not," I said, "because you'd be bound to leave clues as plain as your name, and that would be something he *could* call the police in on. How do you cook mussels, Lorenzo?"

"You're just trying to change the subject," Lorenzo said sourly.

"And not succeeding, I guess." I went back to prying up mussels. Sara said, "When did you find out about it? When did it happen?"

"He must've got some stonecutter down from Williston yesterday. Because it was there the night before. *But not last night.*" He gave those four words a sinister emphasis. "Maybe he's told me to stay off the place, but I get there when he don't know it. There's a fox goes around that house in the night, and so do I."

"What does he do at night?" Sara asked. "Read? Watch television? Or does he just sit there wearing his dark glasses?"

"I never look in the windows," he said with dignity.

"I didn't mean you were spying," she said in a hurry. "When you think of all the good people there are in the world, and this is such a beautiful place, why did *he* have to find out about it?"

"Blame your cousin Seth," I said. "Never mind. He'll be absorbed into the place eventually, when he gets over thinking everybody's out to get him or his treasures, or else he won't be able to stand it and he'll go away. I'm sorry for him, because how can a person like that ever be happy?"

"He's so mean he don't deserve to be," said Lorenzo.

"That's right," said Sara virtuously.

Lorenzo squelched off across the flats, and we finished filling our buckets with mussels. Sara said, "I guess I'll make a candle into a wax image of Cory and stick pins in it."

"As long as you keep it in your room the police will never suspect you when he keels over," I said.

"Don't worry, I'll melt it as soon as the job's done. Hey, Meer, did I ever tell you about the coven I was invited to join?"

"No, and I think you made it up about a minute ago."

"I did not." She rocked back on her heels, complacent. "Well, I just might have been asked, how do *you* know? I knew a guy that belonged to the Church of Satan."

"I wonder what they sing for hymns at their services. 'Devil loves me, this I know,'" I sang loudly, "'for his preacher tells me so; little imps to him belong, he has horns and his tail is long.'"

Lorenzo clapped soggy gloves. Sara shouted, "Bravo, bravo! Encore!"

"It wasn't very good," I said modestly. "That last line was pretty weak." I took off my gloves and blew on my numb fingers, then put on my spare mittens. "I'm through. We've got enough, but if you want to keep picking, go ahead. I'm going up on the beach to look around."

"I guess I'll go over with Lorenzo and dig for razor clams. I can use my hands."

"If you cut your finger on one, don't come running and bleeding to me. You and Lorenzo can cook up a little witchcraft for it."

She grinned. "You'd be surprised at what we could cook up."

"No I wouldn't. Not in the least."

When I got to the beach I looked back. Across the dull sheen of the flats Sara crouched on the sandbar, digging with her bare hands a little distance from Lorenzo. I could hear their voices but not what they were saying. I poked around where the Binnorie Brook ran out of the cranberry bog onto the beach. There was always a trickle of water here because the brook didn't freeze up so near the salt water that sometimes flooded up into it. It had cut away a miniature gorge in the shingle and down through hard sand, and often we could pick up good Indian things that had been thus washed clear of the years.

Finally Sara and Lorenzo came up, Sara dramatically crying that her hands were about to drop off at the wrists. I gave her my mittens, and asked Lorenzo home for a hot drink.

"Thanks, but the tide's coming pretty fast and I got a load of wood I want to pick up at the Neck. Found me a good trap on Kyle's shore too."

"You'd better not pick even a chip off Cory Sanderson's beach."

He laughed. "I don't figger to get in any of *them* scrapes, as the feller said when the schoolmarm asked him to tie her shoelace for her."

"Lorenzo, if I hike over to visit you one day will you give me a cup of tea?" Sara asked.

"It's no place for you. Looks like a bear's den, and somebody was in the other day an' said it smelled like one. I don't change the air all winter. Don't believe in cooling it off."

"Oh, you just don't allow women, in case you get compromised."

"How'd you guess? I don't want Barnaby coming after me with a shotgun and saying I have to marry you."

"Rejected," said Sara, kicking at a mussel shell.

"A has-been at nineteen," I told her. "Nothing left for you to do now but go into a convent."

"Ayuh. Poor young one." He got up and started down the beach toward the dory.

"You'll be sorry!" Sara shouted after him. "Some day you'll know what you've missed."

"I know already. That's what makes me such a happy soul."

Sara and I walked to the end of the beach, and as we climbed up onto Far Point the sixth sense, which life on Cape Silver has developed in me, took over; I stopped Sara in midstep and midword, and we saw at the top of Far Meadow five deer in a moving frieze against the sky. They stopped to graze here and there, unalarmed, unaware of us. We waited, hardly breathing, until the last of them had disappeared into Deepwood. Then we looked at each other solemnly and went on slowly toward where they had been, everything else knocked out of mind by the sight.

When Barnaby came home at the edge of dark, Sara told him about the chipped-off inscription. He was disappointingly unmoved. "Save your indignation for something more important," he said.

"This *is* important. It's symbolic of what he's doing to the community."

"He's doing nothing to the community. He's negative, not positive." He was standing at the table looking over the mail he'd brought from the box. Sara and I were scrubbing the mussels at the sink.

"Don't you call what he's done to Lorenzo *positive?*" she demanded.

He put a handful of circulars in the kindling box. "Good God, they cut down forests for this stuff," he muttered. "As if all of it together was worth one tree."

"You're so crazy about trees—what about Lorenzo?"

"I always thought if Lorenzo stood still in one spot long enough he'd put down roots, but I don't know if he'd be deciduous or evergreen."

"You're so insensitive where people are concerned," she said angrily. "You make jokes about Lorenzo, you won't admit that Cory's been absolutely, inhumanly, *cruel.*"

"Do you realize," I broke in, "that all the conduct usually called inhuman, beastly, or animal, is exclusively *human?*"

"Oh, you two!" She began blindly grabbing at her outdoor clothes, fighting her way into her parka.

Barnaby read a letter as if she weren't there. I said, "For heaven's sake, Sara, *you* know we care about Lorenzo!" Red-faced, her eyes glistening, her lower lip out, she struggled with the zipper that refused to zip. "But the sale of the house is a fact of life. We have to accept it. Even Lorenzo has accepted it."

"That's what you think!" She went slamming out of the

house, still unzipped, and stamping on the crumpled back of one unlaced boot.

Barnaby dropped his letter. "No great loss without some small gain," he said, and took me into his arms.

We had a pleasant little interlude that could have led to greater things if it hadn't been an hour when anyone, not just Sara, might walk in. We separated reluctantly and I went back to scrubbing mussels. In about ten minutes the Boones and Prince arrived, out for a pre-storm hike. Sara came later, as luminous as if nothing could ever dull her.

"How was the show yesterday?" Deirdre asked her.

"Fabulous, I think." She grinned. "I couldn't understand it at all, and I don't think anybody else could but the artist. So we all just looked profound."

I asked the Boones to supper, and Cory Sanderson was not mentioned once that evening. I kept expecting Sara to tell them about the erased inscription, but she didn't, and neither did we.

chapter 9

Rain and snow came in the night, and tapered off during the next morning, giving way to one of those dazzling, dripping foretastes of spring. After lunch Barnaby and I went down to his fishhouse in Deep Cove to work on gear, leaving Sara answering her mail. Barnaby didn't bother to build a fire, the sun streaming through the open door was that warm. Aroused flies buzzed springlike around the windows. Barnaby headed traps and I painted buoys. We had little to say, but we didn't need to talk. In the miniature fjord of Deep Cove the little buffleheads talked and splashed.

This was the sort of afternoon that never lasts long enough. In a little while we heard voices on the path above, and there came Sara, with Kyle Boone behind her.

"Where's Deirdre?" I asked.

"She took Prince to Limerock for his rabies shot." He said it absent-mindedly. He was watching Barnaby nail a heading stick into place, but I didn't think that was the reason for his preoccupation. Sara, leaning in the doorway, gave me a signal of the eyes that told me she had caught it too. So it was no surprise when Kyle said suddenly, "Can I talk to you a minute, Barnaby?" He didn't need to add *alone*.

"Come on for a walk along the shore, Sara," I said.

"Thanks, Mirabell." Kyle didn't bother to make a superficial protest.

We went down onto the shore of Deep Cove, and walked by ledge and hard damp shingle out to the entrance, where we turned north along the bay shore. On the rising slope of Indian Meadow a mist hung over the melting snow. Gulls balanced on wind currents against gauzy puffs of cloud.

"I wonder what's on Kyle's mind," I said.

"Something, all right. Usually he talks to me a little while, as if he had all the time in the world. But today he just said Where's Barnaby? And that was it."

"Maybe he's found out something about Cory that he doesn't think fit for our ears."

"You *mean?*" she breathed, and we both laughed.

Below the Gypsy Field at half tide a low natural jetty ran out from the stony beach, patterned with tide pools that shone like random fragments of sky-blue porcelain amid the almost black rock peculiar to this section. We went out to the end, where tiny surf broke against a twelve-inch cliff. Riding the easy swells a little way offshore a loon called, and I answered. He didn't even act surprised.

"I wonder what Max would say about this black stuff," Sara said.

"It's volcanic," I said. "I know that much."

"Somebody told him you can pick up gemstones on the Andrews, if you know what to look for. We're going to take a picnic lunch out there some day and explore them all. Next weekend, if it's fine."

"A picnic out on the Andrews sounds like heaven. I found an amethyst crystal on Herring once."

"You and Barnaby," she began, and I stopped her. "You know you don't mean it. Besides, I'd rather get Barnaby out there all to myself."

"I think it's just terrific that you and Barnaby after two years of marriage have such a meaningful relationship."

"If there's one phrase that makes me want to throw up. Besides, I thought only unmarried bunkies have those."

Sara giggled. "You'd be surprised how many I've been invited to form."

"No, I wouldn't be."

A boat was coming up Morgan Bay from the Cape Silver end, a big, heavy dory-skiff with an outboard motor throttled down so that she rode gently on the following swells. She looked familiar, but the man was an anonymous figure in bulky oil jacket, watch cap, and sunglasses.

The boat came straight for us, and the man swung one arm high. "It's Max," Sara said. She watched him as if he'd disappear if she blinked. He shut off the engine and tilted it, took up a long oar, and watched for just-submerged rocks as the boat glided toward us.

"Want a ride?" he shouted. It was Scott Thatcher's boat.

"Sure!" Sara called back. "Come on, Mirabell!" If he wanted only Sara, that was too bad, because I was on my way. I steadied the bow and kept the stem from bumping the rocks as Sara climbed aboard. Then I swung myself in after her, pushing off with one foot, and Max poled out with the oar to a depth where he could put the engine down again.

We needed to zip parkas, pull up hoods, and put on mittens out here, but it still had the look if not the feel of spring. I stayed up in the bow facing forward in case the other two wanted to conduct a personal conversation (over the roar of the engine, which meant that anyone within a mile to leeward could hear the whole thing). At a moderate speed to avoid throwing too much water we headed back toward the mouth of Morgan Bay and out past the white tip of Cape Silver. I thought we were aiming for the Andrews, and I felt very squeamish about crossing that seething stretch with a newcomer to these waters.

The dory was beginning to drop suddenly with a thump between seas, and this discomfort was compounded by a deep fast cross-chop where current, tide, and wind were all at odds. I was about to forget my own pride and probably maim Max's by asking him to turn back, when he did so anyway, properly favoring the dory. Once back inside the shelter of Cape Silver, we swung toward Amity, a calendar village set between a harbor full of dancing boats on bright blue water and snowy fields bordered by spruce woods.

Then we went slowly into the upper bay as far as the outgoing tide would let us, jogging so slowly we didn't even disturb the braver ducks. Max had binoculars, and we could pick out Lorenzo's landing by the red wheelbarrow in the entrance of his path into the woods. His dory was gone from her haul-off.

We cruised southward on the Applecross side, just making headway into the surge, the sun taking the honed edge off the wind. The shore was clifflike along here, with uneven walls of rock rising straight from the water. Above them moss-draped spruces and venerable old oaks gripped with their roots the precipitous slope. The snowy forest floor was scattered with cones and broken green twigs, everything trapped in a moving tangle of blue shadows.

I think we were all bemused with the whole scene, because there was no conversation from the stern. I did not even associate Cory Sanderson—or any human being—with what I was seeing, and when I did glimpse roof and chimney through the trees, Cory was still nonexistent.

Then we had to move farther offshore as the water grew more shallow, and I saw the first of his NO TRESPASSING signs like a red scar on the day.

We were well offshore when we came abreast of his house. There was already a band of flats between the line of breaking foam and the beach thickly spread with rockweed and kelp from the storm. Simultaneously we all three saw the glaring splash of white between beach and house. Max whistled, Sara cried out something, and I think I did. What looked at first like a random, far-strewn mess finally steadied into a giant swastika painted on the ledge where the inscription used to be, with huge letters sprawled unevenly beneath it. We didn't need the binoculars to read NAZI GO HOME.

Max shut off the engine. "Good Lord," he said. Sara stared, seraphic with wonder, and I watched her. I had a disagreeable roiling in my stomach. There'd been such a shine on her when she came in at dusk last night.

"There's the man himself," Max said, looking through the binoculars. "He's just coming down over the lawn with somebody." Sara took the glasses from him.

"It's Garfield Willy," she announced.

"What, old Rumpelstiltskin?" asked Max.

"He said he'd get in," I said. "I wonder how he managed it." Garfield spryly led the way around the ledge down onto the beach and the two men stood looking at the paint. Even without the glasses I could see Garfield's emphatic gestures.

"He's happy," I said grimly. "He's in his glory."

"Well, I am too, if Cory's upset," Sara said. And where were you last night? I asked her silently. To come back so pleased with yourself? To affirm my suspicions Lorenzo came rowing toward us from the Neck. He was standing up and pushing on the oars, but he kept looking over toward the defaced ledge.

"Whoever did it," I said, "it's as disgusting as those signs of his."

Max nodded. As if I'd said nothing at all Sara went on. "Well, he won't know which of the clammers to blame so he'll be in an awful state, won't he?" She chuckled. "And he deserves it."

"The rock doesn't deserve it," I said. "And all it's done is convince him that he's among the barbarians. Maybe he only suspected it before."

Lorenzo was holding his dory in one place by the skilful motion of his oars like a fishing osprey's wings. You too, I thought, looking from his alertly turned head to Sara's burnished innocence. What did you hatch up on the sandbar?"

"Whoever did it should take the credit," I said, "and not let somebody else be blamed."

"Maybe Cory'll get an anonymous message about it," Sara suggested brightly. "But I think it was Ruel. He said once Cory was the kind who'd like to stash everybody else away in concentration camps."

We were being carried slowly toward shore and Max started the engine. We barely moved ahead. Lorenzo began to row again and easily caught up with us. He shipped oars and held onto our gunnel.

"You see that?" he sputtered. "You see *that*? Walking around there waving his arms, as if he had a *right*? He's tickled as hell and likely grinning like a jack-o'-lantern. Look at them! Walking back to the house together. *My* house!"

"Mr. Darby, you need a good drink," Max said.

"I need a good rifle. I don't hunt God's innocent creatures but there's a couple of birds I could pick off with pleasure."

"What about the one who defaced the rock?" I asked.

"Never mind losing the inscription. Whoever did that paint job is no better than Cory." I gave him a stare intended to plunge straight to his conscience, but I got no further than I had with Sara.

"Next thing," he said, "that damned old bubblegut will be having Madam President worked in there for drinks, and after that the High Fantods will be having their summer orgy on the front lawn—"

"Their *what?*" Max's voice broke. "So that's what really goes on at the meetings! I should have accepted their invitation, but they just asked me to talk about rocks. Code, do you think? Like the ads in certain magazines?"

Sara said, "Listen, it's all a cover-up for a coven. And Garfield gets to be the Devil all the time."

"Seniority, I suppose," said Max.

"They'll have to do better than Garfield before I'll join," I said.

Lorenzo doubled over, wheezing. "Oh dear, oh dear," he gasped. "Just think about all them women dancing bare-arsed around Garfield! And it's a hell of a lot funnier than watching that old goat strolling around Darby land." He collapsed again, making inarticulate noises. Sara hung helpless and tearful over the gunnel. Max pulled her back. "Hey, Mr. Darby, don't kill yourself laughing," he said. "Come on aboard and I'll give you a tow."

"No thanks. I'm going for a long row to work off my venom." He straightened up, reaching under layers of sweaters and old oilcoat to drag a handkerchief from his hip pocket and wipe his nose. With a maternal expression Sara reached for his glasses, dipped them overboard, and wiped them on her scarf. "Not that you fellers haven't helped," he told us.

"I'm much obliged. Thanks, young woman," he said, taking his glasses from Sara. He held them up to the light. "A little better but not much. I hope you didn't ruin the set of 'em."

"If I did, you can break our engagement," said Sara. He gave her a smile, and pushed out into the wind with an effortless, deliberate rhythm that sent the dory breasting into the long swells from the sea.

"He's quite a guy," Max said.

"If he were twenty-five years younger," said Sara, "I'd—"

"You don't need to spell it out," Max said. "I know competition when I see it."

"But *that* man—" She looked back at the land. Cory and Garfield had disappeared. The swastika showed up indecently against the subtleties of the shore, and no trespassing signs burned like small fires against leafless poplars on one side of the lawn and among bayberry on the other side.

"Well, I guess all the excitement's over for now," said Max. He sped up the engine.

The swells were flattening, the wind had almost quieted, and several small boats were coming out from Amity. Gus Flint's green aluminum skiff, with the dog standing like Rin-Tin-Tin in the bow, crossed between us and Lorenzo, heading for the now-bare flats below the Neck. We waved and Gus made a perfunctory response.

Looking past Gus's skiff toward the Neck, I saw someone on the road, and borrowed Max's glasses. The first painter of the year was working there with his easel before him. I thought he was facing the birches of Goldengrove, and I wished I could see what was on his easel. He wore one of those Australian bush hats, which I could never get Barnaby to wear; he said he'd feel like the White Hunter in a B adventure movie.

chapter 10

W hen we tied up at the wharf in Deep Cove, Barnaby came out on the planks and looked down at us. "I thought maybe you'd been kidnapped."

"He said hopefully," said Sara.

"Well, it went through my mind," said Max, "but then I thought, Any man who steals two women deserves everything he gets. So I brought them back."

"And wait till we tell you what happened!" Sara was up the ladder first. Her story was wondrously disconnected, and by the time Barnaby got it straight he squelched her by being no more delighted than I had been. I think she'd have tramped off on her own if Max hadn't been there. But she wanted to show him Thomas Two's finds on the Andrews and his eager interest was exhilarating to her. It was to us too, in a lesser degree.

"I wish you'd come here while my grandfather was still living," Barnaby said. "He'd have picked your brains bare."

"I wish I had too." He looked around the kitchen, lighted now only by the last glow in the sky. "I love where I live in North Applecross, especially in the silent hours. But out here could be another world altogether. If I lived any nearer to you I'd be a pest, just coming to bask in it."

"If it weren't winter," Sara said, "you might be able to rent Jean and Tony's fishhouse."

He reached out a long hand and gently yanked at her hair. "Hey, sis, I'll remember that. And I'll take you rowing on moonlit nights in spring."

"I won't let you forget that! Only—" Joy was defeated. "I'll be gone then."

"Do you have to go? I thought you lived here." I wondered

if Barnaby felt as I did, not in the way, but invisible. I was just going to say, Nobody's kicking her out, but he got up saying, "I'd better start back. I'll be having to feel my way into the harbor as it is."

"Want me to go around with you?" asked Barnaby, "or is that an insult?"

"Good God, no! I'm relieved. Anybody else want to go? Mirabell—Sara?"

"Sara does," I said. "I'll stay here and start supper."

Sara was at once revived. While she and Barnaby collected their outdoor clothes, Max went to the bulletin board. "Do you mind?" he said to me. "I always read the one in the store, from top to bottom, thinking, Do I have any use for a chain saw, a ten-foot skiff, an orange housebroken shaggy kitten, a babysitter, a washer and dryer like new, or a girl's bicycle?" He skimmed over our items, and then came to what I thought was the magnet from the first; the picture of the Little Mermaid.

" 'Sara waiting,' " he read aloud. "For what?"

As always she answered, "I don't know."

"But she'll know it when she sees it," said Barnaby, like a fond though often exasperated parent.

"Come to think of it," said Max, "she does look a bit like a mermaid. It's the green eyes, I suppose."

Sara wore the archaic smile seen on some ancient Greek statues. I said, "You and Cory."

His head swung quickly toward me. "*What?*"

"He said the same thing. Which shows there's a strain of poetry and romance in the man somewhere, if you dig deep enough."

"He gets curiouser and curiouser," said Max. "Maybe like J. Alfred Prufrock he's heard the mermaids singing, but not to him." He read Shakespeare on mermaids. "Good, but I've got something even better. Written by a friend of mine.

'I think the danger of the ocean lies
Not in the storm, but in the mermaid's eyes;

She closes them for kisses, unaware,
Enfolds the dreaming swimmer, and he dies.' "

"That's very good," I said, meaning the delivery as well as
the verse.

"He passes for an electronics engineer, but he's really a
poet," he answered absently, looking at Sara. "Be careful
when you blink. You never can tell."

"Next time I think it's a loose eyelash I'll check to see if it's
a victim," she promised. Her gaiety was real; she had found
her footing again.

I saw them off, with Barnaby taking the boat out of the
cove, and Sara talking above the engine. When I went back
up the path to the high ground the engine's sound was merg-
ing with the swash and rattle of the rote below Cape Silver.
I stood looking at Jupiter in the west and thinking of what
Max had said. A world of its own. How long it would be
ours, I didn't know. Legally it wasn't ours now, in the sense
that we couldn't pass it on to our children. But in another,
truer sense, it would always be ours, as much as we could
make Jupiter ours, and the rote, and the frosty, salty scent of
this February dusk; and that fox trotting around the frozen
duck pond; and the something else, the replenishing silence
and solitude at the core.

Once inside the woods, the fox barked. A message to the
mate, or to me? I could call it what I pleased.

Barnaby was back shortly from the Shallows wharf. He'd
left Sara and Max still talking. "I think they're good for another hour. . . . What do you think of him?"

"Che sera, Sara," I said, which deserved to be ignored, and
he ignored it. "I like him. Do you?"

"Yes. But I don't know if I like Sara going off the deep end
this quick."

"Cheer up, love, you can't do a thing about it. She's not
a minor and she's here on her own. I'm just thankful she's as
candid and down-to-earth as she is, and Max seems like a very
nice guy."

"Lorenzo thinks so too. He's going to help him with his boat. . . . Is it true," he asked me solemnly, "that dogs, children, and Lorenzo can always *tell*?"

Sara came home singing "The Bonnie Lass of Fyvie." If she was in love, there was no languishing about it.

Barnaby told me in bed that night what was bothering Kyle. Cory had called him up and asked him if he was sure about his right of way. Since they were both on a town road Kyle thought first that it was an attempt at a joke, though it was difficult to associate Cory with humor. Then Cory told him there was a discrepancy in the history of the road, and Kyle realized incredulously that the man was serious. He advised Kyle to look into the matter, and to pass the word on to the Taggarts. He would call the Weirs himself.

"He was too blunt to be pompous," Kyle said, "and he had me almost convinced there's been some wild comedy of errors about the whole area and we didn't own our own land, or something that insane. You know these first paranoid thoughts. . . . Anyway, I'm passing it along as he requested."

"You're not really disturbed about this, are you?" Barnaby asked.

"I don't think so," Kyle said. "But I keep remembering that first horrifying moment. It came down to something ridiculous, but for a man who doesn't want neighbors he's bent on making a damn' nuisance of himself. I guess I'll get an unlisted number, too, so he can't call me, and he won't walk to the house with his little valentines because he's afraid Prince is a killer in a clown suit."

They both laughed about this and went up to the house and had a drink, and then Kyle went home, feeling better.

"I wonder if he did call Uncle Stewart," I said. "Why didn't you stop in there tonight and find out?"

"If there hadn't been a couple of cars in the yard, I would have."

"Barnaby, that nut has to *be* a nut. Or he's trying in an

amateurish way to needle everybody, and I can't figure out why. Just because they tried to be neighborly, or what?"

"I guess I'll have to call on Mr. Sanderson," Barnaby said.

"Can I go with you?"

"If you keep your mouth shut," my husband said graciously.

"I'll be just your sex object," I promised. "A pretty playmate, no more."

"And let's keep it from Sara. She and Lorenzo will have it kicked around until it's unrecognizable. Between Stewart and me we should settle it before it goes any further."

I didn't tell him my suspicions of Sara and Lorenzo and the paint. I wanted to get the truth from Sara first, and then it would be up to her to tell Barnaby. I woke in the morning with that on my mind, tempered by the rather pleasant anticipation of seeing Barnaby and Cory face to face. I was sneakily amused because Barnaby had to make a move at last, instead of sitting haughtily in his ivory tower and telling the rest of us not to be so foolish.

There were still heavy seas offshore, so Barnaby didn't go out, and we left early for the store, planning to be back at a decent hour for making a morning call on Cory. Not wanting to make a point of leaving Sara out and perhaps making her suspicious, I asked her if she was coming with us to the store.

"No, I've got letters to write," she said, looking past my ear. She was far away this morning, and I hoped that was due to a struggle with her conscience.

At the store we found out that the news had gotten around about the paint on the rock. Some people laughed, and some thought, like us, that it was a form of vandalism, no matter what the cause. By now I was ready to discount Lorenzo. He had an abiding tenderness for even the inanimate features of his natural world. But I would ask Sara straight out before the day was over.

Cory wasn't home; the carriage house was open and empty. We sat in his driveway among the spruces, gazing past the end of the house at Morgan Bay flashing in the sun. "With any luck," Barnaby said, "he's put the house on the market and moved out."

We drove around to Shallows and had midmorning coffee with my uncle and aunt. Yes, Cory had called there, and told Stewart there was some doubt as to whether the road from the Darby driveway on across the Neck was public or private. My uncle had been prepared for this by a call from Kyle. He asked Cory what his source of information was, and Cory named Mr. Willy.

"That explains it," Stewart said. "*Mr.* Willy says a lot more than his prayers. And maybe he disremembers things. That's his word for being mistaken, intentionally or otherwise."

"A man of his age," said Cory stiffly, "has no reason to lie."

"I wouldn't be too sure about Garfield," Stewart said, "and don't ever let him hear you say anything about his age. It's all right for him to mention it, brag on it, even add to it, but not for anybody else. If I were you, Mr. Sanderson, I'd forget about the road, just relax and enjoy the place."

"With a public park less than half a mile beyond my driveway?"

"I didn't try to answer that," Uncle Stewart told us.

"Oh lord," said Aunt Jess, raising her eyes devoutly to the ceiling. "What oddities they breed in the cities."

"Well, we can't blame the cities for James A. Garfield Willy," I said. "Why do you suppose he's taken a fancy to Garfield?"

"Hard telling," said my uncle, carefully raising his mug of coffee above the rumpled head of the Aussie in his lap. "Maybe he thinks extreme old age automatically confers sainthood, so Garfield's the only one he can trust around here."

"How did Garfield ever get inside the door?" Aunt Jess asked.

"Oh, we'll probably hear from Garf," said Barnaby. "Some weird and wonderful version of it, anyway."

When we got home there was a note on the table that read: "Hiking around the bay. Don't worry. Love. The Girl of the Limberlost."

"She's been reading the Gene Stratton Porter books in the attic," I said. "In between reading her Tarot cards."

We had lunch and went for a walk. Up in the swamp plenty of little bright green plants gave the lie to the ice, which was snapping all about us as the soft salty thaw of the south wind penetrated the woods. We watched a saw-whet owl no bigger than a robin being discovered by chickadees, and accidently startled the spruce grouse who was spending the winter on Cape Silver. Our local grouse usually startled *us*. We came home by a deer trail through upper Deepwood.

We had work to do, but instead, we got into the jeep and went to try Cory again. There was smoke from his chimney now and the carriage house doors were closed. We went to the back door and Barnaby gave a fine, resounding, authoritative knock. "Open in the name of the law," I murmured.

The responding silence was not that of an empty house. After a moment Barnaby knocked harder. "Shall I go to the front door and surround him?" I asked.

Then we heard steps, and Cory opened the back door. He wasn't wearing the dark glasses. Without speaking, he looked at us with his odd light eyes. Barnaby took his pipe out of his mouth and said, "I'm Barnaby Taggart. My brother told me you value your privacy, so I haven't been around. But I think it's time we talked."

The abrupt approach seemed to disconcert Cory. "Come in," he said. He led the way through a kitchen neat enough to shame me. There were a few dishes in the sink to show that he must have eaten in ordinary human fashion, not feeding from the air like orchids.

In the living room a book lay open on the sofa before the fire; I tried to see what it was without being too obvious, but Cory picked it up and closed it, and put it on a table across the room. I couldn't see Leonardo anywhere, either.

"Sit down," he said vaguely, and began fussing with the

fire; it occurred to me that he was actually nervous. I sat down on the sofa, but Barnaby stood watching Cory, his hands in his pockets. Then he took his pipe out of his mouth and said in a friendly way, "Now what is it that worries you about the road?"

Cory straightened up. "I expected this place to be quiet and isolated. Your brother didn't see fit to tell me I'd be living next door to a public park."

"The Cape Silver Preserve isn't a public park. It's a wildlife refuge to which the local people have always had free access."

"Then it's a public park."

"Call it what you like. Maybe a given day there'll be three or four cars parked by the mailboxes, or along the Shallows drive; the Weirs don't object to that." With a slight smile he added, "There'll be bike traffic, I'll admit that. But some people come by boat and never set foot on the road here. Are you worried about it turning into a freeway?"

"My shore front has become a freeway, or would if I'd let it. They can't get it through their thick heads that the place belongs to somebody now."

"It's always belonged to somebody, Mr. Sanderson," I said, forgetting that I was supposed to keep quiet.

Barnaby said gently, "For somebody who wanted to be isolated, you've certainly drawn attention to yourself."

Cory's cheekbones flushed. "I'm just standing up for my rights. I paid for privacy, but it's been a constant procession of intruders from all directions. Those bums prowling around in the mud out there, crackpots coming to the door—is this my place or isn't it? A hundred thousand dollars says it's mine, and there wasn't anything in the deed about a duty to history or entertaining Boy Scouts, or—" He turned and jabbed viciously at the fire.

"Well, Mr. Sanderson," Barnaby said, "you don't have to be bothered now with people coming to look at the inscription. You can manage the Historical Society with a few well-chosen words—"

"It's taking more than a few," Sanderson said morosely.

"Lorenzo won't come where he's not wanted.

"I hope so. He wasn't included in the deed. Is he safe to be running around loose?"

"He's harmless."

"He threatened me!" Cory said angrily. "He told me I'd be sorry for turning him off the place."

"Meaning that he could be as useful to you as he was to the Darbys," Barnaby said.

"I don't care what the Darbys used to do. If they wanted to let their mentally deficient relatives run all over the place like mice, I don't have to. I can call the exterminator."

I stood up. Barnaby said temperately, "You just had the bad luck to choose a friendly village, Mr. Sanderson. There are some where, if the newcomer isn't actively harassed, he's ignored even if he doesn't want to be. Applecross isn't like that. It's got a lot of good people in it, including the clammers you class as bums. Well, now that they know how you feel, you'll be left alone, I promise you." He was moving toward the kitchen, and I followed.

If Cory was chastened, he didn't show it. He stood in our way, erect and impassive. "What about the road?" he said.

"What about it? You're a good distance from it, with a thick insulation of trees in between. A car or two a day, a lot of days with no cars—you won't know a thing about it, one way or the other."

"That's not what I meant," said Cory. "I mean the legal status of the road."

"It's a public road, a town road, and it ends where the blacktop ends, across the Neck at the mailboxes."

"How sure are you of that?"

My unflappable Barnaby flapped slightly or was flapped; I'm not sure whether that's transitive or intransitive. But for only a moment. "My great-grandfather bought his property from my wife's great-grandmother in 1906. There was a road here then."

"Are you positive the town road didn't *end* at my driveway, and the rest of the way to the Neck wasn't just a path the Darbys used to get to the harbor and the Neck?"

"What else did Garfield tell you?" Barnaby asked.

"I found him very keen and very honest. He wanted to put me right and I appreciate it. He came to do me a favor, not to ask one."

"Well, I told you it was a friendly town," said Barnaby. "Tell me the rest of Garfield's glad tidings."

"He told me that the road down the hill past the Boones' was always Darby property, and it was illegally finished off and made into a so-called public road because the selectmen were so impressed with your great-grandfather's money."

"And what were the Darbys doing while the selectmen stole their land? Was it taken by eminent domain? It should be in the town books."

"The Darby who was living here then was on the board of selectmen. He wanted business favors from Taggart. Your great-grandfather put some money into his Limerock plant or built him a new trawler, or maybe did both, I don't know."

"Mr. Sanderson," said Barnaby courteously, "I can't imagine my great-grandfather spending so much money to get a right of way. He'd have gone across Morgan Bay to Amity to get his provisions."

"Mr. Willy was a young man when the deal was made. You weren't around. He's the only one old enough to remember the hassle when people realized how it had been all pushed through in a secret deal, and onto their backs."

"But the town always had to vote to raise money for repairing and rebuilding roads. So this section would be eventually mentioned in town meetings, or was there always a conspiracy to not mention it? Handed along from one set of selectmen to the next? Not possible, Mr. Sanderson."

"Of course it was mentioned, but people just took it for granted after ten years or so. That's what happens if you can hush up things long enough."

"With Garfield still around?" I asked incredulously. "Who bought him off?"

"Maybe he was a solitary fighter against corruption," said Barnaby.

"You think it's funny," said Cory. "I don't happen to."

"I apologize," said Barnaby. "Listen, what I think is that Garfield could be partly right, but mixed up with something else that happened over the years. I think that the right of way to the Neck ran across Darby land, just a footpath or rough cart track at the time, as you suggested, and the Darbys made over or sold to the town a strip suitable for a decent road."

"It should all be recorded then," said Cory stiffly. "The town would have had to vote either to accept the gift or to buy it, wouldn't they? And there'd be some argument about the expense of keeping up the road for one family. Because the other people over there—the Weirs—they never used it. They traveled by boat, like islanders. There wasn't any right of way across the Neck then because nobody lived there. The track wasn't much more than a cowpath going through Darby pasture, and it was all fenced off at the bottom of the slope to keep the cows from crossing onto the peninsula, or getting down onto the shore at either side of the Neck."

It was strange to hear him talking so familiarly about *our* history.

"Garfield is smart," said Barnaby. "There was a Town House fire about 1914, and a lot of records were burned, so he's on pretty safe ground."

Cory ignored that. "Mr. Willy remembers well, because there was a place where he used to get through the fence on the Cape Silver side. It was always fenced. In his words, the selectmen and Thomas Taggart made a deal, the town's been stuck with the upkeep ever since, and the whole thing's illegal from start to finish. And for another reason too." He was as near triumph as he could be. "The whole property had been left to this Darby's children, because his father didn't trust him to hang onto it. Mr. Willy remembers the gossip about that as if it were yesterday."

"I'll bet he does," said Barnaby. "Did he have any good reason why nobody questioned building this new section of road through the Darby pasture? Because in a town like this there's always someone to question every nickel spent, Mr. Sanderson. And even back then you didn't build roads for nothing. How did Garf explain that?"

"He said Darby and Taggart shared the first expense. It was a couple of years later that it was slipped into the warrant, and the reason it went over at town meeting was because everybody was so worked up about something else. There was some big hassle about the schools that caused a real feud in the town."

"I've heard about the feud," I said.

"We all have," said Barnaby. "Garf must have had a hell of a good time running from one side to the other."

"Can you imagine him in his prime?" I said with awe. "When he's so —uh—creative at ninety-odd?"

"Can you prove he's lying?" Cory challenged.

"Can you prove he's telling the truth?" demanded Barnaby. "As you say, the town books should tell the story. But whatever it is, and whatever was or wasn't here before my great-grandfather's day, this road has been a public right of way ever since 1905 or so, and that takes care of it."

"You're all so damned smug around here," Cory burst out. "Everybody's so well read in the law. Even those mud-crawlers. That Trooper who says I've no defense against a vicious dog. That warden telling me I've got no say below high water mark. Boone. Your uncle," he said to me. "But an old man went out of his way to tell me there's one thing I don't have to put up with, and that's a steady stream of traffic past here to a public recreation area."

"Why do you believe him?" Barnaby asked. "I'm curious. Why take his word and nobody else's?"

"Because he's got no ax to grind."

"Meaning the rest of us have?" Barnaby grinned. "Do you think we charge admission over there?"

"He's found out about the gambling casino in the cellar, Barnaby," I said. "Well, it's a relief to come clean. I'm glad, I tell you. *Glad.*" I buried my face in my hands.

"Steady on, old girl," said Barnaby with a comradely hand on my shoulder and a painful dig of the thumb. "Look, Sanderson, you're causing a lot of your own distress. Nobody's going to bother you—"

"What about that paint job?"

"Most of us are sorry about that. We don't like seeing the shore defaced. I'd be glad to see about cleaning it off."

"It's been cleaned. And it had to be scraped off by hand, bit by bit."

"I'm sorry you had to do it all, and I apologize for the hoodlum element. But I've been talking about the attitude of the town as a whole. I think you'll enjoy it if you give yourself and it a chance."

"I didn't come here to enjoy any damned town. I came here for peace and quiet. I should have taken one of those godforsaken farms out in the boondocks."

"Maybe you should have," said Barnaby. We had reached the back door.

"What are you going to do about the road?"

"Why should I do anything about it?" Barnaby asked calmly. "You're the one who finds it a problem." We let ourselves out. I remember his face, and the absurd pang I felt as we came out into the fresh cold salt wind; I turned back without thinking, something on my lips though I didn't know what, but the door was already closed.

We stopped at the Boones' and reported. "Well, are we leaving it to him to find out about the road?" Kyle asked.

"I've got more to do than give Garfield that satisfaction," Barnaby said. "He's got Sanderson all worked up, and that's enough for him. He's likely to laugh himself to death as it is."

"When I think of him posing as the saintly old sage in

Madam President's article in the *Patriot* last year!" said Deirdre.

"Well, you have to agree he adds a certain richness to the texture of life around here," said Kyle.

"And he's the most precious relic the Historical Society has," I said. "Their living link with the past and so forth. Except that some people suspect him of making up half the stuff just to bring a sparkle to Madam President's eye and roses to her cheeks."

"It makes me sick," said Deirdre, "to think that we've all tried to be welcoming and neighborly and have been insulted for it, and then he takes that reprehensible old bird to his bosom and believes everything he says."

"Cheer up, love," said Kyle, "when Madam President gets her foot in his door by way of Garfield, he'll repent and repent and repent."

chapter 11

The first of March came in with the Canada geese which Barnaby and I heard in a silent midnight. The pheasants and partridges (really grouse) were beginning to pick buds in the birch trees, the first fox sparrows had arrived, and pussy willows appeared. The gulls sounded different in the mornings.

I'm not such a purist when it comes to the simple life that I want to wash by hand anything too big for a basin in the kitchen sink, so I take my washing to Shallows and use Aunt Jess's automatic washer, and the dryer too if I need to. That wasn't so on this particular morning, and I drove a wet load home in the jeep to hang up in the yard. Barnaby was out to haul, and Sara had gone somewhere. I enjoy being alone at times, if I can't be with Barnaby, and this was one of the times. The sea was white-flecked blue and green in the sun, darkening to an almost purple-gray under blowing clouds; each brightening was an alchemist's miracle. I intended to get out as soon as I could with my sketchbook.

I was hanging the last towel when a deer broke out of Deepwood on the far side of the duck pond, and stopped. I could see his heaving sides and hear him blowing hard from where I stood. I didn't move, but the clothes were flapping on the line and that was enough to compound his panic. He bolted off behind the barn with a flash of his flag.

The last time I'd seen a deer run like this on Cape Silver, there'd been five dogs behind him. Barnaby had been here, and he'd driven the dogs off. They weren't from the harbor, where we knew each individual, but from somewhere farther up the road, and Barnaby had posted a warning notice in the store.

This sort of chase isn't common on Cape Silver, but even if it were it would still deliver me a belly-punch. I heard the baying in the woods, and I don't know which was stronger, rage or fear, and I stood there trying to think what to do, run into the house for the .22 and have the pack come out of the woods while my back was turned, or grab up a stick of firewood and wade in swinging, and take a chance on being attacked myself—

When one lone dog appeared I said, "*Oh boy!*" on a long windy groan of relief. He didn't stop to look across the duck pond; he was off on the trail, nose to the ground and long ears swinging, white tip of tail oscillating madly. I ran around the far side of the barn to head him off. One dog alone could keep after a deer for a long time if he didn't drive it overboard right away. Just to imagine the deer's terror filled me with rage.

But I knew the dog. He'd run away to the Preserve before, though not always to chase deer, and he'd been one of the five that other day. He was a basset–beagle combination, and much faster than I, because when I got around the barn he was already out of sight. I heard him from far down the southeast slope. I can never whistle when I want to, but I yelled his name, which was a waste of breath. I couldn't just go home and forget all about it, so I went tramping down the spongy field.

When I emerged from the spruces I stopped to listen, quite difficult with my heart beating so hard, and all I could think of was how hard the deer's heart must be pounding. Damn the dogs! I was sweating, panting, and I felt absolutely helpless. The field stretching down to the Raven Hole was serenely empty in the alternating brights and darks of the day. The sea glittered blindingly.

I kept on going toward the shore, then turned northward into the Far Meadow. Somewhere up around the Binnorie Swamp a conclave of crows burst into noise. Had the chase got that far, then? But they were quieting; maybe it had been a family argument, nothing more. I still couldn't hear Beebee's resonant bark. In a way the silence was worse than knowing for sure that the chase was still on.

I was glad, though startled, to see a man perched on the highest ridge of Far Point. By the Australian bush hat I guessed that he was the same one we'd seen on the Neck the other day. This time his work was taped to a board on his knees, and his box lay open on a flat place beside him. As I stood there wiping my hand over my wet forehead, something moved in a tangle of dead grass behind him, and a basset–beagle head lifted up, and brown eyes gazed at me with luminous innocence. *I've been right here all the time.*

"Beebee, you scoundrel," I whispered.

"Yours?" asked the painter without looking around. It was as if a lichened ledge had spoken. He sounded both gruff and aloof. Disapproval or annoyance, or both?

"No, he is not," I said with spirit. Beebee had the decency to lower his head to his paws, and moved his tail apologetically in the dead grass. "He came onto the Preserve chasing a deer."

"I know. The buck bolted past me." He continued to work and I went a little closer. "He went down onto the shore and then up into the woods by the cranberry bog."

"How did you manage to catch Beebee?" I asked. I was pretty close now, I could see pretty well down past his hat brim and thick shoulder, and the sight drove a blade of jealousy through my midriff. Water colors, and he was damned *good*.

"I heard him before he got here, then the buck went by, and I was ready." The man said it offhand and went on working. I was hypnotized by the self-assurance of that brush. "I spoke to him in my best quarter-deck voice, and it brought him up all standing."

I saw then that Beebee was leashed by a length of old pot-warp, and anchored to a large boulder. He rolled his eyes at me and I patted his silky dome and said, "Beebee, you're more trouble than you're worth." He behaved as if I'd complimented him. I stretched my neck for another glimpse of the painting, and the artist said dryly, "If you want a closer look, come around here."

"Thanks." I was unabashed. I watched in silence while he worked. I'd thought Mussel Cove at high tide offered nothing like its low-tide charms of ledge and tide pools, but what he was doing only proved how limited my vision was. He put in a last dot of red and propped the board against a stump. He was through and he knew it. It was as if the thing had been born complete in his brain, with no doubt at all from the beginning to the end.

He washed out his brushes and cleaned his palette. Neat and methodical, not like me. "I saw you on the Neck the other day," I said. "Were you using oils then?"

"Yes." With his gear tidily packed up, he got out his pipe and began filling it. He was a stocky, graying man with blunt features, wearing horn rims; he was weathered enough so that the rakish bush hat wasn't incongruous. "Would you be the wife of Barnaby Taggart? I've met him."

"I would be and I am," I said. "Mirabell Taggart."

"I'm Steven Caine. I never knew Cape Silver existed until a few weeks ago, and now I can't get enough of it. My wife wanted to look for old glass and china, and picked out the Williston Inn for headquarters. I took a road out of town one day and ended up at the mailboxes on Cape Silver. Since then I've come back whenever I could, and I haven't run out of material yet."

"I hope your wife's doing as well."

"She is! Did you ever hear of Flowing Blue?"

"The Danube?"

"It's china. Today's she's on the track of a tureen. Sounds like an exotic wild beast, doesn't it?"

"Is that the Spotted Tureen, or the one that resembles a unicorn if you see it through fog?"

"Neither," he said seriously. "It belongs to the family of Sidehill Badgers."

"Oh, *that* one!"

"That one." He was suitably solemn. So was I. We stood nodding at each other until we broke spontaneously into laughter.

"Oh my!" he said "And everybody asked us what we'd do with our time when we sold our business."

"What was that?"

"A travel agency." He stood off to look at his painting. "Adequate, as my son would say."

"Does he paint too?"

"No, but he's a great critic."

"All non-painters are."

"Too right." He began picking up his gear. Beebee arose expectantly, stretching and wagging.

"I hope Beebee and I haven't broken up your session," I said. "I hate having anyone come near me when I'm working."

"You didn't interrupt, you can see for yourself that it's finished." He was adjusting a strap over his shoulder; he stopped abruptly. "You paint, then."

"Yes, but not like that. Which is why I didn't say anything about yours. I couldn't think what to say; I was stabbed to the quick, or the heart, or whatever." His smile was not broad, but it was appreciative. "So if I see you again, I promise I won't start talking to you."

"Thank you, and I'll return the courtesy. This place is a paradise for painters, there must be times when you're falling over them every few yards."

"Not really. We're at the end of nowhere. So it's nice to see somebody working out here, especially at this time of year." I unwound the potwarp from the boulder and Beebee gave my ear a lick. "Come on, you old sinner," I said.

"He's a likeable cuss," Caine said. "We've taken to each other, you might say. In spite of his sins."

"Oh, I don't believe he'd ever hurt a deer when he's alone. But he can panic them. That could have been a pregnant doe, too heavy to move fast. Later there'll be fawns. We don't allow dogs to run free on here without supervision, terrifying all the wildlife—I'll have to drive him home."

"If he lives on the road between here and Williston I'd be glad to take him along," Caine offered.

"I don't think you would. He gets carsick and we have to sing with him to take his mind off it."

"That lets me out. I've got no more voice than a cracked teacup.... I'll walk back your way, if you don't mind. I haven't been out to that part of Cape Silver yet."

Beebee with a leash seemed to be struck with Spanish Mildew (a mysterious disease my father used to accuse us of having whenever we didn't move fast enough to suit him). I untied the potwarp from his collar and he became very chipper all at once and led the way back to the house, with tail aloft as if he'd never in his life chased a deer; had never even given it a *thought*.

My blankets had wound themselves around the clotheslines in an ecstasy of abandonment to the wind, and Sara was trying to untangle them. She left off to embrace Beebee, who acted like the guest of honor at a surprise party.

"What were you up to, you criminal?" she asked him tenderly.

"He was chasing a deer, and Mr. Caine stopped him," I said, "by sheer force of personality."

"He's just what we need around here," said Sara.

"Why?" Caine showed a fatherly sort of good humor toward her. "It might not work the next time, or with a different dog. That German shepherd, for instance."

"Oh, Hugo'd never misbehave anyway. And I wasn't talking about dogs. I meant our new neighbor. Somebody really needs to get through to that man before he lands in a lot of trouble."

"Have you seen him this morning?" I asked, wondering what had happened now.

"No, and I stood around on his shore long enough, picking up those little yellow periwinkles and hoping he'd either come out and drive me off, or ask me in again."

"Why does he need to be worked on by sheer force of personality or other measures more physical?" asked Caine.

"To put it simply," I began, "he's—"

"Spaced out," said Sara. "Not on drugs, I don't think, but just naturally weird."

"He's eccentric," I corrected her, but was ladylike about it.

"Paranoid," she said, and I turned with dignity to the clotheslines and the frantic blankets. Sara touched my arm and grinned at me. "You go on, Mirabell, and I won't interrupt."

I wasn't sure of that, but took a chance. "Well, he's not used to living in a place like this, so he suspects any neighborly gestures, and he thinks the clammers may all turn out to be like the men who murdered the Clutter family. Apparently he thought that there'd be not another soul around here but him."

"You said he needed to be reached before he could get into trouble," Caine said to Sara. "Why?"

"He's gone out of his way to antagonize the clammers, for one thing. I walked around to Lorenzo's shore this morning, and some kids were down there talking to Lorenzo and making these not-so-veiled threats. Somebody said next time it wouldn't just be paint on the rocks."

"You see," I said to Caine, "It's not quite Paradise."

"I said 'for painters'," he corrected me. "That doesn't include the lesser breeds. Well, I'll be getting on." He slid the strap of his kit bag over his shoulder again.

"I can give you a lift to your car," I said. "I have to drive this juvenile delinquent home and tell his family what he's been up to."

"Couldn't I do it?" Sara begged. "I love to drive the jeep."

"Be my guest, but be sure you have your license. We're still within the reach of the law down here." I gave her directions for finding the dog's home. "If nobody's there, put him in his yard and be sure the gate is latched. They'll probably be out looking for him. Barnaby or I will call them tonight about him . . . oh, and you have to sing with him all the way, remember."

"What does he like?" she asked seriously.

"His tastes are pretty common. *Down by the Old Mill Stream*, stuff like that."

"Oh, good. I thought maybe he'd been raised on Mozart and Puccini. Come on, Caruso." She gave the rapturous Beebee a hoist into the jeep, and then ran into the house for her license.

"Do you still want a ride to the Neck?" I asked.

"I wouldn't miss it. But I won't get between them, that's all." He put his things aboard and climbed nimbly in. Beebe washed his face, knocking the bush hat askew. Sara came out whistling, jumped from the top step to the ground, and gained her seat by another leap.

"If I'm not right back, don't worry!" she sang out. "I may stop off somewhere."

They charged out of the yard with *brio*, and before they reached the bridge Sara's voice came floating back in "After the Ball Is Over," with Beebee picking up the obligato, and Caine either holding onto his hat or covering his ears, I couldn't tell which.

I finished untangling the wash, and then got out my water colors. If Sara would stay away long enough, and nobody else showed up, I could experiment while Caine's work was fresh in my mind, and burn the messier results in decent privacy.

chapter 12

I went down to the Raven Hole to paint a still life of an old trap and its tangled warp and battered buoy, tossed into the dead dry rockweed at the foot of some bay bushes. I was pleased with the result and saved it to show Barnaby, though I doubted I'd show it to Steven Caine.

Afterwards I was so full of loving-kindness toward everyone that I worked on the manuscript all afternoon. Sara came home with Barnaby in the jeep at the edge of dusk. She'd made a date with Ruel to go clamming out on the Andrews tomorrow morning. "If the weather's bad so we can't go, I'll kill myself. What can I take for food? We need tons."

When we had gone through that, she assured us that though she would be up very early to get ready, she wouldn't make a sound. This we took about as seriously as her threat to kill herself. Sara trying to be quiet made poltergeists believable.

We were just finishing supper when Lorenzo's secretive tap was heard at the back door. He wouldn't sit down and eat with us, but stood by the stove and kept wiping his nose on a handkerchief it was better to ignore. In the heat from the stove the ineffable essence of Lorenzo steeped to greater strength; a blend of woodsmoke, fried salt pork, and clam flats.

"I stopped in to see Cory Sanderson today." His voice trembled. "*She'd* just been there. Got in on Garf's coattails. Knew she would. That old devil's so soft on her it's not decent. Now he's lost his license and she's lugging him around."

"How'd he lose his license?" I asked: "The dollar falls and governments tremble, but for Garf to lose his wheels, that's *real* news."

"Oh, he went through a stop sign and ignored a policeman, and caused the biggest traffic jam in Williston since the flagpole broke off," said Barnaby. "That, added to all the complaints, finally convinced them he wasn't safe."

"If you knew all about it why didn't you tell me?" I asked. Barnaby said unrepentantly, "I forgot," and Sara gazed at him with shocked eyes and said, "Something like that? How *could* you?"

"Go on, Lorenzo," I said. "So she's driving him around. Were they both at Cory's?"

"Just leaving. Laughing and carrying on like a couple of young ones. She was some triumphant, now I can tell ye. Been to ask him if they can include the house in their tour this summer, she tells me, and she's feeling pretty sure he'll give in."

"What a dreamer," Sara said.

"Unless Garfield's accomplished it for her," I said doubtfully.

"I knew it wasn't much use for me to go up there after them, but I had this picture and I took it up there anyway, figgered I'd leave it on the doorstep. It's that old one of Horatio and Eugenia Darby. I propped it up on the back doorstep, out of the way so he wouldn't step on it but he'd see it, and I give the door a couple good brisk tunks and started away—"

"Like hanging a Maybasket," said Sara.

"If anybody ever hung that one a Maybasket, it'd be full of poison mushrooms. . . . Well, he must've seen me coming. He ripped that door open some fast. I shoved the picture at him, said who it was and he ought to have it. I thought he was going to chuck it into my face. He told me he was so sick of people coming to his door on one pretense or another—them's his words—and 'specially the ones who acted like he was just a caretaker, that he was about ready to burn the house down to the foundation and build something all concrete and glass."

His voice was shaking again. He took off his glasses and looked unbelievingly at us. *"He'd burn down Raishe's house."*

"He was just talking, Lorenzo," Barnaby said. "You know how mad you get when Garfield comes to see you, or Madam President starts in on you about giving up your stuff to the Society. And *you're* used to them ... Cory isn't. But just make sure they haven't been ahead of you next time you make a call."

Lorenzo spoke with dignity. "Today he called me a half-wit. No, I won't go to see him again. What's over is over. If I do go now and then just to see how the place is faring, he'll never know it."

Sara said affectionately, "You're too good a person to be exposed to insults. I don't know why Cory acts the way he does. He has to be sick, that's all."

"That word covers a multitude of sins," I said.

"I thought it was charity did that," said Lorenzo, "according to First Peter. Looks like the rest of us'll have to practice the charity, don't it?" He had recovered, at least on the surface, and sat down at the table with us to drink coffee and eat pie.

"Did you ever hear anything like this yarn of Garfield's about the road?" Barnaby asked him.

"Yarn is right," he said, with contempt. "That one started lying in the cradle, from all I used to hear about him from Father and the rest. Why, if I set down all the stories about Garfield Willy and *by* him, they'd fill a book the size of the Sizz Roebuck catalog. Nope, I never heard anything about the road except when they started blacktopping from the post office down to the harbor, back in 1947 or so." He stopped to eat and drink, and I suspected that even Barnaby was in suspense, though he'd never admit it.

"They had quite a touse at town meeting about extending the blacktop past Raishe's driveway and down across the Neck. Some thought it was a waste of money when there was just two families on Cape Silver, and one of 'em summer folks. There was a few ill-tempered remarks passed about the Taggarts, and a few tossed back, I'm glad to say." He grinned at Barnaby and gave him a little bow. "Rich Jordan was Moderator, and he handed the gavel over to Helen Deming—she was town clerk then—and he made a little speech to the effect that the Taggarts paid big taxes and hadn't ever kicked even though they had no vote, and they'd done a lot of good things in town under cover, and the Taggart boys had been off fighting for their country same as the other Applecross boys and one had been killed." Again a nod at Barnaby but without a grin this time. "Anyway, he got a good hand on that, and they passed the article almost unanimous. And that's all I remember about the road. You got any more coffee in that pot?"

"You're sure," Barnaby asked, "that while the argument was going on nobody questioned the legal status of the road?"

"I'm sure. And Garfield was right there too, the old reprobate. No, all the fuss was about saving a few dollars. Tighter than bark to a tree, some of 'em."

"Well, if Sanderson starts yapping again about the road, I suppose we'll have to go through the county records as far back as we can," said Barnaby. "But maybe that was just fighting talk, like telling you he'll burn the house down. How about a game of crib, Lorenzo?"

He left around nine, and we all went down to Deep Cove to see him off. The night was clear and moonlit, with the silent chill of frost. One of our foxes barked in Deepwood, the echoes weirdly ringing. We stood on the wharf listening to the leisurely rhythm of the oars after the dory had faded into invisibility. When we could no longer hear them we knew Lorenzo was out in Morgan Bay, as sure of himself in the night as a seal.

"I can hardly wait for tomorrow morning. I probably won't sleep."

"Last week she could hardly wait to go out with Max Kemper," said Barnaby, "and now listen to her."

"It's my childlike nature. I can hardly wait to do anything I want to do." She stopped at the steps and looked off across the glistening fields toward the horizon. "Besides, Max is so busy I didn't expect to hear from him again right away. One date isn't a commitment." She sounded too indifferent to be true.

"No, it isn't," I said. Barnaby's arm around my waist gave me a quick hard squeeze. Then he said quite kindly to Sara, "You'd better borrow Mirabell's foul-weather gear. If it breezes up you'll need it."

We were all up by five. Barnaby would be in by noon because we both had dental appointments in Limerock for that afternoon, and we were all invited to supper at Seth's. Sara set out with a basket and my oilclothes, to be picked up by Ruel at the wharf in Deep Cove.

I typed magnificently, if I do say so, for a couple of hours. I stopped finally to go out for a short walk along the jeep track as far as the plank bridge over the Binnorie Brook. Starlings and grackles whistled melodiously in a morning that had turned mild and breezy. John Peel's successor crowed from the Gypsy Field. Gulls rose over the half-exposed ledges to drop and break mussels, and saluted each other with urgent cries. We were likely to have much more winter yet, which suited me; we wanted most of the book done by the time it would be pure torture to have to stay in the house. Just thinking of it sent me back in a hurry. I recharged my batteries with a mug-up and returned to work.

Ruel and Sara were back before I knew it, standing in the kitchen doorway, smiling at my surprise. " 'My heart leaps up when I behold a rainbow in the sky,' " I said, having just typed it.

"Thanks," said Ruel. Against his darkness, Sara's blondness was almost a concentration of light, as if she would be transparent if you could look hard enough.

"I'm starved," she said, dispelling the illusion. "I think it must be because my legs are so long." She opened the breadbox. "What about you, Ruel?"

"Not me, I'm not the one with the hollow gut."

"Watch your language," she said severely. She slathered peanut butter on a heel of bread.

"How was the clamming out there?" I asked Ruel. "Where'd you dig?"

"On the bar between Herring and Andrew's. Good clamming too, but I don't expect it to last, with the weather getting better all the time, and more diggers getting around.

"It's so wild and so beautiful out there," Sara said romantically. "I walked on both islands. I don't know which I like best. I saw the ospreys around the nest on the northern end of Herring, by the way." She began to unpack her basket. "Want to see what I've got?"

"You'd think she'd been on a trip to Europe," said Ruel. "Souvenirs for everybody. No wonder my boat was down at the nose coming home."

"Well, I just couldn't leave *this* behind." *This* was a piece of driftwood roughly evocative of a large bird in flight. "For you, Mirabell. You could do a fabulous still life. For Barnaby, one perfectly good bait iron, and the guy who lost it didn't whittle his number into the handle, so Barnaby doesn't have to feel dishonest. And here's something that may or not be an Indian hand ax, and a few other odds and ends." She laid out a collection of sea-worn felsite pieces and odd-textured rocks, and unwrapped from a paper napkin a perfect sea urchin shell like fine porcelain, and from another napkin a horseshoe crab shell, complete. The last thing, set to one side with no fanfare, was a slab of mica schist studded thickly with big garnets.

Ruel's black eyes followed it from her hand to the table with an almost predatory attention. Then, as if he were self-conscious about my seeing this, he winked at me. "She's going to shower her new boyfriend with jewels."

"If she showers him with that she'll fracture his skull," I said.

She explained with large, flustered gestures. "Well, it's *just* because I told *him* about the rocks out there, and I just *happened* to see this when I picked up the sea urchin. That's *all*."

"Of course that's all, honeybunch," said Ruel. "Who said anything different?"

She smiled at him; it was like watching an aerialist recover her balance on the high wire. "Mirabell, Ruel's going to take me to Charlie's and to Cat. The Kittens were all out today, I'll bet I could have hopped across on them from Herring."

"I'm only taking her," said Ruel, "because she conned me into it, same as she did about cleaning off all that paint."

"What paint?" I asked innocently.

"We used up pretty near a gallon of turpentine and wore down two wire brushes, and I never even had anything to do with the mess in the first place. Good thing it was plain old buoy paint. Hadn't had a chance to really set, and the surface was fairly smooth." He shook his head. "God save me from a woman with a mission."

Sara's glance was not complacent but affectionate. "I did—do—appreciate it, Ruel. And I'm sure Cory Sanderson does."

"Are you talking about the paint on the Darby rock?"

"Ayuh," said Ruel. "I know he blamed me, but I've got more to do than decorate rocks with buoy paint. He blamed everybody that came along, just to be sure he got the right one. Everybody but Gus Flint, that is. He was afraid Gus'd set the dog on him."

Sara was blushing. It was so surprising that I couldn't take my eyes away from the phenomenon, and she kept on blushing and looking everywhere but at us.

"I gave him some lip," Ruel was saying, "but otherwise I let it roll off me like water off a duck's back. Time's past when I think I have to lick every son of a b who looks crosswise at me."

"So it was you and Ruel who cleaned up the ledge," I said to Sara. I almost said, You had a guilty conscience after all, otherwise why blush? But I refrained. "Why did you want to do it? The way you talked out aboard Scott's boat that day, you seemed pretty happy about it."

"Well, I was happy to see him so mad and not able to do anything about it," she explained. "But then I kept thinking about what you said about vandalism. I mean, it's not the rock's fault, Cory acting the way he does. And I thought that if somebody cleaned it up out of the kindness of their heart, it might make a dent on Cory. Somehow," she added dubiously.

"You might have felt kindly, but I didn't," said Ruel.

"Come on now, I didn't come down there in the flats and twist your arm up behind your neck somehow, and march you up to that ledge and say, Clean it off or I'll break this arm off and beat you over the head with it."

"Oh no! You came tippy-toeing across the mud—" he put his hand on his hip and tippy-toed across the kitchen floor, and said in falsetto, " 'Oh goodness gracious, do you know how to get the paint off that rock?' "

"Seductive," I said.

"Not that much," said Sara. "He wouldn't stop digging."

"So she stood around till I said I'd meet her there at high tide. I wouldn't waste any time out of a low tide for *him*!"

"Does he know you two did it?" I asked Sara. "The other day I got the impression that he'd done it himself."

Sara's head jerked back as if she'd been slapped. "You see, he's not only a son of a b, but a lying son of a b," said Ruel.

"No, wait," I corrected myself. "He didn't say he'd done it. He said it all had to be taken off by hand."

She slumped with relief, smiling. "Well, that's something, even if he didn't mention any names. Because I went up and told him when we'd finished. I tried to get Ruel to go with me, but he wouldn't. He pushed his boat off and left."

"I'd wasted enough time on that—"

"Son of a b," said Sara helpfully.

"For heaven's sake, what did Cory *say*?"

"Nothing! He just looked at me. It seemed forever. Then he nodded, and I thought he was going to ask me in—he acted as if he was going to say or *do* something—"

"Rape?" suggested Ruel.

"Where is your *mind*?" she snapped at him. "No, don't tell me." She turned back to me. "I had this feeling that he was touched, or at least grateful, but he didn't know how to accept it, and I kept looking at him, *willing* him to commit himself to humanity with just one word, one gesture—"

"Talks pretty, doesn't she?" Ruel said to me.

"I think he was almost in my power then," she said dreamily. "Lost in my green eyes. Then damn it, somebody knocked on the back door. He said Thanks, and shut the door in my face."

"Gee, I don't know how to tell you this," I said, "but we probably ruined the Great Moment of your life. It may have been Barnaby and I at the back door."

chapter 13

W̶e got our car at Shallows and drove to Limerock for errands and dentist; then on to Fremont. Of course we talked about Cory that night. I'd have been glad to ignore the subject, and Barnaby showed his reluctance, but Seth was eager to know how Cory was getting on. I let Barnaby do the talking, knowing he'd keep it short; I'm inclined to get carried away as I warm up. Sara was upstairs with the children. Barnaby left out altogether Cory's questions about the road, so it sounded as if nothing much had gone on since the skirmishes with the clammers and the trouble about the inscription. I was pleased then to tell them what Barnaby didn't know yet, that Sara and Ruel had been the ones to brush away the paint.

"Well, he'll simmer down in time," Barnaby said. "Got any big fights coming up in Fremont town meeting?"

Seth held his head. "Have we!" They were off into municipal politics. In the middle of this the telephone rang, and it was Kyle, wanting to speak to Barnaby.

We heard only one side of a short conversation. Barnaby laughed once, and that was reassuring. "We'll be leaving shortly," he told Kyle. He came back to us looking both amused and astonished.

"I have to laugh because it's so wild," he said. "Cory's shut off the road. Kyle wanted us to be forewarned."

"I certainly didn't do much for Applecross when I took him down there," Seth said. "I'm sorry."

"Aunt Jess says he's the hair shirt sent to keep us from getting smug," I said. "I know one thing, this road business is so far out it's getting to be a real cliff-hanger. Did Kyle say how Cory'd shut off the road? Barbed wire? A locked gate?"

"He didn't say, but they got through all right," said Barnaby. "He called from home."

"Listen, if you stop at their place call us up, for heaven's sake," said Lois. "Otherwise Seth's going to take to biting his fingernails from suspense."

"Seth, I hope the IRS takes all your commission," said Barnaby.

"Don't worry, they're going to."

To drive home from Fremont we went out around the city of Limerock, past white, frozen lakes and among black woods and snowy hills. It's a beautiful drive in moonlight, not that we saw much of it that night. Sara and I were so vocal that Barnaby finally told us his eardrums felt like ocean's wave-beat shore about to crumble under the relentless surf. We shut up so emphatically that after a while he was driven to start talking to himself. "The silence is unnatural," he complained. "Now my head's ringing."

We were driving now through the moonlit fields of Applecross. "There's Max's place," Sara said suddenly, twisting around in the seat to look out. One set of downstairs windows in the old white farmhouse glowed with the richness of light shining through red wine.

"He has red curtains in that room," Sara said. "His stereo's in there, and all his books."

"Should I turn around and drive back so we can all genuflect?" asked Barnaby. I gave him a hard knuckle in the ribs. He didn't take the hint. "I didn't know you'd ever been in his house," he continued.

"We stopped there on the way back from dinner last Sunday," she said in innocent surprise. "He wanted to change from his dress shoes to his boots. When we left, he showed me the sloop in the barn. Lorenzo's been up and looked at her already."

"That's good," I said. Barnaby began whistling "The Devil's Dream." His disapproval was obvious to me but not to Sara, still in spirit back there with Max. I made a mental note to have a little discussion with Barnaby. He might as well start learning now how to live with daughters.

After a few minutes of meditative silence, we came to the portion of the road that passed the harbor woods, going slow in case of deer crossing. The suspense was as obvious in the car as the scent of the unseen salt water and tidal flats. The road dipped into a curve, and a moonlit figure stood at the left side of the road. It was as if a statue had been erected there while we were gone. We didn't speak, and my heartbeat seemed to snap violently into a different gear. Barnaby stopped the car, without a jolt because we'd been going slow, and Sara whispered hopefully, "Is it a ghost?"

The figure stalked toward us, its shadow at heel, and Barnaby opened his door. I seized his arm, and he shook me off.

"Hello," Kyle said. "I hope I didn't wreck your evening." He got into the back seat.

"I'm disappointed, Kyle," Sara said, "I thought maybe you were a Darby ghost come to straighten out the whole business."

"I'd like to locate one who could. Know any good mediums?"

"But Cory would never believe him," I said. We completed the curve and came out on the brow of the hill; from there the road went straight down past the Darby turnoff.

A red Cyclops eye blazed out suddenly on either side of the road and between them hung words of fire: PRIVATE ROAD. NO TRESPASSING.

"Good God," said Barnaby in disgust.

"No, Cory," said Kyle. "Though if he could have managed an angel with a flaming sword he'd have probably done so." Our laughter was like letting go the held breath. We got noisily out into the cold moonlight.

A thick white-painted post had been driven on either side of the road just before it reached the Darby drive, each one carrying a circular red reflector. The sign was hung from a chain slung between the two posts.

I said tritely, but emotionally, "Who the hell does he think he is?" Sara was breathing quickly, as if she'd been running, but she didn't speak.

"When did this happen?" Barnaby asked.

"It had to be this afternoon while we were all gone. Deirdre and I drove to Augusta, and on the way back we stopped at the Williston Inn for dinner. We drove home around nine, and there it was." He laughed. "The effect was weird, I can tell you. This sudden flaming-out at you, so for an insane moment you think you've been driving in your sleep and gone off the track somewhere and you're out in a field, or else you're hallucinating. Of course Deirdre's reaction took care of that."

"I'll bet," I said.

"Is the chain padlocked?" Barnaby crossed the road to the other post.

"No. If it had been, Cory'd have had a visit from the constable. I unhooked it and drove through, and I didn't fasten it again. I came back after I called you, and the chain was back between the two posts." He turned toward the spruces of the drive, standing massive in their pools of shadow, and raised his voice. "At last Cory's got some healthful recreation to keep him out in the fresh air. . . ."

"Then he can't be afraid of the bogey man after all," I said loudly.

Barnaby took hold of one of the posts. "Solid."

"Oh yes, it's a good job. Anyone who tried to kick one down would break his toes. Whoever helped him, they had it all to themselves out here this afternoon. I called Stewart and neither he nor Jess had been on the road."

"Well, what are we going to do?" I asked. "Stand around and stare as if this were some kind of holy vision?" I went to the nearest post and unhooked the chain, and with the metal sign dragging noisily I crossed the road. "If you hear any chains rattling, it's not Marley's ghost."

Barnaby unhooked the other end before I got to it. "Sara, will you please drive the car through?" he requested courteously. She bolted into the car and obliged, stopping a few yards beyond the driveway.

"Barnaby Taggart," I said savagely, "if you replace that chain I'll divorce you. Or brain you."

"That sounds like my wife," said Kyle. "She was all for going directly to the house and calling Sanderson out. I asked her if she was going to be the one to hit him, and she quieted to an intense smolder." We all laughed, more easily now, and with relief that we *could* laugh.

"I didn't plan to replace it," Barnaby said to me. He dropped it on the ground where he stood.

"Come on down to the house," Kyle urged. We were glad to, at least Barnaby and I were. I was all charged up and I knew Barnaby was quietly enraged, and to go home now would mean staying awake half the night. Sara had nothing to say, and when we came into the house she had the pale, plain look she got when she was tired. But then she'd been up since five, starting off with a strenuous morning out on the Andrews with Ruel.

"Would you rather go home to bed?" I asked her when we were dropping off our coats.

"What, and miss anything good?" she retorted. "Hi, Prince! How's my old sweetheart?" She got down on the floor to play with the dog, and worked up quite a bit of spirited noise. She looked better when she came to the kitchen table.

Barnaby called Seth and told him what we'd found. After that we sat around for a long time, drinking hot chocolate and eating crackers and cheese.

"What we've got to have," said Kyle, "is something in black and white that says this section became a town road on such and such a date, period."

"What about newspaper files?" I asked. "Didn't the Limerock *Patriot* always report town meetings all over the county the way they do now?"

"That's a possible source," Barnaby admitted, "but they

didn't always report on every article in the warrant, just the high points. It's only in the last few years that they've taken to printing all the warrants in advance."

"Somebody in town must have a whole set of town reports tucked away in the attic," Deirdre said. "We'll start asking."

"If they haven't already presented them to the Historical Society," Barnaby said. "So somebody'll have to butter up Madam Prezz. Somebody like Kyle. Smooth."

"Maybe she'd expect to be paid in the old-fashioned way," said Deirdre.

"I'd rather die," said Kyle.

Barnaby bit down hard on his pipe stem. "Damn it, why doesn't the man just build a six-foot wall all around his property so nobody can see in, and be done with it?"

"Don't start those thoughts winging through the atmosphere," said Deirdre. "He's likely to put it right across the road, with a gate that can be controlled from the house."

"I'm going up to see him tomorrow morning," said Kyle.

"Why waste your time?" Deirdre asked. "You'll be so polite you won't even make a dent in him."

"Maybe it's just for my own satisfaction, love," Kyle said with a smile. "He can't deny any of us access to our property, or the townspeople access to Cape Silver. No matter what the truth is, which we'll try to find out, the road's been used as a public right of way for too long, so Cory can either give in gracefully, or be forced to. I'm sure he doesn't understand what Garfield conveniently left out. No matter what the rest of you think, I'm bound to make a last appeal to reason."

"I'd like to appeal to his reason with a piece of two-by-four over the head," said Barnaby.

We stood on the doorstep talking for a few minutes while Prince ran around the yard checking all the tires. "Oh, I forgot to tell you," Deirdre said suddenly. "While we were having a drink before dinner at the Inn we met this man who's been painting on Cape Silver for a couple of weeks. Have any of you seen him? His name's Caine, and his wife collects old china."

"Flowing Blue," I said, "among other things. Sara and I have met him."

"Frank Ives introduced us in the store once," Barnaby said.

"Interesting chap," Kyle said. "Not a lot of noise to him. A serious painter, I gather."

"He's good," I said.

"We're going to make a date to have them down," said Deirdre. "And maybe his wife can tell me about some of my old dishes. You'll come, won't you?"

"I wouldn't miss it," I said. "Speaking for myself."

"He seemed like a nice guy," Barnaby said. "Sure, I'll come."

It was so late now that we broke our own rule and drove the car home, rather than back to Shallows to risk rousing the dogs. Sara went directly upstairs without bothering to undress in the warm kitchen, or to take her hot water bottle. Barnaby looked at me with his *Now What?* expression. "She's tired," I said.

"Who isn't?" He yawned with magnificent abandon. "Shall I brush, or to hell with hygiene? Oh well, I'll hate the taste in the morning." He raised his voice. "Sara, your teeth'll rot, and what'll he think *then?* 'Believe me, if all those endearing young charms,' " he sang, " 'that he gazes on so fondly to-day—' "

"If I didn't know better I'd think you were drunk," I said.

"I've got my second wind. I guess I'll stay up the rest of the night and weave sinister plots. I think Cory has finally got to me."

"Then you'll have to do it alone," I said, "because I'm weaving on my feet right now." When I was in my pajamas I took a hot water bottle up to Sara. She mumbled thanks from inside the sleeping bag.

When I came downstairs, Barnaby's second wind had gone and he was in bed. We rolled together like survivors tossed ashore, and I don't know who went to sleep first.

chapter 14

We slept later than usual; I think Barnaby knows in his sleep whether it will be a fit day to haul or not, and this one had squally winds and rain. Perhaps he could hear through his dreams the cannonade of surf on Far Point. Sara was cheerfully herself this morning, and borrowed my rain clothes to go for a walk in the woods. Barnaby and I worked on the book with industry and contentment. After two years I still felt that simply to be alone in a room with Barnaby was a kind of perfection.

I was sorry when the rain let up, and the world came in with Sara, and it was time to think about lunch. She'd been to Shallows and was full of news. One of Garfield's great-grandsons, known more for brawn than brain (people got him to dig cellars because he was cheaper than a backhoe), was bragging about the money he'd made the day before doing a job for one of Gramp's friends.

I was disgusted at having the chain served up for lunch, and Barnaby's gloomy reticence was eloquent while Sara ran on. "Come on," I said to him when we were finishing the meal, "let's go work on blowdowns, or get after that juniper in the Gypsy Field. Something strenuous, anyway."

"I guess I'll work on gear," he said.

"Then *I'll* go chop juniper. And the other day I found a nice little spruce trying to grow up in a clump of alders. I'll liberate that . . . Sara?"

"I've been out all morning. I'll do the dishes, and then maybe I'll help Barnaby and maybe I'll help you. Care to flip a coin to see who gets lucky?"

There was a peremptory bark and a passionate scratching

at the back door. Prince was hysterically glad to be there, and Kyle and Deirdre were just coming up from Deep Cove. It was plain that the red in Deirdre's cheeks was not simply caused by the fresh air. But Kyle was at his mildest.

"I thought you'd be relieved to know that the new laird isn't shutting off you, the Weirs, or us. Just in case you'd like to stop by and pay your respects, pull your forelock, curtsey, and so forth."

"You mean he isn't going to put in a tollbooth or a port-cullis?"

"Oh, no." Kyle's smile was seraphic. "In fact he'll give us all a written, legal, right of way. Of course it won't be trans-ferrable, in case any of the properties pass into other hands. In the meantime the chain and sign are meant to stop—quote —outsiders—unquote."

"You can see the man's insane!" Deirdre said. "Kyle asked him if he'd had legal advice, and—"

"*Dearest*," said Kyle. "Be quiet. I told him he didn't have to give us permission because the road had been a legal right of way since long before I ever came here, and if he didn't believe it he'd better see a lawyer. Without a change of ex-pression he told me that if we forced him into it, we might be sorry. Garfield's his authority," he went on. "He seems to have an almost Chinese reverence for age."

"Did you leave without hitting him?" I asked.

"I didn't even feel like it, I was so astonished. He could be one of those humanoid robots straight out of science fiction. So I told him that if we had to settle it in the courts we would, and I left."

"Always the gentleman," said Deirdre. "Which makes some people think you're either a fool or soft in the head."

"Oh, I could rage around and slam my fist into my palm, but he'd be sure I was worried. He told me that the way everybody's been telling him to relax convinces him we're all trying to throw him off the track, and Garfield's confirmed it."

"So we're going to have to waste our time digging out facts," Barnaby said. "It would be a damn sight quicker to just keep sawing down his posts every time he replaced them, till he got tired of it."

"If he's really off his rocker, he won't get tired of it," I said.

"If he's really off his rocker he could do something worse," Deirdre said. "I wish somebody would do something to *him.* Something nice and final."

"That's not even funny," Kyle reproved her.

"But it does me good to say it out loud. Don't be a prig, Kyle darling. There's no law that says you have to be a gentleman at all times." The unfamiliar edge to her tone made us all uncomfortable.

Sara said quickly, "Maybe the way Cory's acting is really a cry for help. Maybe he wants attention badly, he wants people to know he's *there,* a real person and not a cipher."

"If that's so," said Deirdre, "what about our welcome with the clam pie and apple cake? What about all the other attempts? Wasn't that attention in the most friendly and well-meaning way?"

Sara became silent, sulkily biting her lower lip; after a moment she went out, taking Prince with her. The men were moving into our workroom, already talking about something else.

"Did I snap at her?" Deirdre asked me, penitently.

"No, I would have said it if you hadn't. She's beginning to romanticize him, if you can imagine it. She and Ruel cleaned the paint off the rock, and when she told him about it she thought, or wanted to think, that he was affected in some way. Then Barnaby and I had to show up inconveniently at the back door. So the electrifying moment vanished, never to return."

"Poor Sara," Deirdre said softly. "Once I thought the town drunk was a romantic character because when he fell into me on the street one day he apologized with such elegance. Oh dear!" She laughed. "Over thirty years ago, and it could have been yesterday. When he died of cirrhosis of the liver I wrote a sad poem about the victim of the War of Life."

"Well, I suppose he was one," I said seriously.

"Did anyone ever tell you what a nice child you are?"

The Boones had planned to spend the afternoon walking around the Preserve, so we walked part way with them. We left them in Mussel Cove, at the cranberry bog. As we entered the woods we heard behind us Prince's basso from the other end of the cove, Digger's baritone and Girl's voice ranging from alto to soprano.

We climbed to the pond and stood in old snow, listening to the ice snapping and the forest in motion all around us, the tops circling against the blowing clouds. I put my arms around Barnaby, and he returned the embrace.

"I think I'm depressed," I said.

"Why?" Men always ask that in such surprise, unless they're the ones who are depressed and then you're supposed to know why without asking.

"The longer you forget Cory the worse it is when you do remember him."

"What can he do to us, you nut?" asked Barnaby.

"He pollutes," I said. "Like an oil slick."

That night the Boones let Prince out at midnight for his run, as usual. He wasn't a terribly brave dog, and after a few noisy dashes to scare off anything that might be lurking he was always ready to come in again and have his biscuit and go to bed. This time Kyle heard him barking in the woods and thought he'd treed a raccoon lured out of sleep by the soft weather. He went out and whistled. The dog didn't come, so he went toward the sound.

Prince was up the hill toward the Darby house and Kyle followed the sound, swearing under his breath, sure that Cory was calling the State Police with a complaint that very instant. There was a cloud cover over the moon, but he could still see well enough to follow the old path through the woods to the Darby place.

Suddenly Prince stopped barking, and Kyle thought his whistle had reached him. He kept on whistling, but the dog still didn't come. He went toward the place where the sound had last been, and found Prince lying dead behind the carriage house. He had been shot in the head. Yet Kyle had heard no shot.

Sick with shock, Kyle carried the dog home, not even noticing the weight. He had to break the news to Deirdre, and there was no sleep for them the rest of the night. The frost hadn't gone deep that winter, and the soft spell helped; before daylight they had buried the dog wrapped in his blanket, with his dishes and toys.

After that Deirdre went to bed, and cried herself to sleep. Kyle went to see Cory as soon as he thought the man would be up. . . . There was a thick and dispiriting fog that morning.

"I've got no case against you, Sanderson," he said at once. "The dog was on your property and you could convince the court that you thought he was going to attack you. This is between you and me. *You* know that dog would never attack anyone. He was a loving fool of a dog—he—" To speak in the past tense was almost unbearable, and something in his throat shut off Kyle's voice for a moment, in which Cory said, "What in hell are you talking about?"

"You shot my dog last night," said Kyle. "Out behind your barn."

Cory went grayish-pale. Even through his rage and pain Kyle saw that. "I wasn't out of the house last night," he said. He gestured toward the living room. "I watched a late movie and went to bed."

"You didn't hear him barking? Around midnight?"

"I told you." The man spoke numbly. "I was watching a movie and it was a noisy one. Listen, I didn't hear anything, and I never shot your dog. Believe me. Scared as I am of dogs, do you think if I did hear one barking in the middle of the night I'd go out there looking for it, even with a gun? No, I'd call the police. And I don't own a gun of any kind."

Kyle turned and walked away. He stopped in at his own house and saw that Deirdre was sleeping deeply, so he came directly to tell us what had happened to Prince.

Barnaby was at home because of the fog, and he and I

were working on the book. Sara was trying to adapt a cassoulet recipe to what materials we had on hand. All this now came to a wretched stop. Barnaby hunched silently over the stove as if he'd been punched in the belly. Sara cried in a brief, noisy outburst like a child, protesting and incredulous, and ran upstairs. I wanted to go off by myself and give in; I'd loved Prince as much as I loved the two Aussies at Shallows. My throat was aching with the effort of holding back. But Kyle looked so drawn and exhausted that I had to keep making futile offerings simply because I couldn't keep still.

He didn't want coffee, he'd drunk so much since midnight. But he admitted that he hadn't eaten, so I fixed bacon and eggs and toast for him. Sara came down the stairs and sat on the next to the last one, sniffling now and then. After he had eaten, Kyle told us about Cory's reaction.

"Did you believe him?" Barnaby asked.

"Yes, I did. He went so pale I thought he was going to keel over."

"Maybe he was afraid of you," Sara suggested wanly.

"Maybe I looked that savage, I don't know. But my first impression was that what had happened terrified him. He was as stunned in his way as I had been."

"I'm going out," Sara said. She took her boots and jacket outside to put them on, as if she couldn't stand the kitchen another instant.

"Sounds like poachers to me," Barnaby said. "They may have been after a deer, or even a moose, and Pr___ and the dog caught sight of them and queered the operation."

"That's probably it, the bastards," Kyle said harshly. "Excuse me, Mirabell."

"I'd call them worse, except that my husband would be shocked." We exchanged weak smiles.

"Well, one thing more to feed Sanderson's paranoia," Barnaby said. "The thought of someone prowling around his premises with a gun must have shaken him up. He'll be sure now someone intended armed robbery."

"It would shake almost anyone up," Kyle said. "The trouble with guns is that it's so easy to pull the trigger even when you don't intend to, if you're taken by surprise."

"He may move out after this," I said.

"It's a high price to pay for getting rid of him." He got up abruptly. "Thanks for the breakfast. It made me feel better in one way, at least. It seems like a year since midnight."

Barnaby and I walked part way with him. The fields sloped away from us to dissolve gently into the fog, but you could still hear the old-squaws' woodwind music on Morgan Bay, and the fox sparrows singing. I had never in my life hated a foggy day on Cape Silver until now.

We were among the birches of Goldengrove when Kyle stopped. "I just remembered something. They must have used a silencer."

"Great," said Barnaby. "Poachers with silencers. That's all we need to make a happy home. Are you going to call the police about this?"

"What good would it do? If it were a human being, they'd have to put all the machinery in action and maybe they'd find something. But I don't expect them to do it for a . . . and anyway, the only way they can get a night hunter is when they catch him with the goods or in the act." He left us abruptly, saying "Thanks," without looking back.

We watched him disappear in the fog that lay thickly on the Neck. "Remember yesterday when I said I was depressed?" I said. "The way I felt then is nothing to the way I feel now."

"I know," he said absently.

"I wonder if Lorenzo saw or heard anything," I said. "He's all over the place these soft nights."

"We'll find out; but if we don't have clear eyewitness evidence there's nothing much can be done about it. . . . Still, the word ought to crop up around town somewhere if someone's using a silencer for his night-hunting. I'm concerned now with keeping them off the Preserve. Damn it, Mirabell!" he exclaimed. "If it's true, it's crazy! It's fantastic! The game warden ought to know, and he'll probably tell the police. But

I don't want to go behind Kyle's back and then have them come down and question him, it's hell enough for him and Deirdre as it is."

"I know," I said as he had said it a little earlier. "Why don't you wait just a little while?"

I took hold of his hand and he wrapped his fingers tightly around mine. We walked back slowly along the jeep track, with nothing more to say.

chapter 15

S ara cried by fits and starts all that day, she said she couldn't help it and it would just have to wear off. I kept having bad moments of my own, when I was remembering Prince's chin heavy on my knee while his eyes followed my hand from my plate to my mouth, or I was seeing him race in drunken circles of greeting, and splashing across the mud to meet his friends the clammers. It's a gut pain when you're trying not to cry.

Barnaby was given to longer silences than usual. He and I walked to Shallows after supper. The night was so soft it felt as if the wind were spring itself rushing through the dark, and tomorrow would be full of singing birds. But for us the old excitement was replaced by depression and apprehension.

Lorenzo was playing cribbage with Uncle Stewart in the kitchen, and Aunt Jess was in the living room knitting and watching the "Ironside" reruns. There was a comforting ordinariness about the whole business but when I was leaning down to greet the Aussies I thought how happy they'd always been to see Prince, and now they'd never play with him again. So I sat on the floor with them, my back turned to the men, and blew my nose and wiped my eyes while the terriers licked anxiously at my ears and cheeks.

"Kyle call the police yet?" Lorenzo asked Barnaby.

"I don't think so. The last I knew, he wasn't going to."

Lorenzo cleared his throat. "Even if he did, that maniac isn't likely to give the police permission to search on his so-called property. So I been there already." I had to get up and look. He reached into his pocket and brought out one of those questionable handkerchiefs. He unrolled it beside the cribbage board, it showed the slug that had ripped through the dog's head, and a rifle shell casing.

"Winchester 30–30," he said. "And this lead I dug out of a spruce tree. Down low, where it should be. It's on a line with where the dog fell. You can see the hair and some blood on a rock, and you can see where it went into the tree. Now all they got to do is find the rifle." I looked away, having that gut pain again.

"Simple," said Barnaby. "Just round up every 30–30 in the county." In the next room Ironside put a malefactor in his place with measured cadences. "We could do with him around here," said Uncle Stewart.

"Were you out around that time last night, Lorenzo?" I asked.

"Not on the road or in the woods, dammit. I was out rowing. I hadn't planned on it, but I went outside for a minute and it was so calm and pretty I took a walk to the shore. The dory was dropping curtseys out there, asking just as plain as she could. So off we went."

"So you didn't hear anything." Barnaby's flat tone told me that he'd been hoping for something tangible.

Lorenzo bristled. "You just hold your horses, son. I rowed clear to Amity harbor, and back again, and when I was walking up from the shore I heard the dog barking. That carried some clear, the night was so quiet. Then it stopped, and I figgered Kyle had got hold of him." He reached down to the nearest Aussie. "Few minutes later—I was just opening my door—I heard a car start up and go tearing up the black road. I could tell when they went by mine. Figgered they was cussid poachers, and the dog scared 'em off."

"Where do you think they started from?" asked Uncle Stewart.

"Sounded like they was in that old wood road just before you go down the hill to Raishe's driveway. I went over there this morning to see how right I'd guessed, and pick up the mess. Whether it's hunters or lovers, seems like they can't roost fifteen minutes without fouling up a place with cigarette butts and beer cans, and Lord knows what other nasty things. I been keeping Darby woods clear for a good many years now, and that critter ain't going to keep me from it."

"Obviously he isn't," said Barnaby, "but come on, tell us, were you right and what'd they leave?"

"Well, there'd been a car in there all right. But they didn't leave a thing! By Godfrey, I was some surprised." He was surprised all over again. "Neatest damn killers I ever saw!"

"I suppose that's a compliment," Aunt Jess said.

"That was some nice dog," Lorenzo said sadly, "Not much sense, but—" He left off talking, and rolled the evidence up in the handkerchief as carefully as if it had been a piece of fine scrimshaw.

"To change the subject," said Aunt Jess loudly, "I want to know how long that idiotic chain will last. When are we going to do something about it?"

"You going out to remove it with your own fair hands, Jess?" Lorenzo asked.

"I just might, unless your fair hands get afoul of it first, my lad."

"Why me? That chain could end up on the bottom of Morgan Bay without me having laid a finger on it. What are you all grinning at?"

"You and your outraged virtue," said Barnaby.

"When and if I abscond with that chain," Lorenzo said coldly, "I'll be proud to tell the world."

"From the county jail," said Uncle Stewart.

We all laughed outright then, as if we had been just waiting for something to grab at. Maybe it wasn't much, but it helped.

"We're hoping Sanderson will do something himself without a legal touse," Barnaby said. "Of course we may have to lean on him a little with some evidence. If we find any."

"Don't you love this positive approach?" I asked Aunt Jess. "We *hope*. We *may*. *If*."

"The only really positive approach," Barnaby said with spirit, "would be to strangle him with his chain and drop him overboard. I take it you're not suggesting that."

"Well—" I began doubtfully.

Another excuse for everybody to laugh. It was a good time to leave, before the communal depression could set in again. "Keep your ears open for talk of a silencer," Barnaby said to Lorenzo.

"Ayuh. Times when I'm clamming, I'm near some who don't pay any more attention to Lorenzo than if he was a rock."

"We can't get the dog back," Barnaby said, "but maybe we can find out who did it."

"It'll come out sooner or later," said Aunt Jess. "It's impossible to keep a secret in Applecross. Impossible anywhere, but a little less so in Applecross."

"Lorenzo, have you got town reports dating back to the Year One?" I asked.

"Now that's something I *ain't* got," he said regretfully. "But somebody ought to have them."

The dog's death had sent shock waves around the harbor. People were not only sorry for the Boones, they were enraged, and frightened beneath the rage. It would have been a relief to blame Cory; the shooting would have been simply and understandably the act of a madman, who at least stayed in one place. But Kyle was meticulous about exonerating Cory.

Cory's chain disappeared, but only briefly; Lorenzo would have done better at hiding it. Someone had thrown it into a clump of bare alders in the field, and there the fluorescent red on black caught the light and Cory's attention when he made one of his periodic inspections. He was fastening it back to the posts when a troop of young bike-riders came around the curve and sped down the hill, yelling in exhilaration.

The racket carried to where Kyle was limbing out blow-downs beside his driveway. He walked up the road far enough to get a clear view of what was going on.

Cory stood by the outer post, unmoving, as the phalanx bore down on him. The war whoops and rebel yells suddenly stopped, and the youngsters dragged their feet to brake or dismounted. There was an eerie silence; Kyle could imagine the quenching effect of the motionless figure, the pale impassive face, and the dark glasses.

Then one of the boys said with gruff bravado, "What's that sign mean?"

"It means just what it says," said Cory. "The road is closed. You have no right to go beyond this chain."

"Who says?" a girl scoffed.

"*I* say," answered Cory.

"Dog-killer!" the girl shouted at him. The others picked it up. It was like a noisy conclave of crows, except that words were distinguishable. "*Dog-killer! Dog-killer!* Why don't you go back where you came from? Who wants you? Get out of our town!" It became a miniature but ugly mob scene.

Kyle walked up the road toward them. Cory didn't move his head, so he couldn't see Kyle, but first one child saw him and then another, and the jeers died away. He shook his head at them, and made a gesture of dismissal, not having the slightest conviction that they'd obey it. But they turned their bicycles, reluctantly and not all at once, and began pushing them up the grade. Cory must have known that someone was there, but he still didn't turn his head, and Kyle stepped off the road into the woods and went home that way.

"It was weird," he said. "As if we can't ever meet face to face again. I think the intimacy of that morning, when I was so furious I didn't care what I said and he was so startled, was too much for him."

"It gives me gooseflesh," Sara rubbed her arms vigorously, and after a few minutes she went upstairs.

"In the light of new developments," said Barnaby, "she'll try her cards again."

"Did you read your cards?" I asked her when we were alone in the kitchen getting supper.

"Why?" She was defensive.

"I'm curious. I have an open mind, Sara, you know that. So

come on, give! Did you read them, and what did you ask? Who did it?" It was too soon to be able to ask objectively, *Who killed Prince?*

"No, you can't ask questions like that, because you wouldn't know how to read the answer," she explained. "I just tried again to see how Cory was going to adjust, and the final card was the King of Wands. That could mean absence, departure, even flight."

"Great!" I clasped my hands over my head. She was not amused.

"You don't need Tarot to tell you he'll probably split." She placed the silver around the table with slow, almost dreamlike motions. "What is there here for him? He's turned everyone against him, and even if he says he doesn't care, he *must*. If he really didn't care he'd be perfectly happy. Which he's nowhere near." She stopped at a window and stood looking out at the dusk advancing swiftly over the sea. "And wherever he goes it's not going to be any better for him. I've never had a good reading for him yet. . . . It seems like such a waste of a life."

I went to the store a few days later, where I heard that most people couldn't believe that any of Applecross's night-hunters were equipped with silencers. They'd been doing all right without any, so it had to be someone from out of town. A few others weren't willing to give up Cory as the killer. I was lucky enough to miss the Scourge, but Madam President cornered me by the stationery shelves. "It started with a dog," she told me sternly. "Next time it could be a *child*. There's something very wrong with that man."

"I don't think so," I said. "I mean, I don't think he'd hurt a child. Or that he killed the dog." In my effort to be nonchalant I took five packages of envelopes and a lined tablet off the shelf, none of which I wanted. "Even Kyle doesn't think he did, and Lorenzo heard a car right afterward."

"Personally *I* think he's capable of it." She tossed her head; she really did. One expected a horsy jingle. "Anyone who'd have the inscription chipped off just out of pure spite—that's wanton destruction! It makes me *sick* to think of him owning that wonderful old house and not giving a *damn* for its past." Another spirited toss. "Well, I gave him a chance to redeem himself for destroying the inscription, but he refused it. He'll be sorry when he finds nobody speaking to him!"

"Maybe he'll be happy," I said, and left her. Looking for oranges, I came face to face with another woman, who said out of the corner of her mouth, "She means he'll be sorry when *she* isn't speaking to him. Funny how many people are happy in Applecross without her ever talking to them."

"Well, don't let her know," I said. "Ignorance is bliss."

"If he hadn't shot that dog, I'd like him just for snubbing her."

"He didn't shoot the dog," I said distinctly.

"What about the road, then?" It was one of the farmers in town. "Trying to keep people off Cape Silver?"

"That's just a misunderstanding," I said. "We'll get it settled. He's not used to things around here, that's all. He's confused."

The new town reports were stacked on the counter, and I took one. Arthur Deming, the constable, came in to post the warrant; town meeting was two weeks off. Arthur's arrival changed the subject to the ever-inflammatory argument on the school budget. Nobody even saw me go.

chapter 16

The next day Barnaby and I drove to Limerock with the Boones to do some research on the road. It was a poet's March day, cold and blustery, with swift interludes of sun and blue sky like sudden smiles, just as suddenly gone. The men dropped us off at a major intersection and went on to the courthouse. We had about two blocks to walk to the *Patriot* offices on Main Street, and the store windows were as lavishly decorated for St. Patrick's Day as if the place were an Irish colony. St. Patrick was conspicuously missing, but leprechauns proliferated.

"They all look like Garfield," said Deirdre.

I pointed to a piece of hideous whimsy peeping through green-dyed carnations. "That one looks like Garfield being a Peeping Tom."

From the newspaper files we needed only the late March editions of the years succeeding 1905, but there was no mention of the road in those years. One March there was a big fight about making repairs on the North Applecross school, which had been struck by lightning in a freak storm in the winter. The disorderly part didn't concern repairing the roof and replacing windows, nobody objected to that. But there was a radical element among the younger parents, backed by the teacher and a few of the older people who, according to one passionate speaker, were always in a hurry to spend other folks' money when they owned nothing and didn't pay any more than a poll tax. These renegades suggested putting in water closets and doing away with the perfectly sound old outhouses on which the population of North Applecross had been carving initials, hearts, and less innocent *motifs* since 1870 or so.

Women didn't vote at town meeting in those years, and the few who boldly attended so as to know first hand what was going on, and to prod reluctant husbands in the ribs, were considered by some other women as fast and by others as courageous. So the teacher created a sensation by asking for a chance to speak for her pupils.

With great daring *but* delicacy (the reporter's words) she argued against denying small children the comfort of not having to go out back in bitter weather. Some children put off going, she said, and suffered severely in consequence. Mr. Noah Gammon stated that *he* had been going out back for sixty-eight years and hadn't suffered yet, whereupon someone asked him a question which caused such laughter the moderator had to gavel for order, and Mr. Gammon sat down.

"Cautiously, I'll bet," I said. "I can imagine what someone asked him."

"This suspense is terrible," said Deirdre. "Did they get their water closets?"

"Not at this one. Miss Eleanor Parsons was the teacher's name. Hey!" I was excited. "She became Lorenzo's mama!"

"Great," said Deirdre, "But it kills me to have to admit that Garfield was telling the truth about one story. They did have a big row about one of the schools. So if the road *did* come up in that meeting, the reporter didn't bother to mention it, the other fight was so much fun."

"Maybe they simply agreed to put it in shape without any fight," I said, "but I can't imagine that. Old Noah would have been in there pitching, and plenty of others. 'What, spend good money and time building a road for some high and mighty summer gink? Let him come and go in his fancy yacht.' Oh well, we'll keep on looking."

Finally, in a paper dated 1913, we found the motion made and the vote taken to rebuild the Cape Silver road after unusually severe winter storms and flooding had washed it out.

"There it is!" Deirdre said. "It's a town road all right, or accepted as one. There was no fuss about the repairs. But I'd be really triumphant if we could have found mention of the time when it *became* a town road. So far we can't really prove that Garfield's lying."

"Or that he's telling the truth, either," I said. "Gosh, I feel good about this, Deirdre. We'll have them make us some photostats. And we don't know what the men will find at the courthouse on the original Darby deed, and on the one before that."

"I keep forgetting that the Darbys bought that land from somebody who'd lived there earlier."

We checked through some later years, just to be sure we weren't missing something, and came to the blacktopping in 1947, with a discussion that was just about as Lorenzo had reported it. We had copies made of it as well as the earlier reference, on the premise that it would do no harm.

When we met the men for lunch, we were all really hungry for the first time in several days. Like us, the men had enjoyed the prowl through Time's attic, but they'd found nothing in the old deeds about the road. What they'd wanted was a clearcut mention of it as a town or public way.

"What do we do now?" I asked.

"We either shoot him and bury him in an alder swamp," said Kyle, "or we tell him to take up his posts and come have a drink."

"I think the first method's the only one that'll reach him," said Barnaby.

"Seriously, though," said Kyle, "maybe he'll be willing to consider it a draw. He can't shut off the road. It's been a right of way too long, no matter what its history is. I hate like the devil to haul lawyers in on it."

Barnaby grinned. "And of course we don't want to tarnish Cory's love for us, do we?"

"What about all our work this morning?" I asked. "These photostats and everything? Was that just something to amuse us and keep us off the streets?"

"Oh, they may be enough to shut him up if he comes to the boil again," my husband said indulgently.

"You'd better believe we need those copies," Kyle told me. "And that complete set of town reports if it exists. Right now I don't feel like letting this business die of attrition. Any more crusades you'd like me to take on?"

After lunch Deirdre and I went to the museum to see the show Sara and Max had attended. We were impressed, but not as the artist had intended. The men spent a contented hour browsing in a hardware store. We met at the car in mid-afternoon and drove home in good humor. But as we approached the harbor the Boones grew more and more silent; there was no Prince to greet them, undulating from nose to tail tip and carrying a mouthful of slippers and socks. I began to feel a prickling at the back of my nose and in my eyes. Barnaby was whistling softly, and I realized he was probably thinking of Prince too and trying to ignore it.

We made the turn above the Darby drive and drove down the slope. The chain and sign were still in place. But another sign had been added, nailed to one of the posts, neatly lettered in staring black on white.

CHECKPOINT CHARLIE
HAVE YOUR PAPERS IN ORDER
GUARDS SHOOT TO KILL ! ! !

We reached for the hurting release of laughter, the kind that gives you an excuse for tears. Kyle stopped the car and Barnaby got out to unhook the chain and toss it into the woods.

We changed to the jeep at the Boones' house, and went to Shallows to make a report on our findings, then home.

Sara was getting supper. She'd been around at the harbor and had bought some fresh scallops from Ronnie Deming. When she found out we hadn't yet uncovered anything on the origin of the road she said, "I think we ought to try a Ouija board. Bet got one for Christmas. She's carrying on a flirtation with some Viking, and he says he carved the figures on Cory's rock. Did I tell you?"

"I think I could have endured being kept in ignorance," said Barnaby.

"Who did the Checkpoint Charlie sign?" I asked.

"Hasn't Cory discovered it yet and torn it off? Bet's boyfriend did it after school. He's very brainy."

I went into our room to get out of my city clothes. She lectured Barnaby while he went through the mail.

"What I really think, Barnaby, is that Lorenzo and Uncle Stewart should try the board. You see, the answers may be deep in their unconscious, in memories of stories their fathers told them but which they've forgotten. If you concentrate on the board it acts like hypnosis, and the memories come swimming up from the depths."

It sounded perfectly logical, which was the trouble with a lot of things Sara said. "In other words," he said, "we have met the spooks and they is us."

"Exactly!"

"What depths did Bet's Viking beau swim up from?"

"I think *he's* a direct product of watching Kirk Douglas on television," she said.

chapter 17

few nights later a man in Applecross Center was up
past midnight to see a young mare through the delivery
of her first foal. When it was safely over, and he and
his wife left the barn, they heard a rifle shot from far down
in the pasture. He told his wife to call the game warden, and
he went off across the fields to where a rough track led from
the main road. He had a strong torch with him, but he didn't
use it then. He waited behind a stone wall, and after about
twenty minutes he heard a truck start up and head out. He let
it get past before he stood up and shone the light on it, recog-
nizing not only the truck but getting the registration number
to clinch it. The men in the cab had no time to react to the
shaft of white light suddenly striking through the rear window, because the game warden and the sheriff's patrol were
there on the black road to meet them.

There was a hastily gutted buck under canvas in the back
of the truck. The men resisted arrest, and one threatened the
officers with a pistol, but was disarmed by a surprise move
from one of the deputies. They were taken to the county jail
and booked, and put away for the night.

Lorenzo, who seemed to pick news out of the atmosphere
the way African tribesmen read the drums, was around to tell
Kyle about it early the next morning. He also showed him the
slug and shell casing. Kyle talked with the game warden by
telephone, then he drove Lorenzo to the jail in Limerock. The
poacher's rifle was a 30-30 Winchester all right, but they
swore that neither had ever used a silencer or had even seen
one, outside of the movies and television.

"I wouldn't want one, it spoils your aim," one of them said.

The other said with ponderous virtue that he'd never shot a dog yet, by God.

The game warden, who'd had many dealings with the pair, told Kyle he thought they were telling the truth. "They wouldn't have shot the dog to keep him quiet, they'd have just got out of there in a hurry. Besides, they wouldn't go that close to a house. They're stupid, but not that stupid. They know where the deer are likely to be."

The chain now disappeared completely, and we laid bets on whether Cory would replace it or not. Uncle Stewart suggested that Cory might have even removed it himself, and would then let the issue die out. Barnaby thought he might have gone for legal advice at last, and been advised to drop the whole thing. But I couldn't imagine his giving up that meekly.

But still, it would be nice if it were so. His fanatical insistence on his alleged rights had become merely tiresome. He had enlivened the winter, but we'd had enough of his nonsense. I didn't know what else he could think up, but whatever it was, nobody around here would bother again to tell him to relax and come have a drink.

The posts remained like memorials, each with its red Cyclops eye.

Town meeting day came on the first day of spring that year. The calendar date meant nothing to us except that we could very well celebrate it with a blizzard. The "town meeting storm" was more reality than myth. So it was a surprise to be enjoyed reverently when we had spring weather that week. We heard the first red-winged blackbirds and song sparrows, and more and more Canada and brant geese were seen. There was also one of those epidemics of what the older people called "the distemper." We all had it lightly in our house, and I was the last to get it. With my usual perfect timing I was almost back to normal on The Day, but in no condition for the big baked-bean supper and a long evening on the hard bench afterward.

Barnaby left me the jeep—"Just in case," he said ominously —and he and Sara rode to the Grange Hall with my aunt and uncle. Sara was going to meet Max there. She'd been out with him several times since the museum date, so we'd been having a lot of Max even without his corporeal presence. For the past few days we'd been educated by a series of lectures on the importance of the town meeting as a viable survival of early American culture; as the last stand of pure democracy; as the legitimate and cherished child of the Constitution. We knew it already, but we let her tell us.

I was sorry to miss the meeting, but there was compensation. I was alone, not only in the house but on Cape Silver, except for Digger and Girl at Shallows and all the wildlife, and I loved it. I watched until the sunset splendor faded over Morgan Bay, then I lit a lamp and fixed a light supper, and luxuriously read while I ate. After that I went into the workroom and revived the fire there, and began playing Calum Kennedy records.

I'd discovered Calum Kennedy by accident when I was about seventeen. His songs, some in Gaelic but still entrancing, and some in the beautifully accented English of the born Gaelic-speaker, had done as much to sublimate my unhappy juvenile love affair with Barnaby as the poets had. Between his singing and a picture of him in a kilt I fell violently (and safely) in love.

As he shifted without effort from the rowdy "Barnyards of Delgatie" into the seductive tenderness of "Gin (If) I Were a Baron's Heir," I decided that under certain circumstances— like no Barnaby—Calum would still have a chance, and he wouldn't have to braid wi' gems my hair, either.

After an hour in the Hebrides I had to return myself to Cape Silver, so I went out. I walked down toward the white cliff. My footsteps in the frost-stiffened grass made the loudest sound there was, until a fox barked, and I stood listening until the eerily ringing echoes died away. I looked up and sought out Orion the hunter, crossing the sky in his seven-league boots. Then I started back to the house.

On the way, I heard a car driving fast on the black road. It would be coming along the height of land behind the harbor, and the roar dulled suddenly when the road dipped into the curve. Then the rush of tires grew louder as the car began the long descent toward the Neck. Town meeting's over early, I thought at first. But it was never Uncle Stewart driving that fast, or that loud, and not Kyle and Deirdre either. This was one of those souped-up jobs dear to a generation of kids who are all going to grow up deaf because Noise means Living, man!

Everybody had gone from this end of town, which meant a good chance for drag racing, or the Boones' mailbox and ours were about to be knocked down. Or the Boones' glass doors were to be smashed. Or there could be more damage on Cape Silver than to mailboxes. Last town meeting night a gang had driven over from Amity and committed some fairly expensive vandalism.

The engine had stopped. But the silence was not the same as before, because I was listening so hard that either it or I was full of pulses. I ran in and got the jeep keys. If they had thought nobody was home down here, perhaps the sound of a vehicle coming off Cape Silver could drive them away. I grabbed up the grocery pad and pencil too, in case I could get a license number.

At the mailboxes I stopped the jeep, and listened with hideous expectation for the crash of breaking glass. It didn't come, and I started up again and drove across the Neck. Ahead of me the road ran gray between black woods. I stopped again. What in hell were they doing? I wasn't so terribly courageous; supposing my headlights didn't scare them off?

A chain saw erupted into a nerve-wringing screech, and my hands flew off the wheel. It didn't run for much more than a minute, then there was a pause and it started again. So did I.

The Boones loved their trees almost as much as they'd loved Prince. All I could think, hearing the chain saw splitting the night, was that destroying fine trees was a favorite form of vandalism over in Amity, and some Amity boys had made trouble in Applecross before this.

My headlights picked out Kyle's mailbox. I went slowly up the drive all the way to the house, and my lights showed the trees majestic and unharmed in their solitude. A pair of incandescent eyes glowed at me from a big bough a third of the way up a tremendous old pine.

I drove out again, and up the hill. I would go just as far as the Darby road and turn around and go back home. Maybe Cory had heard the noise—I didn't know how he could *not* have—and had called the police.

When I came to his driveway, I missed the Cyclops eyes in the white posts. The posts lay where they had fallen, one across a clump of juniper, the other half-submerged in the ditch where the hill water ran off like a brook this time of year. I sagged back in my seat and blew like a porpoise. So that was it, and I'd been suspecting the worst. The car must have gone while I was at the Boones'; with the jeep engine running I wouldn't have heard it.

I pulled over to the side, turned off my engine, and listened for another car that might be the police or the sheriff's patrol. Then I smelled burning cloth tinged with kerosene. It was coming from the Darby place.

I tramped on the gas pedal as if I were starting a motorcycle, and made a dizzying U-turn into the drive. Then I came to a bucking stop because a big spruce lay across the way. Swearing, I got out and climbed through the thick, aromatic branches, getting scratched and almost hit in the eye, and ran toward the strengthening scent of oily smoke. After a while I could see the fire through the trees, and hear its soft sibilant voice.

I made it out into the open, my breath searing my throat. What I saw ahead of me in the drive, redly illuminating the face of the carriage house and the entire back of the house and reflecting off the windows, was something I couldn't recognize at first. Then I thought it was a dummy being burned; Cory in effigy. An ugly joke, but maybe no worse than the ones we'd made in words only.

At least the house wasn't on fire. I went around the thing and along the walk to the back door. The house was dark, I could see that when I got past the blaze. Maybe he wasn't even home, I thought hopefully. He wouldn't have gone to town meeting, but surely there was somewhere he must go sometimes, or perhaps he was driving around on the dark quiet roads convincing himself anew of his rights.

From the back doorstep, I saw that it was a fiery cross out there. There might have been some recent movie on television with a fiery cross in it, and whoever planted it tonight (whose old clothes bound around crossed poles?) would have dressed up in sheets if they could have managed it, and pranced around a bit in the firelight. Maybe they had, before I got here. Too bad for Cory to miss the performance.

I stood there getting my breath while the fire died down, turning over names in my mind. Ronnie? His sister's boyfriend, who'd done the Checkpoint Charlie? Ruel and friends? Or some other wits I didn't know so well, from farther up in the town?

The door opened behind me and I squawked in fright like a night heron.

"*Come in here*," someone said in my ear, and took my arm and hauled me in over the doorstep into the kitchen. "What do you know about this?" Cory's voice was pulled out to a fine slicing wire.

"Nothing," I said. "I came to see if you're all right."

"Yes, I'm all right." But he didn't sound it. "Do you know who did it? Never mind, you wouldn't say if you did. You people protect your own, and to hell with the poor innocent caught in the middle."

"Number one," I said, "I haven't the slightest idea who did it, but I'm damn sure they're not *my own*. Number two, if you consider yourself the poor innocent it's nobody else's fault but yours. We've all tried to welcome you and have been insulted for our efforts. Now that I've seen you haven't had a heart attack, I'll leave." I felt behind me for the doorknob. "Why didn't you call the police? That's within your *rights*."

"I did, but where are they? Long live crime!" He was human at last.

"We don't have many troopers around here, and they could be busy at a bad accident or something right now—"

"Bull—" He stopped. If he'd finished it I'd have found him growing more human by the moment. But the restraint could be the remnants of some early training in manners, and that was human too.

I started again to leave and he said quickly, "Did you see what they did with the chain saw?"

"They cut down the posts," I said.

"I knew it! Now don't tell me that it's not a conspiracy with your husband and Boone, and—"

I was too enraged to be anything but icily quiet. "Is it really *impossible* to communicate with you? Do you actually believe all the things you say? If you do, what sort of world have you come from?"

He didn't answer. "Or is it some kind of defense?" I went on. "Some shield to keep anyone from getting near you? But if you don't want to be noticed, you've taken a peculiar way of showing it."

There was a tap on the door and we both jumped. A shadowy, amorphous mass moved weirdly on the outside of the glass. "Mirabell, you all right in there?" It was Lorenzo. "I've been waiting for you to come out, and I got worried."

Cory opened the door so fast that Lorenzo almost fell into the kitchen. "I might have known *you'd* be around." "You set up that thing out there while your partner, whoever he is, was sawing down my posts. Which one of you shot the dog to try to scare me away from here?"

"You *crazy*?" Lorenzo was too astonished to be angry. "Somebody like to knocked me down tonight out there, Mirabell."

"Who was it?"

"Who could tell? He was in a car, one of them low-slung, noisy jobs, takes off with a screech and a roar. Couple of 'em in town. I dived for the ditch and when I climbed out and looked after him, there was two heads in the front seat."

"That's some story," Cory said sarcastically.

"I heard the car," I told him. "I heard it coming from over on the Preserve. That's why I drove across. I thought they'd try knocking down mailboxes, or worse."

"Young hellions," said Lorenzo. "I heard that cussed saw, that's why I came along. I hate those things. And sure enough, they felled a real handsome spruce right across the driveway. All them years of growing, and they could wipe it out like that in a minute. I'd like to top *them*."

"Well, I guess the excitement's over for tonight," I said. "I'm glad it wasn't any worse." The fire had died down to one small persistent flame.

"You don't call it bad, them murdering a tree like that?" Lorenzo asked bitterly. He turned to Cory and said in a more friendly tone, "I'll come over tomorrow and saw it up for you and help you get it to the house. Might as well burn it as waste it."

"No, you won't," Cory was stony again. "I'll take care of it myself. I thought I gave you orders to say off this property. I told you what I'd do."

"Now you just wait a minute, Cory. Let's talk man to man."

I took his arm. "Lorenzo, did you ever think he may not be a man at all, but a being sent here from another galaxy? Wow! Captain Kirk and Mr. Spock, where are you when we need you?"

Lorenzo chuckled, and his arm relaxed. " 'Night, Cory. Get yourself a good drink, and go to bed. And be careful. The goblins'll git ye if you don't watch out."

"Go to hell," said Cory without expression. He shut the door on us.

"And the same to *you*, Prince Charming!" I called through

the glass. "Come on over home, Lorenzo. I could eat something, couldn't you?"

"Ayuh. What you got good?"

"Any number of things." We stopped to look at the smoldering ruins of the cross. "It shook him up some, I think."

"I've got no pity for him! I see they got his posts down, and that's fine. But I can't forgive 'em the tree." We began to walk down the driveway. "Why aren't you at town meeting?" I asked.

"Well, I was kind of worried about somebody trying something when everybody was up to the Grange Hall. I wouldn't want any damage done to the house, or the weathervane stolen off the carriage house. And Cory, he'd never hear anything because he runs that TV at full blast to keep the evil spirits away. Times when I've been around here you could hear those police sirens and gun battles as if the windows was wide open."

"He heard the saw tonight," I said. "I wonder how long he'll stay. I wouldn't be surprised any day to discover he's gone and nobody would know when or how." We came to the tree and condoled with each other. It smelled so fresh and alive, but it was dying and didn't know it yet.

"He'll never be able to clean it up himself," Lorenzo said, "unless he's got unsuspected gifts with a saw. Which I doubt."

"He'll probably get Ol' Buddy Garfield to send the boys over."

"Might've been Garfield's boys who did the work here tonight. You can't ever tell. In the Civil War I dunno how many times Eusebius Willy turned his coat before both sides got onto him."

"You mean Old Squarr Willy?" Laughing like school kids, we got into the jeep.

chapter 18

We were eating cheese nightmares when Barnaby came in, bringing me a custard pie he'd bought after the supper.

"*Ha!*" he said. "A rendezvous, huh? So that's why neither of you wanted to go to town meeting tonight."

"You wouldn't believe the rendezvous we had," I told him. "Thank you, love, for the pie. Sit down and have some and we'll tell you what larks we've been up to."

"Brazen," he said. "All right, tell."

He had seen the sawn-off posts, but had taken it for a sign that Cory had capitulated, and had the posts removed when everybody else was away, just as he'd had them set. He wasn't much concerned with the fiery cross—no one had been hurt—but like Lorenzo he was angered by the destruction of a perfectly sound tree.

"I suppose after you two have been out raising hell all night you don't give a damn what happened at town meeting," he said.

"What happened?"

"Nothing. Wilbur said he wasn't running for selectman again, and then Jeff Ashe was nominated with so many seconding it that Wilbur changed his mind and decided to run for the good of the town—said loudly—and he got it by one vote only."

"Gosh, Lorenzo," I said, "if we'd been there we could have changed the course of human events for once in our lives, anyway."

Lorenzo munched peacefully. "Ayuh."

"Shoreline zoning didn't pass again, but we voted two

hundred and fifty dollars for the County Mental Health Clinic, which tells something, I suppose."

"Sara must have found it pretty dull."

"Well, there were a few Patrick Henry type speeches during the zoning discussion. Like 'I'll be goddammed if some goddam committee is going to tell me what to do with my land.' And 'Anybody comes on my property and gives me orders about my septic tank, I'll defend my rights with a gun if I have to.' Maybe she and Max saw that as the spirit of '76."

"It is in a way—I guess," I said. "Where is Sara, anyway?"

"She told me she'd be home late, and drove off with Max."

"Seems like a nice enough feller." Lorenzo prepared to leave. "Doing real well on that sloop. You have to have a feel for it, like one of those sculptors knowing just what's in that block of marble, and he's got it. Not real developed, of course. That takes time."

We went to bed as soon as he had gone. I felt shaky after the last few days and the excitement of the evening, and my head was light and ringing when I lay down. But Barnaby went to sleep first. My consciousness was a mad collage of voices, parts of faces, disconnected words, sounds, impressions. The cold green fragrance of the spruce boughs when I climbed through them, the quiet voice of the flames and the oily whiff in the smoke, and myself running. I couldn't stop reliving the horror of believing the house itself was on fire.

I was just thinking about going out into the kitchen, and pulling the rocker up to the stove, and reading for a while, when I heard Sara coming cautiously in, and I realized by some low murmuring that Max was with her. I'd left a lamp burning, so they didn't fall into any furniture. There were faint sounds of movement beyond the closed door and then prolonged silence. So love goes on, I thought with a great sense of comfort. The Sumerians wrote about it, and it's in the Bible, and the old songs that Calum sings, and the songs of *now*. It's like the stars.

I went to sleep against Barnaby's back, watching the stars

past his shoulder, and trying to remember all of "The stars of midnight shall be dear to her."

In the morning when I asked Sara what she thought of town meeting she had a hard time concentrating long enough to tell me anything. She didn't run on about Max, or tell me what they did after the meeting, and I wouldn't ask. I hadn't been too long away from it myself.

When I told her about the fiery cross, she seemed to hear it from afar so at first there was a vague "Mm-hm ... uh-huh ..." and then a languorous return from the Land of the Lotos Eaters. "What did you say about Cory?"

I told her again. "That's rotten!" she cried. "Why don't those creeps stay away from here? He's our problem down here and we can handle it."

"How are you planning to go about it?" I asked.

"Play upon his weakness for mermaids?"

She grinned, but colored even to the tips of her ears. "For some reason that embarrasses me." She put her hands to her cheeks. "My God, *blushing*, and I don't know why."

"I don't either, after all this time, when it didn't make you blush before. Hey, has Max picked it up? Maybe it's got nothing at all to do with Cory now. Come on, Sara," I teased her. "Give! Barnaby's not here to ask all the questions as the head of the house. Like, Is he married? On drugs? A drunk?" *Is he?* I wondered to myself. You can't tell by faces or manners, I'd learned at last.

"The only reason I'd get mad at Barnaby for asking would be if Max *were* married, on drugs, or a drunk. He's none of them, at least so far as I know, the young girl added candidly, being the granddaughter of Thomas Taggart the Second whose descendants have the congenital defect of not being able to fool themselves for long. Wow, where'd that speech come from?"

"It's pure Taggart. You're in love with him, aren't you?"

"Yes, but he hasn't mentioned the word to me yet. Maybe he thinks I'm too young, maybe he's naturally cautious about committing himself. But he didn't act it last night," she added with one of her remoter smiles.

Barnaby got his innings later in the week. He asked her casually at supper one night if she knew yet what Max's book was about.

"It's a novel—a thriller—I know that much. He doesn't like to talk about it because he says it's bad for him and bad for the book."

"Where does he come from?" Barnaby persisted. "Does he have any family?"

"He mentioned a sister, but just in passing. And he went to M.I.T. He was a geologist for some oil company, doing exploration in far-out places until he made up his mind to quit and take time to feel the texture of life. He always felt Maine was the place for it. When he was a kid the whole family used to go to North Haven. He doesn't reminisce, but he did tell me that much, and we're going out there some day."

Barnaby nodded. "All right. Thanks for the information. I know you're legally of age, but I still feel as if you're my responsibility while you're here."

"The truth is," Sara said demurely, "I'm only going with Max because I can't have *you*." She burst out laughing at his startled expression.

She was with Max for most of the weekend after town meeting, coming home only to sleep, and to tell us where they had been, and what they had seen; the odd corners and the odder creatures who inhabited them.

On Sunday Ruel came up from clamming in Mussel Cove with the excuse that he'd forgotten to bring water with him. I knew he was looking for Sara.

"She's on her way to Castine with Max," I told him.

"Well, he's more her kind." He drank, gazing out at the ocean with dulled black eyes.

"Don't say that, Ruel," I protested. "She's friendly with Max the way she is with everybody." It was weak, and it wasn't what he wanted to hear.

"I know better," he said flatly. "It's more than friendly. Oh hell, we couldn't have made it anyway." He set down the glass and walked out without the jug I'd filled for him. I took it and followed him.

"I'm sorry, Ruel," I said.

"Ayuh." He went off toward Deepwood, rubber boot tops flapping.

She and Max returned in late afternoon. We were due for supper at Jean's with some other couples, and they could have come along, but Max went home to work, and Sara said she was too sleepy after her long day.

"I never knew being in love could be so exhausting," she said plaintively. "When I'm with him it seems as if I could never be tired again. Then all at once I am. Zap!" Her head flopped over sideways, eyes rolled up and tongue lolling. Then she came back to life again and said complacently, "He says I'm more rewarding to be with than anybody else he ever knew."

"Said for the fiftieth time," said Barnaby, "to the fiftieth girl. What are you rewarding him with?"

"I thought you liked him." She was serious and hurt.

"All right, honey. I'm willing to put you a bit higher on the list. I saw the way he looked at you, and the way he listened to your innocent prattle." He put his arm around her shoulders. "How would you like to be—okay, tenth? After all, he's older than you are and he can't have lived like a monk all those years."

"Well, I'm glad if he hasn't," she retorted, "because I like my men experienced." She took Barnaby by surprise with a strangling squeeze, and smacked kisses noisily all over his face. "Like you, my precious. Like you!"

Barnaby waited until the jeep was rattling loudly over the plank bridge, and then he shouted at me in a voice of doom, "I hope to God he hasn't got her into bed yet!"

"What do you think of her? Just knowing him this little while, Sara would never—" I stopped right there and it wasn't Barnaby's sidewise look that did it. I'd learned early that when I swore that So-and-so would *never*, it always turned out that So-and-so *would* and in fact already *had*.

"I hope so, too," I said meekly. "But we'll probably never know."

"Unless he gets her pregnant—"

"Unless he and she get her pregnant," I corrected him, still meek and mild. Barnaby's pipe all but flinched as he set his teeth harder.

We had a good evening and a late one at Jean's and Tony's. Nobody hurried to go home, because there'd be no day to haul tomorrow with strong southerly winds forecast. When we left the house we all stood around in the yard admiring the northern lights splendidly flaming over half the sky. They would have forecast the southerly shift if the weather bureau hadn't.

"Let's have everybody over on Cape Silver next time," I said to Barnaby when we were driving home. "We've got plenty of room for dancing in the living room."

Barnaby murmured something agreeable. We drove through the woods, sometimes surprising bright eyes like little twin lanterns low at the roadside; we didn't hurry because there was a place along here where deer crossed to graze their way through the Darby fields. "I will never be able to call it Sanderson land," I said drowsily. "As long as I live."

We came to a spot on the rise where through a dip in the trees we could look straight out at Morgan Bay in one direction, and then, as we made the turn but were just at the brink of the descent, we could see the loom of Cape Silver.

In the area between the two vistas, some of the tallest spruces stood out with unnatural clarity against an illuminated sky. "That's funny," I said. "It's not northern lights in that direction. Has Cory sprouted floodlights for protection, I wonder?"

"If he has, they're a damn' funny color," Barnaby said, and then I saw that the sky had the hue of smoke reflecting fire. The recognition jolted me back into nightmare so that for an instant I was again running up the Darby drive toward the sight and smell of fire.

"It's either at the Darby place or the Boones'," Barnaby said with unnatural calm. I thought the jeep was going to take off into space when it leaped forward. He slowed at the Darby driveway as I had done that other night to listen. This time it was more than a fiery cross. A column of reddened smoke was boiling up into the sky, and the dreadfully industrious crackling and snapping was too loud. From far up the road we heard sirens.

Barnaby jumped out. "Drive down to Kyle's," he shouted at me.

The Boone house was all lighted up and Kyle's car was in the open garage. I ran to the house as Deirdre rushed out of the door, talking above the clamor of the sirens.

"We were taking a walk on the beach before we went to bed, and everything was lovely and quiet. We went as far as the Neck, and when we came back this way we saw the glow. Kyle ran in and called our fire chief, Arne Hendricks. Then he went up there through the woods. He said it might only be the carriage house."

The sirens were dying out at the Darby house, and we could hear more cars rushing along the black road as the volunteer firemen from all over Applecross arrived. Far back there was another siren, apparatus coming from either Williston or Amity.

"Come on, let's go," I said. "We can't stand here trying to guess at it."

"Wait till I turn off the stove. I'm supposed to be making coffee." She laughed nervously. "You boil water for the doctor, make coffee for the fireman."

chapter 19

The smell of the fire blew hot and threatening down to us on the path through the woods; the roar filled our ears like a hurricane wind. There was an explosive hiss when the water hit. We came out around the carriage house, and beyond it the house stood wrapped in flame like a martyr at the stake.

A scorching heat reached us. Against the glare the small black figures walked, ran, bunched around hoses as streams of fire played on the base of the house to try to protect the cellar where the fuel tank was. The driveway and yard were full of apparatus and other vehicles.

Deirdre shouted in my ear, "I've got to make sure Kyle's all right!" She left me. There was no wind, and everything was dampened with nightfall so the showers of sparks could do no harm to the woods. They were trying to keep the fire from spreading through the ells, but it was already in the one just off the kitchen. The carriage house doors were shut and I went close enough to see that they were padlocked. So he'd lose his car if the carriage house went. He must have escaped in just what he stood in. That would be why he hadn't called the fire department.

All at once I saw Barnaby's silhouette against the flames. He was talking with a fireman anonymous in rubber coat and helmet, and I had started toward him to ask about Cory when a man running past me stopped and came back.

"Mirabell!" It was Max Kemper. "Is Sara here too?"

"No. We were coming home when we saw the fire, so as far as I know she's sleeping through it all. She'll kill me tomorrow. Where's Cory? Is he all right?"

"I haven't seen him, nobody has. Kyle says the fire was go-

ing strong when he got here. We all hope he was out somewhere—"

"The car's still there."

"Yes, and we can't save it for him if the carriage house
goes. But he could have gone out with somebody else—maybe
an old friend showed up. Oh, Christ, Mirabell, that's what we
have to hope!" He went on.

I walked around the back of the carriage house, where its
bulk cut off the heat of the fire, and then followed along the
edge of the woods toward the front of what was now the
skeleton of the Darby Homestead. There were men everywhere. Ronnie Deming shouted at me, "Hey, Sara here?"

"No!" I shouted back. "Have you seen Lorenzo?"

"Nope!"

I went down to the shelving ledges between lawn and
shore. Ruel and a North Applecross man were adjusting a
hose line that led up from the water to supply the pumper on
the front lawn.

"Hi, Mirabell!" Ruel called. "Sara here?"

"Look, I'd have gone home and gotten her up if I'd known
this was *the* social event of the season."

"It's some nasty mess, isn't it? I hope Sanderson wasn't
caught in it."

"Not him," said the other man. "Tomorrow he'll be swearing somebody set it."

"If somebody did, it wasn't me," said Ruel. "Arson's not
my thing."

"Either of you seen Lorenzo?" I asked.

"Come to think of it, I haven't." Ruel looked around him
in the erratic flares of light and sudden darkenings. "And it's
not like him to miss all those sirens."

I crossed the hose line and picked my way across the ledges
by the unsteady glow from the dying house, and went up on
the far side of it. I was looking for Lorenzo now, but I didn't
find him, and I could imagine his being there and then wandering off in a daze of shock. He should be all right in the

woods, I tried to assure myself. There was nothing we could do about him until he appeared again.

I found Deirdre in the driveway standing by a police cruiser, talking with Bill Cartright. "There you are!" She greeted me. "I thought if I waited here you'd show up sooner or later. Kyle asked me why I wasn't at home making coffee. Talk about male chauvinism! They act as if we'd forced our way into the Club in the worst Women's Lib style!"

"As long as we didn't appear all suited up and carrying axes, they've got no kick coming," I said. Bill laughed.

"But we're not even supposed to *watch*," she said. "Are you coming back with me?"

"I guess I'll have to. Have you seen Lorenzo?" I asked Bill.

"No, but we're more concerned about Sanderson right now."

The woods were cold, black, and silent now, after all the heat and glare and noise. "That wonderful old house," she said. "I'm madder with him than I was before. After all the years it's been there, *he* had to do something to burn it down!"

"Hey, be careful," I said. "If he's anywhere around here he'll be suing you for slander."

"I didn't mean he did it on purpose, but he was careless with a cigarette, or overloaded the circuits; he did *something*, anyway. And I may just give myself the satisfaction of telling him so, if I ever see him again."

"You probably won't. When he comes home tonight from signaling U.F.O.'s or whatever he does, he'll take one look and then leave, and that will be it."

"Oh, probably I wouldn't say anything if I had the chance," she said gloomily. "Even someone like Cory Sanderson must have things it would hurt to lose. I'm just thankful he didn't have any pets to be caught in it."

When we reached her driveway, Jean and her sister Alice Deming had just arrived with a carton of sandwich-makings, packages of doughnuts from the freezer, and hot beverage cups. Uncle Stewart and Aunt Jess drove in behind them with more contributions. Jess came into the house with us, and Uncle Stewart went up through the woods to the fire.

Nothing blew up, and they were able to save the carriage house after all. The men took turns as stand-by crews, those on relief coming down to the house for coffee and food. The younger ones were wound up and boisterous. It was suggested that Cory had set fire to the place for the insurance, and had then left. But this was the usual bad joke cracked on such occasions.

"What, and take a chance on losing that Porsche?" said Ronnie. He said the car's name like an anguished lover; he'd wanted the firemen to break down the carriage house doors with axes to get the car out.

"Why didn't he leave in it?" someone asked.

"Oh, he wasn't too far away." That was said with a portentous wink and slow nod. "I'll bet he knew everything that was going on."

"Didn't he threaten to burn the house down?" Ruel asked me.

"Only to needle Lorenzo," I said. "Did *anybody* see Lorenzo tonight?"

"Looks like this is one thing in town he missed." It was not said cynically.

"But where in hell could he be *not* to know about it?" Ruel demanded. "You can hear those sirens all over town. He should've been right on deck, the contrary old gopher. Looks some damn' funny. Somebody's sure to say he could have done it."

Max overheard that. "Look, Lorenzo could have been sound asleep in his camp the whole time. He puts in a full day, and he doesn't row around all night every night."

"Well, let's hope he can prove it," someone said. "Because from what I hear, this guy's going to nail somebody's hide to the wall."

"He may try to," said Kyle, "but he's the one who has to furnish proof, not Lorenzo."

"Besides, Lorenzo wouldn't harm a shingle of that old

house!" I said it so passionately that there was a startled and stuttering chorus of agreement.

"What we're all sidestepping," Barnaby said slowly, "maybe because we don't want to face it, is the fact that Cory might have been caught in the house. The car's there. If he was in bed and asleep when the fire suddenly blossomed out into what Kyle saw from the beach, where is he now?"

"Oh, hell," somebody muttered. "That's enough to turn my stomach.

"He never called the fire department, either here or in Williston," a man said.

"Maybe because he never had the chance," said Kyle. "He could have gotten out of the house just in time—he could have been shut off by flames from his own telephone—and started out to find one. He'd have been confused, maybe panicky. Nobody saw him along the road anywhere, so he could be lost in the woods. He could even be lost between this place and his. He didn't know where the path was, I'm pretty sure." He got up. "Come on, somebody, anybody. Gather up some flashlights. We can check that area, anyway."

Deirdre and I got a bed ready with an electric blanket, in case they found a chilled and possibly injured and unconscious Cory. "This'll be one offer he can't refuse," she said. "If they do find him, if he hasn't burned to death in that house, I'll be so relieved I'll probably kiss him and he'll die of shock anyway."

"Max has a theory that some old friend, if you can imagine Cory having one, showed up and they've gone somewhere. I hope it's that simple," I said.

"Maybe the police have found him, and he's spending the rest of the night uptown," she said. We went back to the kitchen feeling a little more optimistic. Aunt Jess was doing the dishes. Jean and Alice had gone home, and Uncle Stewart and some of his contemporaries were sitting around the kitchen table. The talk had moved from great fires they had known to the bad state of lobstering. It was nearly three o'clock in the morning.

The searchers came back, having found no trace of Cory in the stretch of woods between the two places, in the fields across the road, or down on the shore. There was a great deal more wood lot on the far side of the Darby place, and there would have to be a more extensive search organized by daylight if the police couldn't find Cory in the meantime.

Kyle, Barnaby, and my uncle volunteered as watchmen at the site for what remained of the night. The other men left for home, and the three took blankets, coffee and doughnuts, and a small transistor radio, and drove back up the hill in Kyle's car.

Deirdre and I made some half-hearted gestures toward tidying up, but were now overcome by such yawns that we could hardly see from streaming eyes. "Oh, the devil with it," Deirdre said. "I'll do that floor in the morning. I'm not so delicate that I can't stand getting up to a dirty kitchen."

"I'll stay the rest of the night with you, Deirdre," I said, mindful that Prince was no longer there, and how we'd missed him all this night of comings and goings. He'd been a born host.

Deirdre turned me down. "You'll sleep better in your own bed."

Aunt Jess left their car for Uncle Stewart, and I left the jeep, and we walked down toward the Neck in a before-dawn wind that blew away any reek of smoke or soot. The stars had the thick, close appearance they sometimes take on at that hour.

"I keep wondering about Lorenzo," I said.

"Oh, he'll feel bad for a time," Aunt Jess said. "But he has that house all in his head where it's safe. Cory will go away now, I think, and maybe somebody who has children will buy the land so it will have a future again."

"But Lorenzo may not get over this as easy as we think—"

"Lorenzo Darby is *tough.*"

That closed the subject as far as Aunt Jess was concerned. We had reached Cape Silver and the parting of the roads. Over in Amity, where there were some very early risers, an engine was warming up. "Good morning, Aunt Jess," I said, leaning groggily against a mailbox. I sighed without meaning to, and my aunt answered the sigh.

"I know. You watched the house die, and nobody could do a thing to save it. But burning the house didn't burn up its history."

She went along the Shallows drive through its ghostly white birches, and I went home through the birches of Gold-engrove. Maybe when I was her age I could take the long view too, but that called for experience. Right now I was so depressed I wished that Barnaby and I could get in the car at sunrise this morning and drive for three hundred miles or more, and sleep tonight in a place where no one had ever heard of Applecross or Cape Silver.

chapter 20

The warm dark of the kitchen kindly enfolded me. The homely ticking of the mantel clock, which we hardly noticed during the day, was particularly loud at this hour of the morning. There were still some live embers in the stove, and I stood with my hands cupped over the sides of the teakettle to warm them. Tired as I was, I didn't want to go to bed without Barnaby. The instant I started to drift, it would all be there against my eyelids, in my nostrils, and in my ears; the sight, the stench, and the sound. The fiery-cross episode had been a dress rehearsal.

More for something to do than with any conscious motive, I went up the back stairs to Sara's room. It was on the south-eastern corner, so even if she had waked up she wouldn't have seen anything from her windows but the sky over the ocean. But she might just possibly have heard the sirens; she might have still been up at that time. I doubted it, though. She'd been too sleepy when we left.

There was a line of light under her door. I put my ear against the paneling and listened, and I heard her humming. I tapped on the door, and followed the tap in.

She was sitting up in bed, a blanket over her head and shoulders, and she was laying out the Tarot cards on the red cover of her sleeping bag. She didn't glance at me, or stop humming; the humming had no tune, and she wore that peculiarly mindless look she could get sometimes. The air was chilly and fresh from a window opened a few inches; the lamp flame shivered in nervous little bursts. I stood at the foot of the bed, speaking, and when she had put down the tenth card she laid the rest of the pack on the table beside the lamp, folded her hands in her lap, and gave me her attention.

"Hi," I said. "Have you been awake all night or did the sirens do it?"

"What sirens?" She had the solemn attentiveness of a young cat watching a fly. "Are you just getting in? That must have been some party."

"It turned out to be. There was a fire."

She lifted her laced hands and rested her chin on them, staring down at the cards. "Don't you want to know where?" I asked.

She shrugged very slightly, and leaned forward to look more closely at the pattern. I saw both the Hanged Man and the Fool and said, "If you're telling your own fortune you're off to a rotten start."

"I'm not reading for myself, and the word is *divination*," she corrected me, too remote to sound rude. "The Fool can be a very good sign in some cases. And the Hanged Man doesn't mean an execution." There was a tremor in her voice that could have been fatigue.

"Is there a card that signifies fire?" I asked.

"Not fire *as* fire. Flames come out of the Tower, but—no—there's nothing for fire alone."

It was all too profound for my present condition. "Good night," I said. "Or good morning. Don't forget to put your lamp out before you go to sleep."

I was ready to fall into bed now with or without Barnaby. The baffling exchange upstairs had completed my exhaustion. Either she was as groggy as I was and therefore hardly taking in my words, or else she was half-hypnotized by her cards, as Barnaby claimed.

I didn't dream of the fire and I didn't wake up when Barnaby came to bed. I woke in gray daylight, past nine o'clock. The northern lights had brought us our southerly wind all right, loaded with fog again. I felt as if the sun had last shone weeks ago, instead of only yesterday. I sat up and looked at the back of Barnaby's head and the way his hair grew on his neck, leaned over to examine his neat ear and the secretive composure of the eyelid gently curved over the bronze eye. I admired the authority of his Taggart nose, and saw that he had tidily scrubbed away all traces of soot before he came to bed. He'd probably brushed his teeth too. I hadn't. I thought philosophically that my sister was right when she called me a slob.

I tied myself into my warm robe and went out to the kitchen, and put water to heat on the gas stove, and built a fire in the range. Cold water on my face had a beneficial effect after the shock wore off. But not much. I went out on the back doorstep. Cape Silver was muffled, blindfolded, shrouded in fog. That cloud sat solidly upon us, and if you don't think a cloud can be solid, your experience is very limited.

I heard a sound inside and went back hopefully, expecting to see Barnaby. It was Sara, dressed, her hair knotted severely at the nape of her long Botticelli neck. She gave me a look both defiant and wretched, and went to the sink to wash. As she disappeared into her towel I said, "Are you coming down with something? That distemper goes round and round. Or is it a cold?"

"It's nothing," she said into the towel.

"Well, your eyes look like two burnt holes in a blanket, if you can stand compliments this early. Mine do too, by the feel. I wouldn't look in the mirror."

She had a hard time hanging up the towel, her hands were so shaky. I took pity on her and left her alone. Besides, I was in no mood for loose talk either.

I felt better after coffee and a whacking slice of our own bread toasted on top of the wood stove. At least the symptoms of premature old age began to reverse themselves. With returning youth I wondered if Cory had shown up at all and, if so, what he'd had to say.

"Where was the fire?" Sara asked. She was standing back to me, looking out at where Morgan Bay would be if everything but Cape Silver hadn't actually been atomized during the night.

"So I did get through," I said. "It was the Darby place."

"Was it like the last time? The fiery cross business?"

"No. It was the house." I saw it in its winding sheet of fire. "It all went, except the carriage house and the car." She didn't turn around. "Cory might have been caught in it, but we don't think so. Well, we have to hope." She gripped the edge of the sink as if the floor were tilting.

"I can't bear to think of anyone being burned to death." She spoke with obvious difficulty. "It's always horrified me— it makes me sick—"

"It does most people. I was too knocked out to have nightmares last night, but I'll probably have them tonight." I told her the story as completely but as briefly as I could. "And all your boyfriends inquired for you."

"*All* meaning who?"

"Ronnie, Ruel . . . Max."

She turned around, almost lively. "Was he there too? What did he say?" She made a cup of tea and came to the table.

I found Max a pleasant change from the fire, and apparently he was the only subject that could bring her a ray of cheer this morning. But in the middle of a sentence she suddenly ran out of momentum and sat looking desolately at nothing.

"You *are* coming down with something," I said. "How about going back to bed with a hot water bottle and trying for some more sleep?"

"Maybe I will," she said in the meek little voice that had the squeak of incipient tears in it. Barnaby came out, looking as fresh as April after three hours' sleep.

"*Good* morning, girls! Aren't you dressed yet?" he greeted me in righteous astonishment. "We're going around to Lorenzo's as soon as I have breakfast." He tilted up my face and kissed me. "I'll fix my own."

"No, I will," I said. "And we'll have a good one. Go on talking." I went to dress, leaving the door ajar. "Did Cory get back?"

"No, at least he hadn't when I came home around half-past six."

"What about Lorenzo?" Sara asked. "This must have killed him."

"I hope not," said Barnaby. "That's why I want to see him right away. It's going to be a lot worse for him than when the house was sold." Barnaby was a little less sunny. "That's why I want to get this over with."

I returned dressed and combed, and began making left-over fish hash into cakes to fry, a meal that is always restorative to both body and soul.

"Cory will be probably glad to take his insurance money and go far away from darkest Applecross," I said. "He must be completely disenchanted by now. Not that he could ever have been enchanted with anything or anybody. I can't imagine it." The first fish cakes started to sizzle in the iron frying pan. "I had hopes for him once, when he was so taken with Sara's green eyes, but there seems to be something left out of that man."

"Blood," said Barnaby, and I laughed.

"That's not fair!" said Sara angrily. We looked at her in surprise. Her color was blotchy and her hand on the table was shaking. She hid it in her lap. "I'll bet you were all having a high old time last night, as if it were a Fourth of July bonfire or some tremendous cookout. Cory's an outsider, so who cares if his house burns down!"

"Hey, wait a minute!" Barnaby objected. "Everybody worked like hell to save that house and nobody thought it was a picnic. A fire like that is a terrible thing, no matter whom it happens to."

"Glad you put that *whom* in there," I said. "Shows you never forget your grammar in a crisis."

"There you go!" Sara cried. "Being funny as if it's nothing! All right, maybe everybody worked hard, but now they're all glad because he'll go away now, and it's good riddance to bad rubbish."

I started to protest, but someone knocked on the back door,

and Sara ran up the back stairs. Barnaby opened the door to Detective Sergeant Blake of the State Police. He'd driven out, police vehicles evidently being exempt from our rule about cars on Cape Silver.

He had a cup of coffee and a doughnut while Barnaby ate his breakfast. He was a thin man with an easy way, and never gave an impression of haste or formality.

"Sanderson hasn't called in or been spotted anywhere," he said, "but the arson squad hasn't found any trace of human remains in the débris. Yet. Of course they're still working up there." He nodded at me. "That's a good doughnut." So I passed the plate again. "It's possible he may be in the woods somewhere. Mr. Boone says you've already combed the area between his place and Sanderson's. We're going to start a broader search of this whole end of town. I don't think we ought to overlook Cape Silver. If the man was confused, possibly injured and in shock, he could have wandered off in any direction. Would you take care of this?"

"Yes, of course," Barnaby said.

"Good!" The detective had a not-overused but very attractive smile. "Volunteers are gathering at the Boones', if you want to come over and choose some."

"Wait a minute," I protested, "he's got me, Uncle Stewart and Jess, the Aussies—"

"I can do with a few more, Mirabell," Barnaby said. "What about Sara?"

"You saw her this morning. She looks terrible. I think she's coming down with something."

"Some of the high school youngsters have been excused from school to help out," said Blake.

"All right, we'll scratch Sara, and I'll go over and bring back some of the kids who know the place." Barnaby pushed back his chair.

"Wait a minute," said Blake. "Your brother was the real estate man in the deal with Sanderson, wasn't he? Does he know anything at all about the man?"

"Absolutely nothing." Barnaby was emphatic. "But I'll give

you his number and you can check with him. The lawyer in the sale was Rex Ashton."

The detective wrote down the names. "I don't suppose he'd ever have talked about himself to Garfield," I said tentatively, but this was lost in the confusion of Lorenzo's arrival. He nodded bleakly at us and gave Blake a desolate stare over his glasses. He refused food and huddled by the stove like a molting fowl that used Vicks Vapo Rub. The heat brought out the full pungence. Occasionally he stifled a bronchitic cough in a questionable handkerchief. His skin was grayish, and he had aged enough to make me feel sick. There was no need to ask him if he knew what had happened.

"You weren't around last night," Barnaby said. "When did you find out?"

"This morning. I had to go to the store." As the detective put away his notebook and rose to leave, Lorenzo blurted out, "*He* did it!"

"Who?" Blake asked with leisurely interest.

"Cory himself burned the place down, the way he promised." The words seemed to emerge in little fiery strips curling in the air, like burning fragments blown from last night's fire. "Set it and run off. Had somebody pick him up, even a *taxi*. Anybody think of that?"

"We'll check it. But why would he want to burn the house down?"

"Because he hated everybody's guts around here, especially mine. The house should have been mine, you know," he said. "By all that's right and moral. I'm a Darby and the only one that stayed home, the only one that cared about the Homestead all the time, not when it was just a convenient roof to camp under." He took off his glasses to wipe them, and I pushed a tissue into his hand rather than see that handkerchief again. "But they never even gave me a chance, never even told me they were selling it! Then this stranger showed up."

You understood from the way he said *stranger* that it was a euphemism for the worst thing he could think of. I could see Barnaby's hands move as if he'd like to throttle Lorenzo into silence. I threw myself helpfully into the breach.

"I just mentioned Garfield Willy, because he's the only person around here Cory ever had much to do with."

"He wouldn't get a chance to talk," said Lorenzo. "That old schemer's tongue is hung in the middle and wags at both ends."

Blake knew Garfield; who didn't? "What makes you so sure Sanderson burned down his own house?"

"*His* house?" Lorenzo half rose, then sank back coughing. Blake waited patiently. Lorenzo wiped his eyes, and said in a scratchy voice, "He never gave a damn for what that house meant. It was nothing to him! And he swore he'd burn it down and put up something all glass and concrete."

The detective watched him, casual and yet predatory, it seemed to me; I wondered if Lorenzo knew he'd just presented the law with a good motive for *his* burning down the house. If he couldn't have what he felt should be his, neither should a cold, ignorant, callous foreigner have it.

"You wait till you catch him, if you ever do," Lorenzo said. "Then you'll find out the truth. I know his kind. Soft as rotten squash, you can threaten it out of him."

Blake's mouth twitched. "Well, thanks for talking to me, Lorenzo. Thanks for the coffee and doughnut, Mrs. Taggart." Barnaby put on his jacket and took the jeep keys off their hook. Lorenzo began to push himself up from the rocker, but Barnaby said with great kindliness, "Oh, stay and have some of those good fishcakes, Lorenzo. It's your dinner time, isn't it?"

"Just about," he admitted. "Not that I've got much feeling for it." He went back to staring at the stove.

Barnaby put his hand on Lorenzo's shoulder. "You have to keep your strength up. *Eat.*" He went out with Blake.

"Excuse me a minute, Lorenzo," I said. "I want to see Sara. Don't go anywhere."

"Don't worry. I'm not about to take wing," he said sarcastically.

I couldn't hear the slightest whisper or creak from Sara's room. "Are you awake?" I said in a low voice against the door. No answer. Well, sleep was best for her, and I could have used some too. The night was now catching up with me. Heavily—at least it felt that way—I returned to Lorenzo, and worked up a great bustle getting a meal for him.

He rocked, sighed, coughed, and whispered curses to himself. When I heard the jeep in the yard I rushed out and surprised Barnaby and myself by hugging him ardently. He responded happily and finished off with a comforting pat on my bottom.

chapter 21

He had brought over Ruel Jason and a younger brother and dropped them at the Shallows line to work toward the Binnorie Brook. My aunt and uncle and the two Aussies would be responsible for Shallows woods and shores. Barnaby and I would take the outermost section.

"I reckon I ought to help," said Lorenzo.

"You're in no shape for it," said Barnaby. "Why don't you sit here in comfort and keep the fire going? I'll bring you out a stack of magazines. You got plenty of tobacco?"

"Even if I didn't have, I wouldn't try that fancy stuff your womenfolk palm off on you," said Lorenzo ungraciously. "They found anything in the ashes yet to show how he set the fire?"

"I wouldn't know," said Barnaby. "They're still there."

"They won't find anything. He'd know how to make it look like an accident. And *you* won't find anything, either." He watched gloomily while I laced my Bean boots. "He's like the song, over the hills and far away."

"Without his insurance money?" I asked. "He can't be rich enough to sacrifice that. Nobody is, these days."

Lorenzo started to answer and had to cough instead. When he'd finished and wiped his eyes he said, "I'm going home. Thanks for the meal, Mirabell. It was a most elegant collation."

"Oh, for Pete's sake," Barnaby protested. "Stay here where there's company for you. Sara'll likely be down pretty soon—"

Lorenzo cut him short. "I'm not afraid to be alone with my thoughts, if that's what you think. You realize how many people'll be tramping up and down my road today and all over my woods in hope of finding Cory's corpse? No sir, I'm not leaving my place unguarded. It's too full of valuables."

There was no use in arguing.

"I'll walk down to the dory with you," I said, "and start my search from there."

"I walked," said Lorenzo. "Stewart picked me up halfway to the store, then brought me all the way down. Wanted me to come home with him, but I had a hunch that detective would be out here sooner or later. I wanted to get my story in before he got his brain too cluttered up with so-called facts."

"Well, you sure did that, Lorenzo," Barnaby said. "Come on, I'll take you home in the jeep."

I was revived by the thought of being outdoors even in fog, and pretty sure that I wouldn't find Cory either dead or alive.

When I got around to Mussel Cove, I met Ruel and Simmy Jason taking a rest on a log, and I sat down with them for a few minutes before going up into the woods. We talked about the fire, the possible findings of the arson squad, the police inquiries, and then finally Ruel got around to Sara.

"She's in bed," I said. "She's coming down with something. Otherwise she'd have been out here too."

Ruel stared into the fog with stoical black eyes, and his younger brother winked at me. I thought it was kinder to Ruel not to notice, and in a few minutes I went back to my job.

Searching the woods was easy, with the snow gone. In many places there are long clear avenues among the taller spruces, and I could ignore those sections and go to the con- centrations of boulders and thickly brushed spots that make good hideouts for deer. There's also a dense mixed growth in the boggy area spreading out from the swamp and brook. It took me only about two hours to inspect them, and finally I went home by way of the mossy rock steps that lead up from the Devil's Den or down to it, depending on your destina- tion. I didn't forget to look into the Den itself. My feet were as heavy as if I were wearing divers' boots, and I was constantly blinking to fight the droop in my lids.

No sign of Sara. I revived the woodfire and took off my boots, and I sat in the rocker with my feet on the oven hearth and wiggled my toes in voluptuous comfort as I sipped hot cocoa. I thought with anguished longing of my bed, knowing that if I fell upon it for only fifteen minutes it would be the essence of agony to arise from it. My mind went wobbling off into a kind of waking dream among the more soporific quotations.

Tir'd Nature's sweet restorer, balmy sleep ... He giveth His beloved sleep ... Sleep dwell upon thine eyes, peace in thy breast ...

They hung weights on my eyelids. And then, like a blow to the side of my head, leaving my brain rocking in its cage of bone, came the words that had never been forgotten since a high school performance of *Macbeth*.

> *Glamis hath murder'd sleep, and therefore Cawdor*
> *Shall sleep no more, Macbeth shall sleep no more!*

Neither would Mirabell. For now, anyway. I went upstairs and knocked on Sara's door.

"Come in," she said in a sodden voice. She was sitting up in bed, all hunched together. Her eyes seemed to have turned dark, because of their shadows and her pallor, and her teeth were trying to chatter. She looked wretched, plain, and slightly retarded. I was upset by the sight, and that made me sharp with her.

"Come on downstairs," I ordered. "If you're sick, this is no place for it. I'll make up the living-room couch."

"I'm not sick. I'm terrified."

"Of what, for heaven's sake?"

"I think something awful's happened to Cory, and I'm to blame." It was wrenched out with a gasp that must have hurt, because she put her hand up to rub her throat.

"How could you be to blame?" I asked. Then I saw the

Tarot cards spilled on the floor in a vivid spatter, as if they'd cascaded off the lamp table. "It's those damned cards! You've been taking them seriously!"

"It's not the cards. They did tell me it was bad, but I knew that already. They just confirmed it." She hugged herself convulsively, but kept on shaking.

"Come on down where it's warm and tell me." I sounded more in command than I felt.

She crawled out of the sleeping bag and wrapped herself in the bathrobe I handed her, then followed me downstairs. She was very quiet. This was worse than if she'd been sniffling or making soft little sighs and whimpers of self-pity. I thought of her sitting up in that cold room laying out the cards and scaring herself literally sick, and I made up my mind to destroy the pack as soon as I could lay hands on it.

She washed her face and used my brush to tidy her hair, then sat up to the open oven door with her feet on the hearth, sipping from a mug of hot bouillon. Now that she had decided to talk, her adult poise was rather chilling, as if it had come too suddenly; as if she had lost her youth overnight with no chance for any of us to say goodbye to it, even herself.

She talked with her eyes fixed on the thin curl of steam coming from the teakettle spout. "Mirabell, I didn't stay in last night and read and play records and go to bed early. I intended to—I didn't lie about that. But then I went out for a walk, it was so beautiful. I started for Shallows, but when I got to the mailboxes, I decided to go see if Cory would take a walk with me."

Glamis hath murder'd sleep. I'd never been wider awake in my life. "You decided, just like that?"

"Just like that." She nodded at me. "Mirabell, I've been seeing Cory. Maybe you'll think I've been dishonest, but I didn't feel I was doing anything wrong, and I've tried never to lie to you." She was solemnly composed. "I mean, I'd never say I was going to a certain place if I didn't mean it. If I intended to go to Cory's, I just didn't say anything except maybe that I was going for a walk. Because I *would* be walking, you see. That was no lie."

I nodded. I must have looked composed too, but *stupefied* was my inner condition.

"Last night, I didn't plan it at all when I went out, because after a day with Max, Max is all I want to think about. But I saw the northern lights beginning, and I wanted Cory to see. I always thought he would begin to love it here if he gave himself a chance."

"Mm-hm," I said, which was all I was capable of. My brain seemed to be dog-paddling in futile circles.

"He never liked to go outdoors much," she went on. "You know how he was. But he was getting over it, and I think I had something to do with that." She spoke with innocent pride. "I think I had him half-convinced nobody was going to murder him for his money. When he pulled that business about the chain, I was furious and I let him know it, but when an obsession grabbed him, he wasn't anywhere near reasonable. I had hopes, though. When the chain disappeared I talked at him like mad, trying to get him to forget it." Her voice hoarsened and she faded into silence, gazing off as if to contemplate the miles and years between last night and now. *Last night, ah, yesternight!* my private delirium rambled on.

"Well, last night he said yes—to taking a walk, I mean," Sara said. "So I thought I was getting somewhere with him after all." She flushed. "I didn't want him to make love to me! That isn't what—"

"I know," I told her. "You wanted to find him out. To make him say he hated parsnips or loved them, had a thing for Leonardo da Vinci, or collected early jazz, and maybe— to explain a lot about him—he grew up in an orphanage."

"That's it, that's exactly it! But I couldn't say anything about it here because Barnaby would say I was wasting my time, and the man might be a sex maniac or something. Well, Mirabell, he *isn't*. At least I'm pretty sure," she qualified it. "You can't tell about these inhibited people, and Cory's very uptight. But I never had the feeling that it was about sex. . . .

He was so terribly proper with me too, like somebody out of another century. Remember how he offered us sherry that first day? After that, it was always tea or coffee; never wine, as if that wasn't suitable when we weren't chaperoned." She smiled faintly. "He wouldn't even make himself a drink."

I was entranced, but I was also in a hurry to hear the rest of it before Barnaby showed up. "And so last night he was willing to go out with you."

"Yes, and going down over the ledges he said he'd missed me; he said it had been like three years since the last time I was there. Mirabell, my heart actually jumped, because he sounded so human. He didn't say it easily, but he said it. We walked on the shore, and the northern lights really performed for us. I could see his face in the glow, looking up as if he couldn't take his eyes off the sight. And we heard geese going over, too. You know how they sound in the night. He listened the way he watched the northern lights, with *all* of him, and I thought there was a breakthrough at last."

Her voice faded. In slow motion she leaned forward to set the bouillon mug on the back of the stove; she seemed to talk to it now, rather than to me. "We walked away from the beach, all along those flat ledges under the Darby woods. I don't think he's been there even in daylight, so I told him how beautiful it is there between the water and the spruces when the bay's all sparkling and the sun is bright. But then I got this feeling I have with him sometimes, that he only half-hears me, he's so preoccupied with whatever's haunting him—"

"*Haunting*," I said. "Do you think it's that?"

"Something is, I'm sure. But I don't know whether it's outside him or inside . . . Anyway, something stirred in the woods above us, and he really jumped, and hurried me away from there. I kidded him about being a city slicker, afraid of a deer, but that didn't get anything out of him. He was in a rush to get back to the beach, and he had a grip of iron on my arm." She pushed up the sleeve of her robe to show me the marks of fingers on her upper left arm.

"When we got back to the beach he let me go, and muttered an apology. We just stood there looking across Morgan Bay, and the lights were sparkling over in Amity, and suddenly he said *Sara* in a different voice, and I turned to him, and he took me in his arms and we kissed."

I sank back in my chair. *Macbeth shall sleep no more.* Her voice went on in a sort of murmurous clarity. "He was like a man in a spell, and it was strange for me too. It was like waking up in the midst of a fairy tale. Not exactly the frog turning into a prince, or the Beast turning into a marvelous man. The thrill that I felt wasn't anything to do with sex." She frowned. "At least I don't think so. It was more like a glad surprise that he was a real person after all, Do you see what I mean, Mirabell?" It was an entreaty.

"Yes, I see," I said. I thought I did.

"I shut my eyes. And then, all at once there was this violent motion, so fast and so sudden I couldn't tell what it was all about; I was shoved away so hard I fell down, and all I could think was, *He's gone mad.* I was scared to death. I rolled over and over to get away, and then the water stopped me, and I got onto my hands and knees to see where he was, before I dared to get up and run—and he wasn't there. He'd disappeared! I might have dreamed him!"

"My God." I had to get out of that chair and see how my legs were.

"And you know what I thought, but not right then?" she asked anxiously. "That he was terribly upset because he kissed me. Maybe he did have a psychosis, and that's his secret. Maybe he shoved me away before he could harm me, and ran."

"It could be," I said.

"I was so scared, I came straight home. I went along the shore around the Neck, and then I ran like the dickens." Her composure was breaking up, she was talking faster and faster. "I wish I'd gone up to the house and seen if he was there. I knew about the fire, I heard the sirens, and from the attic windows I could see where it was. And all night I kept thinking, What if he went completely to pieces, set the house on fire, and went away in the woods and killed himself? He didn't have a gun, that's one of the things he did tell me, but he could have *hanged* himself." Her mouth was trembling uncontrollably now, and she put her hand over it.

"Look here, can you see a man who didn't know the woods at all, going out after dark carrying a ladder, and locating a suitable limb from which to hang himself?"

"All right, but what about the carriage house? He could have done it in there. Or he could have asphyxiated himself in the car." Her panic was contagious, and I had a nasty picture of Cory swinging from a beam or slumped in the Porsche, until from the distant past of several hours ago, I recalled Barnaby telling me that the police had gone into the carriage house through an inside door. If there was no trace of Cory by tomorrow, the outside padlock was to be sawn off and the car removed to a Williston garage for safety. Then new locks would be put on the building all around.

I told Sara, who was relieved for all of a half minute. Then she said, "He's lost, and he could have fallen and hurt himself, maybe died." She gulped as if to keep from vomiting.

"They'll find him," I said. "But you realize, Sara, we'll have to tell the police about this. Or at least Barnaby."

"Oh, *Mirabell!*" she wailed.

"Look, we can say that you and he were walking on the beach and you were looking off at the bay, and when you turned around he was gone." But while I said it I knew it wouldn't be that simple. "But maybe they've found him by now," I offered weakly. "If he's alive, he certainly won't tell about the kiss. And if he's dead, by accident or his own hand, there won't be any need to tell anything."

"I'm guilty," she said desolately. "I did it. I barged into his life. If I'd minded my own business he wouldn't have been out on the shore last night and had this attack or whatever it was." Her eyes were full of tears. "If he's dead, don't you see, it's as if I killed him?"

There wasn't much I could say to that, but I tried. "Sara, I don't believe that the only thing to save him from an untimely death was *not* meeting Sara Brownell. I mean, if he was that close to it, it was with him all the time. Do you see?"

"But he did tell me he'd come here for peace and quiet and that it was just his luck to get a house like the Darby Homestead, with historical significance and somebody like Lorenzo hanging around like the resident spook. So everything was against him, you see. Including old dumbhead Sara, who's going to find out what makes him tick if it kills him. And it probably has."

"Stop that," I commanded, for my own benefit as well as hers. I was shaking too. "We don't *know*! . . . You might as well tell me anything you found out about him. When did all this start?"

"When I went to tell him we'd cleaned off the paint. I made up my mind then that I'd keep going back until I broke him down. Right from the start, when we were laughing and calling him foolish names and Mafia and stuff like that, I'd get this queasy feeling that I ought to be sorry for him."

"I've had it myself," I said. "It's even queasier right now, when we don't know what's happened to him."

"And I wanted to know *why* I felt sorry for him. It was a puzzle about myself as much as about him. Do you see? . . . Well, he didn't shove me away; he seemed to accept me after a while, as if he wanted something around but didn't know how to manage it; and he was afraid of dogs." She gave me a weakly humorous glance. "Barnaby says I'm as good as an Irish setter anytime, except that I talk, which is a disadvantage setters don't have."

"There was something special about you," I said. "Our cousin the mermaid. Remember?"

"Yes. And I don't like to." She jumped up and went to the bulletin board and ripped off the mermaid picture and quotation, and put them into the stove. She stood looking down at the flames for a moment, then replaced the lid.

"Maybe he thought I was still a kid, and more harmless than the rest of you . . . I was making his new curtains, Mirabell. They're gone with everything else now, of course. I saw the sewing machine the Darbys left in the house, and I told him I could sew. We went to Damariscotta one afternoon and got the stuff, because I thought somebody might see us in Limerock or Fremont, and it would start talk. And what was between us was so—" Her hands delicately shaped something fragile—"I didn't want to spoil it."

"You were lucky to get out of town even the back way without being spotted."

"I know it!" Her smile was both rueful and amazed. "It just happened that way, as if it was meant."

"But with all this—did you find out why we should pity him?"

"No, unless it's because he is as he is."

"But good God, Sara, how could you do all this choosing materials, and sewing, and drinking your tea together, without his breaking down a little? Didn't he ever refer to a family? To a previous life, even in some little details? Did you ever get him talking about that Leonardo book, or the stories about men on long solitary voyages?"

"I wouldn't ask. I always felt that if I asked a personal question it would ruin everything. Like trying to take hold of a wild animal. It would either attack or run. He would have run; I was never afraid of him."

"You know," I said, "he was on a long solitary voyage of his own."

"Mirabell, he could have been born all grown up from a computer. Incomplete, and knowing it, and not knowing what to do about it. That's why he let me in, I think."

Her laughter was so harsh it must have scraped all the way. "And, *I* was going to unlock the door and let out the real, warm, breathing Cory. And last night I thought the key was beginning to turn. Well, I unlocked something all right!" Suddenly her eyes ran over, and she choked. "I can't bear it! First Prince and now this!"

She really cried then, going at it with all her might. I was relieved for her. The arid, adult remorse had been hard to take. I went into the other room and made our bed, and tidied my work table. I was so full of apprehensions and premonitions that I would have enjoyed a good howl myself. And then some sleep. *To sleep: perchance to dream.* Shut up, old Will, I thought wearily.

chapter 22

Sara was setting the supper table when the jeep drove into the yard. She headed for the stairs, pleading, "You tell him, Mirabell, please. I don't want to go through it again!"

I let Barnaby talk first. There was no official report from the arson squad yet, but the site was being guarded. All the cottages had been checked from the harbor to Applecross Center. The search had been called off at dusk, but some of the men would patrol the passable wood roads at intervals, in case Cory should stumble out to one in the fog and the dark. His description was being circulated on Maine television and radio, in case he had left Applecross.

"*And* they've checked out the car," he said through jaw-cracking yawns. "He bought it—cash again—and registered it in Portland, and got his Maine license there, giving as his residence the hotel where he was staying. The hotel people said he'd come there in December and stayed until into February. He'd made a couple of trips away in that time. And that's all they knew about him." He got his boots off, sank into the rocker with a groan, and put his feet on the hearth. "If I stay awake through my supper I'll do well."

"I've got a little something here that's guaranteed to rouse you, and it's not a benny, either," I said. Then I told him about Sara and Cory.

He leaned back with his hands clasped behind his head and his eyes shut, showing so little expression I thought once he'd gone to sleep. I waited a moment, and he said, "Go on." So I finished.

"Is that all?"

"That's all," I said. He got up and went to the foot of the stairs. "Sara, come down here!"

"Now, Barnaby," I began like an apprehensive mama.

"I'm neither going to throw her out nor wallop her bottom," he said brusquely. Sara came down, quiet but wary. He pointed to a chair and she sat down, folding her hands in her lap. Visit to the principal's office.

"Sara, you must have heard something," he said. "You're used to being out at night and to picking up sounds. It was quiet last night, no wind in the trees, no run on the shore. So think back."

She relaxed perceptibly, and her gaze became vague, dreamy, fixed on some secret, inner landscape. We waited. The clock ticked, the teakettle hissed softly, there was a gentle bubbling from the stew kettle. After a while she spoke. "Every night I've listened for the peepers, but they haven't begun yet," she said. "But we heard geese. A car now and then, coming down to the harbor. Oh, a boat over there, too. Somebody putting his boat off?"

Barnaby nodded. "Tony had his boat ashore to find a leak. He put her off on the high tide last night. Anything else?"

"Penny barked from over at the harbor. You know how it echoes. It sounded really weird. It shook Cory. I told him it wasn't the Hound of the Baskervilles, or a bloodhound tracking an escaped convict, just a darling old golden retriever."

"All right. Where did you hear the noise in the woods?"

"On those flat ledges under his woods. Oh—you know where that white stripe runs across the rocks in folds, sort of? Max told me the name of that stuff but I can't remember."

Barnaby was patient. "How long after you heard the noise before you were knocked down and Cory disappeared?"

"Long enough for Cory to rush me back to the beach."

"So you were on the beach when it happened."

"Yes, just off the ledges on that stretch of coarse sand. I got it in my hair, and up my sleeves when I rolled over. There's some in my sleeping bag," she said to me. "I've got to bring it down and shake it out."

Barnaby tolerated no diversions. "What did you do then?"

"I was so scared I came right home." Her mouth trembled. "I was a coward. I should have looked for him. At least I could have gone up to the house and called his name, and told him it was all right. Instead I ran home and straight to bed."

And to the Tarot cards. For how long, and for how many times, trying to make them come out right?

"Think back," Barnaby urged. "Was there any other sound before or after? Anything *at all*? Or were you talking the whole time, so you wouldn't have heard other footsteps, anything like that?"

"No, we had long silent spells, when we were watching the northern lights, and listening to the geese. I *can* be silent, as you very well know," she said with dignity. She shut her eyes. "Something . . . something . . . so natural it didn't register like the geese, because that was so exciting, like bagpipes. But I do remember now."

"What, for God's sake?" Barnaby's anxiety at last exploded through his patience.

"The sound of oars," she said. "Not very close, but nearby, and just once."

Barnaby was bound that Blake should hear the story to-night. I groaned, and Sara pleaded. "But *why*? Can't we all get a night's sleep first? What difference will it make? It's not as if they haven't already begun to search."

"It may be important," he said stubbornly. "If we get it over with tonight, we'll all sleep the better for it. We can have supper first," he conceded.

"Oh, *thank* you!" said Sara. "Considering that I don't think I'll ever have any appetite again. *Ever*."

"Oh, you can choke something down," said Barnaby brutally. Then he gave her a hug. "Come on, Sairey Gamp. Some decent chow will do us all good."

He was right; at least afterwards it didn't seem an insuperable task to ride over to the Boones' and call up the police. The Boones accepted the fact that Sara knew something, which might or might not be important, but would rather not talk about it yet.

"Believe me, I wish I didn't know *anything* that was going on," said Deirdre. "I'm delighted to be left in ignorance."

When the detective's unmarked car arrived, Kyle welcomed Blake in, then all of us but Sara took our coffee cups out to the kitchen area. Deirdre turned on the transistor radio that stood on the divider, tuning to an FM station that made a soft but continuous shield of music between us and the two by the fireplace.

We couldn't stay away from the subject any longer; we were too consciously dreading the report of the arson squad, and the results of the search. Yet talk was futile; we ran out of *ifs* and *supposings*.

Sara and Sergeant Blake were together about a half hour, and then he was ready to leave. He shook his head reluctantly at an offer of coffee and cake. "I'm always behind on my day's work," he said. "We need about five more men in this area."

Sara was much more cheerful and even had some color. "Could I have some of that cake?" she asked.

We were all tired so we broke up early. As soon as the jeep left the driveway for the black road Barnaby said, "Well, Sal, how did it go?"

"All right. At least he didn't act as if it was anything great. Of course he took me over it several times to see if I could remember anything else, and I couldn't. I'm so foggy by now I can't even be sure about the oars."

"But you were sure when you told us," Barnaby said.

"Oh, yes! But now I can't hear them. It's as if they've gone for good."

"It's because you're so sleepy," I said. "Just saying the word makes me ache. Did he mention Lorenzo?"

"No. Why should he?"

"Because I've been thinking of him ever since you mentioned those oars, and Barnaby's a liar if he says *he* hasn't been. It would be just like Lorenzo to be out rowing around last night. Barnaby, did he ever tell you what he was doing if he wasn't at the fire?"

"He was in bed drinking hot rum toddies trying to stave off that cold. Said he started about seven and was in a drunken stupor—his words—before ten. He didn't think it was proper for you to hear, so he saved it till we were outside this morning. I'd be a lot happier," Barnaby went on, "if he could prove he was stowed away drunk. If the arson squad gives a positive report, Lorenzo's their pigeon."

"Lorenzo wouldn't hurt that house any more than he'd hurt a person!" Sara said indignantly. "They have only to look into his eyes and see the truth."

"The law isn't concerned with such poetic considerations," said Barnaby.

"It would be better for the world if it was," I said profoundly. "Or *were*?" Nobody bothered to tell me.

Barnaby and I managed about eight hours of sleep, and Sara got a little extra. The next day was a fine one for almost anything you might think of. With a good sleep behind you, you could face with confidence even the grimmer facts of life, at least until the bloom of the morning wore off.

The volunteers would muster at the store today as the search moved northward through the town. We drove there before sunup to see if Barnaby would be needed. Sara went with us. She behaved as if she didn't want to be left alone, and I remembered all the times she had stayed behind and wondered how many of those hours she had spent with Cory.

She talked with an excess of nervous energy. "I wonder if Max will be up there. He likes to be involved. He says you don't really live in a place, you're just roosting for an instant in time, if you don't take part in all the aspects of its life." Across a deep dip between a grove of oaks and a subtly greening slope of pasture, the first blazing orange sun appeared enormous above the horizon. A boat with scallop-dragging gear moved slowly across the opening.

"Did Max search yesterday, Barnaby?" How she loved the sound of his name.

"I don't know, Sara," Barnaby said. "I didn't see him, but I wasn't hunting on that side, remember."

"Did I tell you he wants to buy one of the Andrews, if he can get around the man who owns them? He says it's like conducting peace negotiations. Cat is the one he wants, because it's the only one he thinks he can afford. Imagine owning an island, even a little bitty one. I'm sure he'll get it. I think he can get anything he wants."

"Is that according to your cards?" Barnaby inquired.

"Oh, I wouldn't need them to tell me," she assured him. "But they do confirm it."

"Were the Fool and the Hanged Man for him?" I asked, shamelessly probing.

"I told you they can be very good signs, and that's so even if they're reversed. I'll explain it all to you when we have time," she said kindly.

Barnaby swung off the road with unnecessary vigor, and we came to a sudden stop between gas pumps and store. There were quite a few vehicles parked on the blacktop in front of the barn, and the store was crowded with men and boys. Sara smiled gently all around her. She stopped to read the bulletin board, and there was a shifting of the group like the swirling of sand grains in water, and she became the center of a separate whirlpool.

A North Applecross man was talking by the cash register. "It's the damndest thing. I never set eyes on the feller, but I knew he was in town all right. There are some folks you never think of until you see them, but he's one I was pretty much aware of without ever once seeing him face to face. Saw the car once, that's all."

"It's ironic," Barnaby said, "because he thought he'd be invisible here."

"Maybe it was somebody else he wanted to be invisible to," Max Kemper said, coming in by the back door. "An ex-wife, a bank he embezzled from, or the Mob."

"Oh, you're out of date, Max," I said. "They call it the Organization now, don't they?"

He didn't answer. He had just seen Sara by the bulletin board, and he went toward her as if no one else were there. Their smiles were not secretive, but private.

The boys around Sara grinned derisively, or moved off with overdone indifference.

In a few minutes Barnaby came in. "They don't need me," he said. "They've got a legion of searchers. I want some buoy paint." He began hunting along the lower wall shelves for his colors. The searchers collected at the back of the store to divide and distribute territory, and in a few minutes they were leaving. I saw Sara go out the front door with Max.

A few older men remained, and a young clammer, who was drinking chocolate milk and eating packaged cake. "I said I'd give Parkin's Cove the once-over when I get down there," he said, "but I don't know what in hell he'd be doing this far up from the point, and on the ocean side."

"Well, if he was wandering around deranged or concussed you can't tell how far he'd go," said Mr. Ives.

"Tell you one thing," the clammer said unhappily, "I ain't looking forward to finding him face down in the clam flats, and the crabs been at him." I was glad Sara wasn't there to hear that.

Garfield came in the back door, escorted by the great-grandson.

"Hello, hello, hello! What a den of thieves *this* is!"

"Takes one to know one, Garf," said Mr. Ives.

Garfield relished that. "Speaking of criminal natures, I was struck all of a heap yesterday! Police come over to my house. I thought my sins had caught up with me at last."

"Now maybe you'll stop chasing women and stay out of the bars, Garf," one of the men said. Garfield laughed till he choked, and the great-grandson pounded him on the back. Mr. Ives said in alarm, "For heaven's sake, Raymie, don't beat him to death."

"Oh, he's tougher than tripe," said Raymie.

Short of breath but indomitable, Garfield said, "Turns out

I might be an important witness in something pretty serious now, I can tell ye." He smacked his lips. "They wanted to ask me if I knew anything about where Cory Sanderson went. *Me!* Because I was his only friend in town." He waited for suitable expressions of awe, and then pushed for them. "You realize that? Nobody else in this town went near him. I was the only one offered the hand of fellowship to the stranger in our midst."

"He was a stranger," said Mr. Ives solemnly, "and you took him in."

"I did," said Garfield with innocent fervor, and the rest of us burst out laughing.

"Go it, Gramp!" said Raymie in admiration. "You tell 'em! Proper old bastard, ain't he?" he said to everybody in general.

"Way I heard it, Garf," one man said, "everybody tried to act real neighborly at first, but he wasn't having any of that."

"He figgered they all had axes to grind, that's why."

Barnaby came to the counter with his paint. "What kind of ax did I have to grind, Garfield?" he asked mildly.

"Where *you* been hiding, son? A mite sneaky, ain't ye?" Garfield squinted dubiously at him. "Well, you fellers down there settled up that road business kind of final. Cure was worse than the disease."

"Oh now, Garf," said Mr. Ives. "I hope you're just having a joke."

Still easy, Barnaby said, "Garf, there never was any 'road business' as you call it except right there"—he tapped his temple—"where you made it up. So there wasn't anything for us to settle. The chain disappeared, somebody sawed the posts down to raise a little hell on town meeting night, and I don't think Cory will ever put them up again."

"Because he can't!" Garf said in triumph. "Dollars to doughnuts they've found what's left of him in the cellar hole with his head bashed in . . . if they can tell, and I guess they got ways all right." He screwed one eye up tight and wagged his head at us. "Like that fire over to the west'ard a couple years ago. Clammer murdered two women and set the house on fire. And you *know* Cory hated clammers and they hated him worse, by God."

"Now you listen here." The clammer arose from his nail keg and seemed to stretch up and up in height. Garfield was not abashed.

"Present company always excepted," he said glibly. "Ain't you one of Mose Newcomb's boys? Godfrey, I thought so."

"No, I'm not," said the clammer. "I'm—"

But Garfield was in full spate. "You take those Jasons and their gang, they got no law but their own, never had. Gus Flint, he's got no use for Cory since Cory set the police on him, and Cory he threatened to shoot Gus's dog the way he shot that dog of Boones', and—"

"Oh good God," said Barnaby in disgust, and turned away.

"Raymie," Mr. Ives said, "do you know what he wants? You got his list?"

"Why, he just wanted to come in and visit, Mr. Ives."

"Well, I think his visit's about over. You'd better take him home before he winds himself up into a fit."

"Or before he winds somebody else up," said the clammer menacingly. "It's bad enough to be treated like a bunch of trespassing bums without being called murderers. That guy over to the west'ard was a nut and everybody knows it."

"Of course, of course," said Mr. Ives, and the other men made soothing noises.

"What about Lorenzo?" demanded Garf. "He's gettin' more mental by the day."

"Come on, Gramp." Raymie reached for the old man's arm. Garfield rejected it like an aggressive bantam rooster warning off a rival. "I ain't ready yet! Don't you try to team me around, Sonny."

Raymie wasn't quite as simple as he looked. "Marm'll be having kittens, thinking you're throwing your money away on them fast girls that hang around the bars in town."

Garfield looked gratified. "Say, I'd ought to squirt some

cheap perfume on me, hadn't I? That'd give her a turn." He was still giggling as they went out the door.

"Just for the record," Barnaby said, "all the rest of it was in his head too. You know they found no human remains in the cellar, and we don't think Cory shot the dog. So we'd be much obliged if Garf's pipe dreams don't get repeated around as gospel truth."

There was a general agreement, and Barnaby smiled and said, "Thanks."

When we went out, Sara was leaning on the jeep, gazing up through the bare elm branches at the new sky, and listening to the exuberant whistling of blackbirds. She looked as if the only matter occupying her mind was love, and not even the shadow of guilt had ever crossed it.

chapter 23

Barnaby went to haul, and I swore that neither hell nor high water was going to get me off Cape Silver that day. Neither hell nor high water threatened, and nobody came near us at all. It was a weekday, which helped. We stayed outdoors, greedily getting all there was of this foretaste of the real spring. When Sara disappeared alone I thought of all the times when she must have been with Cory. What had he really said, what had he been really like? Shopping together—I couldn't imagine him in that context; Sara running Joan Darby's sewing machine, and Cory making tea or chocolate for her. Or had she been allowed to become familiar enough to take cups from the cupboard, cream from the refrigerator, talking all the time or singing to herself, and what was his face like as he watched and listened? Had he ever laughed with her?

Finally he had kissed her. No. *We kissed*, she had meticulously stated.

Sara had a date with Max that night for dinner and a movie. Barnaby hadn't got home yet, and Max and I had a few minutes in the kitchen while Sara finished dressing, and he gave me the news. Detective Blake had stopped in at the store for a Coke, and told Mr. Ives that the experts couldn't find any evidence of arson in the ruins. Cory's disappearance was still a mystery.

"I was serious this morning," Max said. "He could have been hiding out from something or somebody. Right now he's probably safely on the run, if that isn't a contradiction in terms."

"And the fire? And that gorgeous car?"

He made a noncommittal motion with his hands. "A useful

accident. He used it as an excuse to disappear, hoping every-body would think he'd been incinerated along with the house. In that case, he'd have to leave the car behind."

Sara came down the back stairs, and Max stood up and went toward her as if she were Flavia on the grand staircase in Graustark.

All this homage was wasted on Sara. "You've been talking about it, haven't you?" she accused us. "That's all everyone talks about, and it's so damned *awful*. The police taking state-ments, the cellar hole guarded, suspicion falling on innocent people—"

Max put his arm around her. "Cheer up, love," he said ten-derly. "The guard's been taken away because it's not neces-sary, and nobody's going to jail because Cory vanished. Unless *you* made him vanish."

"*What?*" She stiffened away from him, looking frightened.

"You might have drowned him in your sea-green eyes. Re-member the dreaming swimmer?" He brushed her nose with a lock of her hair. " 'I think the danger of the ocean lies/ Not in the storm, but in the mermaid's eyes—' "

She laughed uncomfortably. "We shouldn't joke about it when we don't know what's happened to him."

"He's safe somewhere, I know it," Max told her. "I have second sight from my Scottish grandmother. Somehow or other he got a ride up to Route 1 with some coincidental stranger, and maybe farther, so he's well away now, and maybe the stranger's had an accident by now so he can't re-port it. Or he didn't read or hear the news when Cory's de-scription was given." He swung back and forth with her in his arm. "Cory could be out of the country now!"

I could see in her the transfiguration of hope, if not belief. "All at once I'm famished," she said. "Where are we going to eat? My mother used to say all my dates would be first dates, because no boy could afford to take me out twice."

Barnaby brought home a bucket of lobsters, and I boiled the lot. We ate ours hot, by lamplight, in the usual lovely mess of shells, which we pawed over avariciously to be sure we hadn't missed anything. And the pleasures of the evening weren't over when we'd cleaned up.

Nothing much happened for the next few days. The weather was typically April; open and shut, quiet and windy, mild and frosty. Sara and I painted buoys while Barnaby shortened warps on traps in preparation for spring and summer fishing. He brought *Andromeda* around to her home mooring in Deep Cove. More birds arrived to be logged. Lorenzo was not seen on the Preserve. Uncle Stewart and Barnaby went to the cabin at separate times and found him depressed, but not dangerously so, they thought.

We heard nothing about the Sanderson case because nothing seemed to be going on. Cory's car had been taken away from the carriage house and the new locks put on, the site was no longer guarded. Kyle and Deirdre were walking along the shore one afternoon, and Deirdre wanted to look at the ruins to exorcise the last view she'd had of the place at the climax of the fire. They went up over the deeply rutted lawn, and surprised Madam President and a companion climbing recklessly among the fallen timbers in the cellar and groping through heaps of charred wood. The Boones greeted them with good-natured surprise, and Madam President poured out volumes of explanations about saving possible valuable historical finds from the Amity hoodlums who could land on the shore below, and so forth and so on. Kyle and Deirdre listened politely and the reason grew more confused and complex.

"There was a lot about rare old bottles, I remember," Deirdre said. "Strictly for the Historical Society, you understand. Not for *her*, even if there is a fortune in them."

"You have seen a sight very few people in Applecross have been privileged to behold," I told them solemnly, "Madam President embarrassed."

"And it's enriched the quality of life for me," said Kyle. "I did manage to get a word in finally and tell her any bottles would have blown up or melted in the heat. In the meantime the friend, who had been all the while edging away, suddenly yelped, 'Oh, Polly, I left the gas on under the teakettle!' "

"Prezz fairly galloped for her car," said Deirdre. "I thought she was going to take it like a high fence. And then she leaned out of the window and shouted at us. 'There's nothing there anyway. Lorenzo probably swiped everything right under the deputy's nose, including the evidence!' "

"God, I wish there was some way we could frame *her*," I said despondently. All Barnaby did the whole time was laugh.

Sara and I took a lunch down to the Raven Hole one noon, when the wind was from the northwest and the little cove almost as hot as it could be in summer. Barnaby had gone to haul. I had my sketchbook, and Sara brought a book that Max had lent her, and started reading it aloud. "Maybe I can understand it better that way," she said. "Max takes it for granted that I can understand it if I try. He says it'll stretch my mind."

"Maybe it'll do that for mine too, and it probably needs it," I said. I let the words float peacefully by me like little breezes while I did a series of quick sketches of her. When her throat began to get dry, we stopped for lunch. Afterwards, we were comfortably full of food and hot tea, and were so quiet that some buffleheads came in close enough to feed among the floating rockweed.

All at once Sara said, "Do *you* think we've seen the last of Cory? That he's gone away as mysteriously as he came?"

"That's what I'd like to think."

"He'd have to be desperate to sacrifice all he'd paid for the place, as well as his car."

"He wouldn't have to sacrifice. Rex Ashton could get a letter from him any time telling him to sell the land and car and deposit the money in any bank he named." Simple, but flawed. "Still, he'd have to sign things, even if it was just to give Rex power of attorney. So Rex would have to have an address."

"A post office box?" said Sara.

"See? Your mind's stretched already. I never thought of a box."

"Wherever he is, I wish him well," she said sadly. "It'll be a long time before I forget that night." She sat up suddenly, and the ducks flew. "You know, I keep dreaming it all over again, but in the dream somebody else is there. I know it for a fact in the dream, even though I didn't know it at the time. Somebody else, distinct from Cory, shoves me and grabs him. It's all so clear in the dream that it seems as if it must be so. But Max says it's probably because I don't want to think Cory would manhandle me like that. I *want* to blame it on somebody else."

"I thought you weren't going to tell anybody else about that night but the police."

"I didn't mention the kiss. I only said I tried to be friends with Cory and he went out for a walk with me that night to look at the northern lights, and so forth. Mirabell, there's just something about Max," she said. "It's so easy to tell him things. We got into it very naturally, and he understood, the way you did. I mean, he didn't think I wasn't playing with a full deck."

"Did you tell him about the oars?"

"Yes, and he didn't pay much more attention to that than the police did. Oh, and he said maybe Cory thought the noise in the woods meant that somebody had caught up with him at last, and he bolted, and I was in the way, that's all. That's because Max doesn't know about the kiss," she added self-consciously.

"Well, it's all so fantastic anything could be the truth," I said. "Has he made any progress yet on buying his island?"

"Oh, that darned man won't say anything yet, but at least he hasn't said no, so that's progress, I guess. I can hardly wait, but Max is so patient. I guess if you love million-year-old rocks you know how to be patient."

When we were on the way home in midafternoon, yawning soddenly after all that sun and salt air, we met the painter coming down across the field. "Hello, Mr. Caine!" I called, ready to be expansively hospitable and talk about painting.

"Hello." He raised the bush hat, but it was more perfunctory than courtly. "What's going on around here? We've been down east for a week, I've been painting those red rocks on Schoodic, and when I came back they gave me this wild story at the Inn."

"I don't know what theirs was, but there are plenty of wild stories going around."

"I didn't mean to come on so strong. But I was beginning to believe this place was a little enclave of peace and sanity, unblemished by the world's slow stain, or whatever it is I'm thinking of."

"The only place like that has no people in it," I said.

"But it *was* like that down here," Sara insisted. "Until Cory Sanderson moved in and brought his bad vibrations. He was to be pitied, because he was really a prisoner of them, but they've influenced this whole community."

He didn't laugh. "Maybe you'll tell me the true story." He looked encouragingly from one to the other of us.

"I'll tell you what we know." I made it short, and when I finished, he said, "I hope he turns up alive somewhere. I'm very sorry, especially about the house. I drove up there today. The carriage house or barn or whatever it is, is in fine shape, and that weathervane is swimming into the wind as she's done for a good many years, I suppose. But the atmosphere was—" he broke off a bay twig and rubbed his fingers over the coral-pink infant berries. "To me there's something very tragic about chimneys left standing like that."

We agreed, and separated. He was going to stay through sunset, he said; he hadn't yet been on Cape Silver at that hour, and he hoped to make some quick studies of changing lights and clouds over both land and water.

The next day an Amity fisherman took a notion to look around the Andrews for a couple of traps he'd missed in the fall when he was taking up and shifting gear. No one fished there in the winter, but the grounds were rich in the summer, and by a tacit agreement decades old the Amity men fished the northwest side and the Applecross men the southeast side. The Kittens between Cat and Herring, and the bar between Herring and St. Andrew's made the dividing line.

So on this quiet morning, when the sea lay flat as summer silk around the islands, a man went looking for his lost gear. There in plain sight, off the northwestern tip of Herring, was one of his buoys lying like a placid though exotic duck above its reflection. He must have missed it on that day in the fall because of an exceptionally high tide and swift current that dragged the buoys under.

He hooked the slimy line into his hauling gear, wondering if he'd get a complete trap or a battered one. In disbelieving horror he saw, coming up through the water, sprawled over the end of the trap, the body of a man seemingly frozen in the very act of swimming; a swimmer in icy waters where no swimmer could live. One leg was entangled in lobster warp and kelp, holding the body to the trap.

None of us had to identify Cory, which couldn't have been done by his face, anyway, but Sara could describe what he'd been wearing that night. She remembered in detail, because she had liked his clothes. Besides this evidence, there was other identification in his pockets. Rex Ashton was called in, and he said that the hair looked the same. The autopsy showed that Cory had drowned. There were faint marks around the wrists and ankles as if they'd been tightly bound, though they were free when he was found.

Sara's sound of oars was heard again, this time by all of us.

The next day I went down to the wharf with Barnaby at high tide, to help him load new traps aboard *Andromeda* to be set the next day. "And I'm going with you to set them," I told him. "I'm not staying around here with my thoughts. Max is keeping Sara busy, so I don't have to worry about her."

"Glad to have you aboard. Of course I may insist on a captain's prerogatives."

"Is that anything like *droit du seigneur?*"

We'd been talking this kind of nonsense so we wouldn't have to keep imagining the discovery off Herring and remembering all our jokes about the best method of getting rid of Cory. Max had come before noon to take Sara on a long drive to Merrymeeting Bay to see the wildfowl. When she went upstairs to change her clothes, I said to him, "She won't say anything, but she blames herself."

"I know, and it's so damned senseless. But it shows she's a sensitive, compassionate girl and I wouldn't have her any different. We may not get back until late tonight, all right?"

"It's fine," I said with real feeling.

"We won't worry," Barnaby said. His uneasiness about Max's intentions had been swallowed by the relief of having Sara and her silent staring-into-corners out of the house for a while.

So there we were loading traps on this damp, silvery day, and ordinarily we'd have been very happy. The annoyance and frustration caused by Cory's life among us became nothing compared with the effects of his death.

Gus Flint's green aluminum skiff came into the cove and headed for the wharf, with the dog sitting in the bow. We gave up working and waited for them to arrive, glad of the diversion. Gus was not a social man, and the tide was too high for clamming, so this had to be an errand. It was unexpected, but then everything was unexpected lately. Gus slowed down and circled so as to come in gently along *Andromeda*'s outer side. The dog studied Barnaby with dignified interest, and acknowledged my presence on the wharf with a slight twitch of the ears. Then he turned his huge head away from us and contemplated the view. Gus shut off his idling motor.

We greeted him by name, not effusively. His weather-burnt wedge of a face under the old felt hat discouraged any display of familiarity. He nodded at a point somewhere between the two of us.

"What's going on?" Barnaby was admirably direct.

So was Gus. "I was down on Dick Martin's shore helping

him put his float overboard on the high water, and we thought
we saw a deer swimming out from just above Lorenzo's place.
We thought maybe dogs had driven it. Dick, he run for the
glasses. Well, it warn't no deer, it was a hunk of wood, but
we saw something else."

"Well?"

"Blake and another feller in plain clothes are down on
Lorenzo's shore. Looks like they're going over his dory some
finicky. Lorenzo, he's standing to one side with his hands in
his pockets, and there's a trooper standing around too. Not
Bill. It's one of them brand-new ones, looks about sixteen.
Anyway, I figgered some of Lorenzo's friends ought to
know."

"Thanks for telling us, Gus," Barnaby said. Gus pushed
away from *Andromeda* and started his engine. The light
aluminum skiff shot toward the cove mouth, leaving a new
wake to fan fresh small waves out to either shore.

Barnaby swung himself up onto the wharf. "Come on."

The jeep had never bounded so fast along the Cape Silver
track. Crossing the Neck we met Uncle Stewart and Aunt
Jess coming back from somewhere; I saw their astonished
faces behind the windshield as we rushed past. We didn't
meet anyone else, but just as we came in sight of Lorenzo's
road Blake's car turned out of it and went north. "Two men,
but neither's Lorenzo," I reported, "unless they've got him
bound and gagged on the floor."

There was a cruiser in Lorenzo's dooryard, parked incau-
tiously close to his bird feeders. Barnaby knocked and Lorenzo shouted, "Come in!" He and a trooper who couldn't
possibly have been as young as he looked were drinking coffee and eating gingerbread, one of Lorenzo's specialties. Lorenzo was an expansive host, getting out mugs for us and
filling them with coffee from the gray agateware pot on the
woodstove, whacking off big squares of gingerbread whether
we wanted them or not. He introduced the trooper.

"This boy's from way up in Patten, and his father's a

licensed guide. I've been asking him about The Enchanted. The place really exists, you know. Doesn't it, son?"

The trooper nodded. His smile was an embarrassed one.

"Beautiful country," Barnaby said. "What's going on here?"

Lorenzo answered airily. "Oh, it's nothing much. They figger my dory took Cory out somewhere and dropped the poor devil. You want canned milk in that coffee, Mirabell?"

"I didn't even want the coffee, but you wouldn't give me a chance to say so."

"I guess I am kind of wound up. You know this boy's stories almost got me convinced I ought to take a trip away from here now and then? I'd sure like to see the great north woods. But damn it, I got so much stuff to take care of down here."

"We could move all your valuables over to our house," I said helpfully. Barnaby cut me off.

"Let's get back to today, Lorenzo. Did they find anything in the dory? What are you under guard for?"

Lorenzo put more wood in the stove. "Oh, they found a thread caught on a nail on a plank lying on the bottom of the dory, and they think maybe it came from Cory's jacket." He settled back in his chair, the way he did when he was going to tell a story. "Where I've been having that cold, and then with all this hooting and hollering through the woods when I wouldn't leave the place anyhow, the last time I had her out was the day before the fire, and that's when I picked up that plank. It was floating, and I wrassled it aboard. It's short, but it's oak, and it'll make me a dandy doorstep." He rocked comfortably, "Well, tide was out so far when I came in that day, and I was beginning to take sick, aching so I thought it was the real old-fashioned flu, I just put my girl on her haul-off and figgered to take the plank out on the high water the next day. Water-soaked, y'know, and some heavy. And that night I went to bed before it was dark under the table, to try and kill off whatever was trying to kill me. Spinner got me the rum."

"I take it they've gone to match the thread if they can." said Barnaby.

"Ayuh, I guess so. More coffee, George? More gingerbread?"

"No, thank you, sir." The trooper was not happy.

"That Muster Gingerbread sticks to your ribs," said Lorenzo. "Funny thing. If I hadn't hung so close to home because of all these so-called search parties, that plank would've been ashore long before now, and my new doorstep all built. Or, if we'd had some real heavy rain, I'd have pulled the dory in to bail her, and I'd have taken the plank out then. So where'd that thread be now? . . . It's all chance, the way I see it. Like Sara's foolish cards." He grinned. "She better get to work on this puzzle. Maybe she could solve it."

Barnaby filled and lighted his pipe, a useful performance when you don't know whether to laugh or swear or give up altogether. My release was to get up and turn my cold coffee down the sink and put my untouched gingerbread back in the pan. I doubted that I'd ever again be able to stand the sight and smell of gingerbread.

"It's simple," Lorenzo said tranquilly. "If he *was* in my dory, somebody took it the night I was sleeping off my cold. That poor bastard, excuse me, Mirabell, I wouldn't wish that end on my worst enemy, and he was that all right."

"Well, shut up about it," said Barnaby. "If the thread matched up and they take you in, I'm calling Todd Bingham, and *you* keep quiet, understand? Don't go waiving your rights because your heart is pure."

"Maybe he'd like to choose his own lawyer," I said. "*If* he needs one."

"Father always had Lawyer Burton for any legal business, but he's dead now," said Lorenzo brightly.

"Do you have any objections to Todd?"

"No, but I won't need him. Like you said, my heart is pure. Maybe not in thought, but in deed. I must have thought about half a million impure thoughts in my lifetime, but never mind what it says in the Bible about what a man thinketh in his heart, so is he. *Thinking* murder don't *make* you a murderer, so long as it stays a thought."

Barnaby said to me, "How about going somewhere to call Todd? Tell him to be ready. You don't have to tell him why and let half the town know."

I drove over to Jean's. Neither she nor the children were at home, but the dog offered me the freedom of the house and I called Todd's home number. When my sister, Irenie, answered I was so relieved that they hadn't gone away for the weekend that I was practically demonstrative, and she said suspiciously, "Where are you? Have you been drinking?"

"No, you rat," I said. "I'm trying to take your husband away from you. Is he there?"

"Are you and Barnaby in some kind of trouble?"

"Somebody is," I said.

"I knew it," she said in resignation. "That place is bewitched. Here's Todd. I don't know what's going on," she said to him, "but it's not good."

chapter 24

*I*told Todd that within the next hour he would get a call that
would explain everything. When I drove back toward Lorenzo's I met the cruiser coming out to the black road. Lorenzo was in the front seat beside the driver. He waved but
the trooper gazed straight ahead with an official face. I drove
on down to the camp, feeling as if I were going to throw up.

Barnaby came out and fastened the padlock in the hasp. I
couldn't tell him what I'd been thinking; I was ashamed even
to have thought it, no matter what Lorenzo said about
thoughts not counting. But Barnaby put his arm around me
and said, "I know."

"I didn't really believe he could do it," I said fiercely. "But
how can he prove he didn't?"

"Never mind that now. One thing at a time, that's how we
do it."

"Has he been arrested?"

"No. He'd already agreed to make a statement if they
needed him, and Blake just called the cruiser and said they
needed him." He shook his head. "He went off chipper as a
lark."

"But if they arrest him when he gets there, my God,
Barnaby, what will he think *then*?"

"I had the trooper tell Blake that Lorenzo's lawyer was on
his way. So let's get the hell out of here and call Todd." We
kissed with a desperate passion as if we were the ones in
jeopardy and about to be torn apart forever.

For once the telephone booth outside the store wasn't occupied by an adolescent making calls away from family ears.

Barnaby gave Todd the story in about two terse sentences, and when we got to the county jail in Limerock Todd's car was there.

We parked behind it and waited. Barnaby had his pipe, I had nothing. My hands and feet were cold from nerves, and a mean little northeast wind began prying at every interstice in the jeep body, whistling and keening around the doors. Time crawled; we couldn't make small talk when all we could think about was what might be going on behind the dignified Victorian façade of the county jail.

At the end of a half hour I said, "I don't know whether my spine will disintegrate before my feet fall off, or the other way around. Maybe I'll come down with pneumonia first. They don't need to keep him this long just to say what he has to say."

Barnaby made one of his all-purpose sounds of reply, which can be interpreted any way you choose. Ahead of us Todd's Monza gleamed in the late-afternoon gloom, all snug luxury. "I wonder if he locked it," I said.

"He did," said Barnaby. "He *lives* here, where they'd steal the dashboard and the steering wheel if they could."

"But maybe he didn't bother for once, so close to the jail and the sheriff's office. Anyway, I've got to move around before I freeze permanently into the number 4."

The car wasn't locked, and I was grateful for Todd's lapse. After a few moments of looking the other way to show disapproval of both Todd and me, Barnaby gave up and joined me. Now we could stare at the jail in physical comfort, at least. After a little while it began to spit snow, and the cold was creeping insidiously into the Monza, and I kept thinking, They've arrested Lorenzo. It's circumstantial evidence, but it's so good it's the next best thing to seeing him do it.

I was going to have to say it in a moment. Then someone was at the door on my side, tapping on the glass. It was Todd, laughing at my yip of surprise.

"I hate to make you three drive home in that jeep," he said.

"*Three?*" Barnaby repeated.

"Three. Lorenzo's on his way. He drank so much coffee in there he had to make a stop on his way out."

We were too wary now to believe in simple solutions. "What's the score?" Barnaby asked.

"He hasn't been booked, he can go home, but he can't leave town. See if you can't find somebody who knows for a fact he was in his camp all that evening."

"Tell me to find out something easy," said Barnaby. "Like how far space goes."

"You should have seen him in there. Nothing fazes him."

"If you can keep your head when all about you are losing theirs," said Barnaby, "then you don't understand the situation. Which applies to the Peter Pan of Applecross."

"Oh, he swears he understands it all right. But he's armored in his innocence."

Lorenzo reached us, all sweetness and light. "Well, now, this is real good of you to come and get me. Feller just told me a funny story but I can't repeat it."

He climbed into the back of the jeep, chuckling to himself. His mood was contagious, or else we were deliberately clutching at false comfort, but on that cold and bumpy fourteen-mile road home, it really seemed as if nothing could happen to him; how could we ever have been foolish enough to worry?

He wouldn't let us drive him down to the camp. "No need of you going that far, and besides, I kind of like to come to it on foot."

He trudged off into the deepening shadow of his lane. His favorite raccoons would be waiting for him; that was one reason why he wanted to walk down, so they would know who was arriving.

"Oh boy," I said with a groan. "Let's get home and pull up the moat."

Sara hadn't returned from the Merrymeeting Bay trip, though for all we knew she might be at Max's place in North Applecross. We shut out the last visit of winter with lamplight and a wood fire. While I got supper Barnaby went down to put his boat off on her mooring.

Barnaby fell asleep before I did, and I hated to sit up to blow out the lamp for fear of rousing myself and letting in what I'd been keeping away ever since we'd first heard the news about Cory. It was *there* anyway, all the time, but during the day one could keep from staring at it. In the dark, in the vulnerable state between sleeping and waking, you had nowhere else to look, and there he was coming up with the trap. As a variation on that, one could imagine, even while wincing and shrinking back from it, how he got there; but one could not, absolutely not, go so far as to wonder what he thought before he stopped thinking.

I read by flashlight for a while after that, and finally fell asleep. I didn't hear Sara when she came in.

We were up at the first light. I left a note propped against the sugar bowl, so Sara would be sure to see it, and we left to set the boatload of traps. The threat of winter's return had blown away during the night on a velvety southwest wind; the sugaring of snow was melting even before sunrise, and the fields were full of migrating robins.

Andromeda glided through the shadowy fissure of Deep Cove out into Morgan Bay, around the white tip of Cape Silver and eastward across open water. The ducks flew away from us through an opalescent light in which sky and sea seemed to run together in some new medium, neither water nor air. The first light of the sun dissolved the enchantment, but the replacement sufficed.

We passed a cluster of ledges where seals were hauling themselves out to sleep in the sun through the period of low tide, and about a half mile beyond that Barnaby took his marks for setting the string of traps.

It doesn't take long to set a boatload of traps, even allowing for the time used in taking out the buoy and coiled warp from each one, putting in loose ballast from the pile of beach rocks on the platform, and baiting the trap. I shared the work, which meant we were through much too soon. We had a mug-up with us, so we ran toward the south and anchored in the little bay formed between Andrew's and Herring islands when the bar between them was out. This was where Ruel and Sara had come to clam; Gus Flint's boat was hauled up there this morning, but neither Gus nor the dog were in sight. They'd be on one island or the other, just looking around, and I half-envied Gus his way of life. Like Lorenzo, he was as much a creature of this world as the seals out there.

To think of Lorenzo was unfortunate. It also reminded me that at the other end of Herring, on such a morning as this, Cory had been found. I put down my half-eaten turnover and my thermos cup. Barnaby, who had been gazing tranquilly around him, said at once, "Now what?"

"I keep thinking about all our jokes about getting rid of Cory. Hitting him on the head, strangling him, dropping him overboard."

"Remember what Lorenzo says. Thoughts can't be held against you, and if you brood on it, you're neurotic. *Listen!*" The ospreys' whistles echoed in blue space. We leaned together and tipped our heads back to watch the soaring, floating birds. "They're reality," he said, "as much as Cory's death is. Which reality do you choose?"

"It's not a matter of choice," I protested. "It's just that if you forget yourself for a minute, and then remember all at once what's going on, it seems worse each time."

"I know that. But the fact that Cory mysteriously died, and that Lorenzo may be suspected, doesn't take away from the fish hawks, the ducks, the seals, spring, or what you and I have. Those are all facts too. And unless there's a wholesale slaughter of everything, or the sun goes out and pitches us back into everlasting winter and kills us all off that way, those facts are going to remain after Cory's buried and forgotten."

"How about this for a fact?" I took his face in my hands and kissed him. "Not only do I love you, but I like you," I told him, "and I am your sincerest fan. Will you sign my autograph book?"

"Not here, it's too public," said Barnaby. A blue heron took off in stately flight, and gulls and crows flew up from the bar in a black-and-white pattern of wings as Gus's dog came down a turfy slope on Herring. Some of the gulls flew over the boat, calling, and Barnaby said, "See what I mean? The place is full of Peeping Toms."

"Have some more coffee, then."

Gus followed his dog down to the bar and began to dig. We sat there a little while longer, our jackets off to the sun, but we had to go back eventually.

We slipped by Herring's shattered staircase for giants and into the passage between Cat and Charlie's. Small ducks fed in the rockweed lying dull green and gold on the untroubled water around the Kittens, the string of ledges running off Cat toward Herring. A raft of eiders took wing and flew out in a long file a few feet above the water. We could hear the rush of those strong wings above the throttled-down engine.

As the mainland grew larger, so did the thread found in Lorenzo's dory until it was as substantial as a manila hawser. And it wouldn't help to discuss it; we were too old to dream of miracles.

When we headed down the Morgan Bay shore of Cape Silver, we saw a mile ahead the hole left by the destruction of the Darby Homestead. It was the first sight of it for me. The carriage house was unfamiliar—it had always been more or less hidden by the house and the ells. The chimneys starkly caught the sun.

I didn't look for long.

There were a few clammers along the shores below the Indian Meadow and the Gypsy Field, digging fast to race the incoming tide. The ones nearest the entrance to Deep Cove straightened up as we approached, recognized the boat, waved, and bent double again. The Cove was a sun trap now, and the water as glossy as oil. We put *Andromeda* on her mooring and rowed ashore.

"I wish we were rowing to an island," I said.

"And everybody would find us either by fast outboard or

helicopter. Don't you know there are no hiding places left?"

"Remember that book about the highlands of New Guinea? It would be hard for anyone from here to drop in on us *there*."

"What do you bet?"

Sara and Max were waiting on the wharf. I reached for the ladder. "*Good* morning!" I called blithely. The reaction almost knocked me back into the skiff.

"Why didn't you tell me that Lorenzo had been arrested?" Sara shouted. I was ahead so I got the full impact.

"Because he hasn't been," I reached the top finally. "Or *has* he?"

Max shook his head. "Not this morning. But I heard about what happened yesterday, when I stopped at the store just now." His smile was apologetic. "I didn't mean to start a riot."

"Well, what did happen yesterday?" Sara demanded. "He was dragged off to the police station, everybody saw him go! What *for*? Why are they persecuting an innocent man?"

"Be my guest," I said to Barnaby as he stepped onto the wharf. Max put an arm around Sara's waist. Her face was drawn with anxiety and suspense.

"He wasn't dragged off," Barnaby said. "He went to make a statement, and we brought him home. That's all."

"But there has to be more to it than that!" Sara argued.

"Do you know why they wanted a statement from him?" Max asked. "Did he remember something all at once?"

"No, but they think he might have been out rowing around that night."

"He was in bed with his hot rum toddies!" Sara exclaimed.

"He can't prove it," said Barnaby curtly. "I'm going up to the house, I've got things to do today."

"Wait a minute," Max said. "Did they by any chance examine his dory, and find something in it?"

Barnaby nodded.

"I thought so," said Max. "They have to have something to go on. You're sure he can't prove where he was?"

"He says he's telling the truth and that ought to be enough for them."

"But they let him go again," Sara said, "so that must mean they believed him. Or are they going to haul him in again if he can't come up with a dozen witnesses, and put him in a *cell?*" Her voice rose and Max's arm tightened around her. "Sara," he said warningly, but he was unheard or ignored. "They might just as well kill him and be done with it!" she cried. "He couldn't stand it—he'll hang himself—and it'll all be my fault!"

"Sweetness," said Max. "That's not going to happen. They won't railroad him into prison. They'll find out who took the dory that night."

"Whoever it was just has to keep quiet and they'll never know! Or else he's long gone by now. If only—" She jabbed a finger at Barnaby. "If only *you* hadn't kept after me, and after me, and *after* me, I'd never have remembered the sound of oars! *You* made me sell Lorenzo out."

Barnaby's face tightened and grew cold. He walked past her, and she burst into tears, covering her face with her hands while Max tried to hold her.

"She'll feel better after this," he said over his shoulder to me. "She's been pretty uptight."

"I won't feel better," she said thickly from her hands, "until Lorenzo's safe. I just hope Barnaby's satisfied."

"Now you listen to me, Sarah Bernhardt or whoever you think you are," I said. "They'd have suspected Lorenzo anyway, because he never made any secret of resenting Cory. And he rows around at night, everybody knows that. But they never questioned him until they found Cory's body. So you can leave Barnaby out of this." Max enfolded Sara tightly in his arms and nodded past her head at me, shaping the words I'll take care of her.

I went on up the path and left them alone.

chapter 25

When I got to the house, Kyle and Barnaby were sitting on the back steps. Barnaby had just finished telling about the thread. It made me tired. So did the prospect of Sara's continuing dramatics. So did the prospect of getting a noon meal. I was wondering how best to deal with both food and Sara when a man appeared out of the woods beyond the duck pond, where the buck had stood that day. One by one we saw him, and because of his immobility and our somber mood we were all startled momentarily into silence.

Then I recognized the hat, and said, "Oh, it's Caine!"

Kyle shaded his eyes to look. "So it is." He waved. "Good morning, Caine!"

"Come on over!" I called. He came around the pond toward us. There were general greetings and handshakings, and he put down his kit and sat on the chopping block.

"So that's your car at the mailboxes," said Kyle.

"Yes, I've been here since early this morning. I've been discovering the shore all around your uncle's place," he said to me. "Accompanied by one small sociable terrier."

"Digger, the People's Friend," said Barnaby. "His ancestors came from Down Under, like your hat. He must have inherited memories of the good old days."

"Well, he certainly greeted me as if we were old buddies."

"I thought we were going to get together," Kyle said. "My wife called the Inn but you people weren't there."

"We've been down east. Tell me something," Caine said abruptly. "I heard some talk in the lobby this morning about an arrest being made in the Sanderson case. Is it just so much talk?"

"As far as we know it's just talk so far," Barnaby told him. "There's literally one thread of evidence."

"But Lorenzo's a friend of ours," I said, "and when he says he didn't do it, we believe him."

"I've seen him around, and talked with him once. He seems a gentle soul. I can't imagine his drowning that poor devil out there in the dark." His voice roughened. "What a death to die in such a beautiful place. What a death to die anywhere."

"We were all out watching the northern lights," I began, but had to stop because there was no way to go on aloud. Still the words stumbled on unwillingly inside my head. Sara had coaxed Cory out to see the lights; had he seen them again while he struggled to survive in the icy water? And did someone wait out there to see him die?

I knew by the stillness among us that we were all asking the same question. *The poor devil.* If we could feel that way now about him, why couldn't we have felt even a small fraction of it earlier?

But we had tried, and had been repelled. Now he had no defenses against either our curiosity or our pity, and that caused me a twinge of shame. It was as if only Sara had the right to speak with regret or remorse, because only Sara had seen doom in him and tried to make one last contact, however tenuous.

But pity or disgust or rage, whatever he had inspired, made no difference now. For us he would be forever about to drown in a black night sea under the northern lights, swimming the few strokes allowed him before the cold struck into his heart.

And Sara's cards had been right.

I thought I'd said it aloud when Barnaby's hand came down on my shoulder, apparently in a casual gesture. His fingers were warm and very hard. I wondered what my expression was, and assumed a consciously intelligent one, reminding myself of an Aussie listening for a squirrel.

"It's a queer thing," Caine was saying. "The fire and the disappearance the same night. If he was to be killed, why not leave him in the house? I know the arson squad couldn't find any clear-cut evidence, but it seems too much of a coincidence, that's all."

"All the more reason for the fire to be accidental," Kyle suggested. "It was an old house, the wiring might not have been adequate. If someone intended to burn the house down and kill Cory too, it would have been logical to leave him in it. That's why I think it *is* pure coincidence. He might have left some appliance on that overheated, something defective. Or a log fell out of the fireplace."

"Whoever came," Barnaby said, "had to come from away, but he knew about Lorenzo's dory."

"Cory was certainly afraid of *something*," I chimed in. "Now it looks as if he gave up worrying about being found, so he started asserting himself about the road and so forth. He must have decided he was safe at last."

"Or that his nemesis had arrived, made an abortive attempt, and given up. Don't forget the silencer." Kyle's manner masked whatever he must have felt. "Deirdre's talking about Mafia-type executions, and I don't suppose it's too far-fetched these days to consider organized crime."

"Kyle, you're giving me gooseflesh," I protested. "It seems a couple of years ago that we were making all the bad jokes about what he could be. Now I'd like to find out that he really was a gangster. Then I'd stop feeling guilty."

That came out unexpectedly, but they all looked charitably at me. Barney slid his hand down my arm, squeezed gently, and let go.

"Hi, everybody!" Sara shouted from the Deep Cove path. "We've got something!" She came running ahead of Max, abloom with pleasure. "It may not be much," she admitted sheepishly when she reached us, "but you never can tell. We've been down talking to Ruel's friend Spinner on Indian Beach. He told us that the day before the fire he was digging on Lorenzo's shore, and—Oh, *wow!*" She folded up gracefully on the steps beside Kyle. "You tell it, Max. I'm winded."

"As she says, it's not much," Max said temperately. "Lorenzo rowed in from somewhere that day, and he was coughing and groaning. So Spinner suggested he needed some hard stuff to fight it off. He offered to get some at the liquor store in Limerock when he went to town later that day. Lorenzo gave him the money to get a pint of rum, and Spinner left the bottle in Lorenzo's mailbox late that afternoon. It proves that he had the cold and the liquor, at least."

"And he's still got traces of the cold," I said.

"But is Spinner willing to tell this to the police?" Barnaby asked.

"He said he would," Sara answered. "In fact he promised."

"She had only to look at him like that," said Max.

"Rats! He'd do it for Lorenzo!" Indulgently she lifted his sunglasses off his face and began to polish them with a tissue. "A clam sprayed him," she explained to all. Barnaby was at his most wooden, as if Sara were committing intimacies in public.

"Oh, Max!" I said quickly, "have you met Mr. Caine?" I made as much as I could of the introductions. The two men shook hands, and Sara looked pleased and proud, as if Max were her personal accomplishment and a superlative one at that. She gave him his glasses back, or rather he reached out for them before she could put them in place.

"Why don't I make a big pot of coffee?" she proposed.

"I'm tempted," Caine said, "but I promised my wife I'd have lunch with her today. She's probably watching the clock now."

Kyle got up from the steps. "I'm resisting you too, Sara. I'll walk along to the Neck with you," he said to Caine.

"Fine. Maybe I can drop you off at your mailbox."

"I came over this morning to ask you to supper tonight," Kyle said, taking my hand. "It's been too long since we've gotten together for a real meal, not just an emergency mug-up. Barnaby's willing if you are, and maybe I can persuade the Caines to join us."

"I think we'd like that," Caine said.

"Sara and Max?" Kyle asked.

They were standing to one side, arms linked and fingers laced. Sara bemused, Max solemn but with the one-sided smile imminent. "I'm taking Sara out tonight, but thanks."

We parted all in a glow of good fellowship. Max left a few minutes after the other men, saying he had to work all afternoon to make up for the morning, and Sara went to the Neck with him.

"If we're lucky," I whispered, "they'll take an hour or more to say So long until tonight. At least Sara will. She amuses Max, you can see the laugh around his eyes even when his face is straight."

Barnaby gave me a sidewise glance. "I'd better get to work on this woodpile," he said, picking up the ax. "Yep, she amuses him all right, and that's all he wants with her. Good God, he must be thirty."

"And she's old enough to know whether or not she wants to be seduced."

"Don't *you* worry about her?" He split a piece of oak into two pieces and tossed them onto the pile.

"Oh, sometimes I think she may be more in love than he is, because she's a romantic and he's older and more cynical about life. So she could be hurt. But that's part of growing up, and she'll survive. Then at other times I catch a look between them and I think he's in as deep as she is."

"I hope that wasn't a Freudian slip." The sidewise glint was no longer bleak.

"Damn it," I muttered, "it's noon and we can't go to bed, with Baby Bunting likely to hop home any time. So let's take our lunch out on the cliff and dangle our feet over the surf, and say to hell with everybody."

"And if Baby Bunting shows up, we'll drop her over."

"You don't really feel that way," I reproached him.

"All I know is, I wish she hadn't tried to discover Cory Sanderson's soul. And if my brother weren't such a hot shot in real estate, X would have caught up with Cory in the wilder reaches of Fremont." He grinned at me. "What did you say about food? I'd just as soon eat right on this doorstep.

We've got a salt-water view on each side, so what more do you want besides peace and quiet and the two of us in the sack?"

"Some large thick corned beef and onion sandwiches?"

"I can always trust you to make the perfect response," he said. Cheered up, I went into the kitchen, and was slicing onions when Sara returned. She began getting out trays, mugs, and napkins, and made the coffee. She didn't speak, but she looked meditative rather than depressed.

When we took the trays out Barnaby whistled, and drove his ax into the block. "Barnaby's ideal centerfold features food," I said. "It makes me feel very secure."

Sara made an odd little snorting cough that might have been intended for a laugh. "Before we eat," she began in a light, almost breathless voice, "I have something to say. I want to apologize for the way I came all apart a while back, screaming those things. Max said he was ashamed of me, but I was already ashamed of myself. I would have apologized when we came up, but the others were there."

"Apology accepted," said Barnaby. "Did anyone remember to put mustard on my sandwiches?"

"Mirabell did. I'm apologizing to you too, Mirabell."

"Why, for heaven's sake?"

"Because Barnaby's your husband, for heaven's sake, that's why."

"Oh. Well, all right! Thanks!" We began to laugh.

Barnaby and I left before Sara did, to go around and see Lorenzo. His cold was about gone, and he was getting an early start on his garden, digging out alder stumps to enlarge it. "I always plant something special for the deer and the rabbits, y' know," he told us. "And they respect the rest of the garden. Same way my father always planted extra cucumbers and carrots for the kids to help themselves to, and they never set foot in the rest of the garden. *Never did*," he repeated devoutly. "Some different from these hellions today with their cars, they'd just as soon drive back and forth through some old woman's garden patch as look at it."

He didn't mention being under suspicion, and we didn't bring it up. We left him in the foggy almost-twilight, with the quiet shutting in as the birds began settling down for the night. We heard the first woodcock as we walked up the road.

When we got into the jeep, I said, "Barnaby, if they do take him in it will be the murder of *him*." He took my hand and drove around the fog-bound and deceptive curves with the other hand. "We can live only one day at a time. That's what Lorenzo's doing, and we're going to do the same and have a good night out."

"In the ditch, if you don't drive with both hands." I squeezed his hand and put it back on the wheel.

When we passed the opening to the Darby road, it was strange to think that the drive winding up through the dripping forests of dusk arrived at nothing but the tall chimneys and the carriage house.

At the end of the next driveway there was a lighted house, woodsmoke scenting the fog, an open door and welcomes.

Caine had called to say that his wife had already committed them to drinks and a buffet supper with some people she'd met in Williston. He was sorry, and so was she.

"He really sounded it too," said Deirdre. "And why wouldn't they be? We're all so enchanting and intellectual and sparkling down here."

We settled in for an evening of good food and good talk. Kyle and Barnaby had both worked out of the country, Kyle building dams and Barnaby supervising forestry projects for the Peace Corps, so there was plenty to talk about without getting mired in the Case. Deirdre had been with Kyle on almost all his jobs. My experiences were pretty unspectacular, but I could contribute some of the weirder clients of my interior decorating career, and my sometimes abrasive, sometimes astonishing, brushes with the art world when I worked at the museum.

The occasion was a triumph of willpower for us all. Then on the way home Barnaby asked casually, "When did Caine first show up around here?"

"Whatever you're thinking, it's impossible," I said sharply.

"Why?" He was being too sweetly reasonable. "Is it any more impossible than Cory Sanderson being murdered?"

I hate that silky logic that tries to force you into futile sputters of denial. So I tried to be even more reasonable. "This is a nice retired businessman who's a darned good painter, with a nice antique-mad wife who—"

"Have you seen her? Has anyone?"

Patience, Mirabell, I told myself. "I don't have to see her to recognize the type. If it was summer she'd be haunting every lawn sale and buying every old dish and bottle in sight."

"You haven't seen her, but you've fleshed her out on the skeleton of a few words. *His* words. And you know what *he* is because he sets up an easel."

"And he knows what to do with it. I've seen his work."

"That's no sign that he can't do something else very well, too."

"Such as what? Assassination? Hey, maybe that's it!" I

said gleefully. "Cory was a double agent and the CIA wanted him wiped out. That explains everything. Or maybe Caine's a Mafia hit man. Boy, what a disguise!"

The jeep stopped. "You sound," said Barnaby, "about five years younger than Sara, who at her best is a bright fourteen-year-old. I'm just asking a few sensible questions, and you're hysterical."

"I am not," I said, and got out. Fog and silence were one; thick, wet, cold, a lusterless false light like that of phosphorescence in the water. In the dark kitchen Barnaby took me in his arms. "Yes, you are," he said in my neck. "Yes, you are. Hysterical Hermione, the girl I adore. God help me."

"I thought we were going to forget all about it until we were forced to think of it again, tomorrow."

"I was forced to think about it tonight. It's been in the back of my mind ever since Kyle told us the Caines weren't coming. Come on, let's sit down, and you let me talk awhile, huh? I've been listening to everybody else's theories. Fair's fair."

I admitted it, grudgingly and then with more good will as we got ourselves settled in the biggest rocking chair, all by feel. "Now tell me about it," I murmured comfortably. "Why have you picked him for First Murderer?"

"I didn't say I had. But he's a stranger, and he appeared here roughly around the time that Cory did."

"And I saw him working on the Neck the day Cory discovered the paint on the rock. But he was down east when Cory disappeared."

"Quiet," said Barnaby with a rather intimate squeeze. "Schoodic isn't Alaska. He could have driven here that night and then back again."

"Are you going to tell all this to Blake?"

"Maybe he knows it already. I hope so. I don't want to prance up to him with my great idea, all bright-eyed and bushy-tailed, and have him look at me the way I look at Sara and her cards."

"Well, I'd like to see some pressure taken off Lorenzo," I said, "but I just can't see Steven Caine killing either a dog or a man in cold blood. Or even hot blood. He's sensitive and creative, and creative people don't destroy."

"Tell you what. We'll have Sara give him a reading."

I sat up abruptly and managed to punch him in the ribs with my elbow at the same time. He grunted.

"That's my instant karate," I told him, "and I've got another sharp elbow too. So you think my instincts are uproariously funny, do you? Just about as genuine as Tarot, is that it?"

"Mirabell, Mirabell," he said softly, and pulled me down again. "I don't class your intuition with Tarot cards or tea leaves or a crystal ball. But don't you see, I'd be happy as hell to fasten this on anybody who *isn't* Lorenzo?"

He stopped and waited, but there was something in his silence that forbade me to answer; I seemed to be holding my breath, willing him not to say what he was thinking. But no evasions were possible these days.

"We could go on indefinitely thinking up new theories," he said, "each one farther out than the last, but we shouldn't lose sight of the facts. Did it ever occur to you that the only hard evidence points at Lorenzo for a damn good reason?"

"Yes! That he's the victim either of conspiracy or coincidence."

"No. That he could have done it." He repeated it loudly, as if to defy himself. "He could have done it. You know Lorenzo's always lived pretty much in a world of his own choosing, and he didn't think it could ever change. He never believed the Darby place could go out of the family."

"I know," I mumbled. I tried to curl up very small in his arms, but it didn't work.

"So he's been under a terrific strain ever since the first shock, even though most of the time he's hidden it very well. Oh, he's had little outbursts of rage or hurt, but he seemed to get over them. But it could have been working inward on him, like a porcupine quill working through a dog's chest to the heart. And every time he met up with Cory's hostility, the point was shoved in a little deeper."

"You don't have to be so vivid about it," I said.

"I have to lay it all out in words, and to you, because nobody else would listen. They'd be afraid to."

"*I'm* afraid to."

"Listen, honey, everybody sees him as a gentle child of nature, brighter than the deer because he can read, and build boats, but living peaceably according to the rhythm of the seasons and the tides. Which is like categorizing me simply as a bird watcher. But once a lot of people thought me capable of killing my grandfather, and of beating a boy's brains out because he jacked a deer on the Preserve." He tightened his embrace until I couldn't move. "Maybe, given a certain distortion in my thinking which nobody knew about, I could have done those things and felt perfectly justified. That I had the *right*."

"Do we have to go back over that?" I asked unhappily.

"I'm using it for an example. You know I *could* have done it, if I'd been carrying that invisible flaw or wound, or whatever you want to call it. . . . Unconsciously everybody's trying to downgrade Lorenzo into this child who's not capable of adult rages or loves. But he is a man, Mirabell, and you know it, even if everything is sublimated in his possessions."

"And in something he considered his possession, morally or spiritually," I said. "The Darby Homestead. But shooting the *dog*, Barnaby! He'd never have done that!"

"And it would mean he'd have gotten hold of a silencer without anyone knowing, as well as a rifle, which he's never had since he gave up hunting years ago. No, he'd have nothing to do with killing the dog," Barnaby agreed. "And I don't say he had any conscious plans for Cory. But he caught a bad cold, and drank the rum. He doesn't drink often, so when he had a couple of drinks, everything surfaced. . . . Supposing he intended only to *talk* to Cory, tell him once and for all what he thought of him, and Cory wasn't going to turn his back or shut a door on him this time, no sir! So he rowed around there, and he found Sara and Cory walking on the shore. Sara heard the oars, and later there was something in the woods. Something maybe moving along parallel with them."

I shivered and burrowed closer. Some times a good imagination has its drawbacks.

"He was waiting for his chance to talk to Cory," Barnaby went on. "But when he saw Cory kiss Sara—Cory, that prime bastard, and Sara, that young innocent girl—I'm telling you, Mirabell, I can see it all so clearly it makes me sick. I can even see how he's blocked it out, so that when he says he's innocent he believes it."

"We'll never sleep tonight," I mourned. "Why couldn't you have left it where most of us wanted it left, with someone who's come and gone?"

"I wish to God I could," he said. "Come on, let's build a fire to watch, and have some wine."

chapter 27

There was sunshine in the morning, but we slept late, late for us being seven o'clock. When I woke up Sara was cooking. "I hope everybody's starved," she called in to us, "because I am."

"What do you feel so good about?" I asked her when I came into the kitchen. "Oh, I forgot. You're in love. *Peace.*" She laughed. I wondered dimly what had happened last night; one virgin less in the world seemed relatively unimportant compared to everything else I was remembering. Neither Barnaby nor I were in a mood to ask bright parental-type questions about her evening out, but she told us anyway.

"The fog was so thick last night when we got up the road a little way we decided not to go to Fremont. We went to Max's house instead." She paused artfully for Barnaby to raise an eyebrow, but he just kept on eating. "We cooked up some gorgeous jambalaya and played his Scott Joplin records. One thing I like about Max, he's not afraid to be his age. He admits the last rock group he liked was the Beatles, and the rest drive him up the wall. What I mean is, he's *adult.* Like you two."

"I should hope so," I said callously.

I needn't have spoken. "Oh, and we talked about the kind of house he wants to build out on Cat, if he gets it."

"How's he coming on that?" asked Barnaby.

"He's talked with the man on the telephone, and they're going to meet this week. I read the cards last night when I got home and they said Max will accomplish it."

I spoke before Barnaby could. "How could they mention the house, specifically? Is there a symbol for that?"

"No, but everything was in favor of his doing what he set

out to do. It's always good to end with the Six of Wands. It can mean triumph or victory. If it's reversed it's very bad, but this wasn't."

"Well, I'm glad something's coming out right for somebody," I said. "It's sure great to hear good news the first thing in the morning."

"Don't sound so cynical, Mirabell," she said. "I read the cards for the murderer too, and they were very bad for him. He's not going to get away with it. I turned up the Tower, and that is *ruin*." She was as serene as the sunlight. "Besides, Max and I are working on it." She pushed away her plate and braced her elbows on the table. "You know it was quite a while before I remembered the sound of oars. So there could very well be something else. After all, there's my dream of someone else being there. Finally Max admitted that it *could* mean something important. Well, last night he had me staring at the fire and listening to soft music and concentrating with my alpha waves, or is it theta waves?" She cocked her head as if hearing Voices. "I can't remember. He's very into transcendental meditation, and it's fascinating, but I got so sleepy! He said if I was doing it right I wouldn't get sleepy; that I should hold myself at the state just *before* sleepiness. But all I did was yawn in his face, because it was after twelve then. So he bundled me home."

"No wonder," said Barnaby. "There's nothing more disenchanting than a date who can't tell her alpha waves from her thetas."

Sara looked down at her laced hands with a Mona Lisa smile. "Oh, he's not disenchanted," she said. "We're going out again tonight, to that variety show for the Limerock hospital."

Though the day had a late start it was too fine to waste. Barnaby went out to haul at least a few traps. Sara and I took a lunch down to Mussel Cove. We agreed that whoever brought up the Case would be at once brained by a large rock in the hands of the innocent party.

We stayed out until we saw *Andromeda* coming home. Halfway up through the field skirting Deepwood we met a gray-haired couple picking their way down amidst the bay and juniper; they had binoculars and Peterson's Field Guide. They introduced themselves, and said a man at the Williston Inn had told them about Cape Silver. An artist . . . I told them what birds they could expect to see right now ashore and on the water, pointed out the osprey nest on Herring, and wished them a happy afternoon.

While Barnaby was eating he mentioned that Uncle Stewart hadn't gone out to haul, and suggested going over to Shallows to find out why. It was more than a suggestion; it was an offer of escape, because the instant we three were in the kitchen together the euphoria induced by an outdoor morning vanished. No matter how resolutely we refused to mention the Case, it was there with us, a spectral fourth party whose eyes we avoided, whose chains we tried not to hear.

Shallows looked blessedly normal when the jeep drove into the dooryard. The Aussies came flying off the back doorstep to meet us, the birds went up in a rush from the feeders. Beyond the low white house the eastern sea was a summery blue. Gulls followed a homecoming boat in a rising and falling cloud of beating wings as the lobsterman shook old baitbags overboard.

It was even better inside, with the fragrance of an applesauce cake in the oven. The aroma carried a hauntingly familiar undertone; a refrain, as the perfume ads might put it, both provocative and elusive. It was explained by the presence of Lorenzo, playing cribbage. He looked neither harried nor depressed, but determined to skunk Uncle Stewart, who had stayed ashore that day to soak an infected finger.

Naturally we couldn't go home until the cake came out of the oven, and besides, even with Lorenzo present there was an illusion here that nothing terrible had happened. Aunt Jess had a few accounts of local larks (nothing to do with birdwatching), which assured us that the normal life of Applecross was still going on, virtuously and otherwise.

"*Really?*" Sara was saying in astonishment, when the dogs began again outside, breaking up a story that Barnaby called raunchy soap opera. We looked out and saw the dogs surrounding Blake's car as well as two small terriers could, and they were pretty efficient.

"Now what does *he* want?" my aunt demanded belligerently. She went out to quiet the dogs while we waited, arranged like characters waiting for the curtain to rise. Lorenzo was pegging, and Barnaby watched his fingers as if he'd never before seen anyone put pegs in a cribbage board. Uncle Stewart tilted back in his chair, looking over his shoulder at the door. Sara stood by the window, consciously or unconsciously posed in a marble silence.

The timer went off and we all jumped. I took the cake out and turned off the oven. Sara said, "It's all right. He's smiling."

He was indeed, following Aunt Jess in with the dogs, "You'll have a cup of coffee with us and a piece of cake," Jess was saying.

"Or does that constitute bribery?" Uncle Stewart's chair came down into place. "Sit down, Dan."

"Better take that warrant out of your hip pocket first," said Lorenzo disagreeably. "You're likely to bend it all up if you set on it."

"Relax, Lorenzo, I didn't come to arrest you."

"*This* time," he grumbled.

"Don't sound so disappointed," said Aunt Jess. A faint wheezy chuckle was heard from Lorenzo.

"Then what *did* you come for?" Sara asked Blake.

"He's got a few more questions I can't answer," Lorenzo said. "Ain't that so, son?"

"Has anybody claimed Cory?" Barnaby asked. Blake shook his head.

"Poor man," said Aunt Jess. "Lying there like a—a *thing*, with nobody to mourn or miss him." There was nothing to say to that. Aunt Jess cut the cake and Sara poured coffee. I wondered how many times *Poor Cory* or *Poor devil* or *Poor man* had been thought or spoken since we found out he was dead.

Suddenly Sara exclaimed, "I just thought of something!" She slid into a chair opposite Blake and stared intensely at him. "I should have smelled Lorenzo! Woodsmoke, Vicks, fried salt pork, tobacco. And rum on that night. I couldn't have missed it if he'd been there. Excuse me, Lorenzo, for saying it, but you know it yourself." She sat back and folded her arms and smiled triumphantly at the officer. "I never smelled anything of the sort. Just Cory's aftershave. So that's proof positive that Lorenzo wasn't around."

"Have you remembered anything else, Miss Brownell?" Blake asked politely.

"I don't know why you don't give me one of those lie de-tector tests and be done with it," Lorenzo said. "Only gink who can swear I didn't use my dory that night is the one who took it, and sure as hell *he* ain't coming forward."

"I'll tell you what I did drop in for. It's just a little experi-ment of my own, and I've already talked with the Boones about it. . . . Now, all of you except Jess have had some talk with the man, and you think you found out nothing. Well, I'll tell you the little we've dug up, and then will you all re-consider your conversation with him and try again to think if any of it would make sense?"

I don't know what we expected to hear, but even Lorenzo gave Blake all his attention.

"We've been in contact with the bank that issued the certi-fied check. He had no account there, but came in with the cash. One hundred thousand dollars' worth."

"He was a Mafia bagman on the run!" Sara said at once.

"Is there a face card in your pack called The Mafioso?" Barnaby asked her blandly, and she swung her head angrily away.

"Her idea isn't too far-fetched," Blake warned. "In fact, it's been considered, but the people who know a lot more about it than we do have drawn blanks from their sources. The money was clean as far as hard evidence goes. It wasn't the take from a bank robbery somewhere or any private theft that they can discover." He shrugged. "Who knows? Sanderson could have been the heir of some eccentric who'd been putting cash away for years because he didn't trust banks or he was trying to foil the I.R.S."

He gave us a few minutes to think. Aunt Jess refilled the coffee cups, but it would take more than a boiling-hot beverage to drive away the mortuary chill. One by one Blake took us through the sparse words we'd had with Cory. Sara had had the most, yet it all added up to nothing. A *nothing* so obtrusive and inescapable that it became a positive instead of a negative.

Blake got up to go. "Well, I wanted to try it, and it may have started up something after all. If you think of anything else, even some special word he used, some turn of phrase, let me know."

"You fellers must be some desperate," Lorenzo gibed. "Now me, I know I never done it, so I'm not all hawsed up, but you got to pick somebody out of a couple billion people, and that's not counting Hawaii and Alaska."

"You know you're right? . . . Thanks for the cooperation, everybody. And thanks for the mug-up, Jess."

"How about giving me a ride as far as my road?" Lorenzo asked. "I ain't rowing around much these days, since you won't let me use my dory. They're likely to put it in the Limerock Museum afterward," he said merrily. "For all I know they'll stuff me and put me in it."

"You'll be a sensation," said Blake. "Come on." On the way out Lorenzo gave us a burlesque wink.

"Just one of them little courtesies he owes his prime suspect. Elegant cake, Jess. I'll skunk you next time, Stewart."

We sat around rather limply until Barnaby roused himself. "He hadn't got into your morning glory seeds, had he, Jess?" We tried to laugh at that, but it was a failure. Sara huddled in a chair with her knees practically under her chin, her face long and mournful, her green eyes fixed broodingly on the dogs' water dish. A new attack of guilt was imminent.

t was cold driving home. The late afternoon light was both clear and harsh. The intensifying chill meant frost tonight. Another kind of frost seemed to be settling permanently into our souls.

The visiting couple's car was still by the mailboxes, and some bicycles had been added. We noticed them without comment. But our muteness was shattered by the sight of Madam President's Volkswagen in our dooryard.

Barnaby said something he very seldom says, and I agreed with him. "This is *it*," I said. "You'll have to put up a sign. Or else write her a nasty-nice note."

"What's the matter with being nasty-nice to her face right now?" Sara asked. "Come on, Barn, let's see you freeze her to the marrow."

"She has permanent antifreeze," I said.

Madam President and Garfield were holding court on the back steps. Four young girls hung about the railings like maids-in-waiting in jeans and knit ponchos. Three younger boys perched around like attendant pages, and the bird-watching couple stood by like emissaries from a foreign court. Garfield was being a wonderful old down-east character for all he was worth, and Madam President was feeding him the lines. Her laughter led the applause each time.

The man turned to us, laughing and wiping his eyes. "If this was on a record it would far outsell any of these so-called entertainers. This is the real stuff."

"Yep, it's the real stuff all right," said Barnaby. Fortunately he didn't say what he thought the stuff was.

"Do I get a ticket or just a warning, Barnaby?" Madam President called roguishly. "I *had* to drive Garfield to your door. You couldn't expect him to walk it, could you?"

"I could expect almost anything of Garfield," said Barnaby.

Garfield slapped hands on his knees. "Now *that's* what I call a compliment! Like the nice young officer who took away my license. He says, 'To put it frankly, Mr. Willy, you're a danger on the highway.'" He rocked back and forth in soundless laughter. "I said, 'Young feller, me lad, if you was to call me a danger to women, that'd be praise of the highest order.' Yessir, that's what I said: praise of the highest order."

The girls doubled up in delight, and Garfield snatched at a long dark tress. "Don't believe it, do ye? Why, when I was a boy men'd lock up their daughters when they saw me sailing into the harbor."

"But that was a hundred years ago," the girl protested, sputtering with laughter. The little boys fell against each other, laughing without knowing what was funny.

"Ayuh," Garf agreed, "and you want to be glad you warn't around then. I was known as the roughest rooster this side of Belfast. Still could be, with some cooperation." He pulled her hair harder.

"You'd better not get carried away, Garf," Madam President told him. "You wouldn't want to get picked up for contributing to the delinquency of a minor, would you? Or maybe you would!" She nickered piercingly. "It'd make a smashing finish for you, wouldn't it?"

"*Finish* is right, by the time they got through with their rubber hoses, and splinters under my fingernails." He wound his hand up in the girl's hair and jerked her face down close to his dried-apple one. "Sweetheart, you got a cheek like a peach."

It could have been funny, but the girl was wincing, and she tried to keep laughing. The other girls were fidgeting, their smiles uncertain. The woman said to her husband, "Dear, we ought to be getting along."

"Okay, Garfield," Barnaby said, "Now you've established

yourself as Applecross's Dirty Old Man, so let her go. Did you want to see me?"

"Come to think of it, I did. Then I got surrounded by this crowd of blushing beauties, and I forgot."

He loosened his grip and the girl sprang quickly back, and away from the step. "Gosh, what time is it?" she said breathlessly. "I've got to go home. Come on. So long, everybody." She was leaving at a sprint. "Got a big exam tomorrow," she called to us in passing. The others caught up with her, tossing back *So longs* like kisses. The boys went after them, a stampede of shaggy Shetlands.

"Ah, youth," said Sara mystically. She went into the house, giving Garfield a wide berth.

"See, they all know what a wolf you are, Garfield," Madam President told him, and he laughed and clapped a hand onto her solid thigh in the stretch pants and did a little enthusiastic kneading while the merriment rolled on. Barnaby and I walked across the yard with the visiting couple. When they left us they were planning to return in June when all the warblers would have arrived.

We went reluctantly back to the two on the steps. Madam President had got up; I wondered if Garfield had pinched.

"Well, Garfield," Barnaby said, "what can I do for you?"

"Polly here tells me you don't believe there was ever a fort on Cape Silver. Now just what do you know about it, sonny, eh? Who's the elder around here, you or me? No offense, now." He raised hands in conciliation.

"Where do you think it would be?" Barnaby asked mildly. "Where's the most logical spot for a fort out here?"

Garfield's face shriveled even more in a scowl of concentration.

"Think, Garf," Barnaby urged him. "Can you honestly say that anywhere in these woods there'd be a good site for a fort that could watch all the approaches?"

"We must remember," Madam President instructed him, "that they cleared all the land first."

Garf waved a hand impatiently at her. "Ayuh, but it's all

hilly ground where the woods are now. Trees or no, there'd always be a side where they could be snuck down on from. Nope, the best site would be right about *here*." He slapped the step with a leathery palm, and stamped his foot.

"When my great-grandfather first bought the land," said Barnaby, "and was going to build here, the local kids already knew every inch of this ground—don't you think they'd been all over it looking for tomahawks and powderhorns? And their fathers and grandfathers doing the same before them, because they thought there ought to be a fort here? Haven't you done it yourself, Garf?"

"A couple of centuries can cover a site with how much soil?" Madam President persisted.

"I'm talking about these fields being first cleared for pasture a couple of centuries ago," Barnaby said. "Garfield, do you really think an earlier fort would have completely disappeared from here by then? So that somebody who was looking for one couldn't find a trace of any building here whatever?"

Madam President threw back her head. "Old Squire Willy—"

"Now, Polly, Old Squarr could have disremembered just how his grampa told him," said Garfield.

"I don't *care!*" she said passionately. "People have been fooled before! Especially if they didn't know what to look for. Boys cutting alders!" she said in disgust. "*We* may be amateurs, but we're devoted and dedicated—"

Garfield squinted up at Barnaby. "You got any better ideas, Sonny?"

Barnaby braced a foot against the door step and leaned forward confidentially. "How about the southern end of St. Andrew's Island? Imagine that cleared off, Garf. How far could you see in every direction from aloft on a blockhouse up there?"

"By Godfrey Mighty, there was a reg'lar settlement on the Andrews long before anybody darst live on the mainland here. Now they'd ought to have a fort out there, oughtn't they?"

Madam President was not going to be left out. "Barnaby, you must be *inspired*! Mirabell, are you sure he doesn't have a hot line to the past?" She all but neighed with excitement. "We'll start discussing arrangements at the next meeting. What a project for May!"

"Too bad we ain't got a spiritualist in our midst," Garfield said. "Might be he could raise up Cory's ghost out there and he could tell us who done it."

"Oh, you *ghoul*!" said Madam President, gaily slapping him on the shoulder.

"What's your theory, Garf?" Barnaby asked him. "You must have one. Everybody else does."

"Out of respect to the dead I ain't violating any confidences." Which meant he hadn't been in Cory's confidence. "Not that I wouldn't tell if I knew something strong enough to take my oath on," he added in a hurry. "I ain't fussy about having a murderer loose in Applecross. . . . Though there was one back when I was a boy. We all surmised who it was but nobody could ever prove nothing, and Lordie, I ate her doughnuts many a time after that with never a worry about it."

"Tell us about it, Garf," I said, getting into the act though not within his range. He started to speak, but Madam President's volume easily took over.

"I'm not saying anything we don't know when I call Lorenzo peculiar." She gave us her we're-all-intelligent-people-here-so-we-can-speak-candidly smile. "But consider the way he is about his camp, and that trunk of his. What's going to happen to them when he dies? Why won't he let Applecross have what it should have, if he thinks so much of his town?"

"Perhaps he will," I said. "Maybe he's already taken care of that, who knows?"

"Maybe Polly's worried about what will happen if Lorenzo goes to prison for life," Barnaby suggested.

She colored angrily. "I'm not suggesting that he did it! But everybody knows he's been just beside himself ever since Cory Sanderson moved into town!"

"That boy's been seething like Mt. Etna getting ready to erupt. Father saw that, and he told me about it." Garfield was religiously solemn. "I ain't saying a word against Lorenzo that ain't true. The way he acted last time I went down to his camp, I could tell something was awful out of whack. Darbys have some outrageous old tempers. Slow to anger, but man dear, when they do let go—"

"It's these quiet, inhibited recluses we have to watch," Madam President said.

"I'd hardly call Lorenzo a recluse," I objected. "He's all over the place."

"Yes, and at all hours," she said meaningfully.

"Well, I've got work to do," Barnaby announced.

Garfield braced back. "What, ain't you going to ask us in for a drink?"

"I'll give you a drink, Garfield," said Madam President. "Come on—upsydaisy—" she reached down to give him a boost.

"Quit that!" he snapped. "I ain't decrepit *yet!*" He hauled himself up by the railing.

"Such spirit!" she cried at us. "I hope I do half as well at your age!"

"You won't be around at my age," he retorted nastily, "if you don't leave off the rum and all that fancy fodder." He scuttled off to the car and got in without help.

"My, we are certainly rambunctious today, aren't we?" she chortled, but her face was unbecomingly blotched. They drove off leaving a cloud of exhaust lying low in the dampening air. Barnaby sighed.

"I never heard of a fort on the Andrews," I said.

"Neither did I. But who knows? The more I talked, the better it sounded to me. The old-timers handed down a story to our grandfathers about Dixey Bull burying treasure out there, remember? And there was supposed to be a trading post there once, too. Why couldn't that be a distorted memory of a fort?"

"Gosh, why don't we go out there ourselves before anybody else can?" I said. "I'd love to think about something besides what's going on around here. We could spend a day prowling those woods on St. Andrew's. It would be almost as good as a trip abroad."

"Maybe we will," he said like an indulgent parent, but I could see the spark in his eye.

We'd been to bed and were up again, having something to eat, when Max and Sara came home from the variety show held for the benefit of Limerock Hospital. We sat around the table drinking coffee and eating homemade peanut butter on pilot crackers while they told us about the acts. There'd been a hypnotist, a local man who'd left home as a youth and gone into show business. He'd come back to contribute his time for the hospital.

"He was very good," Max said. Sara began describing the act and he sat thoughtfully drinking coffee while she talked.

"You know, Sara," he said at the first break, "I'll bet he could find out what you can't consciously remember. He might be able to take you back to the scene so that you could relive it in its entirety."

"You're joking, of course," I said.

"Why?" His angular face was both humorous and questioning. "If Sara's willing, and he is, why not? She can't come to any harm. She's not a neurotic who'd blossom into all sorts of traumas and hang-ups the instant she went under."

"How do you know?" Barnaby asked, sounding merely amused. I knew better.

"I know she's an intelligent, levelheaded girl—"

"Thank you, I think," said Sara. "Why can't you say I'm fabulous, glamorous, etcetera, etcetera?"

"Well, you are, and why should I tell you something that you know already?" They took time for one of those long drowning looks, during which I felt extraneous, and Barnaby studied the ceiling.

"It needs paint," he observed.

"The hypnosis wouldn't have to go very deep," Max said.

"Just enough to relax her so completely that her unconscious could take over and relive the scene exactly as it was."

Sara rubbed her hands over her arms. "I've relived it enough both waking and dreaming."

"You wouldn't know about it this time. Afterwards, I mean. And you might get the clue. Do you *want* this murderer running around loose?"

"He's probably running around a good distance from here by now. Supposing I did remember some detail? How could that identify a complete stranger who came from nowhere and disappeared into nowhere? How could that help Lorenzo?"

"You can't tell," Max insisted. Then he relaxed and laughed. "Oh, it's just a hypothesis, and the whole thing is such a blank, anyone's idea is as good as anyone else's. The real truth is probably so far from what any of us have imagined, even in the craziest fantasies, that we'd have a hard time believing it."

"I still think I'd have smelled Lorenzo, if he'd been using Vicks and drinking rum," Sara muttered. "Why can't Blake believe me?"

Barnaby yawned uncontrollably, and apologized. Max got up at once. "It's been a long day for all of us."

Sara went out with him for a lengthy farewell on the back doorstep. "It's love," I said to Barnaby. Did you see the way they looked at each other? Talk about hypnotism, they could hardly pull their eyes away." I rambled on, fighting yawns. "I keep wondering if their kids will have lovely dark blue eyes like Max's or tourmaline-green like Sara's."

"You're half a century out of date if love to you means marriage and kids."

"Our love did, even back when we were sixteen and everybody was agin us. It still does."

"Because we're squares, and I'm a male chauvinist who wants to put my label on my woman." He made a growling grab at me, and of course Sara came in just then and said, "Why, *Barnaby!* Should I go out again?"

"No," he said severely, "and don't act as if you just caught your father and mother kissing, and you think it's so cute at their age."

"I never thought of it like that at all. What I thought was, I hope Max and I will be as secure with each other as you and Mirabell are. Each of you is a complete, separate person, but you're so perfect together."

I tried to smile in a manner both modest and all-knowing, but nobody noticed it. "Listen, Sara." Barnaby cleared his throat. "I know you're your own boss, and even if you were under eighteen I'm not your guardian. So I can't tell you not to fool around with this hypnosis deal. But I'm asking you not to."

"Don't worry," she said. "I've already refused. Not that I thought it would really hurt me, because Max wouldn't let anything happen. But I just don't like the idea of letting go of myself. I always want to be right there, no matter what. That's why I've always stayed away from drugs." She grinned. "I can get high without any help whatever."

"The right company helps, though," I said.

"Well, yes," she admitted. "I've never known anyone like Max. He's sophisticated, but he likes to build things with his hands, he loves music, and he gets excited about seeing a deer. He knows all about 30-million-year-old rocks, and he feeds raccoons off his back doorstep. And I'm another of the simple things he loves."

Unexpectedly she kissed us both, and ran up the stairs. Then she came down again. "Hey, I forgot something."

"A hot water bottle," I said. "Your bed'll be cold."

"Yes, but something else. I wouldn't need to try hypnosis anyway. I *do* want to help Lorenzo with all my heart. So when I go to bed I try to concentrate on letting my unconscious memories float to the surface, and I keep getting the feeling lately that I *am* going to remember something."

She took the hot water bottle, said thanks absently, and returned to the stairs. "I haven't told Max yet, because I'll have to dig it out in my own way, Besides, the more you talk about something like that the more likely you are to lose it."

"We won't mention it," said Barnaby, having gotten the message. She said "Thanks, again," and went up the stairs.

chapter 29

The next day was another good one for fishermen. Barnaby left early to haul, and Sara and I frittered the morning away in peace all the more precious for being so precarious.

We didn't mention Lorenzo, but I wondered what he was doing while we were becalmed; building a new doorstep, maybe, even if his handsome oak plank had been confiscated. Or he was cleaning house, which happened once a year, like fiddlehead greens.

Toward noon we heard a big outboard echoing between the walls of Deep Cove, and went to look. Max was bringing Scott Thatcher's boat to the wharf. Sara hugged herself like a child. "Isn't this spectacular? I was just thinking about him!"

When he came in alongside the spiling and looked up at us, he was trying to show an austere face, but his long mouth kept curling up at the corners, and his eyes seemed to be blinking back laughter but not very successfully.

"I'm on my way to Cat," he said to Sara. "Want to come along?"

"Max Kemper, have you had *good news?*"

He pulled off his watch cap and held it to his heart. "I believe so, most devoutly. If it was all a dream, why did I ever have to wake up? Unless it was to see you standing on a wharf with the sun shining through your hair."

"He's either drunk, or a poet in disguise," I said.

"I'm about to become the owner of Cat."

"Oh, Max!" She went down into the boat and took his face in her hands and kissed him. "I'm so happy for you."

He held onto her wrists. "Be happy for *us*. Are you coming with me? I'm in a hurry. It's like being eight years old again on a Christmas morning, and I can't wait to see what's under the tree for me." He looked up at me. "I've been all over the island before, but this time it will be different."

"Yes, it will be," I said. "I'm glad for you, Max."

Sara came back up the ladder. "I'll hurry and get something to wear—*Oh*." She stopped halfway across the wharf, and returned to me. "I hate to leave you alone."

"Why, for heaven's sake?"

"You know. The way things are. We've been sort of hanging together lately."

"Do you really believe there's a killer stalking us?" Max asked.

"No, but I'd feel better if Mirabell came. There's so much grim stuff to think about when anyone's left to their thoughts."

I tried to make a joke of it. "Excuse us, Max, while we talk about you as if you weren't here. Listen, Sara, Max wants you alone with him on this special trip, not a crowd."

"You're not a crowd, and besides, if it weren't for you and Barnaby I'd never have been here to meet Max. Right, Max?"

"Right," he answered promptly. He sat down on the outer gunnel and unzipped his oil jacket. "Go get your jackets. I've got chow and drinks."

"I'll get your stuff, Mirabell!" Sara took off up the path like a track runner. I chased her, but by the time I'd caught up with her at the top, I was admitting to myself that I really wanted to go. So I left a note for Barnaby telling him where I was, in case he came in early, and nearly beat Sara back to the wharf.

There was a slight southwest chop, just enough to scatter the sea with diamonds. We headed for a steep little shingle beach on the northern side of Cat. Max threw out a stern anchor to hold the big dory steady, and made the bow painter fast to a heavy iron staple driven in a flat ledge above high watermark.

"I wonder who put that there," he said reverently. "I wonder how many hands, over how many years, have tied painters there."

"Nobody can remember when it wasn't there," I said. "It's like the cellar hole. Nobody knows whose cabin was there, and when, and what became of him. Now it shows up less and less, and maybe after us nobody will even know it was a cellar hole, so they won't be wondering about him. For them he will never have existed."

"Well, don't sound so sad about it," Max squeezed my shoulder. "It's my cellar hole now, and maybe I'll dig it out and build on it. Continuity, that's the thing. Come on, let's have a look."

Cat was sheltered from the prevailing southwest winds by the long high ridge of Herring, and the northeastern flow was broken by Charlie's. Up where the grassy saucer of the cellar hole was growing violet buds and early strawberry blossoms, it was so warm we shed jackets and turtlenecks.

From here I went exploring on my own. The little island had some of everything, even a minuscule bog with cranberry vines, and signs of blue flag to come. There were the three spruces, and a small coppice of poplars that would grow fast with no porcupines to bother them, and here and there among blackberry tangles and raspberry canes a young pine that could be liberated by an ax. The shore line was richly varied in rock, colors, and contour. There was a minute white sand beach, and another of smooth surf-rounded stones.

The island was a little treasure and I half-envied Max without wanting to take it away from him. Sometimes the other voices came from out of sight in the quiet, sometimes I could have been completely alone out here. The eiders weren't around, but two loons were offering their duet, and the ospreys were piping signals to each other from on high. I watched two male gulls competing for a sleek female who serenely looked the other way while they paced each other down the shore with deliberate steps and arched necks. There was a lot of chasing, both amorous and aggressive, among the small land birds. Ah, love! I thought philosophically.

Finally I joined Max and Sara and the cooler on a flat ledge on the high easterly part of the island. "Max thinks he'll build his cabin up here," Sara said. "You can look out between Charlie's and Andrew's to open sea, and down at the Kittens when they're breaking, and still have a good view to the east for sunrise, and everything open to the north."

"But I promise to preserve the old cellar hole, Mirabell," Max said. "Sara's going to sit in the middle of it on Allhallows Eve. The spirit of the former resident is going to whisper in her ear."

"And they'll hear me scream as far as Applecross Center," said Sara. "Supposing he's buried about ten feet deep in it?"

"That's one reason why I'm building up here on solid rock. I don't want anything knocking on my floor some stormy winter night. You know that Frost poem about the skeleton that kept coming up the cellar stairs?"

"You are *horrible!*" said Sara ecstatically.

"I'm in good company. The Historical Society is hoping to find a fort on St. Andrew's, with cannon and skeletons in armor and all."

"So she did tell them at the next meeting," I said.

"Oh yes. I heard it in the store. Let's eat. I just went around the store with my eyes shut, and took whatever I jabbed at."

"You're a good jabber," I told him, falling to. He'd brought everything to make our own Italian sandwiches, and apologized for having soft drinks instead of wine. We had Anjou pears and chocolate bars for dessert. It was the best-tasting meal we'd had for days, simply because out here there was no association with disaster. Afterwards we lay around with our jackets and sweaters stuffed under our heads for pillows, and watched the gulls and listened to the somnolent swash around the Kittens as the tide came in. Once I rose up to rearrange my headrest and saw that Sara and Max were holding hands.

From time to time a slight puff of wind would escape over Herring and touch us, and the sound of surf on the outer shore of the long island had increased until the world of the Andrews was no longer quiet.

"Come on, let's go over," Max said. "It must be quite a sight."

We went out around the northeastern side of Cat through the passage between Cat and Charlie, and into a tiny notch of a cove on Herring just east of the Kittens. The rising tide flowed harmlessly around these ledges today; all the action was on the exposed southwestern shores.

We had landed close to the Head, and the path to the top crossed the slope at an angle, otherwise it would have been too steep to climb. As it was, we had to help ourselves along by pulling on the tough growth of bay and alder. At the top the wind and the noise hit.

At home we could get the same cold, unremitting pressure of wind pushing the flesh back against the bones and making our ears ring, and we could see the water boiling green and silver and white to the horizon. But I had never stood on the ridge of Herring and seen and felt and heard it like this. The bar between Herring and Andrew's, navigable at high water in most weathers, was a roaring combat area about a hundred feet wide. The combers rushing in from the southwest deepened as they felt footing beneath them, towered and curved, and struck in smoking, hissing chaos. Spray flew up to touch us where we stood, and across the battleground the lower ledges and turf of Andrew's were dark with flung water.

On the lee side of the bar the broken fragments of seas ran away toward the east and spent themselves out of existence.

Max stood at the head of the trail that led down to the bar, his hands in his pockets, gazing out at the heaving line of horizon. Sara seemed entranced by the war of waves below. Looking east between Charlie's and Andrew's I could see a few boats going home, either because they were through or it was too rough to find lobster buoys. *Andromeda* could be one, but it was impossible to tell at this distance, as they kept rolling or sinking out of sight. Turning farther around to get all the view there was, I saw Ronnie Deming's boat moving sedately along in the lee of the outer shore of Cape Silver.

"Look at that one coming!" Sara shouted behind me, and I turned to see one of the biggest seas yet, breaking all the way along the bar to the other island. Sara started down the path. The turf was slippery and I called to her to be careful, but she was too close to the noise to hear me. The tide was still coming in, with crescendo upon crescendo as if rising to some fearful, final climax; yet my brain knew that this was nothing apocalyptic, only the typical southwest blow calling for official small-craft warnings. Our short trip home would be in nearly sheltered waters. I had only to enjoy myself, but I could do that better if Sara were not where she stood at this moment. One slip on the slick, dampened turf and she could skid into the powerful sweep of an incoming or withdrawing sea. Already the water was full of swirling débris lifted from above high water mark, old rockweed, a shattered trap, a couple of lengths of pulpwood, an oar.

I went out around Max, who glanced quizzically at me, and I pointed at Sara. "She shouldn't be so close!" He nodded, and whistled piercingly; she turned and looked up at us. The wind was tearing at her hair, blowing strands across her mouth and her eyes, and she pulled a scarf out of the hip pocket of her jeans and managed to gather up most of the hair and corral it in a pony tail. She mimicked satisfaction, went nearer to the surf. Another big one exploded and spray reached her in an arc of dazzling drops. She wiped her face with her sleeve. Water foamed up over the dead grass not ten feet below her.

"That nutty kid!" I shouted at Max. He smiled indulgently and shook his head, but didn't offer to go after her. Well, maybe I "hen around," as Barnaby's fond of telling me, but I'd rather people would be mad with me for being officious than for being negligent. I went down the path behind her, cautiously.

"Hey, Sara!" I called to her to let her know I was near. She looked around, laughing, her face wet with spray like rain. "Isn't it *tremendous?*" she yelled back. She glanced up past me at Max, and I did too; he looked about ten feet tall up there against the rushing clouds. "Come on down, you coward!" she shouted between cupped hands.

He lifted one hand in a brief salute.

"Come on back a little way," I said in her ear.

"No, wait till this one hits. Watch it!" It rose in a towering wall of translucent green and then began to arch like a cobra's hooded head. Something heavy caromed into my back and threw me against Sara, who plunged forward and down, with me tumbling over her. Frantically scrabbling at air, with no breath to cry out in surprise, we hit the water and the ocean fell in on us.

It flooded my eyes, ears, nose, and mouth with cold brine. Trying not to breathe in, I struggled, blinded, to get onto hands and knees and to find Sara. The undertow seemed to suck the mud and sand out from under me, and before I could half realize what had happened the first time, a second sea broke heavily over me and smothered me in icy foam. Suddenly my hand got *something*; I knew sanely behind my sightless terror that it was part of Sara, the wide leather belt she wore with her jeans. My fingers knuckled into the small of her back so as to get a good grip on the belt; with the other hand I was groping for anything, a barnacled point or rock, a tough trunk of bay or a thorny tangle of rose bush, anything to keep us from being sucked off the bar, battered senseless among the rocks on the way, and drawn into deep water.

I could tell that Sara was vigorously alive and trying to keep that way. Once we were knocked together and I saw her face wide-eyed and sternly set; then we were thrown apart by a new breaker. It didn't loosen my grip on her belt, and I forced my head up to the air again, and giddily blowing and spitting I saw the dry sunny slope above. We had only to go a little way, if we could make it between the seas that alternately threw us forward, then hauled us back as if we were no more than rockweed streaming out on the tide.

Then that clawing hand of mine that had so far found only floating wood, sand, or old shells, struck something hard. The hand was almost too numb to grip, but I forced it to obey and close around the thing. I couldn't tell what it was, only that it was small enough for me to hold, and that *it* was holding. With the other hand I tried to draw Sara to me by her belt, praying that my arm wouldn't give out from weakness and the paralyzing cold.

A new sea gave her a shove toward me, and drove me hard up against something substantial; we were forced down, knocked around, and yanked powerfully, but I was able to hold fast. When the water receded slightly, I saw that I was holding onto an iron spike, protruding from a ship's timber that must have been lying half-buried at the head of the bar. Sara had one arm hooked over the timber itself. But we were so cold, so beaten by tons of water, so exhausted that it seemed only a question of minutes before another wave broke our grip and took us out.

"Hold on," I tried to shout at Sara. Her lips were blue, her eyes staring. I wondered with a sudden dispassionate sanity if we'd been given this moment of respite so we would realize fully that we were going to die.

Like Cory.

Then, hearing the next sea roaring in to the bar, I thought, *Where is Max?* I had completely forgotten him from the instant we plunged overboard. I strained with burning eyes for a sight of his head in the water too, and thought with sick resignation, *He has already drowned.* He must have skidded into us, and sent us all three tumbling into the surf.

If only Sara and I could haul our bodies onto that timber before more water broke over us, maybe we could hold on until the tide turned. But we were so damned tired. Sara's head rested on her arm, her eyes were shut; I looked up at that hatefully empty slope on which we'd stood and laughed, and then I saw Max.

He was standing knee-deep in rushing water a little distance beyond the timber. In my blurred vision he was just a black figure, but I could distinguish a long pole of some kind and he seemed to be holding it out to me.

Couldn't he see I didn't dare let go to reach for it, even if I had the strength, with the water pulling at me? For God's sake, Max! I implored silently. Come out a little way, that's all we need.

Sara lifted her head and I thought she said his name. He took a few steps forward, the pole became an oar, it flew up against the sky and came down just as the fresh comber broke over our heads. Surf must have weakened the momentum of the blow because I never felt it, and Sara's head came up free, shaking off water and rockweed, and we were still holding. But we couldn't wait until the tide turned. Max wouldn't let us.

I had strength, as I'd never had before in my life, to pull myself up onto that old timber and across it into the churning mess of sand and rotten rockweed, chips, and branches. The oar began to prod at me, jabbing wherever it could, trying to drive me back into the surf, but I was too numb to feel it. I stayed on my hands and knees—I couldn't have stood up anyway—and kept my head down so he couldn't hit my face. Behind me there was another crash, but I couldn't look around to see if Sara was still there. I kept working doggedly toward those legs knee-deep in the water.

The oar blade hit my head and flew off, the already split blade separating completely, but he could still use the sharp end like a cattle prod to force us back into the sea. I dived forward in a long wild slide on my belly and reached his feet before he could kick me. I wrapped both arms around his right leg and brought him down.

We floundered around there in the thick soup of tidal rubbish, and I kept my grip on his leg as desperately as I'd clung to the spike, because I didn't know what else to do. He was trying to pull me off, with the advantage that his hands were larger, stronger, and not numbed with cold. He got me by the hair and I didn't even feel pain, but when his hands reached down to my throat and began to pull upwards, at the same time pressing in on my windpipe, I had to give in. He dragged me to my knees; we were both kneeling in the floating detritus, my head held rigidly straight by the unyielding brace of his hands. His face was quite disfigured, seamed and grimacing in a passion of rage.

"You *would* come," he said. "You interfering fool! I'd only planned on *her*."

"Is she dead?" I asked hoarsely. I rolled my eyes toward the timber, but couldn't turn my head to see.

"If she isn't, she will be," he said. "She's too far gone to help herself now."

"But *why*?" I asked, thinking A hell of a lot of good the answer will do me now. But I was too spent and too astounded to be frightened. Besides, now I knew. "You killed Cory."

"Yes, and she might have remembered something. She was on her way to it."

"You're the fool," I said with difficulty. "She never saw or heard anything that could be used against you or anyone."

"I couldn't take a chance on that." He had managed somehow to calm himself; the long limber mouth dented in at the corners in a parody of a familiar lopsided smile. "If you don't resist it will be quicker, Mirabell. There'll have been a terrible accident, both of you lost in the surf while my back was turned."

"If you strangle me, you'll leave marks."

"The pounding around among the rocks will take care of that."

Barnaby, I thought. *I love you.*

There was a weird, harsh cry from where I had left Sara, and it startled Max. I felt the shock in his hands when they moved on my throat. He looked toward the cry. I couldn't turn my head but I could hear it repeated. It made no sense, but Max let go of me and splashed toward the timber. The cry came again before he reached it. I saw Sara's drenched head, hair plastered over her lifted face, her open mouth, and all at once the nonsense became a name I had heard her call before. I swung my head to look up at the rise of the island above me, and I saw the dog silhouetted against the sky.

There was only that instant for sight and recognition before he moved.

chapter 30

Max was dragging Sara up by the shoulders when the dog catapulted by me and leaped at his back. He went down with a strangled yelp across the timber, and Sara was thrown free of him. Trying to get to her I realized that the tide had started to go at last, and she was almost clear of the surf. I fell onto my knees at the timber and leaned forward, reaching out for her. She reached toward me and with both of us laboring with all our might we got her in. The dog stood over Max, growling continuously, his hackles up, his big head lowered to Max's.

Max's head hung face down in the surging eddies. "All right, Hugo," Sara gasped. "Good boy. Good boy. Don't touch. Oh, God, I hope he hasn't been trained to k-i-l-l."

"Right now I don't care," I said callously, "I just wouldn't be interested in watching, that's all. I suppose we've got to keep this object from drowning. Can I touch him, Hugo? Or is he all yours and you'll fight for him?"

The dog flicked his ears and moved his eyes toward me and then back to Max's head. Like me, Sara had found a reservoir of new strength. Talking to the dog all the time, she slipped her hands under Max's head and turned his face free of the water. He was hardly recognizable as the man we had known. He had turned a dirty white color, and he looked dead, but his eyes opened and saw us, then slid to the massive head leaning over him, and closed again.

"Hey, hey!" Shouts and a shrill, soaring whistle; Gus Flint had arrived while we weren't looking. I had never before seen him so red and so upset. "What happened? Somebody drowned? Oh Christ, that dog done something?" He was breathless with despair. "He never—I never knew him to—" The dog went to him, wagging his tail, then hurried back to Max. Gus snapped his fingers and the dog returned to him and sat down, but kept his eyes on Max. Sara still knelt in the water holding Max's head up.

"Yes, he did something," I said. "He just saved our lives. You can get up, Max. Lucky for you *he's* not a killer."

"What's going on?" someone shouted from above. By this time I was past surprise; very cold, with my wet clothes dragging at me, and a strong sensation of sand in my ears. I was still ready to believe in anything, including a group of four people half-running, half-sliding down toward us.

Ronnie Deming got there first. "Is that *Max Kemper?*"

Max slowly and stiffly hauled himself together and got up. He didn't look at Sara, or at any of us. He went over to a damp ledge and sat down and put his head in his hands.

"What was he *doing?*" Bet Deming asked. "It looked so crazy from out there." She pointed toward the open water between Charlie's and Andrew's. "We saw you in the water, I knew that yellow parka of yours, and we thought first this man was trying to save you, and then it looked as if he was trying to drive you overboard."

"Well, he was till Hugo stopped him," I said, and they all looked with solemn respect at the dog, who still watched Max.

"Hugo gets real upset if he sees any rough stuff," said Gus. "Must be something that happened before I got him. And he knows *her.*" He jerked his head toward Sara. "She's always talking to him." Sara sat on the grass and drew up her knees, and put her head down on her folded arms.

"You must be *frozen!*" the other girl exclaimed, and they began pulling off jackets and sweaters. With gratitude I accepted one boy's Irish fisherman sweater, and carried an armful of clothes to Sara. She was completely passive as I stripped off her soaked parka and turtleneck, and stuffed her into another sweater and a C.P.O. shirt. Bet began rubbing her long wet hair with a wool kerchief.

The thunder on the bar was softer now, the seas were flattening and the wind letting go as the tide receded. Gus asserted himself as senior to the rest of us. "Well, this fella's got to be turned in. *You.*" He pointed at Ronnie. "You got the boat for it."

"Yessir!" said Ronnie enthusiastically.

Max had retreated as far as he could without taking his body elsewhere. It was as if he had shut out the sight of us, refused to admit our existence. It was all right with me, I didn't want to admit *his* existence either. Ronnie and the other boy, who must have been the painter of the Checkpoint Charlie sign, went to him and waited politely for him to get up, which he did without a glance at either. He'd brought out his sunglasses from an inside pocket and put them on. He must have been cold, he was wet, smeared with sand and mud and bits of old rockweed, but he ignored all that as he ignored the rest of us.

Watching him and the two boys start up the hill, with the dog and Gus behind them, I wondered if he was sick with shame and remorse or so disappointed and humiliated by his failure that he was sunk in a colossal sulk. I was already beginning to think of him objectively, maybe because I couldn't bear to think of the Max we thought we knew, and whom Sara loved. Or had loved. Whatever was going on in her head right now I didn't even want to imagine, objectively or otherwise.

Bet and the other girl went ahead up the steep track, and Sara and I walked behind them. When we reached the top, the men and the dog were already almost down to the little cove where we'd left Scott's boat, and where Ronnie's group had rowed in. His boat lay a little distance offshore.

Andromeda was coming around Cat. If she'd been a ship of gold with silver sails she could not have been more beautiful to me.

We waited in silence for Barnaby to row ashore, and it seemed perfectly natural that Steven Caine should be with him, bush hat and all. When Barnaby stepped out of the skiff,

I went to meet him and said without expression, "Max tried to kill us. Hugo stopped him."

If his face changed, I didn't know; he moved so quickly and hugged me very hard, his face hidden in my neck and hair for a moment. When he let me go he looked almost the same as usual. He went across to Sara and embraced her, but she didn't respond. He never glanced toward Max, who stood back to us, staring over the Kittens.

Sara and I rode back in *Andromeda*, with Caine, Gus, the dog, and Max, who sat on a bunk in the cuddy with Barnaby's old pea jacket over his shoulders. We took Scott's boat in tow, and Ronnie was to collect Gus's aluminum skiff from the little alder-grown gunkhole at the northwestern tip of Herring, where he'd hauled it up when he'd arrived in the morning to dig clams.

We headed straight up Morgan Bay to the Boones', where the nearest telephone was; also lots of instant hot water, I thought greedily. I was cold, shaky, lightheaded, and had so many places that stung or ached that I couldn't have brooded over the afternoon's events if I'd wanted to.

I didn't know what to do about Sara, either. I kept looking for some break in her impassivity, but it was never there. Barnaby had an arm around me as he steered, and I tried to keep an arm around Sara, but she moved out of reach, out of the shelter of the canopy and went to sit on a lobster crate in the stern. Gus spoke to the dog and pointed, and Hugo went aft and sat down beside the crate. After a little time I saw that she was absently smoothing the dog's head.

Caine stood braced in the cuddy doorway smoking his pipe; he'd had nothing to say from the time he landed on the shore of Herring with Barnaby. He gave me a slight smile and nod once in a while, in an encouraging fatherly way.

"How'd it happen you were still out there at high water, Gus?" Barnaby asked.

"I went beachcombin' after I got my hods full and found me some good new boards and a couple of two-by-fours, way up on the southerly side, near the bar. So I figgered I'd wait till pretty near high water, and then go around and take them off. Well! First thing I knew, it was blowing like a man, and I knew I wasn't goin' nowhere, lumber or not."

He expected the wind would drop when the tide turned, as it often did. He did some more exploring, and then he and the dog took a nap in the sheltered hollow of one of the old cellar holes. "I guess that's where we were when they come ashore and crossed over the Head and went down the other side. There was so much racket for a while, and with the wind blowing away from us Hugo couldn't have heard the voices at first. Then I figger he must have woke up and been wandering around, and picked up their tracks. Well, he's a mighty curious dog, and he must have gone to see what he could see." Pride and affection suffused Gus's voice. I had never been this close to him for so long, and I saw that his narrow eyes in their nests of weather-wrinkles were soft when he spoke of his dog.

"What can we do for Hugo?" Barnaby asked me.

"I'm trying to think. I know he doesn't have much use for a ten-speed bike or anything like that."

Gus grinned. It was the first time I'd ever seen this phenomenon. "Aw, he's happy as he is. He don't want for nothin'."

Kyle had a mooring where he kept his sloop in summer, and Barnaby put *Andromeda* on it. The seas had flattened so much that there was just a light swell off the beach. Gus took Caine and Max and the dog ashore in Scott's big dory, Barnaby rowed Sara and me in his skiff. Ronnie's boat was coming up to anchor.

"You were right," I said to Barnaby, "about that place in New Guinea. The Andrews should have been deserted in that gale of wind, and it turns out that everybody and his brother was out there."

"And his dog."

"Remember my instant karate? Well, in some places it only works when it's backed up by a large unfriendly dog."

Sara was in the bow, and her eyes met mine over Barnaby's

shoulder with a hard, expressionless shine. "We'll be warm in a minute," I said to her but her gaze moved on. Barnaby questioned me silently about her. We knew each other's signals. "I don't know," I said. "I'm shaky because I'm still alive, and also because I don't know what happens next. I don't even know much of what's happened already, to lead up to *now*. What were you doing out there?"

"Well, Caine's been on my mind, and I kept thinking today while I was out hauling that maybe he should answer a few questions. So I came in early—it was starting to breeze up anyway—and there was your note." His mouth quirked. "Fine! I could do without your telling me he had to be blameless because he's an artist. So I cleaned up to go on up to Williston, and I met him at the Neck parking his car. He was on his way to see *me*. He told me he had good reason to believe that—uh—our friend should be given a closer look. And I'm not going into that now."

As the skiff scraped onto the coarse sand in the light frill of surf, Ronnie was dropping anchor out by *Andromeda*. Caine and Gus were walking Max across the Boones' lawn, and Kyle and Deirdre had come out through the sliding glass doors onto the deck to meet them. By the time we reached the house, Max was already out of our sight, taking a hot shower in the guest bathroom, and Kyle was getting dry clothes for him. Deirdre asked no questions, but pointed Sara and me toward the other bathroom. "There's everything in the medicine chest for your cuts," she said efficiently, "and there'll be dry clothes for you in our room. Then some hot tea afterward, or whatever you want."

Sara was perfectly self-reliant, showering, washing her hair, applying first-aid to her scrapes. But her silence was so uncharacteristic it was unnerving, even if my nerves had been in good shape to begin with. I couldn't think of anything to say that wasn't banal, futile, or inane, so I said nothing. When we came out to the kitchen afterwards, Blake was in the living room with the men. Max was secluded in the guest room, and Ronnie's crew were lined up on the railing of the deck outside, supplied with soft drinks and cookies, informally on guard while waiting to give their stories.

Deirdre sat at the table with us while we drank our hot tea. She knew now what had happened, and didn't offer to discuss it. Her only reference was indirect, when Hugo came out to the kitchen and got a drink. "I feel so honored by his presence," she said. "He's like one of these tremendously noble men you can't ever imagine as babies. We're thinking of getting something not quite so awe-inspiring for ourselves."

There was a general stirring of feet and a lifting of voices in the other room. Steven Caine came out and said pleasantly, "Goodbye, I'll see you later." Kyle went to drive him down to the Neck where he'd left his car. Gus passed through the kitchen with a nod to each of us, and he and Hugo went down over the ledges to where Ronnie had brought the aluminum skiff in for him. Barnaby and Blake came to the table and sat down, Barnaby between Sara and me, an arm around each of us.

"He's going to hear your stories now so I can take you home," he said. "All right?" Sara folded her arms on the table and apparently studied the pattern of the cloth.

"Fine," I said. "Shall I start?"

"Please," said Blake. Deirdre got up and disappeared.

I was pleased to be able to give my story without any emotional frills. The whole thing was too immense for any reaction except awe, even when I showed the detective the darkening bruises on my throat and under my ears.

Sara didn't move during the recital. When her turn came, she spoke very quietly; she said her story was the same as mine up to the time we found ourselves in the surf.

"What did you think he was doing with the oar?" Blake asked her.

"He could have been trying to give us something to hold onto."

"You don't believe he was hitting and prodding, as Mrs. Taggart says?"

She returned to her study of the tablecloth. Blake watched

her speculatively. I felt as if she had become a stranger, or even a robot, the real Sara lost sometime during that dreadful camaraderie in the surf when we had tried to save each other.

"Did you see Mrs. Taggart crawl to him and get him by the leg?" Blake asked. She shook her head. "Did you see him put his hands around her throat?"

"I didn't *see* anything or *hear* anything of that!" she snapped. "I was too exhausted, I was just hanging over that timber or whatever it was."

My compassion and discretion went at once, and fast. "My God, Sara, you must have seen him holding me by the throat; you were the one who saw the dog and yelled!"

Her eyes went suddenly hopeless, telling me that *I* was the one trying to drown her now. Then she said sorrowfully, "Yes, I saw him doing it. Yes. And when he was trying to pick me up, he cursed me. Max cursed me. *Max!* When the dog hit, and he fell on top of me, he was cursing me. I'll never stop hearing it, never for the rest of my life. She pushed back her chair and went out the kitchen door.

Blake closed his notebook. "They can go home," he said to Barnaby. "Bring them up tomorrow morning to make and sign formal statements, will you?" As I got up he said, "Mrs. Taggart, he did say to you in so many words that he'd killed Sanderson?"

"I said 'You killed Cory,' and he said 'Yes.' " I put my hands to my throat, remembering.

"All right; thank you. And I'll see you both tomorrow."

I went looking for Deirdre and found her gathering up our damp clothes. "Got a plastic bag for those?" I asked.

"Oh, forget it, I'll put everything through the washer for you. How's Sara?"

"I don't know," I said, "but she came to life a few minutes ago. Maybe that's a good sign. The trouble is, everything will have to get worse before it gets better."

"Except for Lorenzo," Deirdre said. "I'm so happy for him, and I can hardly wait for him to find out he's clear, but oh

Lord!" she said dismally, "that poor child must be going through hell."

"Well, at least she's alive," I offered. "That's an improvement on being dead."

When I went back out through the kitchen, Barnaby and Blake were talking together in confidential tones. "I'll be right along," Barnaby said to me. I waved at him and went out. Around the kitchen door there was a smell of green grass, and Deirdre's daffodils were giving off their late afternoon fragrance. The peepers were already starting the night chorus. Morgan Bay was like liquid light. Black against the glare, *Andromeda* and Ronnie's boat lay hardly moving.

Being alive *was* quite an improvement on being dead. About two hours ago I had been preparing myself to be dead; I had said goodbye to Barnaby. Now he was on the other side of a door from me, and in a few moments we could take hands and go down to the boat and go home. Thanks to the *deus ex machina*, in the form of Hugo, I'd been given my life back again, and in this burnished hour it amounted to a brand new one. I supposed that eventually I'd feel real again and begin to enjoy it.

Sara stood by Barnaby's skiff. She looked so desolately solitary that I didn't wait for the luxury of holding hands with Barnaby, but ran down to her. The kids shouted goodbyes from the deck, and I waved and said I'd get their sweaters and shirts back to them. Behind the glass doors Max sat unseen, waiting to be taken to Limerock and booked.

"Things will be better, Sara," I said, because I had to say something.

"No. Never." Dull and stubborn.

"*Yes*," I insisted, and that was inflammatory. Her head came up.

"Don't tell me I'm only nineteen and I have all my life before me! It's *behind* me. Anything good ended when Cory died. I was responsible for that, and from that moment on Max wasn't falling in love with me, he was only trying to find out what I knew."

"Agreed," I said. "I mean I agree about Max. But you weren't responsible for Cory's death. Whatever Max's reasons were, he was going to accomplish it sooner or later. Maybe we'll never know why he chose that time and that way, but it's not your fault."

I didn't know where all the energy was coming from, but I'd talk as long as she'd give me an opening, and maybe something would take root. "I'll agree with you about Max. But if you're going to give up everything and everybody else because of one—one whatever-he-is—how did I start that sentence?"

"If I'm going to give up everything and everybody—" She was wanly helpful.

"Well, if you do, you're not the person I thought you were. Who's more important to you, the one who betrayed you and tried to kill you, or the rest of us who care about you?"

"Mirabell, stop it!" She began to cry without sound, the tears flowing endlessly down her cheeks, while she mopped them up with her sleeve. I watched sandpipers run along the little scallops of foam while she wept, and decided that now it was all right to be tired, and to look forward to going home with Barnaby.

chapter 31

B arnaby and I didn't touch too obviously, for Sara's sake, but she went upstairs as soon as she got into the house, and we settled in the rocker.

I told him some of the things I'd thought and felt out there with Max, and exorcised them to some extent, though I knew they'd bother me for a long time to come. Sara's devil was worse and there was nothing either of us could do for her except be her friends.

"What about Lorenzo?" I asked. "Who's telling him?"

"Kyle. You know, this afternoon I was just humoring Caine when he said we ought to go find you. I expected to find the three of you innocently beachcoming, and I'd say I'd come to give you a tow home. But when we got there—" His arms clamped harder. "I've got no more words, not even inside my head, because I can't even contemplate losing you."

We stayed together in the rocker in spite of cramped muscles, and kinks in my neck, until the kitchen began to darken. Then he built up the fire and we hungrily discussed supper. "I'll never in my life want another Italian sandwich," I said. "I wonder why I didn't throw it all up out there."

"Because you're too thrifty to waste good food, no matter what's going on." He gave me an affectionate slap as I leaned over to look into the refrigerator. A love tap. Guiltily I went up to Sara, whose love had died before her eyes, and found her asleep on the outside of her bedding. She looked exhausted, almost comatose. I put blankets over her and went back to Barnaby.

My aunt and uncle came while we were still eating our bacon and eggs, and the Boones arrived a little later. Kyle said that Lorenzo would have come, but on these mild nights he didn't like to leave the camp alone for too long at a time.

"How did he act when you told him?" I asked.

"Not surprised. Oh, he never suspected Max, of course, and he was pretty sad about that. Said Max had the makings of a good boat-builder. But he always knew *he'd* be cleared, because he was innocent, and an innocent man has nothing to fear."

"Then what was I scared of this afternoon?" I asked.

Aunt Jess and Uncle Stewart left shortly, telling me they were glad I was still among the living. I said I was glad too. When I saw them off the back doorstep I heard the peepers for the first time this year, and theirs was a song of rebirth if I'd ever heard one.

"You know," Kyle said quietly, "Max must have tried before. He has to be the one shot Pr— the dog."

"Bastard," said Barnaby.

"I wish I could believe that Hugo knew, and was getting in a couple of whacks for Prince," I said. "Well, he did anyway, whether he knew it or not."

Deirdre's eyes filled with tears but she spoke steadily, even with amusement. "The way he used to put up with our mutt's foolishness. Perfect patience, perfect manners."

When they had gone I looked in on Sara again. She slept on, and I went downstairs to my own bed. If I dreamed that night, I didn't remember in the morning. I woke very early to stealthy sounds in the kitchen, which had to be made by Sara since Barnaby and I were more or less entwined. I extricated myself and went out there, pulling on my robe. Sara was pale and heavy-lidded, with delicately violet shadows around her eyes. She had built a fire and was standing by the stove burning her Tarot cards.

We said nothing until she had replaced the stove lid after the last card. Then I asked, "Can you eat something? You haven't had anything since the hot drink at the Boones' yesterday."

"Yes, I'm a little hungry." She sounded surprised. I made hot whole wheat cereal and threw in a couple of handfuls of raisins for extra nourishment. While we were eating by the first light over the sea, I decided that life was going to be tough enough for a while without our having to worry about mentioning Max. At ten o'clock this morning she would be forced to talk about him anyway. So we might as well start now, while Barnaby still slept.

"Do you remember reading the cards for Max," I said, "and saying he could accomplish just about anything he set out to do?"

"Yes." She didn't blink.

"And then you said you'd read the cards for the murderer, and he was going to be ruined, or his project was?"

"Yes. The Tower, I told you about that. I laid the cards out several times for the killer. For Prince's killer first." There was a little wobble in the words, and this time she blinked. "They were always bad, worse than Cory's. But Max's were always *good*. Oh, there was trouble now and then, but nothing deadly. Trouble's normal in every life, isn't it?" She gave me a quick imploring glance.

"Yes, of course it's normal." I agreed eagerly.

"But I took the cards too seriously. I bought them for fun, and then they turned out to be anything but fun. I was beginning to believe them, I was hurrying up to them like a secret drunk to his hidey-hole. So—" She gestured at the stove and said with weak humor, "They made a good hot blaze, didn't they?"

"They got the coffee water off to a great start this morning," I said. "Sara, Max is two people. One's the geologist and boat-builder and the nice guy we all fell for. The other one's got a screw loose. Maybe we'll never know why he hated Cory, but whatever good reason he thinks he had, he was going to kill a couple of innocent people just because one of them *might* have remembered something—"

"And I never did!" she cried in despair. "Even now, knowing it was Max, I can't remember a thing to point to him. . . . But he was such a *perfect* audience," she said with a harsh new inflection, "so I had to go on and on about my impressions and my dreams—talk about a pair of egomaniacs! I just thought of something. Do you think he shot Prince?"

"Yes, we all do."

"And I never sensed a thing! So much for all my delicate perceptions. My God, when I think back—" She shuddered as if with nausea and put her hand to her mouth. Barnaby, coming into the kitchen, said, "Don't think back. It's over."

"It'll never be over, as long as I have to live with my thoughts."

"Oh hell," said Barnaby coarsely. "I don't mean that for you, Sal, I just mean oh *hell* hell."

"Profound, but I get it. I think." She went upstairs.

When we were waiting for our statements to be typed so we could sign them, Blake told us that Max had waived his rights, and had admitted killing Cory and attempting to kill us. He wanted no lawyer and would plead guilty.

On the way back to the car, Barnaby put his arm around Sara. "Take it easy, Sal. I know nothing's much help now, but it takes a hell of a lot to down us Taggarts, believe me."

"My cousin the cockeyed optimist," she said weakly. "But thanks anyway, for not saying you know just how I feel. Because who else could, besides me?"

She looked back at the building. He was in there somewhere. How—at nineteen—was *she* able to hold together? Well, people had survived worse things; it was all a part of the human condition. . . . It would be nice if philosophy could get us through the dreary hours until everything could be sorted away all shipshape and Bristol-fashion.

In the meantime, thank God for "the uncertain glory of an April day." It could very well have been an inglorious wintry one. Sara went off by herself somewhere on the Preserve. Barnaby and I dug up an addition to our vegetable garden. We hardly spoke; our silence together was all we needed. When we were hungry we took our food out onto the back steps, and we were still there, half-drowsy with the sun, when the painter came by the jeep track. Seeing that stocky, energetic figure marching along, bush hat and all, was like taking two giant steps backward to the time before yesterday.

He came straight to us, answered our greeting with a nod, and said curtly, "I've just come from identifying Cory Sanderson, and telling the police all I know. It's time I told you."

We'd gotten immune to surprises. "Be our guest." Barnaby was practically suave.

"Thank you," Caine said with ironic politeness. He sat down on the steps.

"I knew him, not as Cory. I didn't know Max. The first time I ever saw *him* was right here, the other day. But I had the feeling that I'd seen him before, and I went away from here with it eating at me. There was a whole set of associations that I could almost grasp, but not quite. The harder I tried, the more remote my chances seemed, until yesterday morning, when it hit me between the eyes. . . . Funny I should use that simile." He smiled sadly. "Something my wife said. She found a little pitcher in a box of old dishes she'd bought for a couple of dollars. It wasn't a rare or valuable piece, but when she'd washed it and put it on the windowsill, it was very satisfactory in shape and color. 'You know what that lovely dark smoky blue reminds me of?' she said. 'Priscilla's eyes were that color.' "

He has such beautiful dark blue eyes, Sara had said. *A smoky blue.*

Caine took off his hat and scaled it toward the woodpile, and ran his hands through his grizzled hair. "Priscilla Kemper. A quiet, gentle young woman with really splendid eyes. The last time we visited my uncle before his final attack, she was staying there and cataloguing his library. She'd come from somewhere else; my uncle's book dealer in New York had recommended her. She had no family but a brother, and she was tremendously proud of him. He was a geologist for one of the big oil companies, but some day soon he was going to quit, and perhaps teach, and then she would go to keep house for him . . . She wasn't a kid. Thirtyish, I'd say."

He lapsed into silence, turning his pipe over in his fingers as if he'd never seen it before. Somebody had to say the obvious, but Barnaby never does, on principle. So I did.

"Max told Sara he had a sister, but nothing more about his family except that they used to go to North Haven in the summers. What's his connection with Cory?"

Still studying the pipe, he said, "Priscilla was the connection. Cory's real name was Crispin Saunders, and he worked for my uncle too, in a little Pennsylvania town called Tenby. Uncle Steve died last October of a stroke, and Crispin disappeared after the funeral and the reading of the will. When I say he disappeared, I mean he packed up, said goodbye to us, and went away without mentioning his plans. But he'd never been talkative anyway. I supposed he'd get in touch when the year of probate was over, because he was in the will. As executor, I was staying there in the house to attend to the personal things before the place was turned over to the town as a library and a museum. Priscilla stayed on to finish the catalogue. My wife told me she'd caught the girl crying several times, but we thought it was because of my uncle's death; he'd been very good to her in his way, and she seemed very lonely, with her brother over in the Persian Gulf or some such faraway spot. We told her she needn't hurry the job, she could stay on and be helpful in other ways, and I'd pay her. But one day she simply said she had to leave, the catalogue was finished. I couldn't make her change her mind any more than my wife had been able to."

He gave up examining the pipe and decided to fill it. "We finished our work and went back to Boston. A few weeks later my uncle's lawyer sent me an item from the local paper, carried from a Connecticut paper because some people in Tenby had gotten to know Priscilla when she worked for my uncle."

By the pricking of my thumbs, something wicked this way comes.

"It was an account of a suicide by barbiturates—too sadly routine these days—and the victim was Priscilla Kemper."

Wicked, all right. I tried to get my hand unobtrusively into Barnaby's. "He knew we had liked her, that's why he sent it. The item said the brother had been called home from Saudi Arabia. Well, we were shocked and saddened, we wished she had confided in us, but she was past help now, so that was the end of it. Until I saw those eyes again in Kemper's face."

"Poor Max," I said instinctively, forgetting what poor Max had attempted yesterday. Right now he was the brother getting news of his sister's death, and that death a suicide.

"She never referred to him as Max, it was always 'My younger brother'—very proudly. And Kemper's not an uncommon name, so if I'd heard it before I saw him, it wouldn't have meant anything to me in this strange place."

"Quite a coincidence," said Barnaby. "You and Cory and Max all turning up at the same time in this strange place."

"Wasn't it?" Caine agreed amiably. "I wonder how Max traced him. Not that it matters now. I did it, so he could do it."

"It just dawned on me," I said. "Max must have recognized *your* name when you were introduced. It's the same as your uncle's, so even if she never mentioned you in her letters, the name should have rung a bell."

"I thought of that too. But he'd have felt safe, I suppose, since we'd never met. . . . I wasn't positive that he was dangerous, I wasn't positive that he'd killed Crispin. But his sister and Crispin had worked and lived in the same house, and the weeping didn't begin until after Crispin moved out. So perhaps it wasn't just my uncle she cried about. . . . I began wondering yesterday morning if she'd left a note for her brother, telling him why she killed herself. Maybe he had as much reason for hating Crispin as Lorenzo did. It was worth asking him some questions. And I did know young Sara was with Crispin when he disappeared. It made me uneasy."

"Would you mind telling me something else?" Barnaby asked. "You've known all along who Cory was. Why didn't you say so to the police when his body was found?"

"Well, take a good hard look at it. The man's a complete

stranger, dropped here from God knows where. Then he turns up murdered, and I show up to identify him, apparently the only person in the world who knew him. What would *you* do?" he challenged Barnaby.

Barnaby meditated. "I'd wait," I said at once. "Just to see."

He nodded vehemently. "To see if something surfaces. Exactly! No, I didn't like leaving him there, uncalled for, deserted. But I was pretty sure the dog's death had some connection with his. And I was going out of my mind and driving my wife out of hers trying to figure it out. We knew he must have made an enemy of someone, but I'd swear the only one I could think of is straight; he might sue, but not murder. And *then*," he said softly with a beatific smile, "I saw Priscilla Kemper's dark blue eyes in a stranger's face. If I'd recognized them at once, I could have saved you girls a little trouble."

"But they mightn't have got a confession from him so easily," I pointed out, brave after the event. "So maybe it was meant to be this way, with Hugo and then the kids popping up on cue."

Barnaby was still silent, and inscrutable, and Caine said, "Blake had exactly the same expression when I talked to him this morning."

"You do have a wife, don't you, Mr. Caine?" I asked. "A real flesh and blood wife?"

"She's visiting the museum in Limerock right now." He looked at his watch. "There's a display of Leeds and Mocha pottery."

"Well, Barnaby said once that you could have invented her out of a few words. And after hearing a few of your words, I think you could have."

He laughed. "I deserved that! She tells me I'm devious, too, but I honestly believed this was the right thing to do. I'd never have let them arrest Lorenzo without hearing my story, believe me! And something did surface, didn't it? . . . I'm dry as a cork leg."

"Come on in," said Barnaby. "What'll it be?"

They went into the house and I walked around the yard stretching my legs, and my brain too by the feel of it. Big slaty clouds moved steadily from the northwest, filling the sky and blocking out the sunny blue. A few snowflakes wouldn't have been a surprise. I wondered where Sara was; the unknown girl's suicide had disturbed me deeply.

Barnaby called me from the back door. "There's more to the story. Come on."

"I'm worried about Sara," I called back.

"Oh, she's all right. She may be with Jess and Stewart now."

The men had Scotch, but in times of stress I revert to childhood (I admit it) and get at least physical comfort from something hot and sweet. So I fixed my instant hot chocolate.

Before Steven Caine was through talking we knew Crispin Saunders as we'd never known Cory. When he graduated from high school in the small Pennsylvania town of Tenby, he had gone to work full time for Caine's uncle as a chauffeur and gardener, after having had summer jobs at the Caine place all through high school. His family consisted of his stepmother and her relatives in the village, and once he left them he never went near them again.

"The privacy and a room that was absolutely his own must have been precious to him," the painter said. "He was a quiet boy, very self-contained, almost frighteningly efficient when you consider the average eighteen-year-old. I used to try to talk to him, to find out what he wanted out of life, if he had aspirations toward some high goal, but I never found out. Our kids were small then, and he'd put up swings for them, things like that, and they'd chatter on and on as if they never noticed his silence, but he didn't even unbend with children, you see ... My uncle was a widower, gruff sometimes, but good and kind, and there was a warm atmosphere in the house, nothing to stifle a boy. But my uncle once said that from what he knew of the relatives who had provided a home of sorts for Crispin, they were enough to turn a saint into a sociopath."

He liked to read, and Mr. Caine's library was open to him. He went often to the movies too. Alone. He was an excellent driver and mechanic, and when he began working in the house he was as good at that as at handling cars. "Except that he never laughed at my jokes," Steven Caine said. He smiled as if at a memory and then a look almost of pain crossed his rugged face and he said, "Who'd ever have believed it would all end like this?"

Crispin (never called Cris) began to travel on his vacations. If asked directly, he would tell where he had been, but he never volunteered any information, never sent postcards to the other help. He always had a car of his own and as his pay increased, the cars got more expensive.

"It was reassuring to see that something like that appealed to him. It made him seem more human. He liked clothes too. ... The others used to kid him about his secret life, about having mistresses stashed all over the place. He just didn't hear, or seem to. We had a lot of family jokes about Crispin —not where he could hear them, of course. At the same time we knew how absolutely my uncle depended upon him and we were glad that Crispin was satisfied to center his whole life right there; we came to believe that in his own way he was devoted to my uncle."

Mr. Caine was a collector, not of one thing, but of anything that appealed to him, and the acquiring of a new treasure he loved almost as much as the object itself.

He'd had a secretary, a middle-aged woman who had to retire because of her health, so he put Crispin into the job. Crispin might have still mixed the drinks, but the cook's niece came to be trained to answer the door and wait on table, and Crispin took his meals with Mr. Caine, except when the younger Caines came; and it was his own idea to eat alone then. When Crispin was in his mid-twenties, Uncle Steve discovered Renaissance art, and took Crispin to Italy with him, to drive him around, and to be an audience. "You know, I think they talked when they were alone," the painter said, "but I never did know what about. The collection business, certainly. But by the time Crispin had been in the household for ten years or so he must have felt some affection for my uncle if he felt it for no one else. I used to ask, 'Does he like girls? Does he have political opinions?' and Uncle Steve would just laugh and say, 'Crispin's a good boy, none better. I don't ask for a conversationalist, I can do all the talking.' "

The Italian trip was the first of many journeys, but it was the most important, because it was on that journey that Mr. Caine discovered and bought the Leonardo letter.

"You may know that Leonardo's notebooks and papers were eventually scattered far and wide, and God alone knows how much was destroyed. Still, some of the things fell into good hands and have been rediscovered over the years. Mostly his notebooks and journals. But no letters, except a copy of one he wrote to Ludovico Sforza asking for a job in Milan and detailing his qualifications, and there's one written to some cardinal."

He stopped to take a drink. "A Leonardo letter would be worth a fortune, and Uncle Steve found one. It was in some village where he'd gone to look at a Raphael in a chapel. The man who sold it to him swore his family had had it for several hundred years. Uncle Steve felt in his bones—he had a lot of faith in those bones of his—that it was the real thing, and he brought it home fitted into a picture frame under the photograph of his wife, which he took everywhere with him."

The letter was written from Florence to a friend with whom Leonardo had shared a studio in Milan, Ambroglio de Predis. His notebooks were coded with mirror writing and symbols, but the language of the letter was straightforward and full of bad political news about Florence, some nasty remarks about the young Michelangelo, and worries about his future. It tied in perfectly with everything that was known about Leonardo in that period of his life. It was priceless.

"Cory had at least one big handsome book about Leonardo da Vinci," I said, "and it was full of markers. I was dying to get a look into it, but I never had the chance. He must have known quite a bit about Leonardo, with your uncle's training."

"Superficially, yes, but Uncle Steve was no expert. I told you he collected things that attracted him, rare books, carvings, antique jewelry, but he never went very deeply into anything. Anyway, he came late to Renaissance art, which sent him to Italy. He was offered the letter, took it, and came home triumphant, and—" He lifted his hands and dropped them heavily on his knees.

"If it was a fake, I can't stand it," I said. "Tell me I'm wrong."

His smile was regretful. "You're right. If he'd insisted on having it studied by experts in Italy, he'd have been saved a good deal of money and pride. But he was sure it was genuine —going by his bones—and in that case the Italian government would have confiscated it. But when he took it to a quiet and select gathering in New York to unveil it, he found out he'd been had. It was really a magnificent fake, but the man who proved it had run into the work of the same faker before. He was as good as the man who did the Vermeers, remember?"

Steven Caine didn't know anything about this at the time. His uncle told him much later, after his first stroke. "We were alone one afternoon and that's when I heard for the first time that the letter existed, and that it was a fake. Even Crispin didn't know about the fakery. He'd been sick with a strep throat and hadn't gone to the meeting, and when Uncle Steve brought the letter back he told Crispin he was going to keep it for his lifetime, meanwhile deciding where it should go when he died. And he locked it up in his safe. His pride was saved by the fact that he had never bragged to anyone about this treasure, and the men who'd seen it weren't the type to publicize his humiliating mistake. He blamed his material loss on his own dishonesty, and said Kipling was right about the Gods of the Copybook Headings." He laughed. "Quite a man, Uncle Steve. . . . He'd gone rather rapidly from Renaissance art to early American folk art, and at last I knew why."

chapter 32

*B*ut someone on the outside did hear about the letter. It could only have been through some contact in Italy, probably village gossip in a letter to a relative in the United States. The Leonardo document and its sale, bringing riches, would have been an open secret in any small town. About a month after Mr. Caine brought the letter home from the examination in New York and locked it away, he was visited by a stranger who made him a very good offer.

The stranger was a mannerly young man who represented his grandfather, a very successful building contractor. Of Italian parentage, of course.

"And with no Mafia connections," Caine warned, as if one of us had made some involuntary move. "He's thoroughly respectable, a good citizen who loves his country, like most Italian-Americans. He worked his way from the bottom to the top and he deserves everything he's got. Well, his people emigrated from Vinci, Leonardo's hometown, and it's been a family tradition for generations that they were descended from the daughter of one of Leonardo's legitimate brothers. It's been the family glory. He's practically Uncle Leonardo to the old man, and the youngster was a little impressed too, though he tried not to show it."

Mr. Caine refused the offer. He couldn't bring himself to admit that the letter was a forgery and he simply told the boy he couldn't part with the letter while he lived, but that his heir could do as he pleased with it. Crispin was at this meeting, and later he took and recorded a call from old Gioia himself, almost pleading, and raising the price. So Crispin knew how much his employer had paid for the letter, and how much more he was being offered.

"But he wasn't home when Uncle Steve told me the true story, and said he was leaving the letter to me. I could destroy it, keep it, or sell it to someone who collected such artistic forgeries. I asked him why he hadn't destroyed it himself, and he said he'd saved it as a hair shirt; just the knowledge of its existence kept him from getting above himself." Caine drummed his fingers on the table and watched them with tired eyes. "Ah well, I suppose we all have our fatal vanities," he said. "We don't know they're fatal until the blow falls, or we never know it at all, we merely leave a wake of catastrophe. Uncle Steve's little vanity seemed harmless enough; he couldn't stand having anyone know he'd been taken."

"Like all of us," suggested Barnaby. Caine lifted his head, but his fingers went on drumming out a Dead March.

"My uncle told me the truth only because he didn't want me to think I'd inherited something priceless. The final stroke came in October. Crispin was a great help, and he had kept Uncle Steve's papers and records in immaculate order. A week after the funeral he went quietly away, and about a week after that I found out he'd taken the Leonardo letter."

It was like reading a story of unbearable suspense while you are alone in the house at night, only worse, because Cory–Crispin had actually lived and now he was dead. He moved before my eyes in a silent movie, he spoke to us without sound in the hallway of the Darby house; he talked with Sara; without audible words he was enraged, frustrated or terrified. He embraced Sara on a dark beach under the northern lights, and all the motion was that of phantoms against the image of a dead and sheeted figure on a mortuary slab.

I heard Barnaby saying something about the police. "No," Caine said, "and I told the lawyer that my uncle had already given me the Leonardo letter. That accounted for its not being in the safe with the other things he wanted to go through."

"Listen," I said, wanting to get involved in something healthily crass like money and thus escape that gruesome silent movie. "Wouldn't that letter be worth a fantastic inheritance tax, if it's supposed to be genuine?"

"My uncle had taken care of that; he'd given me the written report on the letter, and that's now been verified and accepted. If Crispin had waited awhile—Poor stupid Crispin." His heavy shoulders slumped forward. He said despondently, "This whole thing has made me feel like an old man, and I resent that like hell."

"Do you think he had the theft planned for a long time?" Barnaby asked.

"No doubt of that. But I didn't have any hard evidence to give the police. He'd said he needed some rest, and I told him to go ahead, he deserved it. That is all I knew for a black-and-white *fact*. I knew he'd taken the letter but I couldn't prove it, and besides, at that point I knew the letter was a fake even if nobody else did. I was also positive he'd gone looking for the Gioias, so my first thought was to warn the old man not to buy the letter." He slammed the flat of his hand down on the table and the glasses jumped. "But good God, do you think I could *find* him? I thought it would be simple. Just go to his offices in Newark. Well, he and his wife and the boy were driving through Italy. Informally, no set itinerary. Being out of reach was part of the joy of it. They called home at intervals, and my number would be given them when the next contact was made. In the meantime, my wife pointed out, Crispin couldn't very well sell him the letter while he was out of the country and incommunicado."

So Caine had concentrated on trying to catch up with Crispin. "I had plenty to say to him. As far as he knew, the letter was genuine, and worth a half million or more, and he'd stolen it almost the instant my uncle was in the ground, the man who had given Crispin the sort of life that he could never have achieved for himself, with his hang-ups, and who had left him independent. I'd never have believed Crispin would steal. I'd always seen him as rigidly incorruptible."

"He was rigid about everything," I said. "Look how he

insisted on his so-called rights around here to the point where he looked ridiculous. Maybe over the years he'd brooded about other rights; maybe he believed he'd given *his* life to your uncle, instead of your uncle giving *him* a life. Maybe he resented your uncle's paying an enormous price for something he wanted and then simply giving it away to a museum. Or to you."

His rugged face was impassive and I thought I'd gone too far. "You'll have to excuse my wife," said Barnaby dryly. "She's a frustrated psychoanalyst."

"But she could be right. You can't tell what goes on in the heads of these people who keep themselves to themselves. It's not true that no man's an island. Crispin was one."

"But look at all the lives he's touched and left indelibly marked," I argued. "And destroyed, including himself. He may have wanted to be an island, but he couldn't be."

He smiled, which took away some of the winter from his face. "This reminds me of arguing with my daughters. That's why I can give in so gracefully, I've had a lot of experience. And I never stay mad for very long, so I stopped wanting Crispin's scalp, but I did want to keep him from cheating the old man, however innocently. I wasn't getting any news from the Gioia office, and I figured that my note had been lost or I'd been brushed off as some sort of crank. And when I finally caught up with Crispin, it was too late. The deed was done. He'd certainly sold the letter to someone, if not to the Gioias."

Barnaby got up and put more wood on the fire; he always has to get into motion when he's disturbed and can't think of anything to say. Steven Caine filled his pipe again. I looked out for a sign of Sara but saw nothing human under the rolling clouds.

"How did you trace him here?" Barnaby asked.

"Through a lucky hunch. Do you remember a magazine article about the most crime-free towns in the United States? We were talking about it at Tenby last summer, at the time of Uncle Steve's first stroke, and Priscilla told us she knew

Fremont well from her early summers in Maine. She'd been in Maine last June, and had stayed in Fremont because there was no place for her to stay on North Haven. She said it still had the same atmosphere she remembered, and she went on about all the quiet, uncluttered space still available in the vicinity, and Crispin actually asked her some questions about it."

"Seth told us Cory mentioned that article," I reminded Barnaby.

"Well, it's only two hundred miles from Boston, so after my wife and I got over the flu that kept us occupied most of this winter we went to Fremont. We spent a week there, my wife looking for dishes while I roamed around making inquiries, trying to behave as if I were looking for an old friend I thought had settled in the area. I thought he might be holed up in a motel or an apartment somewhere. But—*nothing*. We were about to give up when my wife, who reads all the fine print on everything, discovered that the Limerock *Patriot* prints realty transfers, and she found Cory Sanderson. Resemblance in the initials, and supposition again, but I found out where Applecross was, and we moved to the Williston Inn. One day I saw him across the street, coming out of the post office."

I was pleased to see that Barnaby was as tense as I was. Neither of us spoke.

"I called to him and started to cross the street, but two trailer trucks came through between us, and when they'd passed he was gone. After that I tried to call his house, but his number was unlisted. I wrote to him in care of both the Williston and Applecross post offices, saying I wanted to talk with him, but he never answered. I went to the house, but either he wasn't home or he saw me coming, because nobody answered the door."

"So it was you he was afraid of," Barnaby said. "At least, you were one of the things."

"Yes, and I soon got fed up with that game. Finally I wrote him a note saying I wasn't going to make waves about the letter, I wasn't making any more attempts to get in touch, and that was a promise. I'd leave it for him to make contact when the year of probate was up, so he could begin receiving his income."

"But didn't you want the pleasure of telling him the letter was a fake?" I asked incredulously.

"I told you I can't stay mad very long. Crispin's theft didn't wipe out the fact that he'd been dependable and loyal for over twenty years. As for his selling the letter, I was never going to be able to find out from him where he'd sold it—maybe it wasn't to the Gioia family at all. And if it *was* the Gioias, maybe the old man wouldn't want to know it was a forgery."

"And if he did find out," I said, "he might be enough like your uncle not to want it known."

His smile was more of a grimace, as if he'd bitten into a sour fruit. "There are innumerable ways to salve one's conscience, aren't there? I was concerned about the deception, but I was even more concerned about Crispin. Believe it or not, he'd become quite a burden on my conscience. So I tried to shrug that off my back by promising him I wouldn't harass him. And I concentrated on painting Cape Silver."

We were quiet, Caine hunched forward in his chair, smoking his pipe; Barnaby standing with one foot propped on the stove hearth, gazing out the window; myself with my chin in my hands, sickly enthralled by what I was hearing, yet longing to free myself and run outdoors to the chilly sanity of the wind rushing across salt water and matted fields.

"Cory was scared by the shooting," Barnaby said finally. "But he must have known it wasn't you. I wonder if it ever occurred to him to worry about the girl's brother."

"I'm sure it never did," I said. "Sara says first he thought it was someone planning armed robbery, and the dog got in the way, but she convinced him it was poachers, even if they weren't ours." Barnaby was giving me that long patient stare which makes me want to hit him. "Well, it could have been somebody from across the bay or across the river, or even from Limerock or Williston, couldn't it?" I demanded. "There aren't enough police to search the whole county house by house, barn by barn, car by car—"

"All right. All right!" Barnaby threw up his hands. "Go on, Mirabell," Caine encouraged me.

"Well, she told him that our local delinquents don't go in for homicide. Yet. Then, if you'd written that you weren't going to plague him any more, and he thought you'd gone back to Boston, he began moving around a bit. The road trouble came up, and he really pushed with that, so he must have felt pretty secure. And if he didn't have Priscilla on his conscience," I said pointedly, "why should you have *him* on yours?"

He held up one finger. "Item: He may not have known that Priscilla killed herself, and walking out on a woman who loved him probably didn't call for remorse in that odd brain of his." A second finger. "Item: If Uncle Steve had taken him into his confidence about the letter, or if I had when Uncle Steve died, Crispin wouldn't have committed theft. He might be alive now instead of waiting to be shoveled into the ground and forgotten."

If he was brutal, it was because he needed to be, and we understood. "But the theft had nothing to do with his death," I said.

"How do we know? Without it, he mightn't have left Priscilla as he did. She'd have had more time to get to him. But my uncle and I, by what we considered a harmless indulgence in a harmless foible, put an irresistible temptation in his way. It's true that the cruellest lies are often told in silence. We deceived him without saying a word." His voice plodded on. "Crispin seized what he thought he had a right to, and he had to run with it, and Priscilla died. So indirectly my uncle and I could be responsible for her death too."

He got up very stiffly; it was the first time I'd seen him move like an elderly man. "I'm bushed. It hasn't been easy, going back over the years with Crispin."

Barnaby cleared his throat. "We appreciate hearing the story," he said with awkward concern, "and we'll keep it to ourselves."

He made a gesture of either indifference or dismissal. "It doesn't matter. The Boones and young Sara may want to know. I'm going back to Williston and my wife, and give in to feeling my years for once. Tomorrow I must bury Crispin."

Barnaby drove him to the mailboxes, and I walked out on the white prow of Cape Silver and watched the graybacked combers thundering in. Sara was coming along the shore from the east, taking the hard way, climbing rocks when she could have gone around them. I backed away from the cliff before she could look up and see me against the broken sky. When she reached the house I was busily washing and drying glasses.

"Hi," I said without looking around. "There's plenty of boiling water if you want a hot drink."

"Thanks." The bottle was still on the table. "Been having a little drunk while I was gone?"

"No, but if I could find a really attractive little drunk, who knows?"

She managed an imitation snicker, and then I looked openly at her. She looked defiantly back. "It's all right. I'm not going to fall apart. I've got all my bits and pieces fastened together with Elmer's Glue and a lot of prayer."

But I thought the repair job was too new and too fragile to stand approving comment. "Steven Caine was here. He told us about Cory because he knew him, and—"

"*Max?*"

I could almost hear the rest of it. *There, I said his name.* "About everything. Do you want to hear it now?" I hoped not; I was too wrung out to do it justice.

"I'll tell you when I want to hear it. Give me some time for the glue to harden." She dropped a teabag in a cup and poured boiling water on it. "Can I go in and play Calum Kennedy? The island songs?"

"I would love that," I said from my heart.

chapter 33

Since there was no family plot back in Tenby to receive Cory, and the Caines had no more ties with the place, Steven buried him in Limerock, on Good Friday. There was no funeral, just a simple committal service at the grave. Stewart and Jess, the Boones, Sara, and Barnaby and I went. Lorenzo had been around to see us, and said he had half a mind to go because he felt so sorry for the poor cuss now that he was gone, but his funeral-going suit was full of moth holes. So he stayed home and painted his dory instead. It was that kind of fine afternoon.

I kept half-expecting Garfield to show up at the cemetery with Raymie (or even Madam President, if she could manage it), hoping to be the star turn, but the word had been kept well.

Mrs. Caine was a stoutish woman with the pale fine skin that sunburns easily, which explained why she didn't spend too much time out in the sun and wind while Steven painted. She had nice eyes behind glasses, a pleasant voice. "I was always sorry for Crispin," she said. "It wasn't easy, because he was so odd. And his death was as lonely as his life was."

"But he didn't need to be all that lonely, did he?" I asked, thinking of our proffered hands, and of the girl who must have offered so much more.

"He didn't know how *not* to be the way he was, so he threw away his best chances for salvation," she said. She must have been remembering the girl, too.

There was a spray of spring flowers from the Caines on the casket. The rest of us had talked about flowers and decided against it as hypocritical, but we sent a joint gift to the

Easter Seal Fund. Once more in spite of himself he had inspired a positive reaction.

Steven read the thirty-ninth psalm. I didn't know it—most of us know only the few psalms we had to memorize in Sunday School—and the very strangeness of it, spoken in these surroundings at such a time, made the words almost unbearably moving, and gave Cory at last the dignity of true tragedy.

" 'Hear my prayer, O Lord,' " Stephen read, " 'and give ear unto my cry; hold not thy peace at my tears; for I am a stranger unto thee, and a sojourner, as all my fathers were. O spare me, that I may recover strength, before I go hence, and be no more.' "

It was finished. Beside me Sara drew a quick shaky breath.

We walked away from the grave without looking back, and clustered around our cars with a renewed sense of life, or perhaps it was an eagerness to hurry back into our routines so as not to think of the short and wretched life of Crispin Saunders.

We all agreed to meet at the Boones for supper on Easter night, and weren't expecting to see Caine again until then, but he stopped at the house just before noon the next day. He had his painting gear, including his easel this time, and he looked rested, and younger.

"I went around to see Max Kemper after the services yesterday," he said. Sara, making bread, turned immobile. "He was pretty remote until I explained my connection with the case and told him I had known his sister for a short time. That brought him to life. Even killing Crispin hasn't spilled his rage and hatred. But he asked me to deliver a message to you both." He glanced at Sara's stiff back. "He wants to talk to you."

"When?" I asked.

"This afternoon, if you can make it."

"Thanks for telling us," I said. I walked out to the yard with him, we talked a few minutes about painting, and when I went back into the house Sara was kneading dough again. Her face was cold. "What's this about a sister?"

"She committed suicide last fall, and Max evidently tracked Cory down to avenge her."

"Oh." A flat, dead sound. Silence except for thumps on the breadboard. Then with a slow, subtle, returning tint of life she said, "You mean Cory actually had something to do with a girl, and she cared enough so that she— Then that was it! *That's* what was haunting him!" She swung around, her floury hands flung open and imploring. "Can't you understand him now? Locked up in all that guilt as if he'd walled himself into a tomb?"

I didn't point out, as Caine had, that Cory might not have known Priscilla was dead. Because we weren't sure. He could have seen the same newspaper item the Caines had seen, instead of hearing the news from Max in the last few moments of his life. Perhaps he was no stranger to remorse, and Sara's simile was too gruesomely apt.

She returned to the breadboard and began kneading again. "I don't ever want to see *him* again. If he wants forgiveness, I don't care. I don't think I could give it, anyway. I'm sorry about his sister, but I loved him and it was real, it went deep, it was in my bones. It wasn't just a kid thing with me, and he knew it, and he *used* it." She was trying not to choke over the words. "Whatever Cory did that meant the girl died, Max is just as bad because he would have killed *me*. And you too, because you happened to be there. How can you even *think* of seeing him now?"

"Maybe it'll help to cancel out that day, or blur it a little." I had been decided from the first, and Barnaby had gone to haul so he couldn't stop me. "But I don't want to leave you alone."

"Don't worry, I'm not going to jump off the cliff. But I don't want to bother with people, even the nicest ones. They're all being so sorry for me, as if I were the Little Match Girl."

"And there are times when sympathy is just unbearable," I said. "I know."

"I'll borrow the Aussies for the afternoon and we'll go visit all the places in the woods that have been under snow for months."

"Hey, maybe you'll find the Easter Bunny! I want all the pink eggs."

She obliged with a faint groan and a weak grin. I dressed for town, making a few silent quips about What to Wear When Visiting the County Jail. We walked to Shallows together, and she had disappeared with the dogs before I could get the car out and turned around.

It was like going to the dentist, only much worse. But the fact wasn't as bad as the anticipation. I didn't have to see him in a cell, but waited in a clean, small room with a table and chairs, and when he came in, the nauseating dread went at once. There was nothing to be afraid of now; that afternoon had gone forever, and there was no sense or health in forever thinking, *What if*—?

He was gaunt, he had dropped pounds in a few days, but he looked fresh and clean in chino slacks and shirt, and the smile was the same. I was embarrassingly conscious of his eyes, after all the talk about their color, and wished he'd worn the tinted glasses.

"Thank you for coming, Mirabell," he said, sitting down opposite me. "It was too much to expect Sara."

"She loved you," I said. "There were no reservations on her side. As far as she knew, it was for life. But no matter what you felt for her before Cory's death, afterward all you wanted was to know whether or not she could incriminate you."

"I attacked him when I did *because* of Sara! I took Lorenzo's dory and rowed around there that night to get him somehow, but I never intended to involve her! Finding them outdoors like that was totally unexpected. And when I saw him take her into his arms, I exploded. To see him touch her like that—after what he did to my sister—can you understand that, Mirabell? *Can* you?"

"Tell me what he did to your sister, Max."

"She tried to be his friend, and then she fell for him. God knows why. She used to write to me about him. She was thirty-two, and shy, and she thought they were a lot alike. But to me he sounded like a cold, bloodless stick of a man. Well, he got her pregnant, and that meant sheer joy to her, but not to him. He wanted her to get an abortion, which to her was unthinkable. While she was hoping he'd change his mind, and see a wife and child of his own as the end of his loneliness—those are the words she wrote in the letter she left me—he disappeared. She waited about a month to hear from him, and then she killed herself."

"It's a terrible story," I said. "For both you and your sister. Maybe if she hadn't been living alone, she wouldn't have killed herself."

"Are you blaming me because I wasn't there?" he asked savagely.

"No, I'm blaming you for trying to dispose of Sara as heartlessly as Cory disposed of your sister. You couldn't stand to see Cory touch Sara, but you planned to kill her in cold blood. Does that make you any better than Cory?"

"Mirabell, you don't understand," he said patiently. "I have wit and intelligence and a profession I'm very good at. I have much more to offer life, and I have the capacity to take much more *from* life, than the ordinary person. I'm far more important to me than either of you two were. Or Lorenzo. I didn't mean to leave anything in his dory, but I didn't intend to rush up to confess, either. Can't you see, Mirabell," he asked with that lop-sided smile, "why I had to get rid of Sara if I could? I was sorry, but I couldn't take any chances. Priscilla was gone, there was nobody I had to think or worry about except myself. I had all my life and all the world—as long as Sara wasn't around to remember anything."

It was said with such a confiding warmth. I listened in a kind of trance; I'd expected remorse, maybe a plea for forgiveness, never this.

I stood up. "What did you want to see us about, Max? Just to explain?"

"You do see, don't you, Mirabell?" He was horribly, winningly earnest. "I was going back to Saudi Arabia. I love it out there. Priscilla always wanted to go with me to those places, she argued that other men took their families along, but I couldn't see it. She'd never have fitted in. I sent her plenty of money, and she had her work."

"I see," I said, walking toward the door. "I do understand you, Max."

"Thanks, Mirabell." He sounded actually grateful. "See if you can't make Sara understand. Oh, there was one thing more. The reason I killed Crispin the way I did. I hadn't planned anything so elaborate or so dramatic. I was simply going to get rid of him, with no frills. Oh, I'd tell him *why*, first, and then let him have it. But the dog queered that." He fell into an introspective hush, staring at the foot propped on his knee, jiggling it. "I'm sorry about that poor fool of a dog. I was sorry the minute I did it, in fact. When he started barking, I should have just taken off, the way I did anyway."

Then he looked up with that bright, mocking, one-sided smile. "But it worked out better because of the delay. You might call it poetic justice. You know, when he walked out on my sister because she wouldn't murder their child, he said she could sink or swim. So that's what I said to him." He slapped his ankle and laughed. " 'Sink or swim, you bastard!' I said to him, and I rowed away and left him in the dark."

I couldn't look at him. I kept my head turned away, trying not to swallow, trying not to be sick, trying not to get up and run.

He jumped to his feet and strode exuberantly around the room. "When I tumbled him over the side I reminded him of what he'd said to her. I untied his wrists so he could get a few strokes in, just to make the agony last a couple of minutes longer, and he tried to hold onto the gunnel but I rapped his knuckles. *Mirabell, are you listening?*" He stopped in front of me. "Don't you think that was an appalling piece of sadism, to say that to her?"

"Yes, I do," I said. I forced my eyes, to meet the proud, triumphant sparkle in his. "Especially when you'd already left her to sink or swim, so she had nobody to turn to, and she tried to make a life for herself with someone like Cory." He was still ablaze as he listened but I thought the exultation was beginning to die down a bit. "Is that why you were so fierce to kill Cory? So maybe you'd feel a little less guilty about her?"

"*Guilty?*" He looked stunned. "About *Priscilla?*" He was repeating it in wounded astonishment when I went out and shut the door on him.

The Winchester rifle and the silencer were found in his house. But we never did find out who painted the rock and burned the fiery cross. Usually there'll be a time of laughter and bragging over cans of beer, and the truth comes out as the tales of pranks grow wilder and richer. But the facts of Cory's death were too sobering. There's a certain rough code of honor that doesn't find much fun in recalling practical jokes played on a man who was under a death sentence at the time.

Ruel began coming to the house again, patiently waiting, leaving, and returning again within a few days. One day Sara gave in and went with him; he didn't take her back to explore the Andrews, as he'd once promised, but eastward to visit some other islands. It was one May morning when the sea was so flat, he said that you could roll a marble from here to Spain. They were gone all day.

After that she began borrowing the car and going to Lime-rock to hunt for a job. She came home one day looking like the before-Max Sara; she had applied for a position as an aide in the new school for emotionally disturbed children, which was opening up in one of the old mansions overlooking Penobscot Bay.

"Of course I'll have to take all kinds of tests to see how fit I am, but I'm sure I'll pass. I'll be living in, so will it be all right if I come here for my time off? I think I'm going to need Cape Silver ... you and Barnaby too, of course," she added hastily.

"That's all right. We're used to second billing," I said.

"Garfield Willy was in the store." She began getting herself something to eat. "With Madam Prezz. She's still furious because Ronnie was taking a bunch out to look for the fort that day." She gave a good imitation of a vocally indignant horse. " 'And they aren't even *members*!' "

We laughed. We hooted. We actually did.

"Now they've changed their plans," Sara said. "Garfield's suddenly remembered Old Squarr Eusebius talking once about the Darby place, so they think that maybe below *that* cellar hole there's something else, and—"

"Over Lorenzo's dead body," I said, and we both laughed again, the way we used to.

The Darby place went to the state, and it isn't yet for sale. Lorenzo is officially in charge. He considered moving his trunk up to the carriage house and bunking comfortably in one of the box stalls, but he has his garden and his birds and raccoons back at his cabin, besides a sheltered anchorage for his dory. He is at the Darby place several hours every day working on the sloop, *Jemima C.* Max gave him the hull and the lumber, and Lorenzo had it trucked down the road and set up in the carriage house. He has been having a good number of inquiries about her, and about dories like his own.

"I'll be ready to hand the place over to the right people," he told me the other day when he brought in a bucket of fresh smelts. "There ought to be a new house built there, and soon. And there should be kids. Of course, then I'll have to put up a building on my own land for my operations, if I do take on those dory orders."

Max is in the state prison at Thomaston. There are long periods now when we forget him, at least I do, and I'm sure Sara is too deeply involved in her work, and in breaking loose whenever she comes back to Cape Silver. She has dates with colleagues at the school, and with Ruel here. Whatever she is thinking when she is as quiet as a stone, we're sure she can handle it. But we never make mermaid jokes now, or recall Sabrina fair beneath the glassy translucent wave.

Max refused to give the judge any reason for killing Cory except that it was to settle an old score. He has a life sentence, though of course that doesn't mean what it says anymore. Still, it will be a long time. He is teaching high school subjects to men who want to finish their education, and we heard that he was ambitious to take over and enlarge the library. Which I find ironic, considering his sister's work.

But, as I said, we don't think much of Max, or of Cory either. We are young and we have our priorities, Barnaby and I. Some of them Shelley knew.

Day and night, aloof from the high towers
And terraces, the Earth and Ocean seem
To sleep in one another's arms, and dream
Of waves, flowers, clouds, woods, rocks, and all that we
Read in their smiles, and call reality.

About the Author

Elisabeth Ogilvie lives in Maine, dividing her time between the mainland and her summer island home. She has, hence, an encyclopedic knowledge of the scene in which this book is set. (The narrator is Mirabell Taggart, who was the Memorable Mirabell Weir of *Weep and Know Why*.)

Wherever she lives, Miss Ogilvie's constant companions are an Australian terrier and two cats who are brothers. One of them has made it a habit of sitting in her lap, while she types, ever since his kitten days. This was fine in his youth, but he's now giant size, which makes typing awkward.

If you had any notion that Maine was isolated from the concerns of the rest of the nation, do not be deluded. "Pot" is prevalent, though it is referred to up east as "whacky tobaccy."